LISA RICHARDSON

Broken Toes

Fozbo Books

First published by Fozbo Books 2023

This novel is entirely a work of fiction. The names, characters and incidents portrayed in it are the work of the author's imagination. Any resemblance to actual persons, living or dead, events or localities is entirely coincidental.

Lisa Richardson asserts the moral right to be identified as the author of this work.

First edition

This book was professionally typeset on Reedsy.
Find out more at reedsy.com

Broken Toes is dedicated to all those who feel lost.
Please hang on.
People are coming.

Acknowledgement

My heartfelt thanks go to everyone who has ever read my work or listened to me waffle on about it. Your time and interest has meant so much.

Special thanks go to my family. My husband and children who have put up with the hours I have devoted to this over the last few years. For their regular interruptions consisting of cups of tea and general conversations, for which I have actually been very grateful.

I also would like to thank those people I am fortunate enough to call friends. I have some incredibly beautiful souls in my life. I myself would be lost without every single one of them.

Chapter 1

The waves can be heard so clearly.

In fact, much more than that, I can really feel them now. All sensations heightened by the absence of sight. Instead, I'm merely feeling what I assume to be the hint of early morning sun accompanied by the caress of the gentle breeze. The force that causes the waves to change the beach, the rocks and all that is left behind. Just as it always does, every single day.

Exhaling, I open my eyes slowly, just the tiniest of windows. Now feeling lost in the moment, absorbing the sounds ahead of me and the sensation of the gradually rising sun. It feels almost meditative. There's a hint of at last being able to let go. To let this moment, this place wash over me. The subtle breeze is now a beautiful veil. Delicately moving over my contours. Eyes closed once again, so I can immerse myself in the sensation. The calm of this moment.

I'm pretty sure that death is not what I am yearning for right now. I'm not standing here, waiting with open arms for the end to arrive. Taking that split second decision to give it all up.

Well, at least I don't think I am.

Death isn't really the reason I am here. In this spot. Poised. Balancing. Yet deep within me, I know and accept that I really need to find out how much I actually want to live. If indeed I even do.

My feet, those plates of stability, trace along the angular yet erosion-smoothed edges of the rock face. My eyes held softly closed. Toes subtly shuffling, moving just enough to carefully feel along the edge, without taking me too far from my spot. This place. This moment. The cliff edge I have passed on foot so many times in recent months was then void of too much consideration.

It holds the most perfect view out to the side of the bay. It really does. A favourite expanse amongst those who desire adventure between the varying rock faces. To explore the crevasses, the remnants of tides gone by. A multitude of layers, buffeted away over the years, to reveal a beauty that continues to change, develop, and grow. Gradually and subtly. On the other side of the rocks, the land is open. Ready and welcoming in its space. That area. Its vastness being utterly perfect for those wanting the sound and feel of the sea rather than to experience the stories told by the creativity of weather and time.

I take a breath in. Just a gentle one. I don't want the decision to not be my own.

Yet despite my care, I almost start to lose my balance. A slight wobble within legs, loss of traction within feet. Without taking control of the moment, I will relinquish my decision to the landscape, the weather, this place. It will have taken my future.

I want to live. Really, I think I do. But can I actually convince myself that I want it enough? Am I enough?

Having steadied myself, I open my eyes fully. Take a second to fleetingly look down. A moment of shock. Though really it shouldn't be. I already know what exists below and how close I am to becoming a part of it. With a small, sharp intake of breath, I step back, just a tiny distance. Hearing the waves crashing reminds me once more of what lays beneath as I try to ease my wayward breath. A heart pounds. I realise it is mine. The beat joins the sound of the waves as though this were some musical improv event. Not really working together, but each producing its own music, sharing the same space. I am aware that the air is cold, not windy as such, but providing a brief movement to remind me of its existence and power. I don't dare look around me. Conscious of how risky that might be. To tempt, upsetting my own stability.

Not wanting to share my moment with anyone else, I pray that no one has been standing away from the cliff edge trying to decide whether to intervene or not. Considering whether that might actually cause me to fall. Would I fall? Maybe I would find I could fly? I recall how I used to dream of that. I'd be a vision, floating above fields, arms spread out over houses. My flight would be low enough to appear as a though I were a balloon, somehow lost by a small child, no doubt now distraught. How wonderful it had felt…to fly. Floating over the waves, filling my chest with hope, calm, maybe a little excitement for a future. A future that was mine to explore.

Having now stepped back, there exists a pause. I'm feeling able to press that button. This decision does not require my immediate action. Looking down, I randomly catch sight of my toenails. An imperfect red. Slightly hardened skin. Yet what I most notice is that they really need re-painting. A completely ridiculous consideration right now. But I'm at the beach. It is the end of summer, and I should have colourful toes to display in my flip-flops. An indication that I'm having some 'down-time'. Yet the difference is that I am not. The reality is that this is not a holiday. This has not been a breakaway. It is almost now my home.

I had been so intrigued by this coastline when we all arrived here before. The hotels, grand houses, balconied flats. A myriad of different colours and designs throughout. So many of them are clearly in view from the main stretch of the beach, which is ridiculously wide and almost as deep when the tide is out. On the other side of the barrier of rocks exists a cascade of greys and blacks, marking out areas for tracking down little fish, pond dippers, and the like. These two beaches sit separated by a barrier of huge rocks. Bouncers keeping control. Such unique landscapes are on either side of this rigid division. Either the expanse of sand or an interest in the delights of the coves often draws visitors. I was told once that generally those who do not live here fall into one of two categories. Those who never arrive and those who return constantly. No one resides in between.

The beach, the cliff edge, it now draws me down. I can now feel it. Even though I have just stepped back a little, it is all drawing me over, pulling me further in.

3

Chapter 2

My name was Georgia Florence. I was a wife, a mother, a friend, and an accountant. I found myself to be all those things, not necessarily in order of priority, it must be said. That was my existence. And I was never, ever late.

My pace quickened and I could feel my heart pounding as if somehow that might help jolt me forward. Maybe it would increase my speed of travel, my ability to get to the station sooner. The sound, against the pavement, mapped out my footsteps for all to hear. My hips endeavouring to take my legs forward at a pace that I wasn't familiar with at that time of day, and in those shoes.

I was never late.

Heels were really not the ideal attire for dashing to catch the train to work. I should have known that. Red heels, bar across the top of my foot. A sophisticated look, not much else. My legs would undoubtedly pay the price for this for the rest of the day. Why the hell was I suddenly running? A question I couldn't justifiably answer. Would it really matter if I was half an hour late? Clutching my oversized handbag tight to my side, I mentally scrolled through the memorised paper diary that sat central on my desk. My eyes imagined darting across the words I recalled, skimming over them as I moved with haste through the front entrance of the station.

I was never, ever, late.

Remembering there were no meetings, just a few accounts to finalise and several new clients to call and touch base with, I could acknowledge that there was nothing that would be heavily impacted by my inability to wake on the alarm that day. The reality was that no one was going to direct a look of disappointment at my tardiness of arrival. There would only be my own disappointment with self. As always.

Purposefully tucking my hair behind my ears, while trying to remain casual, I watched as the train pulled in at the exact moment my feet found the platform. Just a little out of breath but trying to look as though I had arrived leisurely, I paused and waited for the train to come to a complete halt. A gentleman I often saw at that same platform, at around the same time each day, signalled for me to board first. There was a knowing smile. His beard hiding the full extent of his smirk, no doubt. He'd undoubtedly witnessed my last-minute dash through the gate not ten seconds earlier but was refraining from directly referring to it. He didn't need to. His face conveyed the notice. Not in the same critical way I was at that point viewing myself, but maybe with a touch more sympathy. I boarded the train and turned to the right. Heading for my usual seat, in the usual carriage, on the usual side of the train.

The views I knew so well greeted me through the carriage window. With open arms, they cared not that I almost did not make the train. They did not inflict the element of judgement that I inflicted upon myself. The familiarity of the places I found myself passing through provided a small amount of comfort. Those colours. Those shapes. I saw them almost every day. It had become second nature. As the train trundles along the back of different homes, I would find myself noticing where curtains had not been opened as usual. Where trees had increased in height in what felt like days. Leftovers of the previous evening's garden socialising remained discarded. All were small hints provided on the lives I saw flashing by.

I don't think I really knew where it all actually started.

I had no real grasp of the moment I began feeling so lost. Consumed by a desire for more, or maybe just for different. That sense of something missing, of someone no longer there. Pieces missing. Jigsaw incomplete. All I really knew was that the missing part was me.

You see, I wasn't the only one. That I really was sure of. I couldn't be, could I? We all sat on that train, other trains, going to and from work and I was sure others must have felt it too. That unwavering desire for more. The hope of finding ourselves again, maybe once again.

Bumping into our very own beings in the spaces between carriages. Finding ourselves, our future selves. Happy? Together? Or maybe that was just us, but in the past. What kept us all tucked up within our lives? Afraid to do more? These repetitive wranglings ran through my head as I walked, now without hurry, from the station to the office. Self-evaluation. Random wonderings. A conversation almost impossible to switch off. Personal podcast ramblings. It was all such a regular part of my life back then. Considering who else also found that hollow, where once there was a spark. A drive. A determination to move things. To do things. To be everything you could ever possibly be.

I questioned myself constantly. Did I look OK? Could I do my job well enough? Did I even care? Did my boys still need me? I had been going on like that for months, maybe years. Who knew? But the one, most reoccurring question that lurked above all others came up time and time again. 'Was this all there was ever going to be?'

The track ran along behind garden after garden. Occupants barely seemed to notice the existence of us as we passed by. Glimpses of others' lives moved in front of me each day. Like old friends, I welcomed their new day, just as they welcomed their own. Preparing to 'see them later' on the return home. I despised yet found some solace in the regularity of these people I did not speak with on my journey between home and work. Finding myself more settled in my seat, I leant back, getting ready to be updated on the lives of these imaginary old friends. Speed gathered. My breathing had settled. Legs eased and my journey then began.

Chapter 3

'Those toilets really are something else.' Chrissie's declaration had gained everyone's attention as she made her way over to us at the makeshift outdoor bar.

'That's because when everyone around you is a bit older, you don't have to worry about someone else having blocked the loo or finding a sea of fag butts on the floor.' Erica pointed out the obvious to several expressions of agreement. 'And let's face it, we here are very much all of an older age.' Agreement diminished. However, finding humour in reminding us of this fact Erica managed to make light of the passing years, at the same time as she searched through the contents of her bag for something that was clearly starting to distract her.

The sun was beginning to wane, in the gentle fashion it so often did on the best summer evenings. No real breeze, yet still the music carried itself across the field, uninterrupted in the main. Draping us all in a delicate cloth of light-hearted enjoyment. A break from the day, from the entire week, from true life. The bands were mainly those who probably should have retired their instruments and fame some time ago. The outfits undoubtedly not retained from their original height of popularity. Yet for us, it was a chance, for just one evening, to be all that we once were. Casting off all the anxiety, responsibility, and doubt. Or maybe that was just me?

It was Chrissie's idea, as plans often were, for us all to go. She'd seen tickets somewhere and before we knew it, four of us were booked and then committed.

Drinks collected. We all sidled away to find a spot where we wouldn't bother anyone else with our gossip and general catch-up chatter. Occasional dancing was also likely to feature, so we made our camp towards the back of the field. Still close enough to see and hear the bands, but far enough away to avoid the reality of their aging and probably allowing us to ignore our own.

That time of day brought us a peace like no other, even with the surrounding sounds and activity. That rare feeling of being able to really let go of events of the days before encompassed me as I leant down and took a seat on the blanket. Not usually a worrier or an anxious person, I'd recently found it so much harder to move on. To let go of general stuff. It all seemed to just grab a hold of me, sapping me of the strength required to just shake it all off.

Idle chatter about children, updates on health and work issues, accompanied by humorous anecdotes, filled those precious hours. The music was, in the main, just as we all recalled. It dragged us back to a time of bedroom walls fully adorned with endless posters. Popular vinyl purchased on Saturday afternoons from the record shop along the nearest high street. Despite the fact none of us knew each other back in the days of questionable eyeshadow, we'd lived the same times, just separately. We all remembered how those days before made us feel. Then placed together, in that field where history ran excitedly to greet us, the ease of those days before filtered through to the conversations. Many of them were unhurried, light-hearted. All of them undeniably easy, without pressure or judgement.

Just a drink or two with the slowly departing sun and music. That was all it took to take me back to that other time. To remind me how it really had existed then. That other place. That other life. The seemingly endless summers. The ease of existence. All in the glow of my very own mum.

She would have loved that day. Open air, music, all completely her thing. She would have been in that field, much as I was, with a group of her closest friends. However, unlike me, she would have been dressed in some outrageously vintage costume. I'd become too serious for that. Also, unlike me, she wouldn't have felt she desperately 'needed' the break. I never recalled her needing or asking for anything much. My mum always appeared content with her lot, loving her life, never yearning for anything more than the blessings she already had.

I wasn't one to think about my mum every day. Not anymore. That sounds awful, but I didn't. It had been almost twenty years since she left. Yet now and then I found something to bring her back to me. For those memories to come flooding through. Sometimes it was something I wish she had seen, heard, or known about. Sometimes it was something I knew she would have enjoyed. Those moments spent thinking of her sparked a light in me. Dim though it was. That evening was most definitely one of those occasions.

Erica disappeared back to the bar again, returning with more drinks for us all. I was convinced she'd managed a few shots during the journey by the look of her, but I wasn't there to judge. Everyone needed to take their own medicine at times, I figured.

Dusk fell, the shroud signifying the approaching end of the day. Bodies lay on blankets all around, lazily letting the music and peace of the moment wash over them. Voices were heard, idle chatter, laughter, the odd beginnings of an argument. The alcohol, the music of a time before. It all became like a huge sway of peace over and above what I expected to receive from coming. Glancing over at my friends, my extended family, I was warmed and, for that solitary moment, content.

Erica started to look agitated as she frantically dealt with what I assumed were urgent messages on her phone. She'd discarded her vintage straw hat. Anxious jolts of her arms as they moved at pace. Annie looked over at me as if to question whether we should ask anything. I shrugged, to indicate that I had no idea what to do for the best.

'Everything OK?' Annie took the plunge, directing her gaze concernedly over at Erica. Chrissie was oblivious, relaxed out on one of the rugs, singing softly, her eyes closed – I assumed – with a random straw hat draped over them.

I looked up and over at Erica, awaiting a response.

With a brief look up at Annie, Erica replied, 'It'll be fine. Just the usual. Dad's restless and messaging me loads. But the carer should be there in a bit. I guess just running a little late.' Her phone signalled a message received, and she went back to giving it all her attention again. Annie and I shared a briefly sympathetic look between us.

I decided to send a quick message to Simon, just to let him know all was well and that I'd be heading back with Chrissie and the others to our respective houses on the last train. He and the boys had returned from a dinner out. Sounding relaxed in his reply, I told him not to wait up. Comfortable in my long floaty dress and pumps, I then lay back on the blanket. Moved my feet to the rhythm of a song I knew well. Knowing every single word, I played it over in my head and heard the others vocalising their knowledge with me. Annie was speaking quietly to someone on her phone. Something about checking on her kids. It was almost dark, but I closed my eyes. I found rest. I found myself actually present.

Chapter 4

The next day, the beginning of yet another weekend, and I was feeling unusually energised. First up and out of bed. That part not particularly unusual, if I'm honest.

Simon looked peacefully oblivious to my movements as I shuffled tentatively out of our bedroom. I wasn't even sure he had heard me get home the previous night. Chrissie and I had split from Annie and Erica at the station. The location of all our homes meant we often parted in several directions after leaving the train. Chrissie was just a short walk from mine, and although she lived alone, she always insisted on walking back to mine first. Compensating afterwards with a message to let me know she was safely home.

The forthcoming dinner party took my thoughts that day. I ran briefly through the things I needed to organise and arrange as I made my way carefully down the wooden stairs. Jack and Matt wouldn't be up, or at least awake, for some time. Of that, I was sure. The sun filtered tentatively through the delicate stained glass in the front door, as I headed round and into the kitchen. Coffee.

Hugs and kisses shared amongst us all, as Nat and Danny arrived later that day. I'd consciously tried to make a bit of an effort in my appearance, yet seeing Nat so immaculately dressed brought out the inevitable self-doubting within. It shouldn't have bothered me. Not really. Yet it, of course, did.

Nat and I had first met while working at the company I joined after university. She was a marketing specialist. I headed for accounts. I think even then my feelings of inadequacy rumbled away, as I inhabited our very grey accounting department. Marketing, on the other hand always seemed to be so full of colour. Vibrant, gregarious beings of budgets and ideas and schemes. Nat was no different. In fact, we were such different people, especially then, it was surprising we'd had such an enduring friendship. Maybe it was a hidden desire within me to take part in what she was and have it rub off. I looked back to those days and wondered whether I was so dissatisfied with myself that I was really, genuinely, looking for that. No answer was ever really forthcoming.

While not the very closest of friends, there had certainly been a connection between us that had endured for some time. I didn't confide so much in Nat, not as I did others. I enjoyed her company on the occasions we managed to meet up and was genuinely interested to see her do so well. There was, however, an element of, I don't know, maybe competition or jealousy. That never came from her particularly, wasn't her doing. Maybe I should have taken responsibility for my own inadequate feelings? Maybe it was more to do with my relationship with myself.

Nat would demonstrate a different side of life. She'd taken chances, done exactly what she wanted to do. On her second husband, no children. Owned a beautiful house, had so many exotic holidays. She was living. She was clearly and openly very much alive.

Danny – husband number two – seemed to just let her personality roll over him. He became part of her. Moulded to her ways. Although he was quite a character in his own right, Nat was definitely most often playing the part of the entertainer. People were interested in her, what she had to say. He learned to periodically step aside. Danny and Simon got on well enough, although also not particularly close. More of an air of mutual toleration and acceptance that they both agreed to step into whenever we met. It wasn't all that regular an event, which I think suited us all, if I'm truly honest.

I arranged the dinner, giving it my best shot. The pressure of competition waving at me from the background. Plucking a few ideas from friends and books, I kept everything crossed that I wouldn't completely mess it up.

While gathering some drinks, I could hear catch-up chatter coming through from the back sunroom. A place for all occasions. A harnesser of light. My very favourite part of our home and the biggest reason I fell in love with the opportunity that the house gave us. When we first viewed it, I couldn't take my eyes off the light that filled the back. It almost followed us as we stepped through room after room, the rest of the house displaying so many features to adore. A wooden staircase leading to the promise of light, space, and possibilities. Notes and drawings appeared over the years as we tore down wallpaper in room after room. That house had lived such a life and held a lengthy history long before us. All within a collection of bricks and mortar. It emanated hope and love and possibilities from the first moment we stepped in. There was never any suggestion we would not live there. Not make it ours.

'Simon says work is still really busy for you?' Nat asked as I handed her a glass.

'Yes, it has been recently.' Couldn't help but wonder where this opening gambit might head to.

'Working a fair few weekends. I'd call that quite busy, love.' Simon gave a sympathetic glance as he carefully took another glass to pass to Danny. I wasn't totally sure if the sympathy heading my way was a nod to my hectic workload, or the questions being launched.

Feeling the need to justify my situation, I made out it was the time of year that accounts were due to be finalised for many of our larger clients. I'd endeavoured to brush the subject off. Nat, however, wasn't so keen to let it go.

'I would have thought now you're a partner, you'd have others doing much of that work. You don't want to be doing all that still, not now, surely?' Nat used a gentle move of her hand to displace the long dark locks. Not quite a flick, but certainly a purposeful effort. As she leant back into the comfort of the sofa, I couldn't help wondering about the meaning of the words 'not now'. Did she mean now I held a position of authority? Or now I was heading towards my late 40s? Why 'now'? I tried to politely acknowledge the question yet shuffle it along and away. It would do no good to let that query sail around my head for hours on end.

'Well, it's a team effort. Anyway, how are you? How's business?' A light-hearted, almost shrill tone emanated from my mouth. I hoped it wasn't sounding as dismissive out loud as it did inside my head. 'Busy I hope?'

'Yes, but I'm not working as hard as you, by the sounds of it.' Her perfect response hung in front of my face like a huge mirror. Shining a searchlight in the direction of my situation. Her smile was not harsh. In fact, it seemed almost pitying. But the nature of the words didn't take away the fact I was sitting in my own armchair, doubting myself. Yet again.

'It's all good, thanks. New clients coming on board and plenty to keep me busy. But I've expanded the team so I can make time for life.' At that point, she turned to face Danny. Their gaze. Each one meeting the other. Thoughts colliding. Was it me or did I sense a smugness? An almost unpleasant odour left. With his arm draped lightly around the back of her and the sofa, Danny was clear with his glance. Her smile indicated contentment. All at once I saw a joy and happiness I hadn't seen wholly before with Nat. Despite her rather brash words, there was an ease and a softness between them. Danny was clearly good for her. Clearly fitted her remit. For a second, Simon and I were no longer required.

'Well, shall I go check on dinner?' Simon asked as he prised himself from the other armchair and offered a branch of hope to me, bringing me away from my thoughts. Breaking the conversation.

'Great – yes please.' His smile, in return to mine, sent comfort.

Nat seemed to be cajoled into moving the conversation on at this point. She asked how the boys were, noted how lovely the house looked. The usual enquiries, I guess.

'No, we haven't got anything booked yet for next year, have we, George?' Simon refilled all our glasses on his return, as he answered Nat's question before I had a chance to respond.

I looked at him, almost finding myself pleading. I wasn't sure he meant it particularly as an accusation, yet I knew he wanted me to get on with that task. That wasn't the first time the topic had arisen. I couldn't even explain why I'd been so reluctant to get looking. It just hadn't interested me at all.

'Oh, that's always our priority isn't it, Nat?' Danny piped up. Joining the team effort, providing pressure for the cause.

'Yes, I know, but I'll get on to it before too long. It gets delegated to me every year, so I know everyone is waiting. Anyway, where are you guys off to next?' My turn to move the conversation along from what appeared to be fast becoming a fraught point.

Nat and Danny happily provided full details of their up-and-coming escape to an idyllic island planned for early the next year and we then moved on to other, less confrontational topics. Dinner went relatively well after that. Many compliments were made on the choice of food and several glasses of wine down, I started to feel a little less persecuted.

The evening ended late, our guests left and before long Simon and I went up.

'Are you OK?' he asked while we undressed on our respective sides of the bed. I paused for a moment unsure of what he meant. Then I recalled.

'Oh, yes. Yes. You know what she's like,' I dismissed. 'Just a little brazen at times, I guess.' I paused. 'She's living the dream, isn't she? Barely working by the sounds of it. A team of others seemingly taking the flack. Maybe makes you start to question your own life a bit, I guess, maybe...' I trailed off. Concentrated on folding worn-out clothes.

'Do you?' A slight pause before he continued. 'I mean question it?' He carried on getting changed, leaving his enquiry hanging in my space. A direct question, even if dressed up.

'I don't know, really. I think I just see people like Nat who seem to have it all sussed, content with where they are, and find I can't help but look at where I am, I guess.' The clothes on my side of the bed all at once required a concentrated re-folding.

'You do know you're doing OK, don't you? More than OK, in fact.' There was an element of concern seen clearly within Simon's eyes. I paused and looked over at him. His comment deserving of my attention. 'More than that, *we* are doing OK.' He reiterated. I sensed a subtle forcefulness, as he seemed to drive home his thoughts in order to allay my concerns.

'I mean, look around you, George, look at what we have. Successful jobs, great kids. It's just a holiday on an island in the middle of nowhere. We could all do that if we didn't have two teenagers to buy endless pairs of trainers for…' He smiled at me, deftly moving around the room as he placed items in various, very specific spots. Clearly an effort to make light of my apparent deepening anxiety but also a moment to bring me back to what was the reality of our situation.

It was silent as I took in the evident kindness on his face. The uncertainty I felt inside at that moment took me a little by surprise. Needing to break the moment, I rashly claimed I didn't feel I was doing too bad I suppose. My smile, though slightly forced, hopefully encouraged his belief in my statement.

I sensed him watching over me as I continued to gather clothing together, along with my hairbrush, before looking up from my work. My eyes met his, and he moved towards me. Taking my arms in his hands, I felt the more than subtle pressure from him, driving home his statement. WE were all OK.

A light kiss. A dismissed conversation. I paused. Stood still as he left the room for a moment. Padding into the en suite, I felt a sense of gratefulness at Simon's comment and his concern. I just wasn't sure of the truth in my response. Truth didn't exist in spoken words. Only deep within. I know that now.

Chapter 5

'So, how was it last night? You had Nat over for dinner, didn't you?' It had actually escaped my mind that I'd even mentioned it to Annie before she asked. I'd just popped over to grab a catch up with her. Immerse in ease after the previous night.

'Yes, Nat along with Danny. Not sure if you've met him before. He's a relatively recent acquisition.' I took a sip of the tea she'd made and half-smiled over in Annie's direction. Fully aware she would pick up from that all the unsaid words.

'Didn't go well?' As she pulled out a chair from the kitchen table. The scrape of wood on the tiled floor disturbing the gentle birdsong floating in from the back door. 'I know it's not always the easiest of catch ups...' The half-smile on her face had a knowledge contained deep within it.

'You know what she's like.' I noted as I took more of the tea. The light shone in through the door, casting a subtle shade of colour across the wood.

'It was OK, to be fair. Just found myself on a bit of a life comparison session after a while.' Finding a light-hearted smile that I could send in her direction, I carried on. 'I like her, I do, but it just brought out my own insecurities, I think. I probably should know by now, though.' Placing the mug on the table, I shuffled myself into the seat, seeking more comfort.

'Well, there is that, I guess.' Her smile, directed towards me, served as an attempt to provide reassurance. 'But you have nothing to be bothered about do you? Why are you bothered by her?'

There was a pause while I tried to think how best to answer her question.

Giving the enquiry thought. Trying to string my feelings into description.

Before I got to the point of being ready to respond...

'Are you OK?' A notably direct question. One I should well have expected from Annie. Established friends often just know, I guess.

Noting the reflection of Simon's statement from the night before, I mumbled something about being fine and we both drank our tea.

Annie continued to watch me, sizing me up almost, as we sat opposite one other. I sensed she was waiting for me to say a bit more. Open up maybe. Open up to what? Feelings turning into words. A tricky task on occasions. Yet her gaze was found to be more powerful than I at first realised.

'I don't know what to say is the honest truth.' Looking at her directly, perhaps internally pleading for her to suggest, probe, maybe? I wasn't sure what I really wanted from her, but it felt as though I needed something.

'What's wrong? It seems obvious to me that something is.' Annie laid her tea down on the table, giving me full attention. 'What is it?'

Almost a whisper.

'I really wish I knew.'

'Well, start by just telling me how you feel, maybe?'

Even that felt tricky. Not that I didn't want to share with Annie, just the idea of trying to put it all into words. That was the difficult part.

Deep breath in. Exhale.

'I'm just not feeling it right now. I can't put my finger on it, really. Just a bit lost maybe. I don't know, maybe just not myself. Sounds silly, but I'm not sure what else to say.' Silence. I left that hanging for a moment or two, because while I knew that was how I felt, I wasn't sure it actually said anything. Meant anything. Or at least anything anyone would really understand. Including me.

An obvious attempt to just brush it aside.

'I'm sure it will ease. Maybe I'm tired or something, but I just feel like...' Looking down at my hands, I noticed I was wringing them out, blending them together. Annie must surely have noticed it, too.

'You don't have to say anything, you know that.' Shuffling forward, her hand moved across to sit over both of mine, a soft pressure to convey her presence.

'I know, I know.' I placed my bottom hand on top of hers. Her delicate fingers were notably still adorned by the jewels no longer necessary. Understandably unable to let go.

Breathing in to provide strength. My visit to Annie's was not for this.

'I just don't feel like me. I hate even saying that. Sorry. It's just so ridiculous and I can't really explain it, but that's it – I think that's the only way I can describe it.' There, I'd said it. I'd at least said something.

'If that's how you feel, then you have nothing to be sorry for. We all feel how we feel.' Gently, her hand withdrew after a time.

'I know, but what a thing to say! Look at my world. I have nothing to worry about. Nothing to make me miserable. No one would say otherwise. Yet somehow, some days, I just think, *is this it?* For the next however many years...' My expression forced and somewhat acknowledging she may well consider me ridiculous. But the one thing I needed was for her to not hate me for my words. To not believe I was an awful person.

'That's irrelevant. It's about what you want from life. Not what anyone else is doing or wanting. Something obviously feels wrong, isn't making you happy. I think that's fine, isn't it? Do you have any idea where it's come from?'

I'd mulled this over so much. If I could have pinpointed it, then I could perhaps fix it. That's how I saw it. Establish the cause and make it go away. A very logical solution.

'I really don't know. This here is just not me. I don't really even know whereabouts 'me' is.'

'You're lost.' A statement from knowing.

'Yes...maybe I am.'

'Lots of us are, you know?'

Annie exhaled. I felt awful having passed the weight of what had been creeping up on me over to her. I shouldn't have said anything.

Maybe sensing my regret, Annie reassuringly looked over and smiled. Reminded me it's often better to talk. Let the words be free. Even though it obviously was hard for me to put it into statements. She went on to talk about maybe seeking someone professional to talk to. Maybe explore some help. Find someone who could guide me to be able to put it into clearer words, description. To figure it all out.

Running scared at this point, I needed to move things on.

'I'll give it all some thought, I will.' Dismissive, I knew. 'Anyway, how are the kids?' I looked around, wondering whether they were about to pop their heads around the doorway.

'Oh, they're fine. At Mum's for a bit today.'

'And you? Are you OK?' I asked, looking directly at her. Suddenly grateful to be able to turn the tables of concern. 'It's that time of year again...' My voice trailed off, but she knew exactly what I meant. Of course she did. I always marvelled at how she seemed to cope with this annual reminder. Not even a reminder, more a resurrection of the situation, the never-ending pain.

'Yes.' She looked particularly pale for a moment. Her subtle red hair enhanced the change. For a second, we both stopped. I hoped that I could convey in my look at her the sympathy I had. The care I always wanted to give. Annie had, for a long time, been that person with whom I was able to be completely and utterly me. There was nothing I wouldn't have done to change her situation, to take away the hurt I knew she felt. To make things different for her. Nothing.

Yet here I sat, disclosing my own truth. That I was now lost. That I was unhappy.

The birds chirping outside continued, despite the moment, as if to remind us that there were lives still sounding. That spring could still be that time of awakening, regardless of whatever life decided to throw our way.

Annie sighed and took a further gulp of tea; I guessed by way of distraction. Liquid now cold.

'Yes. It is.'

The silence, not uncomfortable, but nevertheless heavy, sat with us for a few delicate moments. I could only guess what was really churning round in Annie's mind. I liked to think that after over twenty years of friendship, I generally had a good idea. But Annie had changed. Events way beyond her dreams and ability to control did that. I knew she was still in there somewhere. I knew that the Annie who quickly became my closest friend at university, was still there. She just needed some more time. Space to re-emerge. I would, of course, give her all the time she ever needed.

Chapter 6

It was 22 years.

Three homes, no pets, two boys, several jobs, plenty of DIY, and a good dose of love.

I quickly realised that the last statement of thought, was probably not what I should have been contemplating as we approached our wedding anniversary. It didn't sound quite passionate enough. However, I was merely being honest with myself. I wasn't stating that I no longer loved him. I was just reflecting on time, maybe. Noting how we had changed, compared to how we were many years ago. We did love each other, of course we did. In many ways I couldn't envisage a life without him. But it was still OK to admit that sometimes I didn't consider that our love for each other was always behind everything we said and did. Not like it was in the beginning. I wasn't the only one coming to that conclusion, surely?

Simon was a relaxed yet solidly dependable man. I found myself realising I was probably being unduly harsh with my previous contemplations. Maybe I was jealous. This man I had created a family with seemed to be able to remove himself from some of the trickier parts of life so easily, just with a smile and a sense of positivity that I was, on occasion, notably lacking.

Found myself concluding that somehow, I seemed to have had painted within my thoughts a picture of boredom and unhappiness. Just a habit? A habit that I didn't want to break? Really? That wasn't true either. I couldn't expect after so many years, for everything to stay the same. We were, after all, much older and had very much changed within ourselves. The weather of time would do that. Was it really an issue if things were different? They weren't awful. I didn't hate him. I didn't *not* love him. Must start to police my own thoughts.

So, we took ourselves out for dinner. Something which seemed the right thing to do, in recognition of the milestone. A relatively successful evening, it turned out. I was conscious not to spend too much time talking about work, and he was careful not to appear too relaxed and carefree. It suited us. We laughed, confided in our hopes for the boys and noted what needed doing next in the garden. He'd grown his stubble out more. I'd not really noticed it before. A new shirt, I thought. Cufflinks I'd not seen for ages. My eyes sought to take him in. To absorb his very existence. Food provided filling for the gaps in conversation. It was relatively easy. It was comfortable. Lacking in the heady romance of younger days but it worked.

Simon had pretty much always supported me in a way that gently nudged my ambition in the direction he knew I needed to take it. I'm not sure I supported him in quite the same way, but if I was honest, I don't think he needed it. He stood tall on his own. His job had its own pressures, managing people, but he handled them without any real fuss. Not any that accompanied him through our front door, at any rate. Working almost four days a week must have contributed to that and enhanced his ability to see the bigger picture. Not being taken down by the tiny details that might hamper progress, excitement, and hunger. By his own admission, career progression was not at the forefront of his mind. He was settled. He had no need to seek for more, and it was evident that his role in care management suited him perfectly.

As my eyes traced his face, took in his oh so familiar features, I could see how he radiated a man who knew what he was. Sat back in the chair, his face carrying a lightness of ease. His dedication to his job was undeniable, but also was his dedication to being a father and a husband. That was his real fulfilment. It was the making of him. Once, I would have said the making of us as a family. Not that it no longer worked. Just that maybe I was starting to see things a little differently. Questioning my own role in all of it.

Our stroll home in the early summer air was delayed by the result of a few glasses of wine and the loosening of our routine. Slightly giddy with the effects, we stopped to take in the late-night lights that led the way. On arriving home, we randomly decided on music and another bottle, long into the early hours. I relaxed a little more, sought to try to push recent thoughts and questions to one side. I did my best to allow myself to ease back and concentrate on our life. Our life together.

Chapter 7

The phone returned to its cradle.

Chatter from the main office filtered through, and on checking the clock I realised my next meeting was in just five minutes. I engaged my brain once again, smoothed clothing as I stood to gather all I needed. Mr Harvey. A regular client, Sam, was an amiable man. He and I had known each other for almost as long as I'd been a partner at the practice and as a result the meetings were always more relaxed than they might otherwise be. His accounts were relatively straightforward and left time for some of the usual banter and catch up. An easier part of the job. An almost enjoyable aspect.

Millie brought the files through.

'Mr Harvey is waiting in reception for you.' I looked up, smiled, and thanked her for the head's up. Taking a sip from my cup, I walked out of the office. My office.

Partnership wasn't necessarily on the agenda when I began studying, although I was driven to find success. And I was really driven back then. To the point of feeling the constant pressure to attain high marks in all my exams. A mere 'pass' was never going to be enough. I would not have settled for that. It all paid off. I was indeed a partner. Ultimately, I had accomplished what I hoped to achieve. I was therefore a success, by all accounts.

The sun streamed fiercely in through the blind and the open window as I returned to my office after the meeting. Requiring a fresh coffee, I hung up my jacket and grabbed my cup. Pausing, just for a second, to catch sight of the confirmation of my achievements hung as a statement on the wall. A small, yet formal reminder of how far I had come and where I now sat. Acknowledging how I had taken a second to stop. Bubbling below my surface pride, I couldn't dismiss the sense of 'what happens now?' A question I had begun to mull over far too often.

The remainder of the afternoon passed in a blur of productivity, coming to an end at around 5 p.m. An early finish. I collected my bag and drained the last of a now cold coffee, before regretting it. Sighing without really knowing why, I made my way out towards the front door.

Millie smiled while wishing me a good evening, as I fleetingly waved to the occupants of the other offices I passed on the way. This place was pretty much my second home. Had been for far longer than I had initially envisaged. However, no reason now to up sticks, it seemed. No better place to go to. My reputation intact. I needed to prove nothing. My fellow partners were generally respectful and inclusive. I guess if I was younger, I might have had a burning desire to take on a new challenge. However, the impetus to prove myself to new colleagues and clients had gone. I couldn't decide if it was down to my own laziness, or age, but I just knew that the drive to find more, to actually seek to be more, was lost.

The streets began to get busy as offices threw out their occupants. Sounds from the increased traffic mingled with the music filtering out from some of the various bars and cafés. All awaiting that midweek release.

Chrissie was already seated as I went over to her.

'Check you out at 5 p.m.!' she mocked with a wink and a grin.

'Yes, see I *can* manage it.' My retort lingered…

'Be more me, George…be more me.' Chrissie's encouraging advice on point, as it so often was found to be.

We managed to catch up on our days and weeks since we had last met up. The history and friendship we shared had created a bed for ease and fluid conversation over food and drink. Sometimes finding myself a little guarded initially, it often only took a little time with Chrissie, before the facade waned.

We had known each other almost as long as Simon and I had lived in the area. I happened early on to seek out a beauty salon for a quick manicure in preparation for an important meeting. Not having been a partner for long, I had wanted to give an impression of authority, of belief in my own ability. Convince them that they hadn't made a mistake, and neither had I. Finding her salon a mile or two away from our home, I had booked an appointment. We chatted as I arrived. Her verbal embrace entranced both me and many others into her salon, some of whom seemed to rarely leave. The kindness she showered people with, the wit of her welcoming personality, meant I couldn't not speak at length with her. Despite events that might have damaged her resolve to give, not once had I seen her generosity cave.

Without much warning, undoubtedly fuelled by the drinks, I found myself questioning Chrissie. Suddenly eager to get a sense of her ideas, her considerations on where I was, or might be.

'Do you ever wonder, Chris, where we go from here?' I had clearly drunk too much. It was obvious. I could feel this was going to lead to an overly open conversation, but it was at that point too late. The gun had gone off.

Looking up, as she casually placed her glass down.

'You mean afterlife?' she enquired of me. I sensed the hint of a smirk emanating from her face. Considering why we were having such a deep conversation so early on a midweek evening.

Realising the mistake in her interpretation, I corrected her.

'No, no. I mean, while we are here, not after it's all over.' Neither of us could help but laugh a little at the madness within the chatter. Then, regaining my composure a little as I removed my suit jacket, draping it behind my being, I rephrased my question to her.

'Don't you sometimes feel like there could be more? More to life than now?' I could see from her expression I needed to continue, to explain. 'Doesn't it feel sometimes that as our careers, our lives all feel pretty settled and sorted, we wonder about what we do next? Where the next excitement comes from?' I refilled our glasses, draining the first bottle, while I awaited her response.

It didn't come.

Then in a moment I realised just what I had uttered. The look on Chrissie's face stopped me in my tracks. She paused and blinked away the glaze that threatened to spill out from her eyes. A more than slightly forced smile accompanied the breath out.

'I'm sorry.' I reached for her hand, noticing the perfectly manicured nails diverting attention away from her empty finger.

'No, you're right, we are sorted now.' Bringing herself a little more upright, pushing up her sleeves, she pulled away and reached for her glass, drinking more, in order to move the conversation on.

'No. I really am sorry,' I repeated. Drinking heavily from my own. Mortified at my own lack of thought about the words I had chosen to use.

Interruption to our conversation came by an awareness of the increasing life within the restaurant. The bustle of people venturing out after work, looking to leave their commitments and obligations behind. Raised, jubilant voices and laughter from ties, suits, and heels. People just like me. Just like us. All stepping off the wheel. Maybe some were also seeking some release, some way of being themselves, just like me. Being just themselves, once again.

'Anyway, in answer to your original question, I'm not sure I do, if I'm honest.' Querying where I was heading. 'Are you not happy then? Or just feeling a little bored, tired, maybe?' She trailed off, taking more drink in, I guess to gloss over the reminder I had given, of a situation that had been neither happy, nor was particularly 'now settled'.

'I don't know. I think I just don't feel the enthusiasm for anything like I used to. It's just not there.'

'Don't you think that's probably natural? You've been in your job for a few years now. We can't go around being all excited and motivated twenty-four hours a day, can we?' Unsure if Chrissie was appearing dismissive or whether she hadn't really understood what I was trying to say.

'I get that, but my head just keeps mulling things over that I can't seem to resolve. It's like a persistent child vying for attention.' I smiled a little at the memory, meeting Chrissie's gaze as if it might lessen the load of my words. Feeling it was probably better to give up. 'It's all fine though, I'm sure it will all blow over. It just all feels a bit lacking at the moment.'

'Lacking in what?' Chrissie's question was valid and somewhat direct. A question I'd found myself asking so many times, without any real answer.

I focussed on the base of my wineglass, moving it round in stilted circles. A distraction from the very clear question my friend had asked. As I continued to focus and concentrate, I knew I needed to give her some form of response.

'I have no idea.'

The desire to continue this conversation was disappearing. Why had I even started it? Wine. That was why I had started it.

Chrissie took my last statement in and looked firmly and directly at me.

'Being honest, George, what is there that you don't have?' Her smile attempted to disguise what must have been an element of sheer disbelief.

I could not disagree.

'I know, I know. Maybe it's more than that but I just can't figure it out yet.' Chrissie wouldn't believe me, I was sure, but... 'I don't take it all for granted. I don't. But I just know that something within me isn't right...' I trailed off.

'Maybe you just need to holiday for an entire year or something.' I looked over to see her broad smile, diffusing the weight of the conversation, on the surface at least. 'Or maybe you ought to seek some help? Find someone to talk to about it. Who might be able to suggest things that I wouldn't know about?' Her raised eyebrows forcing this statement through me. The second same such suggestion.

Chrissie continued to look more intently at me. Help, therapy, something professionally provided. I knew that was what she really meant.

'Genuinely, George. Maybe you ought to consider whether you should chat to a professional? See your GP? How long have you felt like this?' Loud laughter caused us both to look over at the bar area. Young lads in expensive suits claimed the space. Cajoling one another as part of some internal joke.

'Oh, I don't know, maybe a while...' I sat clinging on to my comfort in a glass.

The laughter escalated some more. Over the music playing subtly in the background. An almost irrelevant addition when it was so busy within. Busy with people, with lives, with décor.

This was now getting uneasy. Don't get me wrong, I'd already pondered that same thought before that evening, but quickly dismissed the idea. What would I say? Who would I go to? I felt sure that I just needed to work myself out. To sort myself out.

'Yes, maybe I do.' Providing a prescribed response. That would move the conversation on, surely?

'Then make an appointment. You never know, could be the menopause, depression, anything.'

There was a distraction of dropped plates from the kitchen. The standard cheer from those closest. Beautifully and perfectly timed for a conversation I needed now to vacate. After we returned to face the table, I acknowledged I would seek some help and managed to move things on.

We both smiled and took a sip of our respective drinks. I could sense that taking this conversation further with Chrissie was probably not the most helpful thing to do currently. For me. I couldn't understand myself at the moment, so how could I expect her to?

Chapter 8

The words to one of my favourite songs rang in my ears as trainer covered feet pounded the concrete beneath. One, two, one, two. The rhythmic motion took me along familiar pathways, making my way through the village. The usual route went along the street from our house, past the lushness of the green park and then cutting through and round the back of the main street, to reach the track adjacent to farm fields. On reaching the track, the view was completely transformed. Thatched cottages then sat behind me, and towards the front lay an open expanse, promising a freedom. The fields were home to a changing gathering of crops, as the year's seasons replaced one another. That day, I followed the rough pathway that ran between two of the fields and headed out to the open landscape.

Chrissie and Erica never really understood my obsession with running. Having taken it up about eight years earlier, it had in no exaggeration been a saviour on occasions. Limiting myself to tracks and routes not far from home, generally got out three or four times each week. Trainers had come and gone, but each time I just bought more and made sure I didn't have to stop. I couldn't stop. This became my meditation. In fact, it became my medication.

Those extensive views across land that sat not far from home. They always made me feel as though I might run without limit. Without restriction. Sometimes I really and truly tried to. The rhythm of my feet continued, and the music flowed through into every corner of my brain. While my body began to ache, I knew to continue through and complete the route I had come to need.

Making my way through fields, I became a keen observer of the light breeze and the lifting sun. Completely my favourite time of day. Little else was happening. No busyness of others to concern myself with. Just me. Just my own being, my own existence. I found it right there.

Reaching my usual point, where I would pause with hands loosely on hips, I stood still. Took in the all too familiar view. Checked my watch for time and distance and waited for my breathing to ease a little. Stood in the middle of the path that meandered between the fields, I could look around and see little aside from farmland for miles. I used to hate it. It felt much too open. I'd be exposed. My desire for hills, changes in the flow of the land remained, but I had since grown to love my space. Almost no one could find me when I was out here. I became part of the subtle sounds as they changed with the seasons. The farmers growing and alternating their crops.

Checking my watch again, I decided this was a good time to start my journey back home. I quietly thanked the fields, the track, the views, for giving me the space and peace and with a smile, turned around to find my way back.

Through the front door, I grabbed a water as I moved on and into the kitchen.

'Good run, Mum?' Jack was sitting at the kitchen table munching on some concoction of toast and cheese and what appeared to be peanut butter. His blond hair in need of a cut, I noticed. The wayward locks framing his still pubescent jaw line, skin starting to give way to a hint of stubble.

'Yes, really good thanks.' I smiled. 'Surprised to see you up, though.'

'Football match, needed to.' The reply interjected between mouthfuls.

Questioning myself, I noted, 'I thought that was much later?' Poured myself another glass of water and then leaned round to switch the kettle on.

'It's twelve, but I wanted to get up and chill for a bit first. Are you coming?' Jack's enquiry filled with expectation.

A moment of hesitation. I'd got plans; having been certain it was a mid-afternoon fixture. Yet I couldn't not go. Working out how to change my own arrangements.

'Of course, is Dad going too?' I asked, flippantly. Wondering if Simon had a better idea of when the game was due to start, than I clearly had.

'Yes. He said he'd take me and Jamie over and would stay for the game. It's not too far to travel. Be great if you could come too, though.' The briefest of tempting smiles before he took his attention back to the remains of his fuelling.

Finishing my second glass, I confirmed I'd be there, planting a kiss on his head as I moved over to him. Caught him before he could tempt to avoid my affection. 'I'm off to shower now, so I'll be ready in time. What time are you needing to leave?' I finished making a black coffee ready to take up with me.

'About 11.15 ish I think,' he replied, taking his final bite of breakfast.

'No problem. I assume Matt is out with his mates later?'

'I think so.' Jack left the table. Satiated for the moment, at least.

'He's meeting a few of them to go to the cinema, I think. They're taking the bus as he assumed you'd both want to come and see the game.' He slurped the remains of his tea while making further statements on who they would be up against in the final, if they made it through this match. I acknowledged the update as I left the kitchen door and took the stairs. Slightly annoyed at having the wrong time in my head, but also a little agitated that I would now have to change my day. Giving consideration to bailing out of supporting him wasn't really an option.

I showered, changed, and went back downstairs, where I met Simon in the kitchen. We exchanged a light kiss as he flicked the switch for his own coffee. Then caught sight of the trail of unusual breakfast crumbs Jack had left, clear for us all to follow.

'What on earth was he eating this time?' Simon enquired. The affectionate smile on his face directed partly at me and partly at our now absent son.

'Oh, the usual mess of stuff I think.' I looked over and smiled at him as I finished clearing the table.

'Do you want some breakfast now?' Simon offered as he moved from the kettle to the fridge to find if his weekend treat of a full English awaited him. He pulled items out, stacking them on the kitchen island before grabbing relevant pans. The radio filling the room with an old song I recognised.

'I do, but not 'your' special.' I declined as I grabbed a bowl to fill with muesli and headed over for another coffee. 'I'll treat myself another time, but you go ahead and enjoy.' My hand flippantly gestured towards the pile of produce as we each weaved our way around the kitchen, gathering all we needed to set us up for the day.

I took a seat at the nearby old wooden table that provided our casual eating area. A tabletop worn from a thousand dinners, games nights, bottles of wine. Food smeared over it in years before, by toddlers eager to experiment with the newfound joy of solids. We had a formal dining room put in place only a few years before, but that was always my favourite place to eat. A structure holding so many memories within the grain and knots, reminding me of a subtle sense of loss, almost. Nothing awful ever came from being sat there.

Simon finished getting his food ready and joined me opposite. We shared small talk about my run, the weather, and whether our eldest was actually out of bed yet.

'You coming along today?' Simon asked, devouring the last mouthfuls of his hearty meal.

'Yes, of course,' I responded. Slightly put out that both of them had felt the need to check.

'Why wouldn't I?' Probably sounding a little confrontational as I placed the cup down. Not wanting to make a big deal of it, but still curious.

'I was just asking,' he said. 'You didn't make the last couple of games, so I wasn't sure if it was just me today or not. That's all.' He started to clear the table, taking my things with him.

Not wanting to escalate anything unnecessarily, I still felt compelled to remind Simon that I missed the last two because of work. Heading out the door, towards the rear of the house, I let him know I'd be ready in time.

Cupping my left-over coffee, I moved out through the lounge and sunroom into the courtyard part of the garden. A peaceful spot. It was full of flowers and colour in a very casual way, giving an indication of my lack of any gardening prowess. The work I gave it extended more or less only to a touch of planting, watering, and dead heading as and when I remembered. Simon found the time and impetus to do much more. My enthusiasm for the tasks at the beginning of early spring never lasted once the joy of summer and garden get-togethers took hold.

Birds filled the outside space and chirped their way through the morning. Sounds from behind me filtered through of people moving about and starting their Saturday. I just needed a few more minutes first.

Chapter 9

'Do you think I should do it?'

The weight of responsibility in answering that simple question was far from lost on me.

'I mean, do you think I could even do it?' Her face tentatively searching for some form of guidance.

Millie had joined us about a year before, as an office junior really, but quickly revealed her potential and became my support. In many ways she had kept me in check on the odd day I just hadn't felt present. Millie's ability to take charge of matters had developed strongly over time and while she may have only been in her early 20s, her togetherness said otherwise.

My response to her question was important. I was acutely aware of that. Selfishly, I wanted to steer her away from deciding to do it. It would, after all, mean her departure from providing my support, leaving me to start all over again in needing to find someone new. Yet it was an opportunity that I could see would allow her to flourish. She had so much more to offer than merely the help she gave me. She deserved more exciting adventures, perhaps than that opportunity would even deliver. My older, but most certainly not wiser self, needed to hold on before putting her off as a result of my own selfish thought processes.

'Do you want to?' I enquired.

Her smile said enough, but she continued.

'I really do. This job has been great, and I've learnt so much from shadowing you and working for you. But I think I'd like to give it a go.'

Almost apologetic ambition.

Pausing, looking fully at her. For just one moment. A soul full of enthusiasm and hope and excitement. Excitement in a firm of accountants. Willing myself not crush it. I was there once. I recognised it.

'To be honest, I really want to say don't do it. But the truth is that's only because I, for one, will be lost.' We both managed a smile. 'You are great, Millie. Competent enough to do it and do it well. You must go for it and I'll support you in any way that I can.'

Millie's dark eyes portrayed a gaze of gratefulness and a hint of surprise, perhaps.

'Thank you. I really appreciate your honesty and encouragement. I won't be going anywhere, just studying in the evenings. That's if I even get in.' Rambling. Her enthusiasm and youth taking over her words.

'You'll get in.' A statement of undeniable fact.

Millie and I spent much of the afternoon putting together her application to study. Grateful that she had come to me to help, I endeavoured to be genuinely happy for her. At the same time, I found myself feeling more than a little nostalgic for all that enthusiasm and hope. Her drive.

My mind was reminded of the ecstatic announcement I made to Simon over the phone when I secured the job at my firm. I rang him as soon as I received the call, while heading home from the interview. We both knew this could really be a turning point. A firm of accountants, run by young blood. Young enough to have the ideas and desires to be different. To take accountancy out of the stuffy box it seemed to inhabit for as long as ever. Now my firm. It was still hard to acknowledge that I had played an important part in the firm's development and direction.

The moment I was offered a partnership, I could see our future in a different way. We had outgrown the little house we were in, had started looking for something more. And all of a sudden, it all seemed possible. Simon, at around the same time, was promoted, and we were winning. Winning at life. Winning with each other. A successful team. That feeling of almost 'We've done it'. We ate fish and chips and had a bottle of fizz to mark the occasions. At that point, anything seemed possible.

Chapter 10

The wineglass clear and crisp, filled halfway with a tonic. My tonic. The chardonnay sat smooth and still in the glass, and my finger absentmindedly circled the top as I exhaled quietly.

Resting the glass on my bent knee, on top of my well-worn jeans, I tilted my head back to rest on the sofa. I had loved this sofa from the minute it arrived. Soft enough to welcome you in amongst its grey folds, yet coupled with a firmness that would allow you to escape it when something required you to.

I ran my hand through my hair, hanging loosely, just resting on my shoulders, and I closed my eyes. It was Friday. The week was done. Dinner had been consumed, and I was, for once, trying to let it all go.

'Space for one more?' asked Simon gently, as he lightly touched my leg, causing my eyes to drift open and take in his presence.

'Of course,' I replied. Smiling as he leaned into the sofa, I shuffled over a little to accommodate him.

The music carried on in the background. I rested my eyes, closed again, and felt Simon lean back, resting his glass on the other arm.

'It's Friday,' I declared with the hint of a 'yeah' carrying on at the end. Simon gave a smile and motioned with a gently closed fist his joy at that fact.

That week had felt like two. Work had piled up, and I'd rarely been home. New clients set up, partner review meetings had taken place and much of home life had taken a spot at the end of the line. My time was now. I took a sip of the wine and exhaled again, attempting to release the week.

'You aren't working this weekend, are you?' asked Simon. I could hear it wasn't necessarily a question.

'No. I probably should, but I'm so tired I am going to take a break, I think.' My rational approach slightly unusual. Simon raised his eyebrows and smiled at the same time, indicating his approval of that decision.

'Right now, I think I'll just relax, drink, and then sleep.' Smiling with a sense of relief, I sank a little deeper into the cushions that provided a cocoon as they wrapped around me. My light cotton grey overshirt, similar in tone to the shade of the sofa, allowed me to just happily blend in amongst it all. Disappear.

Another sip from the glass and I felt the soothe of the liquid as it made its way down my throat. I found myself then sitting the glass back on my legs and shuffling just slightly deeper into the envelope of the seat.

Simon moved his hand to place it gently on my leg as he made a start on his own glass.

We both closed our eyes gently and sank back further, enjoying the subtle music that kept us company as the hours ticked by. It was easy. At that moment, it felt easy to stop. To be. More relaxed than I had been, not knowing if it was the alcohol or the fact it had been such an intensive week. Yet here I was, not really thinking. That was the key, to not allow myself to think too much.

Simon and I engaged in some idle chatter. Nothing of great significance or importance but instead just an opportunity to share. As I looked directly at him while we spoke, I traced the contours of his face with my eyes. The ever so slightly increased amount of grey hair. The lines that crept up on him a little more each day. Despite the end-of-day stubble, I still saw that softness that had drawn me to him in the very beginning.

He reminded me he couldn't do the rugby run the next day, already having booked a round of golf in with a friend. I noted that my thick fleece would be required as the weather was always testing on the rugby pitch, regardless of the season, so it seemed. The chat was comfortable. No insinuations of one of us not having pulled our weight, of having forgotten our responsibilities. No heated discussion over who didn't take the meat from the freezer for the next day's meal. None of it. This was how we were years ago. I was sure. That was when it felt easy, looking back. However, I am sure at the time it was anything but. I was sure that those times, a bit of a distant memory, were anything but as easy as I recalled them to be. Maybe we weren't as busy and maybe I was in a better place. Different pressures maybe, rather than none. I found it hard to be really sure, to really remember. The fog of time passing made it so.

Water against panes, just a slight splattering to start with, but enough to cause a rhythmic sound against the windows. Further cocooned, I didn't want to be anywhere else at that moment. I was settled. I was comforted. Desperate to hang on to this moment, this time. Something from the way we were with each other told me Simon might have felt the same.

The rain increased slightly. Simon eased himself up from the sofa and moved to switch on another table lamp to counteract the deepening darkness of the evening. Though tempted to find a few candles, I decided against moving. Instead, I embraced those moments of stillness that I found within me that day. Just in case I found they were gone by the morning.

Chapter 11

The alarm burst into life, as usual at 5.30 a.m. Feeling Simon shuffling next to me and then drifting back to slumber, I sat on the edge of the bed. Attempted to come round and focus on the forthcoming day. Tired, too tired to effectively face the Monday morning I found myself in, but nevertheless I began to heave myself up. I would be brave.

Once showered, I dressed myself in my trusty grey suit. My long-standing colleague. It had remained a smart look, if somewhat unexciting. I often teamed it up with my red heels. Breaking the boredom, breaking out. Indicating I had confidence in what I was doing. A mistress of disguise. The weight of deceit had more recently begun to hang heavy on my shoulders.

Heading out the door before anyone else even noticed I was gone. The walk to the station took me along almost deserted streets. The only real hint of company, the dedicated dog walkers who made the most of the dry early morning. Light sunshine hinted at breaking through when the day eventually arrived. But at that moment, I was caught in the stillness, indicating the time between the end of night and the beginning of day. While I didn't always need to go into the office so early, I often preferred it. Being alone gave me some time to gather my thoughts. Or just sit and dwell.

The oh so familiar station platform welcomed me in. I noticed a few familiar, regular faces. Those who joined me, from a distance, on the daily commute. We sometimes gave half a smile towards the other, not familiar enough to generate a 'morning' but accepting we were not strangers. The gentleman always with the morning paper under one arm and a coffee in the opposite hand. I'm sure he probably ordered the same drink each day. Maybe I was wrong. Maybe he mixed it up with a shot of caramel on a Friday? Imagining the reasons that brought them all to the place I found myself. What reason did they have to journey as I? The ladies with the cases dragged behind them. I guessed taking mountains of work home each day, too much to enable a fashionable over-the-shoulder bag to be of use. The casually dressed, athletic-looking young man, full of enthusiasm for the day ahead. He was alone. Many of them seemed just like me. On life's treadmill. Continuing the same drudgery, the same routine day in day out. Maybe waiting for something. A force of change.

I was, of course, merely assuming all of this. Perhaps I was, in fact, alone in my ponderings? Yet we all seemed to bear the same facial expressions. Tired, bored, maybe. Unable to alight from this wheel we found ourselves tied to.

I didn't grab a coffee generally. Instead, waiting until I got in the office. The train pulled in, only two minutes late. I took my seat and, as usual, met with the gentleman carrying the newspaper. He looked over and took the plunge that day with a full smile. Bringing his face to life for that simple second. Still slightly reserved, but much more than a glance. I gave a half-hearted response, hoping it wouldn't be considered rude. He settled in, opened his paper, and started his drink.

As I sat, gazing out of the window, the train pulled away and the sun began to stretch and welcome us all to another day. The fields flew past, cars just seen fleetingly in the distance, filling the earth with the activity of us all. A sign that the majority of us had arisen once again.

Chapter 12

Arriving one evening at our semi-regular haunt. I got there straight from work, later than the others. A quick call to home to confirm I wouldn't be popping in before going out, I then made my way inside. Annie and Erica in situ at a table in the corner. Chrissie, no doubt running late, but probably also ensuring she got the chance to make an entrance.

'Hi, you, OK? Anyone need a drink?' Greetings with hugs stretched across the table.

'Don't worry, hon, it's fine. We've not long been here ourselves.' Annie smiled at me with welcome warmth, motioning towards their glasses, occupied, already visible at the table. 'All sorted.'

I naturally returned the smile, left my light blue jacket draped over the chair, and headed up to the bar. Still in my work attire. An alternative dress code to many of the others scattered at various tables within. Many comfortably placed, most likely for the duration of the evening. I'd made it out, though, which was the important part.

Before too long, I carried my large white wine to the table, along with a large gin (and small tonic) for Chrissie, in anticipation of her imminent arrival. There was very rarely any need to enquire as to what she would be consuming.

Just as I set the glasses down at the table, Chrissie strolled confidently in. Her hair perfectly wavy, full of its usual red/blond bounce. Greetings took place, and I passed her drink over to her before she sat down.

The conversation revolved around everyone's latest news. The trials, changes, and celebrations of the past few weeks. Chrissie in full flow and as gregarious as ever. It appeared she'd been working solidly in the salon over the previous days. An unusual statement, the point not missed by the rest of us.

Erica elaborated on the increasing amount of time her dad needed her for. Much to her husband's annoyance, I gathered from her tone. I didn't pry. It's not that I didn't care, but just that I knew from previous conversations of late that if Erica wanted to talk, she would let us know. Sometimes, for her own sanity, she found it easier not to talk but just to relax and enjoy the time away from it all that she spent with us. Certain she knew we would always listen, I still respected her decision, sometimes, not to ask us to.

'So, Georgia, is work still keeping you super busy?' Annie enquired, accepting delivery of fresh drink from Erica's hand.

Following our conversation a while back, it wasn't lost on me that she might have started this topic on purpose. An opportunity to check up amongst witnesses.

'Yes, you know how it tends to go. The need to keep a roof, food, nails done, etc.' Not all that comfortable in the spotlight, but clearly, my reply wasn't quite enough as Annie proceeded to mention how tired I looked. I thanked her for her compliment.

Chrissie couldn't help but plough in.

'Really, George, you do look like you could do with a break. Do you get to spend much time with Simon and the boys at the moment?'

I paused, as she knew the answer. We both did. No, I wasn't spending as much time with them as maybe I should.

'It's a bit of a balance at the moment, but it's fine. It'll calm down before long, I'm sure.' Defensive in my response. Those words in themselves an admission. The sort of which I had not clearly uttered until that point. I attempted to give it a flippancy to deflect concern away.

Annie looked directly at me as I took a slightly larger drink from my glass than I perhaps meant to. The intensity of her look left me more uneasy. Unable to cope with the conversation proceeding much further along this track, I deployed some flippancy.

'I know Chrissie understands, but the lucky bitch is out the other side now.' I smiled and winked at Chrissie as the words shakily moved from my lips. Chrissie acknowledged the effort in my declaration and laughed, raising her glass in mock celebration of her own achievements. Her arm draped around me with more force than appeared in an affectionate half hug as she agreed.

'Yes, I can sit back a bit now and wait for you to finish so we can drink together.' Shared laughter filled the place of unease and we all toasted to meeting more often. The ice was broken for that moment. The weight of a situation I seemed to be creating, dispersed for a time.

The evening disappeared before we knew it, turning itself into night. Grabbing food and drinking way more than we should, we later gathered our bags and stood to leave. Thankfully, we had moved the conversation on from my situation, instead discussing Annie's business proposal and Erica's dad's diagnosis. Chrissie managed to lighten a few of the heavier moments as she often did. Her outrageous stories could deter the most serious topic from being continued. Thriving on entertaining. As we set off to leave, I was hit by how tired I felt all of a sudden. Aware of how rough I must have been looking and how immaculate Chrissie still appeared to be. I guessed that could have been due to the fact she would disappear to the ladies every half an hour, and I barely bothered. Attending to my appearance was furthest from my mind.

Hugs all round and promises to see each other again soon. Each leaving the pub to make our way to homes that awaited us.

Chrissie and I walked arm in arm. Taking us back to late teenage years when we'd both staggered back home from similar evenings. Walking only so far together, giving three rings as friends each reached their own destinations. The excitement of getting dressed up at your best friend's house before endeavouring to get served underage at some establishment on the high street. Chrissie and I managed that evening to half laugh our way home before we had to take different directions. Pausing at that spot, Chrissie gazed at me, too seriously, for just a moment.

'Annie is right, you do look tired – have you been to the doctor, like we talked about?'

Not sure if she was swaying a little or if it was my own doing, I was certainly desperate to avoid revisiting that topic that very night.

'No, it's just work and stuff – you know how it is...' Trailing off, I looked away, slightly out of the moment. Undoubtedly the result of several glasses of wine too many. Yet I did feel present enough to know I didn't want to have to answer any more such questions tonight, or ever.

'Look at me.' Chrissie gently but firmly grabbed my elbows and turned my body to look directly at her. There was a moment of stillness, and then we both giggled and fell into each other in a light break.

She composed herself, pulled away, still looking at me.

'I know we've had a few too many tonight, but I am serious.' She steadied herself. 'You really should try to get some help. It's not just work, is it? I'm sure it's way more than just being busy. You certainly don't seem your usual self, hon. Do you want to talk some more?' The last sentence came out with a hint of a drunken slur.

I felt myself swaying a little from the combination of cold air, wine, and food. My guard was down, now out of place.

'Oh, we all have good weeks and bad weeks. I think you just caught me at a low point the other week. That's all. It'll be fine. Honest.' Chrissie looked at me. While she was a bit worse for wear, she still managed to gaze directly at me, presenting her genuine concern.

'I'm here for you if you need to talk, you know that. We all are. Why don't you guys get away? Just book a holiday somewhere?' She steadied herself once more and looked me right in the eye.

Running a hand through her hair, as if smoothing and stabilising her being, before she continued.

'Don't keep quiet, George. You do that too often.' A verbal wagging of finger. 'Trouble is...it *will* kill you in the end.' I looked at her quickly, shocked by her blunt attitude, but assumed the booze was interfering. Looking downwards, I managed to utter the words to confirm that I knew, and I understood, but also that sometimes it was just necessary to get on with it all. Chrissie looked for a moment, paused with concern. Yet all she said was, 'At least get to the doctors – they might be able to help.'

Chrissie gave me an affectionate smile, lightening the mood somewhat. I returned it with a reassuring hug, reminded her to give me the standard three rings, and we went our separate ways.

The black front door allowed me back in, carefully, trying desperately not to wake everyone up. Slipping off my heels and jacket, they disappeared from my fingers, dropping to the wooden floor. The bottom of the stairs, an entrance area for letting it all fall. Pausing, barely breathing for a moment, I held on to see if anyone was disturbed by my error. Pause. Still. Ear bent. No sound.

I couldn't help but notice how different I then felt after a night out. Comparing it to years before, when in my early 20s, I'd have felt giddy and giggly. At that moment, I was tired. Not just sleepy, but so, so tired. Of so much. The weight within had become more and more apparent over the last few months. I found it hard to bear at times. An impossible load. My body ached, my mind a blur. Constantly perceived as having let down my friends and my family. Possibly most importantly I was letting down myself.

And yet most days I just didn't seem to care.

Running unfamiliar fingers through my hair, I stood still, looking. The mirror adorning the hall, bouncing back the current version of me. A woman I no longer really recognised. It wasn't about wrinkles and lines that Botox could fix, if I chose. This was the ingrained markings of a life I struggled some days to wade through. Had no enthusiasm for. Too much to carry as I moved from day to day. I looked at myself, examined the features. Deflated. That was it. That word seemed to fit. Yet deep amongst the disappearance of youth, elements of my mum were pushing forward to be seen. Acknowledged. I could pick them out gently from amongst everything else I saw, including the tiny flickers of my absent father.

Even after a lovely and very welcome evening, what was there? Heaving a quiet sigh, I laboriously climbed the stairs to find some rest before I was forced to carry on the next day.

In the morning I awoke, rolled towards my bedside table, and noted the time. 5.29am. One minute before the alarm would disturb the peace. I lay back down with a heave and closed my eyes for just a moment.

Comments made by my friends the night before still drifted around in my head. I'd been found out. That was at least how it felt. They had seen through me. Broken my façade.

Hauling myself up, I located slippers by the bed and came to standing. Head slightly reeling a little from the night before, but I would be OK. Coffee. Coffee would make it all OK. Having carefully padded my way downstairs, I found the strength to enlist the kettle's help.

Chapter 13

I was flying. Arms stretched out as far as they could reach, and I became almost weightless. Soaring. Gliding. Drifting higher, then dipping a little lower as the wind and my momentum took me. Dodging clouds that appeared in my path. I was safe. Not only that, I was also secure. Smiling, I closed my eyes and felt the wind gently coaxing me over hills, houses, and fields. Open eyes, smile broadening as I felt the weightlessness lifting me. Carrying me for miles.

The wind was gentle yet strong. Strong enough to lift me up, while I made no effort to remain there. I did nothing to help. The wind, the breeze, did it all for me and I merely lay back and let it.

My eyes started to move. Eyelids flickered slightly, and I was aware of consciousness greeting me like an old friend. Gently nudging me to move a little, open my eyes still more and then greet the forthcoming day.

When I could fully see, I was met by the sun gently starting to stream through the window. The blind forcefully holding some of it back. My legs began to shuffle a little as I came around to the living once again.

I noted the time. 7.30 a.m. Late for me, but having remembered it was a Sunday, I didn't rush to get up and meet the various things that no doubt needed attending to. I had clearly been in a deep sleep. Now struggling to come around, I increased the movement in my legs, knowing it would serve to wake up the rest of me.

I turned over to see Simon still fast asleep. Not surprising. I recalled he was up late engrossed in some film or other; I assumed, anyway. We barely spoke much of last night. After the argument. He had made some comment about me not being home enough. Probably a valid point, but I didn't need it at that moment. I didn't need to hear how I should be there for him. How I should be working less now and why hadn't I started looking at holidays? And why was I always so snappy? So miserable. Maybe he'd had a tricky day. I didn't stop to ask. I barely said anything. The barrage of noise washed over me. Don't get me wrong, I had initially tried to give a tertiary response, but then I just gave up. What was the point at that moment? Too much sound. Too little being heard.

I gradually and carefully moved my legs to hoist myself out of bed, trying not to wake him.

With my slippers and dressing gown in hand, I crept out of our room and down the stairs. Heading for the kettle before anything else. Then, with my tea in hand, I moved through to the back sunroom.

The dream remained within me for a time. I took the subtle feeling of peace and opportunity with me into that day. A chair welcomed me as I pulled my dressing gown around me a little tighter. Recalling how magical it had felt to fly. To have nothing holding me down, disappointing me or weighing upon me. I hadn't had such a dream of freedom for so many years. Not since my 20s, I was sure. Was it really that long ago? I was free then. I was happy and embarking on exciting adventures. It all just changed.

At that point, that moment, everything was all so different. I just didn't know or understand why.

Chapter 14

So, I took Chrissie's advice. What did I have to lose?

'Georgia Florence?' A voice called. Hoisting myself from the waiting room seat, I followed the doctor to her room.

Her smile seemed inviting, given with care. Yet I sat there feeling such a fraud. Where did I start? How could I even put into words how I felt?

'How can I help?' Standard question on arrival, of course. A genuine sentiment, I had no doubt. Reliable script.

Noticing the family photos on her desk, a hint of a life outside that office, I took a deep breath in. Tried to be prepared.

'I don't really know where to start.' I had said something, at least.

The doctor didn't jump in with further immediate questions but instead took a moment to really look at me as if trying to ascertain what might be the issue, to save me a job of trying to explain.

'I am not right. I mean mentally. God, that sounds so ridiculous.' What on earth? How did that tell her anything? How did that detail what I felt? Stupid!

'OK, can you describe in what way? Do you have any physical symptoms or is it just how you feel, emotionally?' Her warmth in speech was apparent. However, I found myself guarded, almost wishing I hadn't taken this route, hadn't listened to Chrissie's suggestion.

I was still really holding back. Because the minute I spilt all the words of description that I had to use, I would wish I hadn't set them free. The ridiculous statements would make me ashamed of myself. Confused by my own brain. Yet I needed to give this a shot and I needed to say something, at least. Chrissie was bound to keep mentioning it until I did take action. Simon knew I was here. He might even ask about it later.

'Low.' Pause. 'I feel low.'

'OK. Any physical symptoms or issues at all?' She turned to the computer screen. I guess briefly scouting through my file the 'all about me' section. Maybe to check for any history of mental health issues, look at my background, family history…oh, and I guess check my age. That inevitability had not escaped me.

'Erm, I guess, tired, a little stressed…I think it's more in my head than physical, if that makes sense?'

That warm smile again. Sympathetic. Possibly wondering why I'm here, in a suit, clearly from a role of responsibility, trying hard to string a sentence together.

'Periods OK?'

And that's when I knew where she was going. Diagnosis complete. No further discussion required.

I took the leaflets, promised to look over the websites, and contact her again in a couple of weeks. I walked away.

* * *

Matt and I were huddled over the one copy of *Romeo and Juliet* later that same day. I'd given Simon a brief rundown of my medical encounter. Think he made some joke about hot flushes in an attempt to diffuse matters. I only half listened.

Matt's dark blue hoodie sat loosely on his broad shoulders. Ripped jeans finishing the look. His desk littered with paper and pens and sweet wrappers a plenty. His bedroom an ever-evolving reflection of the fifteen-year-old he was. A teenage personality projected on to walls with pictures, shelves of rugby trophies, and floor with a wardrobe spilt.

Reading and re-reading to decipher and discuss what it was that Shakespeare meant with the words he gave his characters to say. Matt generally understood. He just sometimes asked for a little extra dose of suggestion, more information as needed. Not necessarily an area I would have described myself as an expert in, but I could recall similar studies from my own long-lost education.

Homework.

Always presenting mine on time, I did my very best. Bedroom in later years filled with walls of notes, flashcards, spider diagrams. Revision was a serious issue. I was a serious and determined individual. Driven.

Luckily for Matt, he had a firm grasp on much of his work. No doubt he would ideally have spent all his days on the rugby pitch, but he was old enough now to see an element of the reality of Plan Bs. Not that one existed for him at that moment, but I think he figured getting some half decent exam results would at least give him a chance at whatever he wanted to use them to do.

Strangely enough, I relished those moments over a tattered old schoolbook. Ever conscious that this child, becoming a man, would be leaving before we knew it. Leaving to make his own mark, his own future in the world. The moments of conversation, often of nothing particularly important, were what could sometimes make my day. All else stopped and my only role at that very moment was 'mum'.

However, as Matt grew older, his relationship with Simon seemed to become the one of best fit. We were still close, but it definitely wasn't quite the same. I was no longer needed for the mundane food provision, dressing assistance. I was there for understanding literature, taxi service, and the occasional hug. Simon seemed to meet Matt's needs more. Was I jealous? Undoubtedly so.

Then he uttered, 'I'm glad you're here coz Dad knows diddly about Shakespeare.' Smiling as he carried on making his notes, I took it as a compliment and tried not to wonder whether I would be the selected assistant if Simon knew more about the topic.

'Well, I'm glad you are glad.' I replied. Taking a second to rest my hand on his shoulder. The affection hopefully not lost on him. Yet to diffuse the moment and keep it from becoming uncomfortable for my fifteen-year-old,

I messed his hair up as I moved to sit on his bed.

I stayed. I stayed whist he completed his work. He still asked me to do that occasionally, just to be available. And so, I just did it. Always taking in his room. Smiling to myself at the contrast of Lego figures and aftershave.

Idle chatter between bouts of work filled the space. I let him lead the conversations. He would sometimes just use those moments to off load. To share concerns, or sometimes to just ask what was for dinner. I was there for all of it, every last drop.

All work completed, I paused and just looked at him for a moment. He tidied his books together, leaving them to the one side of his desk and started telling me about the highlight of his geography class. Something about a joke between him and a couple of his neighbouring friends that filtered along the row of desks and made the end of the lesson much more enjoyable than the beginning had been. I was listening, well, half listening. I was soaking him in. Absorbing my son's happiness and the man he was fast becoming. The calm of his father and possibly the drive to academia from me. Feeling so often taken aback by these people we made. These humans we created. It was apparent they would never truly understand the joy they had given me, given us. Or the sadness they would bring, as I knew my time with them, guiding and enjoying them, was not limitless.

Chapter 15

'Off for a bit of lunch. I'll be back in about an hour.' My voice carried over to Millie as I stepped out the door. 'If Mr Smithson calls, tell him I've chased up a response to our query at HMRC and I'll be in touch as soon as I hear. He's bound to call again, but there's nothing else I can do for a day or two now.'

'Lunch? Most unlike you, but good. Get some fresh air,' Millie replied. 'I'll let him know.'

'Thanks. See you in a bit.'

I rarely nipped out or did anything much for lunch in those days. It was easier to just keep going most of the time and get more work done. Slowly ploughing through a bit of salad or pasta as I went. However, that day I just felt stifled. I had a headache forming and needed to escape. The desire to leave the office and not return felt almost overwhelming as I walked down the stairs to reception. However, I knew I would, in fact, be back in a while. Though nothing to actually stop me leaving. A perk of partnership, I guess, but I just knew I wouldn't.

Heading out, the sun was shining directly in my face as I pulled the main door open. It was an encouraging day, with a gentle May breeze. Making my way down the high street, I searched for my sunglasses in my bag as I walked. Found myself heaving a sigh as I strolled along, heading towards the little sandwich shop I used on the very odd occasion. The queue was out the door and I took my place as I eyed up the menu. The lady in front of me turned around as a noise further behind in the queue grabbed her attention.

Following her gaze, I also turned and looked briefly at what appeared to be a small child having knocked over the floor sign. As I gazed back, the visibly older lady in front gave me a small smile. Not particularly feeling the impetus to make small talk or greet new people, but also not wanting to be rude, I granted her a light smile in return.

'Such a lovely time in life, isn't it? Youth?' She looked again at the child, then back at me. Her smile further extended.

'Yes, it is,' I plainly replied. Also thinking how quickly the exuberance of youth often comes to an end. I looked up, overly concentrating on the high-up menu, to make my choice.

The lady in front was served, which thankfully ended our chat, and before long I was leaving the sandwich bar with my lunch in hand.

Walking back down the street, I made my way towards the small park. Hoped it wouldn't be too busy and thankfully it wasn't. Finding a free bench, I took a seat. It felt both alien and yet comforting to be sitting in the fresh air and as the sun beat down, I tried to relax a little. My lunch sat on the bench next to me and I gazed around. Not many people in the area, not surprisingly. It was a small park, tucked off the main street, and it had no play areas or cafés. Just trees, some plants, a small path running through it, and a few benches. Most of the other seats were occupied, yet still it felt empty.

Taking my head up high, looking over at the taller trees and the clouds, it actually felt good to stop for that moment. I don't know what caused me to pause that day for lunch, but I was grateful that I had. As I sat there, I could feel my breath gradually slowing down. I purposefully observed the birds in the trees, the tops of the branches. The pattern of wood against the blanket of blue. The endless sky. I looked over at the other benches, the people also enjoying the chance to stop for a moment. An older couple was across from me. They sat laughing together and munching on what looked like sausage rolls. Then they stopped laughing and just sat in silence watching the birds hanging around on the path, hunting for odd crumbs. Comfortable in each other's company, clearly. I found myself watching and smiling...

Unwrapping the sandwich, I took a first bite and noted my shoulders dropping a little as I waded my way through the food. Still taking in the detail of the beauty around me, I found myself looking upon things as if for the first time. Allowing the air to drift across my face, sun bringing me light. My head became full of the words *I wish it would all stop. I wish it could just stop for a while and allow me to think, to catch up.* Acknowledgment that I felt a need for some time and space. I found myself finishing my sandwich and drink and still sitting in the park. I had no enthusiasm for anything else. Not my kids, my husband, not even my friends on occasions, all of which sounded awful and terribly selfish. But that was the reality of how I felt. Sometimes, no, often, I didn't want to be with others. I didn't know what I wanted to say when I was with them, and I felt anxious about how they felt about me.

It was difficult not to consider how long I had really felt like that. Months, possibly years, maybe? Could it really have been that long? Creeping up on me like a ghost of a past life? I had started to look over the information from the doctor. But it was almost too much of an effort to do so. An effort to face help. Maybe take it on. Consumed by a deep reluctance to change everything.

Chapter 16

The phone vied for my attention once more.

Group chat had been busy. Not for me, though. That day, I just needed air. Unable to entertain others, forced to make small talk. It wasn't within my capabilities. The sound of the outside filtered in through the open window, set free to welcome it in. I'd tucked myself up within the corner of the sofa in the sunroom. Magazine discarded precariously on my lap. I should have been working. The laptop and files, all abandoned on the floor. Cast aside. My mind was unable to focus enough to even reach out for them.

Now and then I would look up from the magazine that I wasn't really involved in, prompted by a movement in the clouds above. Aware I was focussing on sounds from the inhabitants of trees, the gentle breeze moving the bamboo that ran along one side boundary. No formal music required.

As the front door opened, I heard the familiar greeting let loose from Simon. Weekend meeting completed, he joyously came through and popped his head briefly round the door.

'Hey – I'm all done now for the weekend.' Broad smile, tie lacking, bag held loosely by his side. 'Cuppa? You OK?'

'Yes, fine and yes, please.' Forcing a smile as I looked over. Providing the required facial feature, before I took my attention to the magazine, hoping that my request would bring an end to the conversation. It did. For a moment.

Tea arrived and Simon perched, slightly precariously, on the arm of the sofa, a clear intention of not stopping long.

'Have you finished the work you had on the go today?' Casting an eye to the fallout at my feet, he took a sip of his coffee and adjusted his position to be more comfortable.

'I've not even started, is the truth.' My smile somewhat forced, my expression clearly indicated an element of 'and so be it'.

'Not like you – you, OK?' His arm lay along the top of the sofa, as a remote form of affection, while he looked at me intently.

The conversation continued flippantly. Skirting around, careful to not unlock a depth of concern.

'I've just not got the enthusiasm for it at the moment and so I didn't even start. It will keep, it's fine. I'll deal with it on Monday.' My tea was hot, but I persevered to take a sip and found the burning sensation almost relieving.

I'm not sure what else I might have expected him to say.

He moved to stand up, the conversation clearly almost wrapped up.

'We need to get that holiday booked, love. It will be good for all of us.' He focussed intently. Really looked at me as if trying to present the remedy to my problem, tick that task off my list.

'It will be good for *you*. Good for you to have something to look forward to. Have you had a look?'

A break. Even that thought brought me no immediate joy. It would not be the answer. I was sure of that. Then – anyway. I informed Simon I'd had a quick search, but I would look over it more soon. Forcefully, he reminded me there wouldn't be much choice if we didn't get booked before long. Time was running out. I resisted the urge to tell him I was very much aware of that. Another argument over some trivial matter would bring me no comfort. It would only serve to exacerbate the feeling that his sight of me was superficial. Notice my face. My eyes. Surely, he'd see that my shoulders or hair must reflect the way I was feeling. Maybe if he just really stopped and looked, he'd see. He'd notice me.

As he exited the room, the slight patter of water against the panes accompanied the end of the scene.

I went back to the magazine, forced myself to look over pictures of lives dreamily successful. People building their lives, achieving, content. Did those people have to get themselves together before they headed for the photo shoot? Had their perfect homes come about after days of tidying and cleaning, removing all remnants of reality? Maybe they were in fact emotionally lost just moments before they opened the door? No one would know. Deemed success was no guarantee of happiness. Not ever. Doors could hide so much. Even the most beautifully crafted ones.

Sighing, I gave up and tossed the magazine to the side. Flipped over my phone to see an abundance of unread messages in the group. I didn't even want to start trying to play catch up with the chat. Motivation no friend of mine.

I gave up. Decided on taking myself off for some peace. Jack and Matt were both out, but the opportunity for quiet wouldn't last long. Their voices would soon trip through the house, reaching me as soon as they made their way up the stairs. I didn't have long.

Rain knocked against the glass as I lay back in the bath. A storm was building, and the forthcoming tension I could feel was escalating around the house. The sky seemed unusually dark for an afternoon. A turbulent wind working its way up to punishing everything in its path.

Leaning back against the cold porcelain, I closed my eyes. I couldn't recall the last time the opportunity to soak had arisen. The heat of the water turning my skin a shade of deep pink, but I didn't care or really notice much. The solitary candle flickered intermittently as a result of the wind creeping through the window left ajar. It complimented the mood. I sank deeper into the water.

Trying to dismiss the urge to cry, to give in to feeling completely helpless, I instead released an emotion filled breath.

The weight of the increasing storm outside could do nothing to lift me up.

After drying off, I sat at the dressing table and studied my face in the mirror. My shoulder length wet hair hung limp and dragged my face down towards the floor. I had been considering whether to get some snappy, short cut but never actually took the plunge. The old me would have done it. I would have courted the view of a close friend or two and then gone and cut it off, regardless. Rebellious. I might even have had a different colour put through it. Not anymore. Would everyone notice, make comments? Would I regret it? Is that the sort of cut for a professional woman in her 40s? The real me would have changed my clothes to fit the cut, regardless of my job. Things had become too sensible, too conformist. How many times a day did I now smile? Laugh? I decided not to consider that too much and began to brush my hair.

Dry hands began to play about with putting it up, scraping the sides away with clips, leaving the top hanging forward. The water droplets continued to find a landing on my face, but for that small moment I saw a glimpse. A fragment of who I used to be. Taking my hair sharply away from my features. Revealing a different person. For a second, I could see the prospect of something positive. Maybe there was something inside that moment that I could build upon. Even if so, that was not going to be the day to try. Strength had abandoned me. Long left me behind.

Chapter 17

Cold hands clasped in tight fists. My feet mirroring the shapes produced.

Eyes are closed and yet I can clearly visualise my toes. White from the pressure of stopping the blood as they cling for life on the edge. Cuts starting to open on the bottom of my biggest toes. Incisions made by stones and shards that line up on the edge of the cliff top.

Just a few centimetres keep me solid. Keep me from disappearing before I have decided. A few centimetres stand between me and an end to this pain. The pain caused by making myself a priority. Trying to find my life again. That is what I thought would happen.

Pain seeps up from the top of my feet, tendons through the muscles and round to my calves. There is a rigidness within my legs, desperately trying to support and protect my toes. My almost fractured feet.

Chapter 18

The air turned colder as the breeze gathered pace. I shuffled rhythmically from one foot to the other, almost appearing to have a casual dance on the sidelines. Neck involuntarily burrowed into my shoulders as far as it could possibly hide.

A long brown coat and patterned scarf hid several other layers of clothing. I was prepared. Having done this many times before. I knew only too well how the wind would rip across the fields, slicing through each and every one of us as it went. This Sunday morning was no exception.

'There you go.' Annie handed me the much-needed warmth of a coffee. That morning's saviour against the unseasonable weather.

'Thanks, hon.' I took a sip and then instantly regretted it as the heat scorched my innocent tongue.

'Any changes?' Annie enquired as she chose to hold her cup with two hands, taking in the warmth from a sensible perspective initially.

'No – not in terms of tries but some good play from what I can see, and the little I know of course.' I updated her, while deciding to adopt her approach with the coffee. 'No injuries so far, which is always good news.'

Matt's interest in playing rugby had been a regular weekend event for about four years, the last two alongside Annie's nephew, Tom. This provided the opportunity for company and lift sharing. Often opportunities for myself and Annie to catch up in the cold. Matt had built up some amazing friendships as a result, and while I didn't claim to understand all the rules, I did enjoy seeing him play. Very occasionally, Simon and I would both go along (normally when the weather was more amenable) but that day was my turn. While the thought of huddling in the bitterness of the English breeze didn't always appeal at 8 a.m. on a Sunday, I played my part. Standing on the sidelines at that moment, I was both proud and freezing. The sidestep shuffle continued as I held the coffee a little closer and a little firmer.

A roar went up, catching me a little by surprise, as I couldn't see the area of play from our position. Apparently, our team had scored. Evidenced by the gathering of the team shorts and huge grins coupled with congratulatory slaps on backs.

'Yes!' shouted Annie exuberantly. Always so keen to celebrate her nephew's achievements. I didn't know if she had a better view than I did or was paying more attention, but she seemed to have spotted the event earlier than I had cottoned on. Tom looked over and sent out a delighted grin over to Annie's direction.

'I can't tell who scored,' she uttered. 'It might have been Matt.' Feeling pride, even at the unconfirmed success, I tried to catch his eye to wave congratulations, but he was enveloped within his team and the moment.

'I think that puts us in the lead,' Annie remarked, while quickly messaging her sister-in-law to provide an update. I briefly acknowledged the statement before taking a drink of my slightly cooler coffee. Instantly feeling comforted and a touch warmer, I went in for more.

'So, how have you been?' Annie's enquiry caught me off guard. No direct eye contact made in the process, yet I knew she saw me.

'Uhmmm, OK I guess,' I replied. Not sure what else would be an acceptable response. Not sure what else I wanted to say.

'I'll accept that response for the moment, but I don't want to find you curled up in a heap on your kitchen floor all because you didn't open up.' Looking directly at me, she firmly smiled. Her shot meant with the best of intentions, though a little uncharacteristically forceful. She then moved in and put her arm around my shoulders, giving me a shot of additional warmth.

'I'm here.' Is all she whispered.

The moment was disturbed by the appearance of one of the other player's mums. I didn't know her all that well, but I'd nevertheless already made my own mind up. Just from a few previous meetings. It was the immaculate make-up, hunter boots, wax jacket. I shouldn't have assumed anything, but of course, I did. The wind seemed to step up a bit as she arrived and I found myself regretting dashing out the door earlier with muddy wellies thrown in the car, hair roughly tied back, and a small splash of mascara at the most.

'Hey ladies.' The greeting accompanied by a broad smile.

'Hi,' we replied in almost unison. Not wanting to appear impolite, but also keen to not get involved in too extensive a conversation.

'Great to see you...' The greeting an opportunity to display her beautiful teeth, encased by perfectly applied lippy. 'Haven't seen you for a while, Georgia – you picked a good morning for it, although cold as normal.' She smiled broadly and half motioned towards the clear, bright sky.

I felt hurt instantly (was that me being extra sensitive?) Then realised I had no recollection of her name, yet she knew mine. I found myself silently trawling through the alphabet, waiting for one of the letters to jump out at me and help my memory.

At the same time, not able to let it go, I launched a defence.

'I am here quite often, most weeks to be honest. Maybe I'm grabbing a coffee when you arrive?' Not sure why I felt that need. Her face instantly looked a little confused.

'Are you?' She questioned. 'Oh. I must have just missed seeing you then. Well, better catch up at the other end. See you later.' She disappeared off with a flourish of some form of perceived superiority. I passed a look towards Annie. Still not having been able to recall her name.

Why should it have mattered to me? Yet I stood there trying to recall the various Sundays and the results, as if to test whether I actually did attend as much as I thought. Hoped.

'Before you even start mulling over what she said, just leave it. You know what she's like.' Annie dismissed the moment.

'I'm not sure if I'm more bothered by what she said (which I will admit I am a bit) or the fact I can't recall her name at all.'

'Genuinely don't even bother.' Annie's affectionate hand sat lightly on my arm for a moment before she turned her attention back to the game. The play moved further towards us and a group of players almost blended into one, gathering pace, heading in our direction. A collection of muddied knees, faces full of exertion.

'It's Jessica, but I really wouldn't worry – best forgotten.' I gave a flippant smile and inwardly tried to note the information for future. Still trying to recall…I knew I had missed last weekend but the weekend before I was sure that was the week Matt had left his boots at home and we had to turn around almost as soon as we arrived to get them…Then the week before that…

I could see pockets of games and Sundays, but I couldn't find the memories. Where was the detail? It should have been there, tucked away. Confusion and panic began to rise within.

My thoughts were then interrupted by the whistle for half time. Shaking myself out of negative thoughts, I pushed a tear away from one eye.

The rest of the match played out, and I concentrated on the action. Matt managed to avoid major injury which was more than could be said for his top. Annie updated me on her plans to set up her website. Her enthusiasm was enviable.

Saying our goodbyes to everyone, Matt replayed a few moments from the game as we walked towards the car. Still fired up from the action, his tired smile served to remind me of what was important, the joy he was immersed in. My doubts from earlier nudged aside. I tried to refrain from being so self-critical. However, the burn on my tongue still lingered.

Chapter 19

It was clear Simon was annoyed. Unhappy with me.

The holiday would have been sorted before. It should have been. He would have dealt with it. However, he knew I was picky and so had left it to me. Simon struggled to decide, always just content to go anywhere. As a result, I had generally been the one to make the decision and put arrangements in place. That year, however, I had failed. Not gotten round to it. Then it seemed I might be too late.

So, there I found myself, searching, yet again. A quiet Sunday morning, Simon pottering in the garden, boys still in bed and I was sitting, laptop on, coffee poured. Just searching.

Generally, we would head for the sun in foreign climes. At that time though, everything I would normally have looked at seemed to already be fully booked. The odd little apartment appeared on the screen, but nothing I thought would be universally acceptable. Nothing at all. Just because I hadn't sorted it. Hadn't been organised enough.

After a time, I found myself just absently scrolling through pages and pages of Google's finest. The screens blurred into one and I was lost with images of beaches, cocktails, and sunsets. After a few more 'checking availabilities' and getting nowhere, I leant back in the chair and cupped the coffee mug as though it might bring about some more direction, and also luck, in finding a place to escape to.

Glancing up, I saw Simon. Out in the sunshine. Adorned in his familiar gardening shorts and top. The sun streamed through the branches of the trees to the left. The light forming rays that gently sat over the plants and lawn wherever it hit. Little breeze to disturb the quiet and aside from the occasional bird and train in the distance, it was peacefully quiet.

I watched him. Sat and watched my husband. So considered in the way he tended to the plants that needed support. The flowers wanting propping up against the trellis. He seemed to find pleasure in the tender way he looked after each individual one. Enjoyed the journey of learning and success.

Stopping for a moment, I acknowledged my luck. So many failed to find someone suitable to share their lives with. Yet sometimes I found myself so hung up on our struggles to find a balance. I couldn't appreciate my situation. We were essentially two different people, mainly with a common cause, trying to work together. Every single day. Yet, that feeling that maybe he didn't always follow me, see me clearly, seemed to gnaw away at me. Our relationship was good. It did mainly work. I could see that.

Finishing my coffee, I decided another was in order. Popping my head out of the French doors to offer Simon one too, I then made my way into the kitchen to make refreshments for us both.

The view out of the kitchen window, to the front of the house, was just as calm. The shutters gently allowed the sun to find its way through the slats, gliding onto the kitchen worktops and over the cupboard fronts. As I waited for the machine to produce, I couldn't help but stare outside. Took myself away for a moment. The machine made the familiar sounds, and I finished the drinks, taking them back through to the rear of the house.

Heading for another round of holiday searching, I started typing away to discover. The search results began to be interspersed with adverts and suggestions of holidays in our own, slightly less sunshine filled, country. We hadn't holidayed at home for years. Thinking back, I located memories of cottages, some surprises with the weather and plenty of rock pooling. The boys were much younger then, of course. Would they find it as enjoyable now? Bearing in mind the lack of options I was coming across, I decided they probably didn't have much choice. None of us did.

After a time and yet more coffee, I came across a few possibilities on the south coast. After further checking with Simon that he just wanted me to get on, find something, and book it, I pressed the 'pay now' button. Suddenly doubtful of my own abilities in this simple task, I panicked a moment. Certain that I was making some mistake. But payment had already been made and we would be going. It was a week by the sea. Simon was adamant we needed time together away as a family and I'd fixed it. Accomplished something.

'Finally!' He congratulated me on 'ticking the task off my list'. 'It will do all of us some good. Let's just pray for the weather.' He finished his coffee, handed me his cup, and went back to tending his garden.

Simon made it clear he thought taking time away from work, schedules, and commitments would help me to 'process' whatever it was that I was struggling with. I couldn't quite work out what he meant by that? 'Process'. Maybe 'get over it'. Whatever 'it' was. Well, I'd booked it and now I would keep my fingers crossed he would be right.

Chapter 20

Leaving so early in the morning meant an opportunity to relish the quiet calm before the world awoke. Taking turns in driving, Simon started, and we set off with Matt and Jack lazing in the back.

As I began to relax, the music subtly drifted across me, surrounding my settled body. The sun just starting to rise for the day as we drove along the motorway towards the sea. With at least another five hours to go, I allowed myself some time to drift. Eyes gently closed, though not asleep as Simon might have perceived me to be.

I was acutely aware that part of me had already written off the week before it had started. Placing pressure on what seven nights away might achieve. But as the boredom of the motorway ended, we entered the undulating countryside that welcomed us. Our journey had become a little more convoluted, but the beauty that surrounded us made it worth the task.

Our accommodation was situated just off the main road that led down to the bay. The driveway sat on an incline, with the pathway running alongside and leading to the front door. Lavender plants took over part of the entrance, forcing us to brush past them as we entered. The scent as we opened the door of the cottage lingered.

The following day I found 'my place'.

It was the perfect spot. A place where I could sit and look out to sea and just about make out the shapes of others there. Boys riding the waves on body boards, along with other visitors and no doubt some locals alike. The water was typically cold but not enough to put anyone off making the most of a day of coastal sun.

It wasn't that I didn't want to join them, but instead I was absorbing the quiet moments so lacking in my days, like so many others. That snatched week wouldn't provide enough to recharge. I knew that. But I was allowing myself to be wrapped in a warmth and solitude I realised I had missed.

I know now that this was where it really began.

The location seemed to be all you could want from a break at the beach. Feeling the air on your face. Our real home provided a lovely setting, but there was always an excitement about being at the beach. As a family, we'd had some great holidays abroad, but there was really something about our homeland. England. For me anyway. As the years passed and we became more financially able, it seemed the thing to do, to holiday abroad. I was now reminded that while those were treasured memories, maybe this place would turn out to be much more *me*.

I sat taking in the view spread out before me. The way the hills and cliffs cocooned the beach kept us all safe as we enjoyed the sand and the sea. Watching Simon and the boys, I felt no need to be anywhere else. The sun draped itself gently over me, like a veil, allowing me to subtly observe life. Not a strange feeling. I was used to the sensation of being a bystander.

The wind blew a gentle breeze, kept somewhat at bay by the curve of land that sat behind me. The cliffs appeared somewhat imposing, but I only felt their comfort. My toes gently played with the sand as I sat, legs outstretched and arms behind, propping me up. Swishing, moving through the sand, taking it from side to side. My solid toes, smooth skin, painted nails. Complete.

Watching my family, I was reminded of how detached I could sometimes feel from them. As though I were some ghostly apparition, the need for my physical presence gone. Such an overreaction in my head, yet it wouldn't disappear. Like so many other thoughts I couldn't lose. Had I chosen to move to one side, or had they?

What more could there be in terms of happiness and a sense of achievement than having a family? How many don't ever get that chance, don't find the one they want to be with forever? How many never get the chance to create life? My boys were everything. I was a proud mum. Proud of what I, what we, had achieved in creating a life for those little humans when they arrived. Proud of nurturing them, helping them to be good people. Yet I felt painfully aware that in many ways I was already becoming a little surplus to their needs.

What would my own mum have made at my attempts to raise others? Regretful that she never got to play her part, my dad's opportunity now lost, too. I had accepted the situation was unlikely to change. The distance between us had opened gradually through the years. Fuelled by hurt, maybe jealousy, but certainly loneliness. Events outside of our control had laid bare gaps that previously existed but were now painfully visible. We were different people. He had his new life, and I had mine.

Thoughts disturbed by the return of the sea drenched bodies, talk of ice cream, who held the waves the best and asking on how much of my book I had managed to read. I cast my eyes down to where the paperback sat, the first page not even turned.

Chapter 21

Our first few days passed in a blur of reasonably relaxed conversations, extensive trips to the beach, and individual cafés that lined the small-town square area. Boys were off getting to know some of the younger locals, Simon and I stealing time for drinks alone, taking in the sun and air.

Watching the boys as they ventured into the sea once more, I was conscious that the time we had with them doing this would end. There would be that gap where they adventured with friends, not family, and where their thoughts and ideas passed between them and their peers rather than to us. Inevitably, a sadness filtered into my being, a sense of time slipping away uncontrollably.

As Simon and I took a stroll alone, we made various comments on the surrounding scenery, before stopping to peek in a few shop windows, sometimes venturing in. It was relaxed, and yet I still found myself feeling a little guarded. Taking the plunge to share, I opened up the conversation.

'Do you ever think we should have done things differently?' How much had I actually considered the question before I let it go? Thankfully, the art shop's interior offered a distraction while we strolled through. Suddenly aware of how serious I was sounding; I almost felt the need to retract my question. I hadn't actually intended for this to be a deeply contemplative discussion. It just seemed to flow from my lips.

'Erm, in what way do you mean?' Simon turned from looking at some of the larger paintings, to flicking through prints stacked up to the side. A hint of some concern over where this was going emanated from his lips, yet his hands were occupied in deftly pushing and pulling through the collection of art in front of him. Thoughts of answering his question, but the truth was, I had no idea.

'Do you mean, where we live, the fact we got together...?' A slightly hopeful half smile accompanied his comment, as he looked over before moving on from the prints to casually continue through.

The distraction offered by the talent on the walls didn't stop him from considering the question. Still, we continued to slowly meander through the shop, taking our time over both words and paintings.

Now it appeared to be my turn to give thought to my response to a question and the conversation I appeared to have started. I continued to follow him.

'I mean home, jobs, where we are, where we live. That sort of thing. The map of our lives together.' I was consciously attempting to bring some flippancy to the moment. Reaching to casually touch his arm as I spoke, quietly.

He stopped looking and turned directly to me. Conscious to also be quiet in his voice. The shop wasn't overly busy, and it was big enough to enable several groups to take in the beauty that had been produced. Luckily, other conversations were louder than ours, providing cover for the moment.

I looked back at him.

There was a pause. He seemed to be considering my question further.

'I don't think I do, to be honest.' Breathing out, he looked straight at me. He questioned. 'I feel happy with where we are, don't you?'

That million-dollar question.

What else could I say in the middle of an art gallery? What else could I say when I didn't actually know?

'Yes, of course, just curious, to be honest.' That one dollar lie.

We moved further through the gallery and out the same way we had entered. Sun streaming in from the sea and almost simultaneously we repositioned our sunglasses, and he reached for my hand.

'Just being somewhere like this, wondering what it would be like to actually live here, well it just gets me thinking. Whether if we'd done things differently, made alternative decisions, this would be us. Cottage on the coast, raising surfer dudes…' I trailed off and managed a small smile of disguise, which he reciprocated as we walked down towards the beach.

'We make decisions as we go, don't we? All of us. Depending upon where we are, what we've chosen to be and do. I'm not sure there's any great point in looking back. And then wondering.' His natural desire to avoid the heavy consideration of events and feelings came to the fore. While he was, almost surprisingly, engaging fully in my ponderings, there was an unease which emanated through his words.

'Yes, I do agree. I just think it's sometimes interesting to consider what we could have done differently.' I could sense this conversation would need to come to an end rapidly, as it was clearly making him, maybe both of us, more than a little uncomfortable.

'Is this your way of saying you want to give up accountancy and head for the beach?' His smile made it a light-hearted suggestion. Trying maybe to mask any concern.

The air was fresh but not unduly cold. Yet I felt far from warm at the flippant suggestion.

'No, of course not, just pondering, wondering really.' I hurriedly sought to push the idea away and the tension it created within me. 'I guess sometimes when we stop, all of a sudden there's time and space to think. Dream, consider. I think when I have that time, all sorts of things can just enter your head.' I smiled, adding to the jokiness of my statement.

'I guess.' Simon smiled back. I took it as a genuine gesture of happiness and care. The hint of concern I felt from him previously appeared lifted. Then, without hesitation, a change.

'You, OK? Happy?' Searching my face.

Without hesitation or consideration, I answered.

'I think so.' Somehow, I hoped that would be the end. Yet as soon as the words were out, I realised I wasn't helping him and certainly wasn't bringing any closure.

'Think?' He looked at me again, the seriousness no longer subtle. The air was turning. This was not what I wanted. This was not right. Not for now.

'No, of course I'm happy. I'm just tired, to be honest, that's all.' Glossing over seemed second nature. My hand reassuringly grabbed his arm, in part deflection. I was on a roll, though. A proper conversation where I could share my thoughts. I needed to grab the opportunity. At risk of causing concern, I needed to give it a go.

'I do wonder sometimes if there is more, though. I don't mean about you and the boys, just whether there could be something else, another way of living.' Pausing to try to gauge his response, I found nothing in his face to give anything away. Knowing I was sounding both unhappy and ungrateful. I waited. Aware that I had not uttered such a complete sentence to him, about all this, until that point. The acceptance, or assumption, that he would not understand had always stood in the way.

There was quiet. Quiet apart from the rise and fall of the waves in the distance. The smell of the sea water bouncing along the air. We reached the wall that separated the beach and the small town. Below, on the sands, an abundance of people gathered, just enjoying the coast. Enjoying being. Enjoying where they found themselves that very day.

Leaning on the wall, he placed his hands behind and turned to face me directly.

'I'll be honest. I don't know what else we could wish for, George.' His eyes demanded my attention. 'Obviously, we could do different jobs, or hobbies, but we have so much. So much to be thankful for.' Reaching for my hand, he smiled directly at me in an attempt to end it. He was telling me the truth. I knew he was. He was trying to tell me I had everything. That I had nothing to question or need. His words were wrapped in a warmth I don't think I had anticipated.

'I know. I just...' Trailing off seemed the best response. The only one I could find at that point. Where could I take this now?

With a breath in, I straightened up and let it go. Breaking the exchange, we both gave appreciations of the area and the luck we'd had with the weather so far. Deciding to move on and walk a little more purposefully, the conversation as was, abandoned. Aware that the change was mainly due to his concerted efforts, I was however thankful.

Chapter 22

I gave in.

Book discarded on the blanket; I made my way down to the water's edge. Jack and Matt in full flow ahead. Body boards under arms, shouts of joy and anticipation, waiting for the right moment to ride.

The wind was doing its best to whip up the surf. It skirted along the sea, losing pace as it hit the shore, and then gently moved across my face. Over to the left I could just make out Simon, having invested in full surf attire, taking tips by the look of it from a more experienced thrill seeker.

I waited. The sea gently lapping at my toes as each one gently sank into the still sand. The grains giving way to the weight of my being.

Matt headed over to me, sailing most of the way, with Jack following a few feet behind.

'You have to come in, Mum!' Jack shouted over the sound of the surf. 'Here, have my board!'

Touched by his motion, I took the board from his outstretched arms at the same time a wave almost covered him. His laugh at the incident, so free and natural. A moment of pure joy on his face.

'I've no idea what I need to do, so you'll have to teach me.' I let him know he was now the guide. He showed me how to watch the way the waves built and described the moment to take the plunge. The board felt awkward in my arms. I'd spent hours watching all three of them take to the surf, seemingly natural in their ability to become adept at riding the waves. Time would pass as they made their way back and forth, becoming part of the surf, at one with the tide. Then it became my turn.

Still fumbling somewhat with the board, I made lengthy steps further out to sea. Each one was taking me slightly deeper into the water. A touch colder than I had anticipated it would be. I kept going, mindful that Jack would not accept me retreating now. And I didn't want to. I didn't want to move away from that smile and from this time.

Once we had moved out far enough, Jack told me how I should now turn around to face back towards the beach. Then we had to wait. Wait for the moment when the surf arrived to carry us back to shore. We needed to get it right. I watched Jack for instruction. I watched his smile, the way the sea dripped from his hair onto his face. His grin never left. He was poised. Ready to give me the nod to go.

Having no idea on when 'the right time' would be, I watched him, concentrated on him. Finding myself smiling helplessly, excitement building within. I was once again a child. Cares had left for just that moment. My son and the surf had made sure of that.

'GO!' His call startled me for a second and then I realised. Looking over my shoulder, I had to time the lift off right to be able to hit the wave when it was ready. Anticipation had filled me and on his command I jumped. Clinging on to the board that I had launched with a second's notice. I did it. I was holding on, an unforced smile filling my face as the wave carried me along the sea. A squeal, a shout, laughter, all found coming from within. I couldn't contain the thrill, didn't want to. Tempted to look back for Jack but fearful of ruining the moment and ending up a mess in the water, I held on and rode. Flying, hovering on the waves, just teetering on the sea, heading towards the shore. Hitting the shallow water just meeting the beach, I came to a standstill. Laid over the board, I stayed in place, catching my breath but more importantly laughing. Laughter spilling from my core, without control. The next moment, Jack and Matt were both in front of me, helping me up off the sand. Laughing. We were all just laughing.

Passing the board back to Jack, he took hold of it and went back out to try for the next wave. Matt paired up with him and I watched them head out, looking to time the surf perfectly and together. Aware that the smile had not completely left my face, I turned to watch them every few steps as I walked back to the space, my space on the beach. Smile still fixed upon my features.

Later that day, I left all of them, lazing at the cottage, eager for a little stroll on my own. Simon was taking a much-needed break, sprawled along the sofa. I felt no need to rest. The sun was beckoning me out and so I left.

'Little breezy today.' The voice was light, unfamiliar, and I turned to see its origin. A friendly looking face greeted me, walking up the path towards where I stood. Having left the cottage, my walk had taken me around the roads off the main track that lead to the bay. I'd come to a spontaneous standstill just outside a cottage, colourfully adorned with mesmerising foliage. Those words, as I found, came from a woman a bit older than me (I assumed), with a smile as broad and relaxed as I'd ever seen.

'Yes, yes, it is. Still lovely though...' Trailing off, I found myself a little nervous, as if caught doing something I shouldn't.

'Are you here on holiday?' she asked as she reached the front of the cottage. Coming to a standstill, she looked directly at me.

'Yes. Yes, we are. I'm...erm...here with my family just for a few days more...' Trailing off once more. Not sure what else to say.

'I thought as much. You tend to recognise pretty much everyone who lives here. Especially in the winter, once the holiday makers have gone and it's just us left.' She continued to smile. Welcoming me.

'It's lovely...isn't it?' She motioned towards the cottage; clearly aware I had been admiring it. I was, at that moment, caught in the headlights. Caught doing what? Just stood in front of a cottage while out on a walk. Admiring the beauty of the flowers creating an arch over the entrance. Yet I found myself feeling awkwardly guilty.

'I was just walking by to be honest. It is beautiful, though. Is it yours?'

'Yes. Only recently acquired but I do rent it out. Well, I will be. All year round, ideally. Sorry. I'm Mary. I always forget to introduce myself, sorry.' Holding her hand out in a slightly apologetic fashion. I took it lightly. Her welcoming smile overshadowing the slightly awkward feel of the moment.

I found myself to be more than a little fidgety. Subtly, I started to look around for Simon and the boys.

We shared a smile, mine cautious, as I introduced myself.

'I'm really pleased with how the roses have grown, despite my intervention.' She almost sounded apologetic.

'Gardening is not really my speciality but I'm glad I managed to have some success there.' She smiled, motioning towards the yellow flowers that were set around the brick entrance porch, hiding the front door away a little, from any passing onlookers.

'I'm not great in the garden either to be honest.' My smile masked the slight discomfort I found within myself. 'They are stunning, though.'

'Oh, thank you, that's really kind. The cottage itself is lovely too, but I do think a nice view as you walk up the path makes a real difference.' Her words were inviting, welcoming, capturing my attention.

'I imagine it will be fully booked before long. It's a perfect location, too.' Motioning slightly over to the direction of the bay. Aware that I might have sounded as though I were enquiring, I told myself it really was more about polite conversation. Mary was turning out to be a very welcoming distraction on my walk.

'I think the summer months will be easy to fill, but who knows? Not everyone wants to be here once the sun's gone in.' Still smiling, she headed up the cobbled path towards the front door. Looking back, she invited me in. 'Come and have a look inside if you want? I was just popping in to check it over.'

Without consciously deciding either way, I found myself joining her, heading into the cottage. Moving through the delicate scent of lavender from the bushes strategically placed. Glad to be removed from the main road, I turned my head briefly to cast a glance each way, checking I'd not been seen.

I followed her in. The front door opening directly into a sun-filled lounge/diner. Curtains slightly closed, still giving an insight to the stream of light that would undoubtedly fill the room if given the chance.

'It's not the biggest, but for a couple or a small family it will work well, I think. The neighbour's quite amenable too.' Her smile accompanied by a slight, knowing wink. 'I live next door.' She confirmed with a chuckle.

Marvelling at the ease and happiness emanating from this woman, I found an overwhelming desire to follow her lead.

She continued to show me around. I had given no indication of wanting to know more, but she carried on, nevertheless. As we moved back out towards the yellow frame, I was handed a piece of paper. Her number. Information I did not request. Mary had asked no questions. She seemed to have no need for details or for information on my reason for taking a peek. Mary gave me what she thought I needed, wanted, before I even realised myself.

The front door was locked behind us and a comment was made about the forecast for rain the following day and how we should go enjoy the beach before it arrived. Then, with another broad smile, she was gone.

I looked at the slip of paper.

An unusual gift.

Quickly checking both directions, I moved from the safety of the path slightly hidden from view, onto the main stretch down to the beach. Hoping that Simon and the boys had stayed at our cottage, rather than returning to surf as they said they might, I decided to head back to them. I'd left them for a stroll. A harmless walk, exploring the beauty situated a little away from the beach. Sometimes, it seemed, life had something else in mind.

Chapter 23

'You missed some classic Jack, failing massively at surfing today. How was your stroll?' Simon tucked ravenously into his seafood platter. I found myself thinking carefully before my response.

'I'm sure I did. It's such a nice beach. Perfect for you three to get stuck into.' Concentrating on my fork and the plate of food sat in front of me, I continued, though stepping carefully through my words. 'It was nice. Just good to have a quiet walk and explore.' I avoided his gaze as I spoke. Like some dirty secret I was having to bury for fear of it spilling out, out of control.

'You should come in again. Let go, just get involved.' He looked straight at me as I took another mouthful of my meal. As difficult as it was, I looked directly back at him. Feeling a touch defensive.

'Maybe I will tomorrow…'

It was just the two of us, dining out at a small and comfortable café we'd seen earlier in the week. It was busy, but not bustling. Other diners noticeably relaxed, intermittent laughter amongst the constant jazz playing in the background.

A semi-comfortable silence overtook our meal. The warmth of the atmosphere within the café couldn't help but surround us as we embraced the evening, yet I was a little on edge. Still conscious of what had happened today. It felt as though some secret assignation had begun. Unable to rationalise the innocence of a conversation with a stranger about a beautiful cottage, I tried to concentrate on the moment right in front of me. As our plates were cleared, Simon looked at me and smiled. Reaching across the table with his hand, seeking out mine. 'This is so nice. We should do this more often.' Just a statement.

I smiled. Still slightly uneasy and searching for the correct, the prescribed response. 'Yes, it is.'

The moment felt done. Yet, leaning back a little, taking a sip from his glass Simon said, 'It's been a while since we were able to do this, without one of us having to disappear off to attend some meeting, rugby game or whatever.' I managed a slightly lopsided smile, tempting myself to be more grateful for, and present, in this.

'I'll admit I didn't really expect much from this week, but I've really enjoyed it so far.' His gaze disturbed by laughter, a little too loud for the setting, flooding out from a nearby table. We both looked over and smiled, nevertheless.

'The weather has been amazing considering we're not abroad. I guess it is true that a break is a break wherever you are. It's a change of scenery, a different routine that makes the impact.' He genuinely looked relaxed. My silence thankfully seemed to go unnoticed. Genuinely wasn't sure what to say other than just agree. Which I did.

I looked at him. Really studied him. Taking in the relaxed texture to his face now. Something I wasn't sure I did anywhere near often enough.

His grin was almost infectious. Yet while I increased the extent of my smile in return, I still couldn't really feel the sincerity I was aiming to convey.

Further laughter from a table in the corner, the aroma of rich sauces, flavoursome dishes elevated into the atmosphere of the café like a mist of life. Breathing its joy and energy and gratefulness into the sea of diners. Tables all appeared full; the café busy without being excessively cramped. Exuberant owners dancing from table to table, sharing their joy at being able to welcome strangers along with friends into their home.

We chatted a little more about the week and he asked me where I had walked. I was suitably vague yet trying not to appear to be hiding details. The more I talked, the more guilty I felt. Guilty at looking at a cottage? That was really all I had done. I was trying to convince myself of that.

Having finished our meal, we decided to take the chance for an unhurried stroll along the path that ran a little bit back from the cliff edge. The conversation was light, noncommittal, and as we walked, I felt his hand seek out mine. The smile between us is soft and genuine.

'Let's head down to the beach – it's so quiet.' I followed him down the steps and took off my shoes to feel the soft sand wrapping my feet with each step. Starting to sink before quickly rising up out of it. It was quiet – he was right. Mainly just a few older children enjoying the waves. Appearing to be friends who had perhaps come out for an evening. Over to the far left were a couple of families with much younger children darting in and out of the sea. Two children, smaller still, babies almost, trying desperately to find success in sandcastles before the sea took away their prized creations.

We held hands and walked along the beach, away from the sea and those people enjoying the evening sun. We remarked at how lovely that time of day was and how living inland was both a blessing but also a disappointment when such amazing places existed. It was easy conversation. Surprisingly so. Yet I remained a little distracted. This was lovely. This was easy. But this was not life. Not our life, not the reality.

'Do you ever think you could move somewhere like this?' I asked. Curious as to what he might say. Whether something he might say would impact; could assist.

He thought. Then answered with care and consideration 'Back to that conversation?' He questioned, but with an attempt at a gentle smile.

'I don't know that I could, George. I love the scenery and the food – that meal was amazing. But this isn't real, is it?' He understood the impact and the moment, just as I did. 'This is great, but it can't be like this all the time if you live here. Can it?' He looked at me as if asking for my input, but I knew it needed no real response in terms of an answer to his question.

'I guess not, but I don't know. I guess to embrace this you'd need to leave everything else behind, wouldn't you? I mean we couldn't move here and still do our current jobs could we? It's a different life. It's a calmer life.'

'Yes, but we are on holiday here, so that instantly makes it calmer. Don't you think? We are different people here. The normality of life is temporarily removed. I'm sure those who live here don't have it perfect.'

I can tell I'm pushing a point he doesn't agree with. Maybe even causing further concern.

'What's all this about? The conversation the other day?' He studied me, continuing to hold my hand.

Say it's nothing, I tell myself.

'It's nothing. Genuinely.' I furnished him with a smile, directly towards him, to reinforce my words. His gaze remained. Everything paused. That point where maybe I could open more, continue this line of discussion.

We edged round to the left following the rock face where it met the sand as they sat side by side, each of such differing texture enjoying the space right next to each other without question.

At a point of solitude, we stopped and took in the setting sun. We had moved on. Some idle chatter about the beauty of the colours took us from the conversation developing further. Thankful for the diversion. Not completely sure what I was seeing, what I was feeling. Just thankful for a change of beat.

The walk back took us past the café again and the light-hearted enjoyment and conversation could still be heard from outside. The energy from the owners and waiters continued to filter out, flowing into the street. Right at that point, the commitments of our lives were not the priority and instead just being us was. Seeking to immerse myself in this space, this peace, this love.

Chapter 24

The rest of the week passed without much change or issue. We all ended up spending most of the time together as a family. I gave a form of surfing another go. Success limited. Coloured cheeks deepened. An impressive amount of ice cream was consumed, and we rediscovered a few card games long forgotten. The sunsets continued to amaze. To calm and comfort. Walks still tested our legs before wine bottles were emptied.

Several times, we ended up walking past the cottage. *That* cottage. I almost held my breath on each occasion, aware that it bore no importance to anyone else. The prospect of bumping into Mary became somewhat of a worry. I endeavoured to remind myself that nothing had actually happened. Nothing of consequence had taken place. Yet the sense of deceiving others along with me unnerved me somewhat. Why was I still thinking about that place? The details a panic-infused blur.

I recalled a conversation with Annie many years before that holiday. Annie was always what Chrissie would refer as a little 'woo'. Not sure I can even properly describe what this meant, but Annie often felt things happened just as they were meant to. Maybe a courageous belief, bearing in mind her own experiences in recent years. Or maybe that meant she feared nothing. Everything was always as it should be. People came to all of us for a reason. Events took place with a purpose. I couldn't say I agreed with Annie's theories but whenever random, unnerving events took hold, I would find myself stepping back to that conversation once more.

I couldn't even cast my glance towards the cottage. It felt risky. The faint smell from the roses climbing over the archway entrance caught me each time we walked past. An abundance of flowers gathering, trying to tempt me in.

On the last day, I left the boys packing and Simon checking the car over, having volunteered to head down to the shop for journey provisions. With a sense of apprehension about the return to a life I struggled with, I grabbed my light blue cardigan and slid on my bright red flip-flops, for what I assumed would be the last time. I walked out the door. A light-hearted 'back soon' belied my inner cautiousness and worry, and I stepped out onto the path.

A slight sadness accompanied my walk. Unsurprisingly, really, as there was always an inevitability about taking a break. At some point, we always must return. Trying to tell myself that maybe I could return to my life armed with a different outlook. An alternative perspective? I still had another week off work to settle myself. Find changes that I could make. Maybe even find myself some help. Help to let go of what I could not change. Help to find why it was all too much and yet not enough. As I walked down towards the path, I was aware that I was trying to convince myself of the possibility of all these things.

Nearing the shop, I caught the view ahead. The sea, as always, washing over the expanse of beach. I tried to mentally capture this sight. A snapshot. A negative held to keep it with me as I left. Take it and hold it close. This view, this provider of silence, this bringer of hope.

'Hello again.'

Abruptly, I stopped in my tracks. Taken aback. Having been focussed on the view ahead, I had completely not registered that I was approaching the cottage. She took me by surprise with her greeting.

'Sorry, I didn't mean to startle you. I just noticed you heading this way – down to the beach I presume?' Desperate to look behind, I tried to angle myself to talk to her but be able to see out of the corner of my eye, towards the top of the hill.

'Oh no don't worry – I just wasn't concentrating really…Hi.' Jumbled words, I tried to provide a smile to indicate a calm lightness of mood. 'We head back today. I'm just off for some provisions for the road.' I smiled and casually looked over towards where we had been staying, scouring the path for a hint of Simon or the boys. None. I appeared safe.

'Ah, often a hard task when you've spent the time relaxing. Having to return to a reality. Not what you want to do.' She smiled with a knowingness.

'Yes. I'm not entirely eager to get to back to work and life without the eating out, the beach, the sea, and sun,' I replied. A flippancy bounded from my lips.

She slowly nodded. An understanding gesture.

A pause. A knowing silence?

'I don't mean this with any pressure, but do feel free to contact me if you decide you want to come and visit again? As I say, no pressure at all. You might not want to all come back again...'

There was something in this statement, this suggestion that I couldn't describe. I don't quite know why it felt so important at that point, but I found myself giving her my number too, so she would know who called, if indeed I did. That transaction.

My nerves. An unexplainable apprehension about two people having exchanged numbers outside a cottage. This place where the roses would unfold so gently, merging their yellow with the streaming sun appearing to float in off the sea. The rays that cast a golden hue around the porch to the cottage, blending with the warm yellow and sunburnt orange flowers.

She told me she would leave me to get in touch if we wanted to stay there in the future. Her parting shot was an encouraging, 'I think you'd enjoy some time staying here again. You look as though you've taken a lot from the break.'

Making a mental note to throw her number away, we said our goodbyes. My heart beating with a nervous energy. The feeling that I had been presented with something. An idea. A possibility, a solution that I hadn't even sketched out lightly. Left with hardly being able to concentrate on the task I had volunteered for.

Taking the supplies back to our lodge, I passed the cottage again. Maybe I could have found an alternative route, but it was the most direct. The boys would expect to see me heading up the hill. Looking out for my return. It really was a beautiful sight. Tucked away like a child's den under the dining table, unseen but encasing of ideas and imagination. A gem. A hideaway.

The drive back home was filled with the usual congestion, snack requests, and changing of accompanying music. I spent most of the hours drifting from thought to thought. Forcing myself to concentrate on the road when it was my turn to drive. Simon and I entered into wistful and light conversation. Nothing that required my attention too much. Instead, I looked up.

Chapter 25

I could go. I really could let go. Close my eyes, let the wind take me and do what it wished.

A release.

I wouldn't have to work out what to do. The cliff and the breeze would decide. The hurt I've caused would no longer be mine to carry.

My eyes are fixed, gazing far ahead. The blue of the sky expands further than I can hold. If only I could blend in as I leapt from the edge. It would stop. The feelings I carry, that weigh me down like a shroud of the heaviest material, would just stop.

The wind wraps around me. My toes dig into the ground further, a reflex. Almost causing me to cry out, *Let me go. Please let me go.*

Chapter 26

The next few days, and beyond, were a mixture of unpacking and reorganising routine. Interspersed with lazy coffees and afternoons spent reading, or generally pottering about. The boys got back in touch with friends and disappeared off for much of the time, as seemed customary teenage activity. Simon spent two days at home before he returned to task.

I attempted to throw myself into getting the house back into some form of post-holiday order and embraced the chance of running at leisure. Seeking to absorb the dwindling rays of warmth as the summer began its long goodbye. I worked through a few mindless magazines and half a book. Not having Simon around all the time appeared to give me a peace and space I probably needed at that point.

Despite my best efforts, the encounter with Mary never really left my consciousness. Consumed by a ridiculous feeling that I might actually come across her once again, at some future destination. Nervousness at this prospect, interspersed with a resurgence of those intense feelings held before the holiday, took me to a place of almost constant confusion. I tried to use gazing into the garden intently as some form of distraction. Sat absently wringing my thirsty hands. Hours passed, with no real sense of where to go next. No real desire to achieve. To achieve anything. The week had in many ways taken me nowhere. I found myself back, just where I had been.

My latest cuppa became drained while taking in the view beyond the large sun-streaked windows. I made a mental note that the grass needed cutting, having grown madly while we were away. The flowers bloomed brightly, roses displaying their beauty proudly. The positivity of their colour not lost on me, however, not a reflection of my own exterior at that point.

Time is sometimes the greatest enemy. It allows space between waking and sleeping that requires filling. If you can't fill it with joy, with purpose, what do you fill it with? Thoughts. Endless images, worries, but even more than that. A nothingness. An all-consuming void.

Light conversations on work and day-to-day triviality filled gaps in the evening. Simon made flippant comments on my apparent enjoyment of time for nothing. Not in a way I would take offense to, more a sense of pleasure at my relaxing. Although a lack of dinner prep clearly caused some issues. It hadn't even occurred to me. So much I could have attended to. But I didn't.

The return to work, in some ways, was a welcome break. An escape from time.

Caught the train, watching once again the various lives pass me by. The windows offered a glimpse into the days and evenings of those who found home along the trackside. I caught dinner parties in full flow, family movie nights, and couples drinking out in the open air. The rhythmic trundling accompanying all I witnessed. A woman sat staring from the viewpoint of what I assumed to be her bedroom window. Was she looking out for me, the way I looked out for them? For just one moment, we played a part in each other's existence. Observers of an alternative. Was she sad? Lost? Waiting? As the carriages heaved forward, taking us on our route once again, I resisted the temptation to place my hand against the glass, as a symbol of solidarity between souls uncertain.

The weeks went by, the familiar houses and people appeared day after day. Save for the bedroom window occupant. When the train stopped in the various stations along the way, I caught smiles. Almost able to make out words uttered in conversations and those in heated exchanges. These were people's lives, their adventures and disappointments all played out for us on our travels. The moving audience. What went on in other homes was often a great secret, yet here, for some, it was out in the open for all to witness, to judge, to sympathise with.

Were many of those people happy? Did they like where they had chosen to make their home? The Victorian terraces lined up along the side of the tracks. Was that really where they all wanted to be? Were they all doing exactly what they wanted to do? There must be an interest in watching the trains go past as much as there was in being part of those travelling carriages. The ability to see inside when they stopped at the platform, maybe wonder where we were all headed to. What exciting lives we lead?

Perception. The enemy of the harshness of reality. We see our friends, our family, total strangers, and all we do is observe and perceive. Imagine what really exists in people's homes, lives. I was sure, if they heard them, many would find my thoughts and feelings completely ridiculous. I had everything. So, what was bothering me? What did I feel so aggrieved to be missing? The holiday gave me a few days of calm upon our return. Yet here I was, now several weeks later and feeling just the same. The sense of not enough. Even uttering the words was ridiculous. I was never sure that was exactly how I felt, but it's as near as I could get at that moment in time.

That life was not enough.

My attempts to talk more with Simon failed. I think it is fair to say he was bored. Bored of my questioning conversations. Apparent lack of enthusiasm for him, amongst other things. While he listened, he had nothing to add to that which had been said on holiday. Short of telling me to 'get over it', he made it clear, enough was enough. I had tried. I could say that, at least. As I slipped back into the routine of life and work and all that connects with those, I could at least say I tried. The distance I felt developing between us may have been created by my own actions, but I was adamant I had tried to ask him to help.

Chapter 27

Erica came bounding in, running late.

'Sorry. I had to double check Mark was going to be back in time to collect the kids from after-school club. Have you all ordered yet?'

'No. We were waiting for you. It's not a problem.' Annie, almost apologetically, responded. The pub was pretty quiet, and we'd managed to secure our preferred table in the corner.

'I'll grab a drink quickly. Anyone else?' A collection of 'Nos' saw Erica head off to the bar alone, as we arranged ourselves to accommodate room for four.

The pub was a mixture of both old and new, oak beams floating without effort above our heads, accompanied by quirky pieces of art situated on the walls and windowsills. A distinctly appropriate feeling for a local pub. We'd been visiting for years, in fact probably since we moved into our home. Luckily, the pub ownership hadn't changed much in that time, and they knew us well. It was a favourite for all of us. Mulling over the changes and challenges of life. And sometimes to mark those things and to celebrate.

Erica returned, we ordered food and noticeably all began to relax into our seats. The conversation drifted from work to home, to kids to news on others we all knew.

'I love those!' Chrissie exclaimed, as she looked over the new earrings that Annie paraded a photo of. Her waves of hair only serving to add to the exuberance displayed. 'When are you going to get selling all the jewellery? Have you thought how you're going to market?' Chrissie's genuine enthusiasm got us all hooked in. It was always apparent how much her own business meant to her. The one thing that really kept her going when it all came out about Michael and the subsequent fallout. The one thing he couldn't touch.

'I don't know to be honest. I think I've just been concentrating on getting the things made and seeing how that goes. Though I have started to look a little at how to set up a website.' Annie clearly spurned on by our encouraging interest.

'I'll need to take tips from you on getting going. It's not so easy with the children and work, but I'll get there.' Annie looked directly at Chrissie, clearly thanking her for her support. Yet I could tell she was a little embarrassed at the reaction to the sideline she'd been working on. I think we were all so proud of her efforts. A crutch to help her cope. Something for her, something positive to focus on.

'I love them.' I encouraged Annie with a warm smile and a gentle nudge. 'You really need to get up on Facebook and take marketing tips from Chrissie. Who knows where it might lead to...?'

Annie, thankful for our comments, closed the photos.

'How's your dad?' I asked Erica, turning to her, tempting her to take part fully in the conversation.

'The consensus is that more care will be needed before much longer. The dementia isn't going to get better. That's the reality of it.' She didn't even look up from her drink. Focussed on the depth of colour, sat inside the crispness of the vessel. The weariness of the burden still clearly etched upon her down-turned face. I often wondered if she just felt that there was no end in sight. No positive end, anyway. Chrissie became the first to offer sympathy, and we all provided encouragement and consolation for her predicament. When her mum was alive, it was just as tough. A terribly lonely responsibility.

'What will you do?' Annie quietly asked. Her hand reaching to place it over Erica's.

'I just don't know,' Erica replied in almost a whisper.

I'd not seen her this way before. Erica always had a steely persona, no doubt hiding a deeper existence, but nevertheless appearing resilient. I was never naïve enough to consider that to be the real her. Did I really even know the real her?

'Anyway.' Breaking the flow, almost as though she realised she might be showing some of her truth. 'How was the holiday?' Directing her question to me, of course. Her smile undoubtedly belied the pain she felt in her own unresolvable situation.

I was struggling to decide how exactly to answer the question. These were my closest friends. Those I would always be most honest with, I believed. Yet what should I say? Part of me wanted to give them the standard 'yes fine, caught some sun, great to have some time away from work.' There was, though, a part of my being, desperate to start the truth.

For me, at least, my pause was glaringly noticeable.

Chrissie looked hesitant, reading my delay.

'It was good, thanks. The boys loved the surf. Made a nice change not to have to do the whole airport thing to be honest.' I smiled and concentrated on taking a sip of my drink. A large one. Warming its way into my very being. Chrissie looked at me a little more intently.

Breathing.

'It gave me some time to think, though. Well, consider more I guess.'

Silence.

Erica's face became the first to focus and probe.

'Consider what?' Erica was always bound to challenge.

I'd started, and I needed to now continue.

'Most things, maybe everything, I think. It just kind of happened.' The drink continued. I was now half wishing I'd not started this.

'Wow, that's a deep holiday.' Chrissie offered a smile to lighten the frame of chatter. Downing her glass at the same time.

'What needs thinking about? What's bothering you?' Annie calmly asked, casting a glance to Erica as if ready to deflect any confrontation.

'I know you've not felt great for a while, George, but...?' Chrissie stepped up.

Backtracking a little as a result of sensing the atmosphere, I proclaimed how I just found time to re-evaluate my work/life balance. That I was giving more thought to what options I might have or changes I could make to maybe avoid getting so wiped out.

The food arrived as a welcome break. Moving glasses, making space served to cut the thread of chatter. I thought.

'I think sometimes you just need to find a different mindset. Maybe start to look at things differently.' Erica rekindled the matter, offering advice between mouthfuls. 'You are so lucky. You have the career, the fulfilled marriage, lovely home, great kids. Maybe you just need to really stop and take all that in?' She moved back to focussing on her food, concentrating hard on loading her fork, having planted her seed.

'I think that might be an overly simplistic way of looking at it, although I get what you mean.' Chrissie came to my defence, sending the ball back to Chrissie to defend. 'I'm sure George isn't ungrateful, just maybe tired, confused?' Looking over at me as if to ask whether she was on the right path.

'I'm not saying it isn't, but we can all feel things aren't right from time to time. Sometimes maybe we need to just look at what we have with more thanks. Or go and get some HRT or something.' Erica's clarity of thought was obvious, even with her attempt to lighten things up.

'Like Chrissie said, I'm not ungrateful, Erica.' I sensed the tension building, but felt I needed to iron this out a little more. 'The break just gave me a chance to think about what I want to do for the next twenty years. What I want to have in my life. It's not moaning about the situation I'm in. I am lucky, but I can't see myself doing this same thing forever, living this way to the end.'

Erica and I had, on several previous occasions, found our viewpoints existed some distance apart. She was often forceful and certain in her ideas and views. I wondered sometimes if it was because of the way her life was currently panning out. It must have been so hard to see your parents leaving you as they were. Watching the glimmer and spark in their eyes fade as age stole the warmth from their being. Took away the people they were. Having been the child, she had now become the adult in those relationships. I never had the opportunity to do that, but it wasn't an experience I necessarily felt I'd missed out on.

Erica had, when relaxed by the consumption of several bottles of wine, opened up about how things bothered her. It was, though, a relatively rare event. The pain of watching parents change, deteriorate. The wanting to catch them before they fell was too much to bear. Alone.

I understood where she was coming from. She would have looked at my life and felt I should be grateful, constantly grateful. Yes. Perhaps I should have been. Yet I wasn't.

Choosing words carefully, needing to break the silence.

'I don't disagree with you, Erica. I'm genuinely not as ungrateful as I might sound. But this feeling just won't budge. I can't shake it. It's more than whether I appreciate my life or not.'

'Could it be the realisation we're all getting older?' Chrissie's almost forced smile attempted to bring a touch of light-heartedness to the situation again.

Erica was not going to let this drift, though.

'No offense, but from where I sit it does sound a little ungrateful. I don't mean to be rude but trust me, I'd swap places with you in a heartbeat most days.' Erica looked directly at me at that point, forcing on me the intensity of her words. Understood. But I was not her.

Returning her gaze, I stopped for just a moment to acknowledge her situation. The look dissolved, and we each returned to join the others in devouring our meals, serving as a welcome distraction.

Instigated by Chrissie, we all motioned an acknowledgment that yes, time was passing, and we were not as we were twenty years ago. The table was busy with drinks and food, items passing, yet I found it almost impossible to just accept that that was all it was. For me, anyway. That was all I needed to do? Accept that youth was leaving? Just appreciate all that I had and the people I shared it with? Surely, I had done that? No. This feeling went way deeper than the superficiality of that assumption. More than an unwillingness to be grateful.

We all ate, passed further conversation (lighter in topic) and ordered more drinks. Erica grabbed her belongings and shuffled through to leave. Her time out was up. As she moved out the door, her dark hair sat gently on the collar of her coat. I couldn't help but wonder what her head now pondered. How she felt about the comments I'd made and how she now felt about me.

Sensing my thoughts, Chrissie interrupted.

'She has a point, there is no doubt, but you and only you know how you feel. If things aren't how you want them to be, then what are you going to do?'

'I'm not sure to be honest.' I'd had a little too much to drink. Pause.

'I've lost myself.' There. I'd said it and yet it wouldn't make sense unless they felt it too. 'I've lost my purpose, my impetus to get up and live. I don't think I can merely go on accepting this and being grateful for it.' Taking my gaze away from Chrissie and Annie. I could still feel their glances lingering. Feeling both that I'd said too much and yet probably not enough.

'I'm sorry you feel that way.' Annie's face was a concern. Her vision concentrating on my being, I sensed. 'Don't you think maybe it could be something you need to talk to the doctor about more? Or seek some private help, maybe a counsellor? Have you spoken to Simon much about it?'

All options previously considered. Maybe only fleetingly for some, but nothing said was new.

'I honestly don't believe the doctor is the way out of this. I did go, and I was given various bits of information, none of which seemed to really give me the answer. If I went to a counsellor, what would I say? I don't feel right? I'm lost, grumpy, living a life my friends want? It just won't work. I know that's what everyone is going to think, but I know it goes deeper.'

'And Simon?' Annie gently tried to prize out a response to this part.

'He doesn't really get it.' My eyes couldn't meet theirs as I let this out.

'Have you really tried to talk to him?' Chrissie pressed. Picking at leftover food on her abandoned plate. A distraction for me or for her, I wasn't sure.

'Yes. I think so. Mentioned a few things on holiday but he's happy. He's settled and content. What's he going to say?'

I almost wished I'd stopped about half an hour ago. This was so far out of my comfort zone.

No one seemed to quite know what else to say. To suggest. I carefully looked over at both their faces, paused for study, almost trying to commit them to memory for some uncertain future. Chrissie's sparkly eyes, flawlessly made face, and abundance of red/blond hair and curls. Annie's quietly considered features with a subtle beauty missed by many. These were my friends. Yet I was at risk of alienating myself from them by following the thoughts I had through to some form of conclusion. Had I looked at myself in the mirror and really considered whether what I felt was nothing more than boredom from the satisfaction of having achieved goals I set myself in life?

The conversation ended with Chrissie reiterating how she really thought I ought to consider seeing someone about it. Someone professional. Annie then, most likely in an attempt to move the topic to something more positive and also taking advantage of the fact that Erica was not there, divulged her latest development. A man. A prospective light on her horizon. Early days, she was keen to confirm, but he seemed nice and both Chrissie and I found ourselves in awe of but pleased for her even considering going down that path again, after the last year or two.

These women were everything to me. We had all helped each other through so many darkened days since we met. And celebrated all those little and not so little wins. These women came with their families and pizzas to help us spend our first night in our now home, as we meant to go on. In celebration. They had looked after my boys when needed. I stayed with Chrissie overnight when her husband finally admitted the details of the horror that awaited her. So many good times, consoling times. Even Erica, sometimes slightly aloof, would hold you up at a moment's request.

I couldn't help wondering if I was really more afraid of losing this family than losing myself?

Chapter 28

It was raining, but I still ventured out.

The droplets splashed against my face, my eyes, sliding down as a waterfall in slow motion. I'd decided on a different route, not wanting to head to the familiar fields and tracks. Instead, I left home and took the path, as if I were heading to the railway station as usual. But I wasn't. This was a Saturday, which this week meant an escape from work. There was, however, to be no escape from myself.

The morning early and grey. The boys were still asleep or still in bed at least. Simon rolled over. That being the extent of his movement at that point. Dragging myself out of the warmth to move amongst the harshness of a miserable autumn day. My conscious attempt to do something positive. To escape. There would have been a time where Simon and I would have escaped together. Gone exploring out somewhere. Now I ran. And ran far. Ran often.

Before I got even a mile from home, my hair was dripping relentlessly, and the constant patter of rain soaked my skin. Lightweight sports T-shirt gripped onto every curve. Stuck there. Not letting go.

Switching off from the physical needs of my body led me to run without feeling, without thinking. I passed the shops. All, at that time, closed. Though some starting to prepare for the rising of the shutters and the welcoming of a brand-new day. A day of customers, idle chatter, catching up with regulars.

Legs covered in splashes of mud, washed with rainwater. I couldn't feel the cold. Feet pounded the path without hesitation. This had become the only thing in my life that I was completely comfortable in doing, in achieving. I would take control of this. The rest of my time in those days seemed to be filled with a sense of something about to change, and drastically. Some days, the feeling was immense, overpowering. Almost as though there was a predetermined plan that would not be subject to change.

That day I gave my whole attention to striding past shops, benches, and then reaching the small park near where we lived. On passing through the iron gates, I decided to slow down for a time. Droplets steadily slipping off the edge of my loosened fingertips as I walked in. It was empty as far as I could see. Normally there would be various families, small people with trikes and half consumed packets of crisps gripped tightly in hand. Older ladies such as Margaret and Barbara who both lived along the way from us. I would see them here whenever I was passing through. Taking up a bench, chatting. Laughing. As I walked and thought of them, I noted at how well they had settled into their lives at each turn. Both now widows, yet still taking life by the collar and declaring a determination to continue. Life had dealt them some difficult times over the last eighty years or so and yet look at them. They were regularly perched on the park bench, chatting, seemingly without concern or worry. The very depiction of a joy of life in abundance.

The sense of dismay, maybe regret, could be overwhelming. I picked up my pace.

The space within my breastbone became a little tight, and I could sense my breathing was more laboured than before. As I turned out of the park, I jogged gently towards the back of the railway station, where I could cross the tracks and head out towards the fields found a little further away. Although aware that I had come some distance already, a route less familiar was still calling me.

After a time, the need to slow down and walk more increased. Disappointment and frustration had to be cast to one side as my chest felt tighter and I continued to seek breath, but without ease. Not wanting to stop completely I managed to at least walk at a steady pace. Breathing becoming more a struggle. The tightness took hold, grabbing my core, and the shock of the situation aggravated it further.

Before long, the tears began. Part in frustration and part in fear. I was now walking alone, in the rain, on a path not far from the station I frequented so often. A quick glance around and I thankfully noticed no one close by. The weather and time too much of a deterrent, no doubt. My pace slowed down even further, it had to, before eventually I came to a stop. Noticing, while stood, an offshoot of a well-trodden route leading into the woods. In the hope of finding some guaranteed solitude, I took the route and came across a lonely bench. Made to, by my own body, I sat.

I couldn't breathe.

I couldn't reach a breath deep enough. Willing myself to calm down, ease the panic, slow everything. Concentrate on getting air. The tightness just increased. The centre of my chest emitting a pain I was unable to merely breathe away. Stood behind and leaning over the back of the bench, oblivious whether anyone else could see me or was wondering what I was doing. Silently the tears continued to fall, just as I grasped tight hold of the wood. Certain that splinters would soon fracture my skin. Cause the life force to seep out. I clung on tighter still. Fingertips pressing hard against the inscription left by a loved one on this memorial. Slow. Slow it down I told myself. Fingers turning paler with pressure. The only colour now escaping in cuts and breaks.

Eyes closed, concentrating on the gripping within my chest. Attempting to visualise its release. Willing it to be so. Arms outstretched, strong, straight, head dipping below the level of the bench now. Maybe this would help. Giving my chest space to absorb. I willed my lungs to fill. Prayed for them to continue to provide life. Attempted to concentrate on calmly filling them. Visualising inflation, deflation, rise and fall. After a time, I could find a subtle and slow easing. Focussing on the space I so wanted to create. I needed to create. Yet still the tears fell. They filtered in the rain that already had me drenched and for which I was strangely grateful. Gently straightening myself up, I placed my face in my hands and just wept. It came. I could not prevent it. Breath still laboured, but slowly becoming just a little easier. As

I left the tears to make their own way, the pounding in my head lessened until, after a while, it became a more subtle numbness.

Pulling myself fully upright, I was grateful to acknowledge that no one appeared to have seen me. Wiping my eyes with the backs of my soaked hands and sleeves before I ran them through my hair to try to tidy up the soggy mess. Pulling myself up. Pulling myself together. Breathe in. Breathe out. Breathe in. Breathe out.

The feeling of exhaustion hit me, and I observed a heaviness within my body that I couldn't recall having felt before. The rain continued to fall, although lighter, captured by the dense trees before so much of it could find me. I would not be drying out anytime soon. The canopy of trees overhead provided some shade. Some comfort.

Deciding it was probably safer to sit for a while, I looked up. The tightness continuing to ease, so gradually. The panic lessened, moment by moment. Perhaps I was seeking some sign. Some greater being. Something.

Having calmed my breath even more, I ran my hands through my hair. Noting a pause in the rain, I stood up. Took time to stand and take in the air. Turned skywards. Then stepped forward to try to regain some composure. My legs could hold me. They actually could give it a go. Breathing in. A cautious breath. All had stopped.

For one moment, there was nothing. I closed my eyes. I stopped. Nothingness. Visualising my lungs slowly filling. Straightening up. Noticing the witnessing trees, I would walk through. Through further into the woods, just walking. Taking the path, hearing the train tracks rattling with the weight of their load. I had no real idea how long I'd been out. I could have gazed down at my watch if I hadn't felt the need to concentrate on placing one step in front of the next. Air became crisper as I found myself leaving the woods and greeting the park once more. Drying out. The sun stretching its limbs, trying hard to break through the clouds to spray even the tiniest bit of sunshine on all those that needed it. Passing through the iron gates, I saw Margaret and Barbara up ahead. Walking today, not sitting. I wanted to smile at them, just for a second. The effort was too much and so instead I concentrated on pretending to look intently at my watch as I passed. They were out early, or I was running late, well into the day. I had no idea which way round it was. I had to concentrate on being able to get home before I ran out of steam, or breath, again.

Taking myself over the threshold, I grabbed a water and went straight up to change. A light and breezy 'hi' welcomed me, but I dodged replying with anything more than an indication that I needed to get dry after the weather had taken its toll. Grateful that I'd managed to get upstairs without being seen or stopped, I took the journey into our bathroom.

A hint of the tightness within still remained, as I changed out of my sodden clothing. Breathing was. however, markedly easier. A moment of consideration took over as I sat, still damp, in a luke-warm towel. Bitter, broken hands covered my softly closed eyelids. Resisting the urge to give in to a repeat of the woodland episode, I quickly checked the door was locked. Palms, skin, tight. Red raw, my wedding band slipping easily round and round over and over.

Chapter 29

I studied the impatient article. Its constant ringing, agitating every winding vein within my head. What? Who now?

Chrissie. What could she possibly want? We'd only spoken yesterday and at length at that. I let it ring and ring, yet still it continued. A determined interruption. I couldn't speak to her. Not then. I meant nothing by it. I just couldn't find the strength to reach and pick it up. To engage in some exchange. Instead, a hideaway beckoned me. Disappearance from view. There was, of course, always the possibility she might genuinely need me. That thought, I did consider. She might need help, maybe some sort of emergency. Still, I let it continue to shout out.

It stopped. Finally. I paused. Grateful for the ensuing silence. Then it began yet again.

I really couldn't. I still couldn't answer it. My head was pounding, I could hear my heartbeat quickening. Please stop, please leave me alone. The words filling my mind as my hands pressed tightly over my ears. Trying to shield them from the intrusion. I tried so hard to drown out the relentless ringing. Willing it to just cease.

It stopped. It gave up, and I was grateful.

I hadn't realised my eyes were so tightly closed until I opened them. Releasing hands from the side of my head. They had been screwed so tightly shut the world became a confused blur when I first saw again. A haze of mis-formed shapes. What was wrong with me? It was just a phone call.

On opening my eyes, I realised that they were wet, as were my cheeks. So much upset from an avoided call? Not just one call, but the final straw in a series of calls. Pulls on my being. People wanting my time, my conversation, me.

Sat on the floor by my side of our bed. My back pressed up against the divan, legs still pulled up tight against my torso. An embryo shielding. I couldn't even recall how I came to be there. Feeling silly. Ashamed and embarrassed. I couldn't even face answering the phone. My phone. Pulling my knees even tighter to my chest, an involuntary rocking motion began. In an effort to stop it, I squeezed my knees hard. So tight to my chest. The phone, discarded on the floor, by my side.

Pushing the device further away, I wiped my eyes on the sleeve of my shirt. Still in my office clothes, noting the appearance of mascara streaks on the pale blue material. It would wash, it would be OK.

This was madness. I was completely unable to cope. The need to hide away had clung on to me all day. I'd held it together just to get to the point of getting home. Leaving work early, feigning a headache to give me time to be alone before the others all returned.

Using the bed for support, I dragged myself up. Continued to wipe my eyes on my sleeve, not caring about the damage being done.

Stumbling a little as I made my way to the ensuite, I figured I'd best have a look at my reflection to see how much of a mess I had to clear up.

The phone started again. Too far from it to see who it was but I could hazard at a guess. Chrissie obviously needed to desperately speak to me. I resigned myself to giving in and returning her call. Just not then.

A splash of water eased my face for just a second. I was a mess. An abomination in female form. That was an accurate statement, not merely an expression of how I was feeling. Maybe it was, in fact a recognition of both. I realised I really could no longer cope. This must now be the end of pretending that I could.

Aware that the boys would be back soon and Simon not far behind them, I needed to tidy the situation up. The best option seemed to be to take my make-up off, rather than try to repair it. Checking the clock in the bedroom, I had time to change and wash before they all appeared. Dragging off my formal clothes, I made a mental note to immediately wash them to ensure the make-up didn't become a permanent addition. As I removed layers, I saw the blood. It was everywhere. The top of the inside of my thighs were covered, my underwear and trousers too. A sense of panic started, even though I, of course knew what it was. Yet recalling how the last one had only finished the week before.

I needed to move on and get myself cleaned up. In the shower. Dried and at least a little more together, I took the wash load down to get started. Hoping the machine was up to the task.

Having switched the kettle on, I left it and reluctantly headed back upstairs to collect my phone off the floor. Glancing down, turning my phone over and over before settling on the screen. Chrissie. Eight missed calls. I should call her. I really should.

Steadying the phone, ready to redial, knowing that I must. Yet I needed tea first. I needed to ease my nerves and calm my thoughts for a moment. She would have gotten hold of someone else; I was sure. Trying to ignore the guilt I felt at not having picked up and not even having called her back as soon as I could, as I made my way cautiously down the stairs. Entering the kitchen just as the kettle finished, I abandoned the phone on the kitchen worktop and grabbed my favourite mug from the cupboard. The largest one there was in our house. A delicate red flowery pattern, the curves of those flowers working their way around, embracing the whole.

Before I'd finished stirring, the front door opened and in they came. Chattering away to each other about some incident at school. I didn't catch much apart from something about a history teacher forgetting his facts on the Second World War. As their laughter echoed through the hall, they made their way into the kitchen and barely uttered hello before one of them opened the fridge.

'Hey, Mum, guess what? Mr Stimpson couldn't remember the exact words used by Churchill in his address to parliament and Jacob knew it and told him but he wouldn't believe him and...' Jack trailed off or at least his words did to me. But I kept smiling and making the relevant noises to indicate I was there. Sort of.

'Kettle hasn't long boiled,' I called to them both, as I collected my cup and phone and started to head out of the kitchen. They remained there, chatting and laughing about their days, and barely noticed I'd gone.

Heading through to the lounge where I felt guaranteed of peace of that moment. It was likely they would head upstairs to hibernate for a while and hopefully settle on some homework before dinner.

I turned over my phone once again. Settled on the sofa, placing the cup carefully on the unit behind the seat. Missed calls and two messages. The most recent was from Simon, saying he was meeting a friend for a quick drink and would be home a little later than normal. The other one from Chrissie. *Georgia, will you for god's sake PLEASE call me!!! xx*

Chapter 30

'How long has she been like this?' Uttering in hushed tones, hoping to not disturb her as I edged carefully through the front door.

'She rang me, in a state, around lunchtime and I managed to convince her to let me go over a few hours ago. Once I saw her, I thought she'd be better off here for a bit.' Chrissie gently closed the door behind me. I didn't stop to take off my hoodie, just slipped out of my shoes.

I peered around the door to the lounge, and she was there, amid a large throw, curled up on the sofa. Childlike. Her eyes gently closed, make-up clearly visible down each cheek and a puffiness of skin clear to see.

'Come through, I'll make us coffee.'

Chrissie and I walked softly through to the kitchen, and I took a seat on the stool, after closing the door protect her from the details of our conversation.

'Thanks for finally answering my call – but where the hell were you?' I was sure she didn't mean to make it sound a critical enquiry, but nevertheless, I was on edge. Already unnerved. Attempting to come up with something believable, I mentioned a meeting I had online, that meant I couldn't have taken a call.

Seemingly accepting of my statement, she made the drinks and brought them over to the breakfast bar.

'So, what did she say?'

'Not much to begin with, really. She rang me to just say she was starting to get some information together on care providers and asked if I knew of any or had any suggestions.'

'She needs to put more care in place now then?' Clearly, the situation for Erica's dad was declining.

'I think so, yes. She just sounded in a complete panic. She was jabbering away. I could hardly make out half of what she was trying to say. I asked her to slow down and tried to find out where she was. She just couldn't seem to control what was pouring from her lips. She was just a mess.'

Pausing to take a breath, along with coffee, I remained silent. Trying to take in all Chrissie had divulged.

'Did you end up going over there at that point, then?' I couldn't recall a time when Erica had ever felt the need to actually ask for help. From any of us. Undoubtedly, it was more likely that Chrissie had made the decision that Erica needed it.

'Yes. I just went straight over, basically bundled her in the car and brought her here. She was just in pieces. I've never seen her like this before.' Chrissie was clearly equally trying to digest all that had occurred before her eyes.

'Did she say exactly what the matter was? What brought all this on?' I was listening with one ear to make sure Erica wasn't stirring and picking up our conversation, or even the fact that I was there.

Chrissie lowered her tone.

'From what I can gather there's been some heated conversations with Mark. He wants her to stop being her dad's main carer. Thinks it's about time she devoted all her time to him and the kids and got a care home sorted. He's been a complete arse about it all, from what I could make out. But nothing new there, is there?'

A sigh of despair came from within. I knew Mark had been anything but supportive. Jealous, maybe annoyed, inconvenienced, but certainly never helpful. It always just appeared to the rest of us that he left her to get on with it all. It seemed now that it was way more than that.

'How can he be so heartless? Her dad would be lost without her.'

'I don't know. I just don't know how to help, but she is a complete mess right now. That sounds so awful to say…' Chrissie's voice at that point a barely audible whisper. 'But she is.'

Chrissie continued.

'I guess this has obviously become too much now. Whatever the conversation was, it's pushed her too far. Balancing care, home, kids, job with Mark doing less than nothing to help. At some point, she was bound to crash.' The concern clearly vocalised by Chrissie's sentiment.

We both sat despondently, considering the situation. After a time, following more coffee, stirring sounds came from the lounge.

Without discussion, Chrissie went in alone to see Erica and offer a drink. I heard mutterings of apology and self-disgust. Recalling getting in touch with Chrissie just brought back the reality of Erica's predicament. I felt caught between wanting to go and see her, try to help, and a fear that I might not be the best face for her to be confronted with. I knew Erica, or I thought I did, and I wondered if now her guard was down, she would feel even more uncomfortable with me having seen the façade fall.

Chrissie took the plunge on my behalf and announced that I'd come to see if I could help at all. Not strictly true, but I went with it.

Tentatively pacing through. Peering round the door, I found myself genuinely saddened to see someone I really didn't recognise. As I greeted her, the tears started to fall once more. Heading over, I couldn't stop myself. Comforting, hugging harder than maybe she felt comfortable with. Her shoulders convulsed and heaved, and the wetness from her soaked face leaked onto my shoulders. I cared not. In that moment, the overwhelming sadness I felt for her situation enveloped me beyond all else.

After a time, I let her go, and she dried her face. Making light comments about how awful she must look. We managed to raise a laugh and a smile, somewhat forced.

We spent time talking calmly about what had happened before Erica rang Chrissie and what the situation now developing looked like. Erica's openness surprising. A level of despair, a sense of giving up. A sense of loss. I was aware that I'd never seen her openly vulnerable before. An immense feeling of wanting to help her. To be with her. Yet at the same time aware of my own inability to look after myself. Chrissie suggested Erica stay the night with her, but she refused. A sense of her firm exterior returning. She was adamant she just needed time to correct her features and then head home.

Despite pleas from both of us, she was firm in her belief that she had no choice but to carry on.

Chrissie drove Erica back, and I sat and waited for her return. Making fresh coffee for her arrival, I considered the events of the afternoon.

Chrissie returned. We mulled over Erica's predicament. Wondering how to be those friends who would support. Without doubt Erica was going to be reluctant to let us in any further and if she could help it, would not get herself in that situation again.

After a time, I headed home, greeted by a family giving support, welcome, and warmth. Dinner was cooking, later than normal, but all very much under control. Music filtered throughout the ground floor. I filled Simon in briefly on the reason for my departure, and he passed on the love sent by his drinking companion. House comfortable and cosy and the boys chatting eagerly about their day over our family meal.

Inwardly scolding myself for recent moments of doubt. My seemingly selfish behaviour brought a sense of disappointment. I might be kidding myself on any long-term change or fix but for one day, one evening, I found I was grateful. Aware that Erica, in my position, would feel that even more so.

Chapter 31

The force of sensibility took over.

Despite the fact I had promised myself I would not be returning, the episode in the woods had made me a little uneasy.

'Georgia Florence?' Déjà vu.

Hoisting myself up, I followed her lead. Remarkably, the same doctor I saw last time. Suddenly aware I might be quizzed on my homework from the last visit, I start to put together some vague response in my head.

The same warm smile, same leather seat.

'How are you?'

'Err, OK, I think. I just wanted to check out about an episode of breathing trouble I had recently.' Suddenly feeling a little under the spotlight. Wanting her to just deal with the breathing problem, just talk to me about that.

'Yes. I see from my notes you had an episode of being short of breath. What were you doing immediately beforehand?' She was poised, ready to add to the notes on her screen. Fingertips at the ready, having already accessed the system. My notes. Me.

I started to relay how my run in the rain had not ended as expected and how my chest felt at the time. Keen to highlight I'd not had anything before or since, but being sensible, thought I should mention it.

Had I experienced an anxiety attack any time before that?

Maybe naively I was stopped in my tracks. I couldn't explain why, but I hadn't given it a name. Hadn't googled it, considered what it might be. I felt so stupid.

Inevitably, the conversation then reverted back to our last chat.

Yes, my periods had been a little all over the place. Heavier than usual? Yes. No, I hadn't really put on any weight or had any hot flushes. Memory lapses? Some.

Tapping away, I awaited her next question.

Started to feel annoyed. I didn't want the enquiry. It had been an issue of shortness of breath, which was what I'd contacted her about. I didn't want further questions, a label, a prescription.

She talked breathing exercises, relaxation, more websites to look at. Would I like to discuss a prescription? It just might help.

No.

Did I think maybe some form of counselling or other talking therapy would help?

No. Help with that?

The disappointment of the consultation sat weighing down my mind as I awoke the next morning. That sense of having wasted my time. No answers, no understanding.

The sun started to peak through the gaps in the blind and I sat hunched over on the bed. I couldn't even recall what day it was for a moment. Tuesday. It might as well be a Monday or a Thursday. They were all the same. The same alarm, the same process of pulling myself up to get started on yet another same format 24 hours.

I no longer felt I wanted to be involved in this same old life.

I turned to look over at Simon. Still sound asleep, waiting for his alarm, due to go off an hour later. I could never understand how he slept through my alarm and not his own, but he had it down to an art. In the same way he seemed to have developed a complete inability to notice the detail within. I couldn't recall the last time he'd really looked at me, noticed how I felt. I'd stopped drawing attention to it some time ago.

The water cascaded over me, trying its best to open every pore as it travelled. I stood tall and leant my head back, washing my hair off the night of rough rest. Wakening my skin at least. The water washed away the night's patchy sleep as it moved with ease, over my head, down my back. I ran my hands through my hair, closed my eyes and let go a sigh, born not of wakening but of perhaps wanting to not.

The temperature of the shower left a mist that clouded my vision, mirroring my mind. I begrudgingly got through the motions of dressing and clearing my things from the bathroom. Then I headed downstairs for the next part of my daily routine.

Making the coffee, sorting through my bag, popping a slice of bread in the toaster. No radio, no company. Not then. Distracted, I forgot the bread until black. Felt annoyed and then tried once more.

Once I'd finished breakfast, I took a look at myself in the mirror that had been perfectly positioned above the hall table. It was easier to use the ground floor when the others were all still in bed. I often, but not always, left the house before them. Sometimes more than a little bitter at this fact.

I could hear the train running as I put the small table lamp on in the hallway. They would have started in earnest a short while ago. Taking people like me to places like mine. The rhythmic trundling of the older style carriages, keeping the city and beyond going.

With the sound in the background, I glanced at my reflection. Just a quick check to make sure my makeup was doing what it needed to do, and my hair looked relatively acceptable. My pink shirt and navy trousers worked. An easy, much-used outfit. It looked just as an accountant should. But it was definitely not me.

Pausing for a moment to look deep into my own eyes. Stopping. Not really recognising the face staring back at me. Not recognising this woman I seemed to have become.

Time was getting on and in whatever form I found myself that day, I must head for the train.

Chapter 32

Undoubtedly, I'd had enough. Too much, even.

That slightly giddy feeling somewhere between relaxed and drunk to the point of feeling sick was where I found myself. The release needed, yet the expected headache the next day would most certainly not be.

I concentrated on refocussing on the sounds that surrounded me. Chrissie was at the bar, trying to speak over the volume of idle chatter and heated conversations. She too, a little beyond relaxed, and trying to put together the order she needed to give. It was proving a little difficult, by all accounts. Across the table, I sought to engage with Erica as she chatted to some familiar faces at the table next to us. The first time I'd seen her since that afternoon at Chrissie's. Despite my messages, enquiring after her welfare, no real honest response had been forthcoming. The standard reply of 'I'm fine' just repeated. A standard reply I was all too familiar with using myself.

Annie held her phone close and desperately tried to hear the caller before collecting her coat and heading outside for a better reception. I took her face to read an element of urgency about the information being received.

Erica laughed. Not a natural laugh but more of a flirty, trying to impress, type noise. For a moment, I forgot she was married with children and assumed she was trying to make headway with the group of young men nearby. Recognising a couple of faces, I felt sure they must be a good ten years younger than even the youngest amongst our group. I was though, not there to judge. Not anyone.

She engaged in more conversation, her 'tactile with drink' nature coming out and with one last overexaggerated laugh, gave them a wink and returned to attend our table.

'How old are they?' Curious more than anything, I managed to make her hear me above the surrounding conversations. The pub hadn't been this busy for such a long time.

'Oh god knows but hey, good company for a bit and it's nice to chat to a few new people.' She clearly was a little further on than I was.

'Don't tell me that you wouldn't be interested in a little flirt if they came on over.' I nearly spat out the sip I was taking at that moment.

'Erica,' I exclaimed. 'That is the last thing I'd be interested in – God what a headache.' Erica seemed somewhat put out by my reaction.

'A little bit of fun, is that what you are afraid of?' Unsure of her retort.

'I don't mean it in a rude way just making a comment.' She downed a sizeable gulp of her wine. Played with her hair a little, coy smile to the side, glancing back over to them one last time.

Chrissie finally made it back from the bar with the first two drinks, breaking the tension for a moment. Erica then replayed our conversation about our table neighbours. Chrissie agreed with me. No desire to get stuck in. Erica mocked us both, while we carefully reminded her of her status. Her expression confirmed all our thoughts.

Annie returned, clearly more than a little anxious. Babysitter issues. She could stay for a little longer but not much. We drank, Erica drank more.

The conversation then came to take a more awkward turn. Erica clearly took offence to my comments on her socialising. I was out of order in making such comments over what was, after all, nothing more than a touch of fun.

Even as I drank, I could clearly see Erica was determined to keep it going. I tried to bring the conversation to an end, started to feel more than a little uncomfortable. Annie distracted by more calls, disappeared outside again.

'It's OK for you.' The words tumbled out of the preceding break in conversation.

I wanted to exit the situation right there. I really did.

'In what way?' There seemed to be a lull in the surrounding sounds that made it easier for our voices to be heard.

'Every way.' Had I heard a slight slur of venom in her voice?

'Come on, girls, this is getting more than a little heavy now – there's no need.' Chrissie's attempt at diffusing the situation as she eased up from the table, heading out towards the ladies, failed.

I couldn't help myself. I'd had too much.

'What do you mean *every way?*'

Chrissie still away from our table.

'I mean literally everything. You have a great husband, kids, house, job, money. No responsibilities of your own. Simon is always there for you. You have it all…and yet you're still unhappy. Apparently.' She glugged the last of her wine. Some of it slipping down one side of her mouth. Realising, she wiped it away quickly. Almost visibly straightening herself up in her seat.

I sat. There was silence in our conversation at last.

Unable to dismiss the feeling I had to come out and correct her. To tell her straight and to her face that yes, I had all those things. But was that what life was about? Because I had all of that. Did it mean I was supposed to always be happy? Maybe Simon wasn't always the husband everyone saw? Maybe I had been feeling unfulfilled in my work? Yes, my house was lovely. I did have more than enough money. But did that make me a bad person for feeling sad, unhappy, angry sometimes? Feeling there was more to life than I was seeing, feeling trapped? Should I always be full of smiles just because all of that was true? I was not a bad or an ungrateful person just because I was struggling. She really had no idea. Erica knew nothing of what my reality was. The thoughts my head nowadays contained. The anger I felt in listening to her judge me in that way.

And so I did. I said it all. Drink infused barrels. Loaded and discharged.

Creeping into the house, my home, I took just a moment to notice and stand amongst the silence.

Chapter 33

Eyes poised. Just staring at him.

Just standing and staring. In the same way that I had done so, thousands of times over the years, yet this was the first occasion for quite a while. He was older now. He didn't need me checking on him, making sure he was asleep. Most of the time, I was tucked up well before he was.

That time, though, it felt different.

I stood, as any other mother, taking in his profile, each turn and dip of his face. Wanting to commit each part to memory. Still hints of the baby within, yet now covered with spattered areas of stubble.

I stood.

Contemplated our journey to now. Had I been a good mum? What would my own mum have thought of my efforts? She missed out on seeing Simon and me as parents. Missed out on passing over advice, babysitting. Being there to witness many of the 'firsts'. Would she think that I should have done more? Or maybe less? Maybe I should have worked less? Perhaps if I had been around much more, they would be wanting me more now?

What would my dad think? He had the opportunity to play some part in our life as a family, but it just hadn't happened. His new wife hadn't done anything to facilitate or encourage involvement. Although, if I was honest, by the time she arrived, much of the damage had already been done.

I jolted a little as he stirred. Turned over, flung out a leg, and sighed. Not wanting to be seen standing in the doorway, I edged back at his movement and carefully closed his bedroom up.

It had been a late night for me. Simon and I had had a heated conversation over the boys and their studies. It appeared we did not share the same opinion. We clearly couldn't reach any sort of middle ground and in the end, Simon decided he wanted an early night. It was obviously more about removing himself from the room I was in, but that was fine. Space between us was good. Increasing. I stayed up. Watched some inane reality TV. Found myself finishing the bottle we had started over dinner and without thought, opening another.

The next morning at work, I sat, just continuously moving a paper clip round, gradually gliding it from my finger to the rest of my hand and back again. Considering it. At my desk, gazing out of the window wondering, toying with the idea. Considering how I could change this whole situation. How I might be able to try to fix myself. Put me at the top of the list.

The most selfish thing I could ever do.

Yet as the paper clip travelled around each finger, I opened my palm and spread my knuckles. Considering. Feeling the sense of emptiness, I had been living with. The sun outside sent shards of light through the blind, hitting the desk, and smothering the paperwork. It beckoned me to follow it outside. I gazed over to where the light began.

I stopped and put the paper clip down.

Chapter 34

Slamming the door as I left, my heart pounding in my chest as I walked quicker than my heels would safely allow. Out of the house and onto the street. No idea where I was going to go but there was a need to get out, to breathe.

I attempted to slow my heart rate down a little, gain control, by trying to breathe a little deeper still. My chest tight, I could feel pain, though not the sort to overly worry about. This was different. This was frustration. Anger and upset all balled up into a controlled explosion. I had let go more than I had done in almost forever, but I'd still not dared release everything. I could have said so much more, told him how I really felt. But why? He didn't understand or maybe he just didn't care anymore. Even worse, he considered me to be overreacting. Simon just didn't get it. Me.

How could that be the case after twenty-two years together? Surely, he should know me more than anyone else. Yet he didn't. Not really. Somehow that seemed to be my issue rather than his, though.

My pace slowed slightly, and I was glad. I was making too much noise with my heels and my panicked expression was likely to start to draw attention. That was the last thing I needed. Trying to casually look around, wanting to know that no one was witnessing what was happening. My bag gripped tightly in hand. The only person I saw was an older man with a walking stick, slightly hunched over. Walking along the other side of the road. I didn't think he'd taken any notice of me – thankfully. I looked the other way to see relatively empty streets. Unusual for early afternoon. Questioning it for a moment, yet not lingering too much on that train of thought, as I needed to get control of myself.

Walking past the bakery, the newsagents, having a good look in the windows. Making sure that no one I knew was in any of them. I must have seemed a little out of control, overly on-edge, slightly manic. Trying to slow myself down further, until I was walking at a regular pace, with my bag casually slung over my shoulder.

Strangely enough, I found I was at least no longer crying. Often tears would escape when I felt full of rage, but not quite so much on that day. I couldn't quite figure it out but was glad that I didn't have to be overly concerned there might be make-up all over my face. I, hopefully, appeared to be relatively together.

My pace became quite sedate and less panicked. Breathing much the same. Thoughts turned to the things we'd both said, the things maybe I should have said sometime before we reached that point. Hindsight made me feel I hadn't made my feelings clear enough before, hadn't asked for the help I needed, the understanding. Though whether Simon was capable of giving it, was a different matter. A great father, easy companion, but how much could he or did he help me? Had I really and truly asked him to?

The park approached ahead, and I found an empty bench. Without the reason for direction, I concluded I may as well have a seat to decide. To consider where to go or what to do next. The bench was mainly clean, and I sat, perched cautiously, huddled at one end. Grateful that it had turned out to be a dry day. Aside from a small family playing football on the grass and a touch of traffic following the main road through to the other end of town, the area was still. The sky demanded my gaze; the clouds suspended in the all-encompassing blue, providing a ceiling of comfort to the trees around the edge of the park. It occurred to me that I couldn't recall the last time I'd really and properly looked up for any length of time. As I'd walked along just then, even other times, I suddenly realised I just didn't do it. I didn't raise my sight. I looked down, maybe ahead or around, if I was curious as to who was about, but never up. When had I last seen this beauty all around me? Observed it. Absorbed it. Taken in the quiet air, the life around me?

There was something truly entrancing in actually looking towards the sky. Taking it in and noticing its beauty. Confronted with how small a part we all play and how much there is that we don't see or don't become a part of. Aware of some slight discomfort, my attention turned to my feet. A broken heel evident on one of my shoes. My red shoes. My confidence getters.

Yet another broken element. Unconsciously, feeling a sense of change. Impending, inevitable alterations. There would be no continuing in this vein. This could not go on. I had crossed the line. If I really wanted to go back, apologise, explain, discuss, and start again, maybe I would be able to? But inside, I didn't think I really wanted it enough.

I ran back over the argument in my head, recalling the hurt. Simon and I didn't argue that often. Well, we hadn't. We usually tried not to let things get out of hand. Maybe as part of that, we just accepted things that might otherwise annoy others. It hadn't been a perfect marriage, but a relatively happy one. We had kind of rolled along through life, not rocking the boat too much, each aware of our roles in the house and family. Maybe we had been playing the game wrong all those years? If we'd argued more, let those frustrations out, we might not have reached the point that we did that day. I had hurt him with the things I'd said; I knew that. I had said things that I don't think, until that point, I realised I even felt.

It had all started just because he couldn't believe I had forgotten about parents' evening the following night. It was an important one to discuss Jack's GCSE options. I admit I hadn't been on top of everything lately, but surely everyone forgot things once in a while. I was relatively organised, but I was not perfect.

'But it's on the calendar.' He pointed out. 'The calendar you insist we write things on because you refuse to become part of modern-day society and store everything on a phone.' He wasn't shouting, but he was firm in his statement. Clear in meaning.

'I made a mistake, Simon. I forgot, but it's not the end of the world.' I wasn't really giving him my full attention at that point, I will admit. Tidying around, putting a few bits of kitchen finery away.

'We've discussed it all with Jack anyway, and he knows which subjects he wants to take. It is just a formality, really. Just checking it through with his teachers. Come on. I don't see the need for the reaction.' Cupboard door closed, I glanced over. His gaze was lowered. Hands in the pockets of his perfectly tailored trousers, rocking back a little on his heels. Leant against the table, the worn wood providing support. I stopped and looked at him. He raised his head. Slowly. Before saying,

'It's not you. That's really my point. This is not like you. You're usually so organised. It's painful, and this isn't the first thing you've overlooked. This is important, George. This is our son's future, and you don't seem to feel it matters enough. What is going on?' He said it all so slowly, low with an air of thought and carefulness. His palms moved, cupping the edge of the solid structure. Knuckles whitening under the pressure of grip.

'For goodness' sake, Simon. I'm absentminded sometimes. So would you be from time to time if you were trying to juggle a home, demanding job, and life in general. You work a few days a week. It's flipping easy for you.'

The sound shocked me more that the action. Would there be a mark from the impact of fist on wood? Reverberation of sound lingering.

'That was what we agreed when you took the partnership. You were ecstatic. But the only way we could accommodate it was for me to drop my hours. You even suggested it for god's sake. Quality father and son time of an afternoon after school, you said. So now it's my fault, and the decision was wrong?'

He moved away, rubbing the side of his hand as he went. Starting to put things forcefully in his bag for work.

Heart pounding, shock having momentarily taken away my ability to put the right words in the right places. Gathered together something.

'I never said it was wrong, but it is easier for you. Of course, it was the right decision, but right now I have too much to deal with. I'm not superwoman. I forgot. That's it!' I could feel rage working its way through me like a fire gradually taking over. Out of control. Both infuriated and upset. How could he have such anger towards me, just over that one thing?

'I'll change my client meeting or get one of the other partners to step in. It's not the end of the world.' I gave in. Trying to close it down.

He didn't speak. His eyes directed straight at me. That sense that there was so much more to this than one forgotten meeting. Looking intently at him, as he looked straight back at me. There was something else. I could just see it.

He let out a gentle, yet forceful sigh. Then spoke low and softly. Clearly meaning every single word.

'It's not *just* this.' I felt my heart quicken as if anticipating a confession? Was there something I was missing, something he had kept secret?

'I don't get you at the moment. I don't feel you're really ever here.' He looked away, stood with his hands now leaning against the kitchen worktop, leaning over or maybe on it. For more support? Anger rose within me, mixing with the darkening feeling of dread. Walking over to him, I peeked around to the front of his body, as it leant over, wanting to make sure I could see his face and he heard what I wanted to say.

'What is that supposed to mean?' The tears started to well up, more through anger than anything else. I wouldn't let them fall. Not one. 'Of course, I'm here. For god's sake, I am here for you and for the boys. One goddam meeting and all of a sudden...' I trailed off.

Moving to look straight at me he pronounced, 'You are missing the point. We all need you to be an active part of this family and I have no sodding idea where you are half the time. All those things you mentioned on holiday. What's happened? What happened to our family? You are so absorbed with work, the girls, and yourself. You're never here. Not for us. I don't mean physically, although to be fair that too. I kind of thought that our son's parents' evening would register with you.'

Words. So many to take in. Digest.

'How many football and rugby matches have you missed recently? How many? The boys want to feel their mum is interested in the stuff that goes on here.' With that, he walked out of the kitchen to the hall where he busied himself getting a coat and picking up his shoes to put on before heading out.

My chest was tight. I was angry. Upset and enraged.

'Who pays for this house?' I half screamed. 'Who carries the burden of the mortgage, the cost of the life that we all wanted? Nice house, holidays, that life we'd dreamed of and I was given the opportunity to make happen. Who carries that burden, eh?'

I could feel my voice starting to crack. Giving way.

'I do so much of it and there's so much pressure. Work, what people expect me to be. But sometimes I just don't feel as I did. I've the doctor assuming I'm bloody menopausal and wondering why I'm not popping pills to deal with it. Pressure from the girls to be that person who finds the answers to everyone's problems. Pressure to be the perfect mum all the time.' I barely caught breath before he walked towards me and stood so close, I could see his chest rising and falling heavily through his pale blue shirt.

'Wife?' he questioned. Gaze intent.

I was off guard. 'Wife? What do you mean?' I asked. Feeling angrier and more uncertain by the minute.

'If you have to ask, we really do have a problem.' A solid statement.

I was taken aback. Thinking I probably knew what he meant. Yet still the rage within me rose. An abnormally fire-filled force, pushing its way through my veins and every limb. What about my needs in all of this?

He started to gather up his things and head towards the front door. Still further back in the hallway, I grabbed my bag from the banister, wanting to have the last word, to make him see but also needing to get out.

I barged past to be at the door first. I found courage to speak close to him. He didn't feel like my husband at that moment. He was an acquaintance, a colleague, distant. I looked at him, made him look at me. Made him listen.

'Who is here for me? Who helps me?' I spoke slowly and calmly, words I had never externally voiced. I forced them straight at him. The fire propelling them forward.

He appeared to stall before responding. Clearly choosing his words with care.

'You never ask. All you do is mumble about how something is missing. Maybe we should have done things differently, you...none of that means anything to me. If you want help just say it.' His voice so controlled. Each word perfectly formed to ensure I would understand every last syllable. The silence, then palpable, sharpening the air.

Out of control in my response, as the words almost fired out of my mouth in retaliation.

'And if I did? Should I even have to ask?'

Looking directly at him.

I asked again. 'Who looks after me?' Struggling to hold back the tears but determined to not let them win. 'You don't even see me. You don't even look at what I'm doing, how I'm managing. You don't see me at all.' No – I would not let him win. The anger felt was almost too raw in its rage that it placed a stopper to prevent the moisture cascading out. I would not cry.

'I would happily give this place up, move somewhere smaller if that was what you and the boys wanted. But I don't think you do. Yet you want to be able to say that you do it all, make me out to be a useless husband. I look after this house and those boys when I'm not working. I cook the odd meal. You will *not* make this out to be my fault because *you* have changed. Because maybe the GP is right, because you don't care anymore, because this is not enough. All of this is not enough to satisfy *your* need. Yet the rest of us are more than fuckin' happy with our lot and so should you be.' The words were far from controlled by this point. The volume hammering them home as each one was uttered.

I didn't doubt they'd been stored within him for longer than the last ten minutes. We continued to stay close by the front door, almost touching freedom, each of us wanting to air those words we'd kept in for so long.

I had to break the moment of silence.

'I am not ungrateful, and I do care. Of course, I care. Everyone just expects too much of me. I'm not the young person I was. Things are changing. Maybe I am changing, but no one wants to know. You don't. You don't even listen.'

I looked away fearful of where this would go.

'No one listens properly. No one really understands. Not even the girls.'

'Then get help.' Was that a softening I heard in his tone? Not that it made any difference to how I felt.

'Oh, I hadn't thought of that. Yes, I'll do that then. I'll get help so you don't have to moan at me about missing appointments. God forbid I should make a mistake, and it's my fault I haven't 'solved' all my issues. Haven't spent hours with a counsellor discussing my childhood. God forbid my family should care about how I am and try to help. God forbid I should just want to live a little, have more to my life than a constant bloody train ride and watching you prune the roses!' I couldn't help it; it all came out before I had a chance to stop it.

'What is it you expect me to do? You don't even ask for help. You don't even really say what it is that all this is about.' He raised his voice further and I could see the uncontained anger clearly etched all over his face.

'After all these years together, Simon, I would have thought you could see, could tell. Should I have to spell it out? Beg for bloody help? No! You should know, you should see, and you should care. I don't have any of the answers. I want someone to help me find them.'

Before he had a chance to respond, I pulled the door open and barged past him before slamming it behind me.

Laughter filled the air as the small boy playing football with his family made a run up to kick the ball and landed flat on his back. He laughed. His dad paused to see if it was OK to laugh before bursting out in joy, too. The rest of the family laughed once they could see the boy was safe. He picked himself up, went to kick the ball once more, and the game continued.

Found myself smiling at it all, remembering Jack and Matt's younger years. How we did exactly the same as this family that I was observing from a distance.

A few tears found their way down my face, and I wiped them away hurriedly so as not to draw attention to myself. Not allowing them to make any imprint on my face. Not that anyone was around really, but still. My bag was its usual state of untidiness as I sought out a packet of tissues located in an inner pocket.

A lone walker passed slowly by where I was sitting and then a little terrier came trotting past after. The gentleman looked up and gave a gentle smile as he moved slowly past, using his stick for assistance.

Simon would quite possibly still be home now. I could imagine he'd be late heading off for work. I wondered what he was doing, feeling. I'd exploded with words I hadn't mentioned before. Hadn't put together. My mind began to wander back to the argument...retraced the steps.

At that point, my phone went off. I rummaged to grab it from my bag and looked to see who it was, though with no real intention of answering the call. It was Chrissie. Had she spoken to Simon already? Had he spoken to her, to discuss my failings between them? Or was that just a coincidence? Either way, I wasn't able to speak to her right now. I wasn't going to speak to anyone.

A sense of impending change was now overwhelming me. Life was moving at a rapid pace. What that looked like or meant wasn't clear, not then. As I reached back into my bag to replace my phone, I saw a crumpled, loose piece of paper in there. I took it out, smoothed it a little and turned it over, wondering what it was. A scribbled phone number. Instantly, I could recall its origin. An option.

Chapter 35

That was it.

That was the moment from which there was no going back.

Yet the reality felt very much like someone else's. I became no longer really in control of my own actions and calls. My hands made plans and reservations without instruction.

A meeting at work scheduled for 9 a.m. Get it done. It would leave the day for unrest and silent treatment possibly, but I would at least then have offloaded. I needed to complete this part of the puzzle first.

Nine-fifteen, the meeting still awaited. Feeling on edge, I couldn't start anything else until that moment was past. Finally Andy, our managing partner, indicated that he was free, and I stepped into the unknown.

I took a seat and as the sun pattered in through the blinds I sought to take it as a sign for me to continue. To do what I seem to have set out to do now. To start a journey that, in many ways, I had begun many months ago.

He took the news with surprise but also consideration. Disappointed, but if it was a sabbatical, then as far as he was concerned, I would be back and that made it less of an issue. Keeping my options afloat, I confirmed I was fully intending to come back.

I left.

The sigh of relief waited until I sat back in my own office. Pausing for a moment, I held my head supportively in my hands behind a closed door. The pounding almost unbearable. It would most likely be a couple of months in order for plans to be put in place, but he had understood that the sooner I went, the sooner I would be back.

Word would be out before long, but I had specifically asked that it wait until next week. I had other conversations to have first. There would undoubtedly be looks, comments and questions from those brave enough to venture. I had not indicated where I would be, just that I would be in touch once settled and provide forwarding details and contact information, but for now, I needed to drip feed the reality to all those concerned.

Chapter 36

I deserved to be happy. I deserved to be happy. A mantra I hoped would maybe dilute all the guilt I felt.

It was us. Us and the house. The house we created, the home we loved. Just us and home.

Not sure how I even started the conversation. It was in some ways easier, as we'd barely spoken with love for weeks since I'd stormed out. The resentment, lack of comprehension hanging in the air, threatening to drop at any moment. And that time was now.

Deciding not to flower it up too much, I shot out the words. It had seemed easier than plotting some gradual build up routine. My weapon had been released.

If only at some point, he'd tried to help me fill the gap within me. Helped me to locate professional help, convinced me I needed it. Or just spent time listening to my words. Found all those expressions that were left unsaid. But none of that had occurred.

'Are you serious? What the...'

I'm not sure what reaction I had anticipated.

Silence.

I had said it. I had decided.

Looking down, I was aware of his gaze, his staring right at me in nothing short of complete and utter disbelief. He stood opposite someone he no longer knew, or even recognised. The reality was that I didn't know her either.

Still just stood. He said nothing more, but as I looked up, I witnessed the tears in his eyes. Sensed the frustration and anger. A sadness. The sheer incomprehension of what I had just uttered. The tears started to drip from his eyes, slowly spilling out what I'd done. What I alone had created that I could not now undo. The words were out. Things had been said that must be shared, and yet there was no explanation for any of it. I wondered if he had seen it coming. Simon's jaw was clenched with a mixture of anger and confusion as he tried to contain the tears. Taking his hand to his face, he wiped away the water before running his hand through his lightly greying hair. I wondered if, to begin, with he thought it might be some form of sick joke, or a test. And then he realised the truth.

'What about the boys?' he questioned. That was the point I had struggled with the most. I loved them. They were mine. My flesh and blood, my heart, my everything. But I couldn't continue to leave myself behind. I couldn't continue to ignore the feelings of having lost everything of me, of having given all I was and more.

'I will have to tell them soon. I need to decide what to say,' I replied, with care, controlling every word.

With disgust at my apparent misunderstanding.

'I don't mean telling them. I mean what you're doing to them. What half decent mother decides to leave, abandon their children?' The anger began to spill out from him with every syllable as the words were almost thrown from his mouth. Spat out at me. I could sense the rage expelling from his chest, with the complete inability to understand how, in any shape or form, I could even contemplate this. Let alone actually do it. My husband's anger was rising.

'Have you really even considered the impact your actions will have on them?' He propelled with fury. 'Have you given any consideration to anyone else in amongst your dream for a perfect, permanent holiday?'

I understood his anger.

'Of course, I have.' I retorted. As I moved towards the door to the room, thinking a change of location might diffuse the situation somewhat. 'I've thought of nothing but.' Immediately I uttered those words, I realised exactly what I had said. I had hurt him even more. Said I'd not thought of him, just the boys. That I'd clearly been concerned at how I would be impacting their lives and yet not his. Not what I meant, but it was now too late to change it or even clarify.

Edging out of the room, he grabbed my arm as I started to make my way through the doorway.

'You seriously are going to abandon everything you have, everything WE have together for the fulfilment of some mid-life menopausal crisis where you get to selfishly put yourself first?' The anger was clear. His face close to mine, I could feel the heat of his breath. 'You are giving up everything to please yourself? Is that what you want? Is that what a mother does? Those boys will be scarred. You will destroy them if you do this. Destroy me.'

The tears flowed freely down his cheeks and while he was clearly fuming, he was also, I assumed, upset. I found I had no tears and yet no idea why.

'I will still be their mum.' I looked him straight in the face. Studied his eyes, the hint of aging lines across his forehead. The tan left over from the break that became the catalyst for all of this. Aware I was hurting, hurting him.

'I love them, and I will always be there for them. I don't know, maybe I'll come back after a while or maybe they…' I stopped. Whatever was said would be wrong. It would only do more damage.

'You are not the woman I married. I genuinely have no idea who you are, or who you are becoming.' His gaze lowered as he let the words escape, releasing my arm as he did so. No physical harm had been administered. He had held my arm so gently, just enough to make me stop before I tried leaving the room.

Capturing his gaze, I agreed.

'No. You're right. I'm not.' This had probably been the case for some time. 'I don't know what's happened, but what I do know is that I can no longer live like this. I can no longer continue in the same way every day, doing the same things for everyone else. I cannot waste my life being what everyone wants me to be. This is my life too. My right to do something that makes me feel whole, that makes me feel me, again.' Somewhat surprised at the calmness with which the words escaped my throat.

'You're right. I'm not me. I don't know what I feel, what's wrong. But I have *got* to do something about it. My life matters. I matter.'

At that point, he released my arm, released me, and I left the room. Heading down through to the sunroom. Just a few moments later, the front door banged shut. Tears gently, quietly, slipping away and down my face.

Chapter 37

The one constant. My feet.

Wondering what might happen if I ran and didn't stop. Could I actually leave my thoughts and actions behind? I tried. I really did try some days.

I ran further than I had done for a long time, the day I told my boys. My sweet, kind boys.

No matter which route I took, my head and feet would pound. No amount of sunshine, or rain, or distance changed that.

When I finally gathered myself to speak to them, I went with the truth. To a point. Simon had wanted to be out of the way for fear of trying to get involved. I think it was more about leaving me to face the consequences of my own mess. They were aware he and I had been distant. No discussions had been forthcoming but clearly, they realised we were no longer sharing a bed. You couldn't hide it all.

What was worse? The screaming? The tears? Or Matt's stony silence. Not even looking at me after a time. Stumbling for words of reassurance, a promise to return, declarations of love and pride and all that a mother constantly feels. I could still hear Jack's tears, uncontrollable, as he ran out of Matt's room, bashing into the door frame on the way, before slamming his own bedroom door shut. I started to go after him, but Matt made it firmly clear that I should stop.

Sunday morning. Today I found myself greeted by clouds but without rain. A small hint of sun. Not enough to create heat, but still warmer than the house I lived in. For the next few weeks, anyway.

Not yet fully daytime and the sun was still easing itself out of bed. My favourite music filled my mind. Drowning out the words that had been uttered amongst the silence of a once buoyant home. Words that can never be unsaid. We'd all gone too far. I, for one, had stepped on to a ride with no ability to jump off. No harness. No refund if it wasn't what I expected or hoped. Sometimes I caught myself wondering if I could step back. Return to joint cups of coffee, questions about how our respective days had been. Instead, we had statements of a finality or at the very least a long break.

The sun became more. It stretched and covered the land before me. A subtle glow as it rejoiced in the beginning of a new day for it, for all. It seemed to be beckoning me to continue to use my courage to find a way forward and to find myself.

What if?

I loved those words. I always had done. The blanket of possibility, the intrigue of not knowing. Life didn't always seek to offer that, or maybe none of us craved it enough? But for me, right then, in tiny moments of excitement, if that was the right concept, the words 'what if?' were a huge beacon of light. A beacon I clung on to. In the dark days of planning an escape while sharing a house with a man I no longer had any real relationship with, I was forced to see children who looked at me in disbelief. The gap on one side of the bed, separate meals, the depth of darkness from a comment regarding the disappointment in me that my own mum would have felt. Had she only been there to see it. On those occasions, the possibility of 'what if' might just have saved me.

Chapter 38

Stood in anticipation of the door opening, I waved reluctantly at her neighbours as they meandered along on the opposite side of the road. We'd chatted a little at various parties, BBQs, and other excuses for celebrations, but right at that moment I was in no mood for a catch-up. *Please don't cross the road to talk,* I pleaded inwardly, as they strolled along with purpose. Relief filled me when I saw them turn to concentrate on a conversation they'd been having with their son. After our brief waves of recognition, they moved on, and I turned back to face her home.

She was in. I knew that. After a short time, she opened the door. The large, ornate front entrance swung to one side as I straightened up. I'd dressed that day as if for work. My dark blue trousers and crisp white shirt accompanied by heels and a long jacket. Dressed with a sense of purpose. With an air of needing to achieve things in those twenty-four hours. I had hoped my clothes would give me more confidence and comfort than they were realistically capable of.

Her familiar and engaging smile greeted me. She had no idea.

'Hey! Come on in. Lovely to see you.' The words tumbled out as she extended her welcome and stepped aside to allow me into the entrance hall. A place I had envied for many years. The opulence, the glistening crystal. Carefully placed, individually produced vases. Not my style and certainly not befitting a family home of boys, but such a beauty to behold. A clear representation of the success from the hard work she'd delivered.

I had, in recent times, wondered how happy all of that really made her.

Years before, she was certainly anything but. I'd spent a lot of time with her, to get her through those tough weeks, and knew she was very much the other side of the worst of it. Yet, I pondered whether the items she filled her home and life with had been sufficient compensation for what went before.

'Coffee??' she asked as we went down to the kitchen. My heels tapped their way across her tiled floor. Chrissie's doing likewise.

I didn't concern myself with leaving my coat in the hall, as I wasn't sure exactly how long I would be welcome to stay. Answering her offer of a drink by way of a slightly downcast affirmative with thanks, I was reminded of previous afternoons where coffee would have been just the beginning. Then had arrived the wine, the gin, and whatever else Chrissie could find in her cabinets. She never let any of us down. Provided for us all.

'What's been happening, all OK?' Chrissie casually enquired, pouring the coffee as I moved onto a stool at the end of her kitchen counter. Allowing her space.

Searching for courage, I took a deep breath, as though trying to keep it subtle. I really wasn't sure I'd be able to say it. That was though the whole reason I was there. The reason I'd asked to 'just pop over for a quick coffee and catch up'. Now I found myself so afraid of facing the judgement. There would be one. I could not expect otherwise.

Chrissie looked over at me as she slowly placed her mug back down on the counter. The bright blue blouse she wore contradicting the complete lack of joy and calm her face now displayed. Utter disbelief. Complete horror. I didn't expect her to understand, although she often had in the past. But this was so different. Of such magnitude, it was impossible for her to sympathise. Despite the depth of friendship, this was an abhorrently selfish act. If I were her, I don't know that I would have understood. I didn't really even understand it myself.

The silence that followed hung heavy in the air. I dared not stir my coffee for fear of breaking it. That might lead to me having to answer questions. I might need to seek to justify, explain, and I could not. I had almost made a conscious decision now to not try to reason my actions. Instead, I had resorted to embracing the numbness within. Quickly but gently stirring the milk in, I cupped the mug for support.

Still no sound from Chrissie. Until she let her breath go and it cried out as if carrying with it so many questions, she was unable to voice.

Finally.

'How have the boys taken it?' Her question barely audible, her face appeared paler than I'd ever seen. She wasn't even able to look at me at that point. Instead, gazing past me. I had let her down in letting it get this far.

That one most important question. How exactly had they taken it? Should I tell her the truth? That Jack had cried himself to sleep that night and had barely looked me in the eye since? That Matthew had chosen not to speak. Maybe I should have gone on and highlighted how they were no longer young children, and they could understand a bit more of what was going on. They might not like it, but could almost think of it as a bit of a holiday/work placement and knew their dad was around still.

'They're adjusting.' Is how I decided to leave it.

Part of me wanted to just let go and spill all that I felt, almost beg her to make me find a reason not to do it. Something to stay for, a way of working through all I had become, but I didn't. If I talked, I might not stop, and I had worked so hard on keeping it all together. I had cried, many times, not for what I was about to do, but for the loss of me. I had no real idea who this person was that I had become, but I couldn't seem to shed the skin.

'I knew you had had some problems with Simon, well I guessed you had, but this? Do you really need to do this? Walk out on everything? Leave your boys? There must surely be a better way?'

While I was concentrating deeply on the mug in front of me, I sensed her stare. Picturing it in my mind, too fearful to meet it.

'No,' is all I could say.

'I genuinely don't know what to say, George. Are seriously telling me you're walking away? Moving away? That's it? That's the answer?' Volume raised. 'What about marriage counselling, a trial separation? For god's sake move in here for a bit if it helps??? What happened to getting medical help?'

It was clear I wouldn't get away with just telling her and heading off. She deserved more, anyway. The trouble was I was running out of energy to have these conversations. There was no naivety, no thinking I could just say bye and run. That was never going to be the case, but I was hit with such an exhaustion about it all.

'I don't know Chris. I don't know.' What else could I say? I needed her to not be mad or upset, but that was of course beyond her.

Hearing her exhale, I wondered where we went from there.

'This is not what mums do. You know that George. Women don't destroy homes. I just don't know if those boys will ever forgive you. Do you really know what you're doing?'

Hands gripping the mug some more, I moved my gaze from the worktop. I had to meet her look.

'I don't know what else to say to you. Apart from I guess I'm sorry. I've got myself into a corner now. I don't honestly know what else to do. I need to try. I need to do this for me.'

I could see I was causing her so much pain.

'This is so extreme, George. This is just so wrong.' The tears of disbelief fell. Just as Simon's head and yet I remained committed.

We talked some more. I held in any tears that might have been trying and we hugged before I left. Stepping into the sunshine, with my jacket still in place, I was now shaking. Knowing that everyone else would be aware before long, I would need to prepare for the fallout.

Chapter 39

The days that followed found me fastened to a surreal fairground ride, travelling in the slowest of motion. A ride I didn't particularly want to be on, but the fare had been paid. Didn't want to be at work. Constant references to 'when you've left'. Didn't want to be at home. Solitary confinement to what was 'our' bedroom. Attempts at some sort of reconciliation with Matt and Jack, quickly dismissed.

'What else would you do?' I asked. Stirring the coffee absently and vastly in excess of what the dissolving sugar required. The café relatively quiet, a touch of lunch time murmur but only at a volume that still enabled us to hear each other with clarity.

Without moving from her intense gaze towards her own drink, Annie remarked,

'I really don't know, hon, but I can't help but think there must be an alternative.' Her tone soft, somewhat concerned. It wasn't unusual for the two of us to meet without the others for a drink or a spot of lunch. Of the three of them, I'd known Annie the longest. Our friendship the easiest of all. She never offered judgement. Not even now, amongst all this chaos that probably warranted it. Maybe, secretly, that was the reason I'd been happy to meet with her. The most likely to not offer great challenge to my ridiculous plans.

Lunch arrived and as we tucked in, the silence required me to intervene.

'It's hard to find any other option. I've looked for one, trust me.' Such a feeble sounding response.

'I'm just really concerned there may be no turning back. That this might be a more final decision than you realise.' She looked at me, intently. Asking, with her eyes, for me to reconsider. She didn't say anything I hadn't thought about already. I was merely being reminded of the truth she spoke. The truth I knew.

'Maybe there won't be a Plan B. This is certainly all I have currently. And I know that it makes sense to no one but me. If I'm brutally honest, I don't know that it 100% makes sense to me either.' I paused, taking a drink from my coffee cup. A larger gulp than I perhaps should have. The richness of the warm liquid, causing a welling within my eyes.

The atmosphere between us still felt warm but was becoming tinged with a sadness of things somehow coming to an end.

'I just worry.'

'I know, and I am sorry to put you through this, but what else can I do?'

'Stay? Find another way to make things better for you all?' Her look was almost pleading, and a pang of guilt hinted at making me wonder whether the decision was, in fact flawed.

'I've told Simon I'm leaving. He hates me. I get it, I'm rejecting him. That's how it will seem to him, anyway. But it really is way more than that. He won't get it. He doesn't get it.'

'I think you're wrong. He'd take you back – you know that.' There's a forcefulness in her words that takes me a little by surprise. Trying to recollect if I'd heard that from her before and decided I'd probably not put her in such a position previously. This was all new.

The waiter popped over to just check we had all we needed. We each smiled in acknowledgement at the same time providing the hint of wanting to be left alone. The lunch rush had subsided a little, causing us to be careful and lower our voices a bit so as not to share all with the strangers within.

Shuffling in my seat, I tried to find the right words to say. 'It's just so much more than all about him.'

Annie's gaze locked with mine. Each fighting to hold ourselves together. A part of me desperately longed for her to make this right. To help me make sense of how I felt and make me work through whatever it was that was forcing me to abandon everything for the promise of a new future. I wanted to ask for her help. But I didn't.

We ate.

We made small talk.

We tried desperately to relax.

Our plates were cleared, and more coffee arrived.

'In a small way, I do admire you, you know.' Out of nowhere. I stopped and looked directly at Annie. Her smile said all I needed to know. That our friendship was unaltered. That my seemingly selfish actions would not change the bond we'd had for years. I didn't need to seek her support. She clearly would willingly give it. The bond between close friends would sometimes transcend the most difficult of events. She knew I was there for her when her world changed forever. However, that was not her doing. It was all out of her hands, and she had had to fight for her future in a completely different world.

She understood the value of life and how short it could sometimes be. This was a choice I was making. I could not, in any way, claim that this was not my fault.

'I don't think *admire* is a word that anyone would use in reference to me right now,' I responded with a half-hearted smile. 'Please don't think I'm in any doubt as to the hurt I am causing. I really don't mean to, and I'll do my best to cause no more. Chrissie and Erica don't believe that I'm sure, but I hope that you do.'

Leaning back, more relaxed. 'I'm sure they do, in their own way...' she remarked.

'Well, I guess I'll find out.'

'Have you spoken with Erica since the pub incident?'

I shook my head gently.

'I've not tried a great deal, to be honest. Maybe I should have, but I didn't think she'd want to talk.'

'Do you regret it? I mean things that were said?' Annie trailed off, gazed away from me, and clearly wasn't quite sure what to do about ending that conversation. It seemed as though she might inadvertently be throwing full blame in my direction.

'I guess so. I just couldn't help myself at the time. That's all. I do stand by some of it though…'

I continued.

'We live very different lives.'

'Maybe not as different as you think.' Annie's gaze concentrated on the cup in front of her. Her delicate fingers working round and round the edge. The drink managing to maintain some level of stability as its container circled gently.

I looked at her with more intensity than ever before. Taking in those words, trying to work it out. I deflected my own opinion.

'I doubt very much she would agree with you on that. As far as she's concerned, I have nothing to be sad, depressed, or whatever about. I have everything I could want. But I selfishly want something else. I can't really argue with that summary, but there is a bigger picture.'

Annie interjects.

'I think you're being hard on yourself. Maybe you're being too quick to dismiss that something might have triggered all this for you. Who knows?'

'Not me.'

Considerations over the issue with Erica plagued my mind for the rest of the afternoon. We endeavoured to move on from such deep discussions, though the reality of it all still hung in the air. Collecting coats, thanking staff, and heading out into the sunshine, I was consciously thankful for Annie. Acutely aware that I, at that moment, had no idea when we might do this again…

Chapter 40

'What the fuckin' hell are you doing?'

No hello. No courtesy in those first words, after I'd answered the call.

'Hi, Erica.' Tone flat. Poised to listen, no doubt be made to.

'Genuinely. What drives that head of yours?' I could almost feel the heat of the words through the phone. She continued, barely drawing breath. 'I think there must be a mistake. Are you having a mid-life crisis, an affair, or something?'

I didn't want to pause for too long. She would fill any gap she was given. But although in some ways I'd been expecting this outburst, I found myself lost at what might be a suitable response. 'I'm sorry' would never cut it. Any form of explanation couldn't be loud enough for Erica to hear. She was a volcano of emotion at the best of times and right at that moment, I wanted to be anywhere but in her vicinity.

'As I said to Chrissie, I know you won't understand and I'm sorry I can't change that. This has however been building for some time…'

'Building during what? During your date nights at fancy restaurants, while you've counted the pounds in your bank account, while out shopping? For Christ's sake, George. You have bloody everything. Every-bloody-thing. Stuff people can only dream of and it's just not enough for you, so you decide to piss off?' She had taken her aim.

Barely heard at this point.

'That stuff is not what life is about, Erica. You know that as well as I do. This isn't about not having enough *stuff*. This is about how I *feel* and as much as I might like to, I can't change it.'

'It actually makes no sense. The only thing I can put it down to is just your complete and utter selfishness.' I could almost feel her spitting those words out as the utter disgust and disbelief she held for my actions overwhelmed her very being.

'Why else would anyone who has everything, and *more*, decide it's not enough? Why would any mum decide leaving her kids was the best thing to do?' Her voice became hurried as though she needed to offload everything quickly before she ran out of steam or before her anger got the better of her. Visualising her face at that moment, how her expression would turn taut, her brown eyes void of the deep warmth that they often held.

'Erica, I know how you feel. I get it. I'm not surprised but I—'

'Your poor boys.' A statement. Almost shouted. An interruption within my attempt to make some valid reason, or an important point, when there was none.

Silence. What could I possibly say in response to that?

'What are you doing to those boys, you selfish bitch?' Her voice had slowed down, softened almost to a whisper. She needed no more volume than that to be heard. "Those boys you apparently love so much. They don't deserve this. And Simon. I'm sorry, George, but I can't see any reason you could ever justify this."

I got it. I really understood the disbelief. The feeling that she didn't know me anymore. I was no longer the person I had been. Nothing could change that. Not there.

I felt her frustration. The anger.

The end of the call. The phone line dead.

I'd be lying if I said I hadn't spent time reconsidering my actions. Erica's words stayed with me for some time. How could they not? Yet she said nothing I hadn't previously thought, hadn't wrestled with. I was a bad person. A cold-hearted person, who put herself before everyone else. That was now how many would remember me. That was how a part of me saw myself. Yet I also grappled with the point that I did in fact matter. That my sense of self and purpose remained important.

My life was important. *My* life was too short. What if I did nothing and the years just slipped by...

Chrissie's text message a few days later was loud and clear. Conveying a message from the masses. Society's verdict on my chosen actions.

You're a mum! And a wife! Don't we all have desires and dreams but, for God's sake, George we have responsibilities and sometimes what you want shouldn't come first.

'I am still a mum.'

Despite my desire to delete the message, pretend it never reached me, I had to respond. I was still their mum. Mum to Matt and Jack. They were mine.

No notification sound. I continued.

I'm sure if Simon did this, we'd all have a bottle or two of wine, moan about him and discuss how the boys will cope, etc., but it would be OK in the end.

That was a step too far. Despite hurriedly checking through settings and menus, no option to cancel the message, delete it before it was received, could be found.

Chrissie knew what it felt like to feel lost within the world. Ignored. Her ex-husband had made that quite clear for a large part of their marriage. The impact of his selfishness and undeniable arrogance still lingered in her life. Part of it still lingered in mine.

No reference to my last message when the phone emitted a beep once more.

You have to know there are a million and one other things you could do rather than destroy the lives of those boys and your husband. You must know that. You will take the lives of those boys and trample all over them.

A further beep.

You can't even justify it, can you? You can't genuinely sit there and say, 'I have a good reason for doing this and I will be better for it'. You just can't.

Time passed before I decided to eventually reply.

No.

I waited some more. Although it would in many ways have been easier to just pick up the phone and thrash it out. However, that wasn't Chrissie's style.

What happens though if I do nothing? I needed her to think about that and left the message delivered for five minutes. No response.

At what point does how I feel, matter? Is it when the boys have left home? Is it when Simon has left me because he's found somebody else who's happier, more lively, more interesting to be with? At what point do I matter?

I can't answer that. The reply arrived quickly. Exhausted probably by the way in which I challenged her concerns. Exhaustion was hitting us all.

No more messages. Chrissie had given up and was conscious that I may have taken her back to a time when selfishness ripped her world apart, reminding her of those awful days. If for no other reason than that, I was then truly sorry.

Chapter 41

Erica arrived to open the door, not lingering to welcome me in. Chrissie busy with the coffee or maybe just avoiding having to see me first, perhaps? I took what felt like a long walk down the immaculate hallway to the familiar open-plan room.

'Hi.' With a muted smile Chrissie glanced up as I approached the breakfast bar. I placed my bag on the floor but kept my coat on as I politely reciprocated the greeting. It didn't feel appropriate to remove my jacket. That might indicate I would be stopping a while.

Erica made her way over to take a stool at the bar. She moved a cup towards herself and focussed heavily on the coffee, an excuse not to have to look up at me. I waited for someone to break the silence, feeling as though I'd been summoned to meet my fate.

Annie gently became the first to take the plunge.

'What time are you leaving?' she asked. Erica looked over at me, waiting for the answer to see how much information I would give. Meanwhile, Chrissie continued to busy herself, stirring the coffee and adding more sugar for taste.

'Erm, I don't quite know at the moment to be honest,' I replied, almost apologetically. I shot Annie a half smile and hoped she could find the gratitude in that look, as my gaze went back down to my coffee. Silence ensued.

Then Erica dived in. 'You haven't changed your mind yet, then?' She almost spat the words at me, the disgust obvious in her tone.

'No.' As if being reprimanded by a stern headteacher I gazed back down at my coffee again, wanting the time to leave to come sooner than it would.

'I am still going,' I stated, not even looking up.

Walking around the bar top, Erica headed towards the plate of biscuits Chrissie had set out by the coffee pot.

'I still can't quite believe it, I'm not going to lie.' Said with an air of authority, before biting into a biscuit that halted her pursuit of honesty.

'All because what you have isn't enough!' The sneer in her last statement in between biscuit munching was clear for all to hear.

'It's not that it's not enough. We've been over this.'

I'd barely finished my sentence.

'Then what the hell is it? I don't see anyone else here deciding to piss off because they're bored of all they have. Let's face it, even with Annie's home life, she's still here.'

Annie looked up, not quite sure how to take that comment. A momentary look of sadness at having been reminded of and almost ridiculed, for her situation, was clear for me to see, if no one else.

Half-heartedly apologising Erica carried on. "I don't mean anything by it, Ann, I'm just trying to make a point.' She then walked back round the bar to resume her coffee. I looked over at Chrissie, surprised at her reluctance to get involved. A by-standing part of the community.

I needed to stand tall.

'I'm not suggesting for one moment that any of you understand this. But I can't ignore it anymore. I can't think straight, I just can't go on. Not now. Haven't you ever had a feeling that you're missing something? And that something is you?'

'But what about being a mother and a wife and a friend?' Chrissie came to the party. Reminding me that my choices were not those recognised by a society for whom my actions were incomprehensible.

'Why?'

'What do you mean why?' Erica chipped in, not understanding my question.

'I mean why? Why is my life so much less important than yours or theirs?

That doesn't mean I don't love you, or them for that matter but why can I not have my life? If Simon was walking out would that be OK? Yes, of course it would!' I felt my temperature rising and the anger in my words become more apparent.

And I was far from done.

'I am *not* a selfish person. I am *not* a horrible person! Should I just wait for the boys to leave home? I'm not getting any younger but in many ways this time, right now, could just be my start.'

'It will never be enough though, will it? Your life will never be enough for you.' Erica cut my thoughts dead.

'You are a complete mess.'

The air was frozen. The momentum lost for that second.

Quietly I spoke, my head down, concentrating on my drink.

'Maybe you are all better human beings than I am. But I am sorry. I've gone too far now.'

Collecting my bag from the floor, leaving the rest of my drink, I turned without making eye contact.

'You know you'll regret it.' Erica still could not leave the matter alone as I headed to the front door. I stopped. Unable to decide whether to reply. I decided not to and made my way back down the hallway of one of my best friend's homes, not knowing if I would ever want to come back or even be welcome to return.

Chapter 42

I'd been awake for hours. Felt Simon shuffling around in our room, my room, as he came in to get a few things he must have desperately needed. He and the boys were going out for the day, just to see a local rugby team take on opponents in a cup game. It had been planned for some time but no doubt the activity had now been extended, so as to ensure they would all be out and gone in time. Now that it coincided with the day I would put flesh on the bones of my plans.

Daybreak carried a weight within it that was felt by all. I expected to have regrets, to panic and seek to apologise for all I had done, maybe ask if I could stay? Yet I did none of that. A sense of sadness of course and maybe a certain amount of nervous anticipation but regret was not the overwhelming feeling at that moment. I couldn't say I was full of doubt. I still felt, even if that was more than a little misguided, that the decision I had made was what I needed to do. Regardless of the reason or the history behind it, I was no longer present. Not really.

The quilt cocooned me to the point of comfort, but I knew I needed to get started. There was a journey to be made. Bags had been gradually packed for a few days now, tucked away in my wardrobe so as not to throw it all in the faces of the others, especially Simon. He'd barely set foot in what was our bedroom for the past few weeks. Only as necessary to collect a particular shirt or pair of shoes that he required. I considered whether he might move back in here, after I had gone. Or would it hold too many memories for him to feel comfortable sleeping in that bed again? Our bed.

Pausing momentarily, after having swung myself up, I then rested on the side of the bed. My eyes settled over onto the side table. The photo that remained there of Simon and the boys. All splattered with mud from some rugby game a few years ago. Filthy, cold, and wet, they all still stood beaming from ear to ear. Simon's gaze lovingly settling on Matt who seemed to take the award for the least amount of skin available to be seen. My fingers lightly rested on the photo, tracing the outlines, as I became aware of the tears starting to form.

As I stood up, I collected the photo and took it with me to my bags. Opening the door, I faced the near emptiness of my wardrobe as it stood before me. The bags were neatly stacked up on the floor inside, leaving only a few old dresses and my collection of formal office attire, hanging amongst the vacant space.

The bags lifted out easily, surprising really as the spaces within had been fully utilised. I popped the photo in the top one, snuck in amongst the jumpers. It was the start of the summer season, but you never knew what the British weather would do. More importantly, I had no idea when, or even if, I would be coming back.

I had left out an outfit that would be comfortable to travel in. It sat waiting on the upholstered grey chair that sat to one side. In our room. My room. I had bought it many years ago as a project. It had been moved from room to room as we played around with layouts and colour schemes. Eventually I gave up and found someone else to bring it back to life. Turned it from a tired old, worn-out seat to a beauty offering support. A place to rest feet, leave clothes. It sat still, waiting.

Heading to the shower in the ensuite, I started to undress. Finding a slowness of pace, a quiet to every limb. No noise from beyond these walls. Had they all left?

Standing still, I let the water drip carefully over me. Eyes closed. Breath barely there. Still. Surreal.

Once showered I checked the time. No reason particularly to do so. Force of habit, I guessed. The cottage was available already. No pressure on leaving or what time I even arrived. Checking the time again, receiving an element of structure to the day. Having cast my eye on my watch, my eyeline picked up the reminder indicated by my empty left hand.

The girls. Not one of them had been in touch since the previous day's unpleasant affair. I could attach no blame to them for the outcome. There were no words I could give them, no excuses to make, that would enable them to understand for one small moment how I felt and why I was doing this. I had seen a flicker of something from Annie, something that might just have signalled she was sorry for the other's reactions. I knew from our previous lunch that she was less angry than the others. But I couldn't be sure. She, the one with the greatest reason to resent me, to see me as the fool that I was. Yet I felt she also saw me as someone in need of help. She would have given anything to be in my position. A complete family. She didn't need to say it. I just knew it. Her world had been shattered by something completely out of her control. Yet she watched me as I shattered mine.

Chrissie had walked away. I could see it so clearly in her eyes, the day before. The stony glare, the raised voice. She had called me out for what I was. Erica too.

Dressed, I started to pack the last few personal things in my bags. Deciding not to pause for one last look around the bedroom I had shared with Simon for the last twelve years. Stepping out. I did not look back.

Chapter 43

There are so many ways that people seek to end it. To remove themselves from this very earth. From whatever situation led them to the point of even giving consideration to it. Does the edge of a cliff make it any easier, quicker? More poetic? Preferable to the other options available?

My toes are now clinging on so tightly to the eroded rock face, that I can feel a depth of pain in the skin underneath, beyond that felt before. Sensing the blood seeping from cuts that are jagged and rough. My mind envisages bones starting to crack sharply, gradually, under the pressure of keeping balance. These images, making themselves at home in my head, seem to make it all even worse. As though a few incisions to the soles of my feet could really make this whole situation feel even more of a mess. It's almost laughable that a picture I've conjured up, of a situation I cannot see, could make things more traumatic.

I sense the fresh air. Taste it on my tongue, even though it remains set in my mouth. A slight hint of salt, caught on the waves of a gentle breeze, captured from the water below.

I did it. I put myself first. That's what I did.

I am important.

Chapter 44

Driving down, heading along the main road into town, the slight sense of some form of familiarity welcomed me in. Sea opened up ahead, appeared on the horizon, while I clung on to the twists and turns the tarmac. A sense of relief at having made it without getting too lost or too upset, coupled with a hope that I wouldn't allow myself to fall at the final hurdle.

Waves rolling ahead, beckoning me towards the shore. Not much before them I needed to turn off to locate what would be my home for a few months, at least. Plans had been put together and changes made, but I had no idea for how long they would all be needed. Or whether it might even become permanent. Work had been accommodating, viewing it all as a sabbatical, a career break. I gave them as little information as I could get away with, yet enough for them to take my request seriously. Or my statement. It wasn't as if I was going to change my mind at that point.

Pulling into the upward slope that was the drive of the cottage, the lavender bushes swayed in the breeze, just as the waves rolled forward and backward. I created enough room to escape the car without interrupting their flow. A blanket of purple rain around the base of the cottage at the front enticed me in with its encouraging aroma. I turned off the engine. Paused. Sat there, for just a second, to take it in. This was it. I had done it.

Tentatively allowing myself the most subtle of smiles. A trickling of relief.

Taking a deep breath in, not intentionally, I opened the car door and stepped out into the mild sunshine. Standing as I closed the door, a small stretch ending this part of my journey, my gaze filtered across to the hills. A glimpse of the waves sat around the edge of the fields, dots of wildlife in the distance.

My hands swept casually through the lavender as I brushed past, setting little droplets of scent free. Reaching the front door, I knelt down to locate the key safe box. Just where she had said it would be. Keying in the number I had quickly scribbled down on a scrap of paper, I released the key to the door. Opening freedom.

Stepping forward and over the threshold, I was greeted by roses, in a vase, on the table. And a note which read:

Welcome, Georgia. I hope you had an easy and safe journey. There are a few provisions in the fridge and the kitchen cupboard to get you started. It's not much, but it might help. Shop at the bottom of the road opens at 7 a.m. If you need anything, just call, but I'll catch you later in the week.'

I'd paid her two months up front, so she really had no need to be in touch, but it was a kind and welcoming gesture. Placing the note back down on the table, I moved through to the kitchen to take a peek. She had been so generous. Looking through the fridge and cupboards, I could see her kindness meant I did not need to hurry and find provisions. OK until the morning and a bit beyond. Meal planning was not top of my list of things to do. In fact, my jobs list was pretty empty.

Usually, *we* would be arriving. Simon starting to unpack the car, the boys checking out the facilities, in younger years wrestling for rooms. Then we'd head off to explore.

Yet there I was. Just me. Alone. There I was, amongst the silence.

Determined not to dwell on it or allow any negative thoughts a pathway in, I carried on through, checking out the rooms. The neatly made bed, plumped sofa cushions, all coming to me as though I hadn't seen them before. Yet now it looked so different. Now I was staying.

Figuratively taking myself by the hand I headed back out to start unpacking my little beat-up car. I travelled relatively lightly for the situation, a suitcase, and a few travel bags along with my handbag. Closing the door behind me, I let go the last of my luggage just inside. Jacket off, draped over the dining chair, I went to go put the kettle on. The slight temptation to celebrate the start of whatever this was, would be, with the small bottle of wine left, was tempting. But no. I am OK, I reminded myself. This is OK.

The kettle sprang into action. Shoes came off, and I stepped, barefoot, over to the large window that gazed out at the hills and tracks beyond the road. Outside, I could hear the distant waves clearly, but inside it was more muffled. I could just about see the edge of the sea if I stood far to one side. Imagining the flow, the cool sound, the wash. Opening the window, I let in life.

Tea warmed my throat, and I chose to rest up for a time, sinking deep into the sofa. Now that I didn't have to concentrate on driving or navigating my way, I found myself replaying over and over the last few days, or at least parts of them. Some had become so hurtful I had to shut them away, in a box, in the depths of my memory. The enormity of what I had done would creep slowly over me if I let it. Despite the relief, despite the peace, I was also conscious of feeling more than a little numb. Cold. Still. I guess a little in shock. Ultimately, though, I could not help but feel, at last, free.

My phone had been placed on the coffee table and I knew, from having checked it two minutes previously, that there were no messages. Not a single one. Hurting. I was hurting. Yet, of course, they all hurt too. All of them. Of that, I was so very much aware.

Closing my eyes for a time, tempted to drift off somewhere. Yet something reminded me of the reality that sleep might not be my friend that night. An afternoon snooze would not be helpful to the cause. Finishing my tea, I pulled myself up and dragged my feet back into my pumps. A stretch and a check around before I moved out of the door to make my way to the tides, hoping they might just greet me with open arms.

Chapter 45

Sunday. I had no concept of that to begin with. As I came around from a restless, yet deep in parts sleep, I gradually opened my eyes to a tiny slit that allowed enough light in for me to be aware it was day. The bed wasn't uncomfortable but just markedly different and reminded me that I was, in fact, not at home. Solitary. I rolled over to the side where I thought I recalled the window to be. That, at least, was a little familiar. I always had the window side of the bed at home. As it was, at least.

Stretching a little, I opened my eyes some more. The sun streaming in through the thin white curtains, a pointless accessory for anything other than framing the worn wooden window. I rolled over, rubbed my eyes, and then attempted to open them fully. Another sigh and I pushed myself up. Looked around the room, casting a glance over my unfamiliar surroundings.

Getting out of bed, I made steps towards the kettle. Milk had been left for me in the fridge, which meant nothing had been required from the shop when I headed out briefly the day before. My stroll had taken me just along the front, avoiding a step down onto the beach. Instead, I had just taken in the sea breeze from a slight distance, wanting it to welcome me into its embrace.

Kettle seemed to take an age to boil. I spent the time gazing out of the kitchen window, pulling the sleeves down on my pyjama top. Feeling, I guess, more than a little spaced out. Surprisingly not feeling overly lonely at that moment. My own company was the only person I seemed to need at that point.

The coffee tasted pretty good, and I sank down into the worn blue sofa as I worked my way down the mug. Tipping my heavy head back, I let my breath just go. Escaping not as a sigh of despair, more an expression of both peace and freedom. The horror that would be felt by the outside world, to that acknowledgment, was not lost on me.

So, what now?

Having left all that I knew, everyone I loved, to be here, to be alone, I sat there with no real plan. Was I hoping to follow some dream, take some unknown journey? The strain of the last few weeks and months began emerging to the fore. Yet while I had set out on that path, I was acutely aware that no reverse option would exist. There was only one way to go.

The first cup finished. I went to make a second take it with me to the shower. Surrounded by a surreal reality. A quiet nervousness existed within. Anticipation abound. Taking hold of the situation, I showered, dressed, and headed down to the beach. Clarity would await me there as the breeze hit my face, I was sure. Well, I hoped so, anyway.

An outfit of three-quarter jeans, t-shirt and hoodie, something I barely used to wear before, now covered my very being. Aware that I was attempting to dress as I assumed would be expected on the coast. The norm. And I needed to fit in. I needed to feel part of it. To enable it to allow me to feel that and to take me in as its refugee.

As I stepped out of the front door, Mary stepped out of her door in the neighbouring house. She waved, and I briefly waved back. She looked as though she might be about to say more and strike up a conversation, but I quickly ducked my head down and without being rude, scuttled off. The hint taken.

A walk down to the beach, steep but smooth. Much of it was pathway, until you got closer to the top of the bay where the rocks took over. A light breeze existed, just enough to push my hair away from my face and give journey to the scent and calm of the sea.

There weren't that many people out and about, not at all as many as I had envisaged. But it was, after all, the beginnings of spring. The weather relatively good, but holiday makers were scarce until the main season really got going (I was told) and the hordes of families no doubt descended, just as we had the previous year.

I thought it would feel strange, even disconcerting, to be there alone. I'd be lying if I said there hadn't been an element of that. After all, the last time I'd visited was to have been our final family holiday. Unknown at that time, of course. Or was it? Did I sense more than I accepted then? A randomly booked break that I thought, or hoped, would fix so much. I had no idea. I thought, or hoped, that just that one week would give me back myself, refresh the energy I was lacking and bring an end to the months, maybe years, of self-unrest. The realisation had hit me, as I stood alone on that coastal path, that I had expected too much from a single week at the beach. Maybe, though, it just couldn't deliver that in seven days and so it had given me the chance to come back for more? Made me return.

Instead of heading down onto the beach, I carried on walking along the cliff top. Following the path along a route adorned with a variety of homes, guest houses, and numerous hotels. I could hear soft murmurings of the chatter of people starting to leave their accommodation for the day. The sound of discussions on directions and weather forecasts. The exact conversations had with my family the previous summer. For a moment washed with a sadness of my own making. A harsh reminder of my boys, those children I'd left behind. If I stopped to actually and fully face the whole situation, I'd have to acknowledge how much I missed them. Longed for their very beings. I'd have to give in to the recognition of that, which might take me away from my journey and cause me to question the very decisions I'd made. Yet, there was no point in pretending otherwise. What sort of mother would I be if I didn't miss them? I was in no doubt that many others would have a clear answer to any question concerning my parenting. Yet what about Simon too?

I almost physically, but more mentally, stood myself up straight and carried on. One foot placed carefully in front of the other. Toes supporting my journey forwards.

Wandering along, I looked out across the bay. The number of people out for a stroll was starting to increase somewhat. Some no doubt holidaying there, but mainly residents, I assumed. Which group did I now fall into? Where was my place?

I promised myself I'd find the courage to call the boys later, although part of me wondered whether they'd want to even talk to me. Our goodbyes had been several days before. I'd done my best to keep it together, to be positive in this temporary break and reassure them of my love. Yet I couldn't bring myself to send a message to let them know I had arrived safely. I had let Annie know with a brief, one lined text.

For many people, what I had done would be unthinkable. Completely unforgiveable. I knew that. I knew that most people would consider I had been selfish beyond measure. But what I had done was try to fix what I had come to believe was a complete crash of my own mental health. Fix the unknowing, the illness, in the only way I thought would work. But from the outside, all everyone could see was that I had put my own desires and needs first. I had placed more importance on me than on them. My children. And of course, my husband.

The word *divorce* had not been mentioned. It was only left that I was going. What that meant for our family life, for our relationship was at that moment in time, an unknown. Void of long-term plans. That should have scared me. I should have been distraught at that fact. Acting on a whim? Finding myself in an area I hardly knew. Yet this was in some ways all I had been searching for, for such a long time. To live. To be alive. I'd been searching. Looking for something to make me, me. I wanted at times to scream out for someone to make me whole again, help me find a route to feeling better. Yet the path I found had taken me much further than I had ever envisaged. And no one had joined me for the journey.

Deciding that what I needed was to just look after myself, I looked for the comfort of another cuppa, spotting what looked like a tea shop ahead. I couldn't recall venturing this far round when I was here before. Striding forward, making my new steps.

The tea shop wasn't too far along the road, and I decided to head in and grab a cup to take on my stroll along the cliff top.

Found myself greeted by an overly friendly looking lady with a wide smile and short dark hair. She asked for my order, and I paid her before stepping aside to await the drink. We engaged in little conversation, predictably mainly about the weather, then I collected my tea and moved out into the sun.

Almost using the cup as a crutch as I walked along, I felt its comfort warm my slightly bitter hands. Finishing up, and with nothing else to do that day, I carried on strolling up and around the top part of the bay to explore some areas not previously encountered.

The path plateaued out, and I took a seat on a bench placed perfectly at the top. Taking in the sea breeze, I stopped. For a time. Absorbed the silence and stillness I had needed, had craved for so long.

Sometimes, as humans, we make decisions and take actions without any knowledge of what the consequences might be. Sometimes we purposely give no such thought, or care, as to what might happen as a result of our own choices, to both us and others. I wasn't clear where I sat at that moment. Had I been purposefully reckless, selfish? Had I even considered what might actually happen, after I made my decision? Unsure of any of it, I just knew I had an alternative place to live for a while and some savings to get by on. They wouldn't last forever, but would be enough to begin with. I'd not taken too much, conscious that Simon would be needing reserves more than I would. Mary had said that there were always jobs available in the buildup to the summer season if you weren't too fussy what you did. There were plenty of tea rooms, shops, and even a few art galleries that needed help with the additional customers. I would have a look around and see what could be found, just not that day.

Without purpose or intention, I found myself releasing a sigh as I stood and watched the waves. A sigh accompanied by softly closed eyes. An involuntary movement, helping me to start to let go of the weight, the unrest that had been at my core for what felt like an age. Another sigh and then I opened my eyes. A tentative but spontaneous smile.

The next day, I woke earlier. Wanting to give myself and the day some purpose. However, it quickly became apparent that it would be a challenge. An emptiness of structure, of purpose. Moving from sofa to kettle to window, not sure what I should do. After a time, I dragged myself into clothes for another walk down to the sea.

I couldn't do it. Calling the boys had been too much for me to attempt the day before. If I rang them, I'd have to face what had happened and so I chose to almost ignore it and instead sent a very short message to each. No reply had been received. Not then. Maybe in the next few days, it would come.

The sea at 7 a.m. was calm. Yet empty. Mirroring the way, I felt, with no one else around. As the day continued, the feeling of stillness around would undoubtedly diminish but for that time, I would immerse myself in the atmosphere of the sand and the breeze.

Purposely, I made it to the beach wearing cut-off shorts and a T-shirt, with my treasured blue hoody loosely thrown on. Flip-flops made my intention of an early paddle easy. As I stepped my way carefully down the steps to the sand, I stood straight. Not hunched; I was not looking down. Such a simple action, but one that I acknowledged had escaped me previously. By looking up, I could witness to depth of sight across the sea. I could take in the gentle breeze, feel the stillness. All this time I had been focussed on looking down, avoiding eye contact, so consumed with whatever I must do next, whatever someone else wanted from me. From that first moment, when I felt the sand gently disappearing under my bare feet, I felt able to adjust the direction of my gaze.

Having removed my shoes, I could sink my feet gently into the sand while moving through the beach to the sea. Standing tall, noticing the empty beach, I took my time. Walking gently, but with purpose. Still, it was early. As I reached the wet sand, my feet sank even more and the only way to keep from getting stuck was to avoid standing completely still. Moving to stand still.

The fresh water used its rhythm to periodically cover my feet. I closed my eyes. Just for a moment. Concentrated on anything other than the chill embracing my feet. As I exhaled, I opened the view. The breeze brushed my face, and I found myself smiling, just.

I was Georgia Florence, and I was standing still.

I was Georgia Florence, and I was looking up.

My eyes closed again, my broad smile in relief. Not quite genuine happiness. A huge difference. But whatever the reason I was smiling, it was a start. Thinking of only myself, for just that moment.

The calm was broken, yet not shattered, by distant voices. I turned around and saw a couple of people over to the right. In amongst the rocks where the young most likely gathered to look for treasures of the sea left behind by the tide. I suddenly felt a little embarrassed but at the same time reluctant to move. So, I looked over, acknowledged them, and then turned back to look out to sea.

My heart stopped for just that second. The people were what looked like a father and son, out early to find the best pickings. For that moment, just that brief moment in time, the calm disappeared, and I remembered where I was only last week. With my family. With my boys.

Pausing to acknowledge the feeling. The situation. The unthinkable.

I looked back over to the side of the beach. In order to remove myself from the memory, I collected the bag I had discarded further back on the beach and moved away from the sand. Walking past the family in the rocks, hearing the squeals of delight at the small boy's finds in amongst the grey formations.

The image hit me hard. Within those few seconds, reality had moved into view and stung like an insect with no care for its own demise afterwards. Vengeance.

As I walked hurriedly from the sea, from the sand, climbing the solid steps, I felt my heart pounding. Struggling to get my breath. Reaching the top, I took just a moment to look out over the rocks again, out to the sea that had given me its time.

Perched at the top, on the grassy cliff, feeling more than a little out of breath. I had dumped my bag by the side of me and slumped down next to it. Hands cradling my head the water droplets trickling down my face.

Not tears of regret. Tears of release.

I needed to compose myself. While it was quiet and still early at that moment, before long, there would be more people mingling around. I would need to gather myself. I started to collect my bag and straighten myself out.

'Often hard to get going again after you've stopped to admire the view,' a voice commented from behind me. I turned around and found myself greeted by Mary, holding the lead of a sprightly dog, still panting with excitement and excursion.

'Yes, it is a lovely view,' I replied, being mindful not to appear aloof but really not wanting a great in-depth conversation.

'Have you settled in, OK?' she enquired, glancing briefly down at her dog, settling contentedly on the grass.

'Yes, I have. Thank you so much for the provisions and flowers. You really didn't need to.' While I didn't really want to get too heavily involved, I was keen and polite enough to thank her for her efforts.

Motioning towards the sea. 'It really is a beautiful spot,' she continued. 'I've only lived here the last five years, but don't regret it for a moment.' She smiled. Hoping I'd dried my eyes sufficiently, I hoisted myself up in as dignified a manner as I could muster, then stepped forward.

'Well, you know where I am if you need anything, but I'll leave you to enjoy it. I really do think you will.' Her smile captivating and knowing at the same time. I watched her as she strolled back towards her own cottage, four-legged friend trotting happily alongside.

The interlude had distracted me for just enough time, and I forgot the realisation I'd been grappling with. Collecting myself together a little more, I started to head back towards my own cottage, a good pace behind Mary. I took the opportunity to have a brief look in some of the shops on the way as they opened for the day. The moment on the beach had gone, the peace no longer so obvious.

Strolling through the streets of buildings which almost seemed to have been constructed built purposefully to lean over and cast an eye on the beach, I noticed more faces milling around. Checking my watch, I was surprised to realise it was a little after 10 a.m. An explanation for the increasing busyness around.

I walked past the shops selling surf boards and wetsuits, relying upon my recollections from before. Images of novice surfers laughing amongst the waves, pulling me in. Photographs in my memory, popping in and out as if poking my consciousness, daring me to face facts. I needed to concentrate on something else. Avoid any great thoughts of doubt that might be ignited. Counting steps, rhythmically strolling. That was it. My feet would take me away from the truth.

Chapter 46

Later that day, picking the phone up from where I had discarded it on the sofa, I deftly turned it over in my hand. No sign of the familiar shrill ring indicating a message. I could kid myself that the lack of full Wi-Fi signal in the area probably meant that the mobile signal was lacking too. That would however lack greatly any honesty. I could envisage the girls messaging each other, having set up a 'what the hell is Georgia doing' group. What else could I expect? Nevertheless, I felt hurt. Despite the fact I had left, it was I who felt rejected now. Left out. Maybe even abandoned.

I couldn't help but rummage through the apps, hoping I'd missed some contact from someone. Nothing. No silly Snap Chats from the boys, kisses from Simon. No gossip from the girls. Not a thing. I tried to take a deep breath as I tossed the phone back on to the sofa, before easing up and heading towards the fridge.

The floor felt bitterly cold against my feet, but I focussed on getting to the wine I had bought earlier that day. I grabbed the bottle from the now relatively empty fridge and made do with a glass tumbler. Making a mental note that wine glasses would need to be on the shopping list if I was to stay a while.

The wine was chilled. In a way, still slightly soothing, as the strength passed down my throat. After an initial drink, I topped the glass up before placing the bottle back in its home. Gazing absently out of the kitchen window at the view, I then paced back to the sinking sofa and the empty phone screen.

Still no messages were waiting for me and so I switched it off. If I didn't, I knew I'd be constantly and eagerly checking it too often. Tossing it to one side, like a discarded shoe, hoping I could forget about it. Maybe I could if it wasn't so easily visible. I could sense the breeze increasing on the other side of the glass, whipping up the atmosphere. While inside the cottage was protected from the wind, it remained bitterly cold.

Unable to help it, I grabbed the phone and switched it back on. Jack and Matt. The screen lit up with one of my favourite pictures of them larking around in the garden. It was easy. Their faces alight with silliness, the fading sun in the background casting a glow around each head. Unable to prevent myself from taking the photo in, from smiling, running my fingers delicately over their faces. Tracing their features. My face, the skin running over my cheekbones. Damp.

Not knowing whether I would get a response, I sent each of them a message telling them just that I loved them. Simple. I had told them a million times over the years. Even as their lives developed and they no longer returned the sentiment out loud as often, I always made sure they knew. Proud and so glad to be their mum. To have been a part of their lives. The fact that I was not there right at that moment didn't alter any of that. That was the truth.

Having said what I needed to say, I switched the phone back off. The ability to call was not mine. Not then. Before it switched off completely, I made one more quick check for messages. I had to. None.

In search of some form of normality, I started to hunt around for some music. I began by opening drawers, unsure on how the Wi-Fi might cope with my playlist, but more intrigued by what I might find that meant something to someone else. I'd spotted the CD player in the corner on arrival. An earlier attempt at finding a decent radio station reception had failed and so I went hunting for an alternative.

Several drawers later, I stumbled across some CDs. Most pre-dated my taste, but miraculously I found a few I recognised. A small flicker of interest spurned me on to firing up the player and trying it out. As the music started, I felt a small sense of comfort, the welcoming of an old friend, being surrounded by a trusty jumper.

Watching the breeze, holding the glass, I stood at the window. Moving a little to the music. The moment took me by the hand and led me to experience an opening of calm. Some peace and quiet. The situation still intensely real, but for that moment I would wholly concentrate on the present and leave behind the truth. My sight glanced over at the discarded phone. Resisting the temptation to go switch it on, desperate for contact, the music served as a useful distraction. Yet also a reminder of a time gone by. Of my friends, my life before I felt I had none of any worth. Darkness started to creep in and I pushed it to one side, taking another glug of the cold wine in order to encourage breath and the barrier to reality.

Eventually, the wine and the music came to an end, and the breeze had escalated. The colour disappeared from the world outside and night came to greet the cottage. I pulled the aged, flowered curtains together to shut out the turbulence I felt building. I could still hear the waves in the distance. Once the curtains were together, it seemed right to give in and bring an end to the day. Spotting, just out of the corner of my eye, the still and unoccupied phone. Switched off and silent.

I could just quickly check. The boys might have messaged to say goodnight. What time was it? As I checked my watch, I it was gone 10.30 p.m. The boys would most likely be in bed. They wouldn't have messaged. They wouldn't have wanted to.

The hollow feeling in my chest threatened to return after I had quelled its fuel over the last few hours. Obsessed with the phone. Frozen with the desire to turn it on, to find some kindness. What if I did, and no message appeared? I'd feel worse. Destroyed. The yearning to be missed. Wanted.

I was unable to work out whether the boys would have consciously decided not to call or contact me, or whether it was more likely Simon might have distracted them from doing so. He would never have done anything like that before, but I had pushed him to behave in a way unexpected. I couldn't blame him for wanting to protect them from further hurt.

Another three days passed before I received it. Just a single 'x' from Matt.

Chapter 47

Two weeks had already passed since my arrival. Fourteen whole, individual days.

I'd managed to pass all those hours somehow, many almost as if I were merely on a break. A holiday from a life. I occupied my soul with walking along the well-trodden coastal path, paddling in shallow spring-chilled water and giving my feet the chance to fight against the sinking sand. Space. I even found a small trickle of joy in some of those passing moments. A sense of opportunity, maybe? Conversations with strangers. Dinners for one. That place was, in its own way, encouraging me. Giving me a glimpse of all I might really be. I'd actually done it.

Yet in amongst all that activity, there were of course moments where I questioned whether I was merely relying upon a choreographed façade. When I produced a smile, was it really genuine, meant with a spontaneity of feeling? Yes. I think it was. At least on occasions. Eating alone was tough, but I did it. Found conversations with fellow diners and staff alike, an enjoyable break from the permeating solitude.

It however became apparent that I was however starting to drop off the edge somewhat. Gradually, over a period of a few weeks or more, I found I began to struggle to even leave the cottage. It became so I couldn't. Not even to go to the shore. The weather attempted to entice me with its light, high clouds, and gently streaming sun, but it made no difference. I stayed put as much as I could.

Barely getting dressed, I spent days moving from bed to sofa, sometimes then back to bed again. Made my way through endless cups of coffee before moving on to not quite endless glasses of wine. I ate without tasting, drank without feeling.

The CD collection wasn't full of my favourites, but I managed to work my way through it. Interspersed with random hours of an intermittent local radio station. The TV felt too much a link to an outside word I was no longer an active part of. The remote control gathered dust in the corner. My phone had become an item to despise. Failing to provide me with the contact I didn't necessarily deserve yet somehow craved. Little in my mind really made much sense.

Following on from the acknowledgment I'd received from Matt, I'd had a couple of brief 'check-in's' from Annie. She hoped the weather was suitably lovely, and that I had settled into my accommodation well. While holed up in the cottage, I replied a little, with as much positivity as I could produce. Trying hard not to sound like a holiday brochure.

From the sofa, I could see the hills and pathways that lay across the way. Almost ignoring the sea, I would waste time concentrating on those walkers who appeared like ants in the distance. Chartering their progress as a lazy spectator. The great undressed often curled up on the sofa, hugging my coffee or wine, depending upon how difficult the day had been.

Some days I, almost in a ritualistic fashion, repeatedly checked my phone, felt disappointed, then threw it across the sofa. Suddenly my lack of routine gave me too much time. Time to be, time to think, to worry, to be upset. This time I seemed to have craved for so long was fast becoming my enemy.

It was morning. I knew that only because the clock told me so. The quilt had been pulled over my head, unknowingly during the night, and as I poked my way out of the top, I felt the also now familiar warmth of the rays easing their way through the glass. I lay still. My heart heavy, my head pressured.

No movement took place for some time, not until it needed to. Pacing tentatively across the floor, I found the bathroom. The cool water cleansed my hands and as I dried them on the nearby towel, I evaded the face looking back at me once more. Turning around, out of the bathroom, facing a choice. Head back to bed or find the kettle. Even caffeine was no great temptation that morning. Grabbing the quilt as I eased myself in, edging it tightly up to my chin. Head resting back on the pillows, I closed and hid my eyes.

As the tears gently fell, I let them finish their journey, down past my chin and onto the plain white material. I made no noise. No heaving, no animalistic reverberation of uncontrollable sobs. Just the quiet release of the water I had retained within.

After a time, the need to return to the bathroom could not be ignored. Having dried my face, blown my nose, I managed to find some courage to face forwards and look. The features staring back at me, not wholly recognisable. A sensation or realisation that the face had been mine. I had owned those features for some time. Though well hidden. My hair lank and dull, desperately in need of a wash and a hefty brush through. The dry skin, shining a light upon the lines of experience staring to creep though. A red nose and sunken eyes that belonged to someone else. I wished.

Pulling my dressing gown tight around myself, hands running fleetingly through my strands. Cold water brought a reprieve from the tightness within my skin, for just a solitary second. The towel dabbed at the water droplets, mixed with tears, and left a harshness to my skin that no amount of cream would be capable of repairing.

Trudging back to bed, still no coffee but with tissue scrunched up in my hand, I climbed in between the sheets. Slumped on one side, arms wrapped around the pillow tightly. Hoping I could pretend it was another human being, another person, a force of reassurance.

When I woke it was late afternoon.

The soaked material, an indication that even sleep couldn't quell my upset. I lay there for a time, moving only to see the result on the clock face. 4.47 p.m.

Aware that my body had been void of food for quite some time, I accepted that I probably ought to consume something. The comfort of tea and toast gave me the spirit to not head straight back to bed, but instead find myself some comfort on the previously discarded sofa.

The solitude of the cottage had done me no favours. I was acutely aware of that. Yet at the same time I had needed it. Placing the empty plate and cup on the floor, I let myself sink deeper and deeper into the seat. Maybe hoping to be taken within its folds. My dressing gown tight around my worn body, I once again drifted off to a form of sleep.

Woken by a noise, it took me a moment to realise where the sound was coming from. Feeling disorientated, almost having forgotten where I was. Convinced that the phone had been switched off, then surprised to find it was the sound of a message having arrived.

Unsure whether to reach out for the device or not. Did I want to be troubled by the contact? See what it required from me? Then there was a second of hope. The promise, possibly, of it being someone who wanted to know how I was, share some news? Looking around to see where I might find it, it appeared, poking out from the side of the sofa. Almost tucked away in hiding.

It took a moment for me to locate the reason for the sound. Matt.

Chapter 48

Exhaling sharply, I knew that day must be *the* one. It must be the day I called.

The message from Matt had been just what I had needed. The push required to actually pick up the phone and speak. Still feeling slightly reluctant, I had at least managed to get up and dressed. Made myself look as presentable as I could, even if the only person to see me, would essentially be me. Hours in bed washed from my body, an attempt to do something acceptable with my hair. Employed creams and lotions in an effort to complete the mask.

I kept going over Matt's short, yet meaningful, text. A tiny glimmer of light. A hope that maybe my attempts at further contact would not be pushed aside. I would be brave.

It was late morning. Easter holidays and Simon should be at work. Not expecting for one moment he would want to prevent contact, but it seemed an easier option to call the boys when he was most likely to be out.

It rang. Shakes consumed me.

The ringing persevered. I considered that he was probably unlikely to pick up. He would know it was me. A text was one thing but faced with the confrontation of a direct call…Then it was answered. Initially with silence.

'Matt?' I could clearly hear the nerves in my voice and hoped he hadn't noticed them.

'Mum.'

That word became so much more than a statement. An acknowledgment. Maybe even a metaphorical hug.

'Hi, mate.' Keeping it light. I paused. 'How are you?' As soon as the words escaped, I wished I had picked something else to utter. Those words opening the conversation up to a discussion I almost hoped to gloss over. Selfishly. The most outrageous of questions. Yet it had tripped out of my mouth so simply, I just couldn't stop it in time.

'Uh…OK, I guess.' I wondered where this was going to go and what I could possibly say next. Then…

'How are you, Mum?'

More than a little surprised at this response. The sentence felt weighted with so much more than was said. A thoughtfulness I'm not sure I really was due. The pressure I felt, to choose the right words in response, was immense. I took my time, gave it thought.

'OK thanks. I'm doing OK.'

We chatted lightly some more, mainly about school, rugby, the usual important aspects of his life. He asked how the weather was and I considered making a comment on how constant sunshine could become so boring. Then thankfully I thought better of it. The time was not right for such flippancy. Not then. Probably not ever.

Matt mentioned that Jack was out. He'd gone out on his bike with Tom. I smiled momentarily at the image of them both out together. Taking money for snacks, trawling the paths and tracks, before returning home no doubt with oil adorning his fingers.

'Would he be OK if I rang him sometime soon, do you think?' Treading so carefully, I wanted really to be sure that I wouldn't cause Jack any further hurt. If he really wouldn't be able to talk, then that would be fine. I would accept it. I would wait.

'I think so.' Matt's confirmation didn't feel forced. I took that as permission to give it a go.

Maybe I should have actually addressed the situation we found ourselves in? Verbally acknowledged what had happened. Yet it was undoubtedly easier for both of us, I think, to skirt around it. It was as if I was away on work or some girls' mini break. That I'd be back in a few days to catch up properly. Have a hug.

Neither of us could ignore the pauses, the lightness and consideration given with each word. As the conversation tailed off a little, I found myself quietly wiping away a tear or two. Trying to keep any evidence of it out of his line of hearing.

I could sense he was getting ready to go. We'd covered the small talk, managed a light laugh. I wouldn't be able to hold on to this time with him for much longer. Hold him forever. I needed to be cautious, gentle, in that moment.

The end was close. I just needed to ask.

'How is your dad?'

Sensing from the initial silence that I had put too much on Matt.

'It's OK, you don't have to answer that. Forget I asked.' Hurriedly dismissing, retracting my enquiry. I felt awful for even letting the words spill out. Yet I wanted to know. I seemed to need to know he was OK. Despite everything.

'It's fine. He's OK. Well, he's not, but he is, if that makes sense?' It was Matt's turn to scramble for the right words to say. Undoubtedly felt he'd been caught in the middle. Not knowing what to do for the best and probably not wanting to say anything at all.

'Maybe you should call and ask him?' A tentative suggestion from him. I knew he didn't mean it harshly. I knew he was just trying to keep out of it. Maybe he thought if Simon and I spoke direct things might change. We might be able to bandage whatever the damage was.

'I'm just not sure he would talk to me. I think he's too hurt.' Or maybe the truth was that I wouldn't be able to find the right words to say to him. Maybe I just didn't want to face the matter. Coward.

'Try, Mum.' Is all he said.

Holding back further tears that had built up from the weight of the conversation, I released him for the rest of his day. Reassured him I'd be in touch again soon and that I would call Jack too. I made sure he knew I was always going to be just at the end of the phone. That I loved him. That I loved them all.

Then everything went quiet.

Chapter 49

I found myself feeling just a little more positive the following day. Well, I'd managed to convince myself to feel that way, at least. Wallowing, for that moment, had been cast to one side, and I knew I must get up and force myself to move on.

I decided I was going to get up and get out. Maybe I could speak to someone, anyone. Real people. In the flesh, actual human beings. I needed to find some way of making an income, anyway. The savings would only last so long. Mary had mentioned that there would undoubtedly be work available and so I hoisted myself up to go and locate it.

Coffee and a little toast before I pulled back my shoulders in an effort to appear in control and confident. Nerves consumed me as I forced myself out of the door, a deep breath steadying my physical presence as I went.

Another breezy, yet sunny day awaited. Legs were becoming used to the journey of walking downwards on the way into town and were definitely getting better at tackling the upward stroll home. Home. A word that meant so much more than accommodation. I had decided I would call this place home, for now, but just to myself. Pushing to one side any fear I held of not being able to go back, of not being able to rethink my plans. No such Plan B existed, but I needed to feel there might actually be options. Just in case. I knew that I wasn't really making any sense, but at that point nothing was. My priority was to attempt to preserve my own sanity if that was at all possible.

I made a little effort in appearance that day, leaving the well-worn hoodie at the cottage. Three quarter trousers and a smart top were almost as comfortable, yet not so 'surfing' attire. Dressed with a sense of purpose but lacking in a plan. That was me. Propelled by selfish impulses, I set off. Passing tea shops, ice-cream kiosks, and surf shops, I casually kept an eye on the windows but saw nothing that might indicate there was work. I guessed, as it was still relatively early in the season, it might take a while for the area to build up work possibilities. Yet I carried on looking.

Stopping at the ice-cream café situated on one corner, an unexpected chill swept over me momentarily. We'd visited that place almost every day when we were all together the previous year. I found no desire to turn the clock back to that time. Nothing would have changed. Still, I was conscious of a hint of melancholy wash over me, as I found myself visiting the café again. This time, I was alone.

I ordered a cone, careful to choose, or maybe just without thinking, a flavour the boys would not normally want. I gently took hold of the ice cream and smiled, just a little, as I walked away from the café, out into the strengthening sunshine. It became busier as the day unfolded. The emergence of couples and small families, all enjoying rays on faces.

No work was spotted on the main stretch and so I made my way again over and up, following the cliff face and main road that led out of the town. Only a handful of cafés and restaurants existed along that route, but I had nothing to lose in taking my task in that direction. Deciding that on the way back I would try the food bar on the beach, my thoughts were then disrupted by a rhythmic noise I vaguely recognised. The sound of my phone ringing.

Not normally an event of any real kind. But that was before. This time I was cautious to even hunt in my bag to find it. The sound persisted, and the volume increased. My breath began to feel tight, a little laboured. Nerves increased; heartbeat escalated. I could almost feel a sense of panic, nervousness, fear. Coupled with a hint of excitement, just a small amount. The desire for it to be Simon, Chrissie, any of them. Someone. Someone who wanted to talk to me. Maybe find out how I was. Who cared? And yet despite all of this, I still found I could make no move to silence or even answer it. I couldn't pick it up. My body seemed to physically find it too much to even try.

It went quiet. They had given up.

Resuming the walk, winding my way between people and across the road to head through the main area of activity. Surf boards, fake tattoos all seemed to line the path, and I moved around as best I could, smiling at strangers as they let me by, and me them. Crossing over the road once more, I moved towards the café I had been in previously. Maybe they would have work? Peering in the window, I saw nothing but busy tables and helpful staff. Plenty of staff. I moved on.

Still, I had not opened my bag.

The breeze seemed to have dropped a little, and the walk became easier. As I followed the bend in the road, I noticed another tea shop, a little more tucked away. I hadn't been aware of this one before and decided to at least grab a drink before carrying on with the task in hand.

An old-fashioned bell rang as I made my way over the threshold. An announcement of my arrival. Grateful for the fact it was relatively busy, I was, despite this declaration, able to slip in almost unnoticed. Heading towards the counter, I couldn't help but be drawn to the decorations. An eclectic mixture of hippy and beach and tradition. Prints and paintings adorned the walls, chairs in a rainbow of colours. I found myself consumed.

I was about to place my order and run when I caught the smile of one of the waitresses – I assumed – enquiring whether I would like a takeaway or to stop awhile and enjoy a seat; she motioned to a small table in the corner. The wooden structure, dressed with shells and candles, tucked into the alcove. I confirmed I would stop. Just for a moment. Making the decision on my behalf.

While I settled, seated in the corner, she finished serving a man and a child I assumed was his young son. They all clearly knew each other. The man encouraged his son to thank the waitress for the cake she gently passed to him for the homeward journey. Promises of popping back later in the week accompanied their exit back out into the sun. I found a warmth of appreciation for the beauty in that brief scene which took the place of holes within my soul.

The waitress took my order and walked back to behind the counter. I caught her deftly moving about, singing along at intervals to the music playing in the background. Some of it I recognised. It quietly played, not intending to overpower the atmosphere or require any attention.

The walls were an extensive collection of art. Beach prints, black and white creative photographs, quotations. Interspersed with plants and candles and washed-up beach fodder. Character. A place you'd not find again.

Above the door I caught sight of a long, distressed looking piece of wood. Sanded to within an inch of its life, its words protected by a subtle sheen of wax, or varnish. Art.

'A reason. A season. A lifetime.'

Distracted from my observations, my drink arrived. Accompanied by a small piece of cake.

'I thought you might like to try some. It's on the house-hope you don't mind.' Her smile broad, unexpected. Noticing the cake, I thanked her and found myself smiling back. Had I looked in need of something more? Or was it just the realisation of a new customer and an enticement for a return?

'Isla, could you pop this in the window for me, please?'

Thoughts broken by the appearance of another member of staff from beyond the counter area, handing something to the waitress. She obliged without discussion, just a smile and acknowledgment before heading towards the large window. Pushing the sign against the glass, she then returned to behind the counter. Cakes were refreshed, before clearing tables and filling dishwashers. I found myself, without conscious decision, following her activities. Aware I might then find myself in a tricky situation of having been observed doing this, I changed gaze to focus on the walls.

Isla, as I now knew her to be, cleared the table beside mine. Catching her sight, I smiled.

'Thank you for cake,' I began.

'Oh, you're very welcome. Hope it's OK. I actually made that one.'

She looked hopeful of a positive response.

'It really was. Thank you so much.' A random act of kindness. Brought about by this random visit.

I continued with my tea while sat, just taking it all in. My mind wandering, absorbing the atmosphere within the café. The mood from the art, interspersed amongst other customers quietly chatting. The occasional laugh. Isla popping in a line from the song now and then. A quiet confidence about her own sound.

Gathering up my simple bag, I went over to the counter to pay for my pit stop. Thanking Isla again, I left with a sense of grateful joy. Just a simple gift.

Heading out the door and turning left, I caught sight of the poster in the window. The note requiring staff for the summer season, and maybe beyond.

'What do you need from me, as I'd be really interested?' I enquired of Isla, motioning towards the sign. A split-second decision.

'Wow, that was quick. Hold on, let me just grab Tilly, she can fill you in.'

The lady who had previously popped her head out came through to where I stood. Arms full of bangles and string flowers. Her blond hair swept up in a casual bun, stray strands cascading down in a bid for freedom.

'Why don't you pop in tomorrow and we can chat about it? Have you much experience of this sort of work? Not that it necessarily matters but it's just good to know.'

Hesitating, I replied, 'Not for a while, it would be fair to say.'

'Look, not to worry, but let's chat about it all tomorrow, 10 a.m. OK?'

I smiled my thanks, more genuine than I expected it to be, and uttered, 'Yes, thank you. I'll see you then.'

Grabbing my bag to me, I stepped out once more. The fresh air and sun surrounded me as I left, glancing a smile towards Isla as I went.

Finding a sense of having done what I had set out to do, I still continued with my stroll. Reaching a perch on an area of rock, where I could look out to the smaller, more secluded bay. The others found fascination in the open beach and I found comfort and peace in the coves. Different needs.

Reminded of the earlier call, I realised I must find some strength and check on who rang.

Simon.

Shocked back into acknowledging how I got there. Wondering about the reason for the call. No message left.

I really should contact him. There was obviously a reason he had made that leap. Was it urgent? Breathing deeply, I pressed to dial his number. Thinking it might just go to message, he picked up. My hands visibly shaking.

'Hi.' That was it. That stilted opener, frozen of emotion, was the greeting.

'Hi. Erm, sorry. I think I missed your call. I was just walking and must have not heard the phone ring as it would have been stuck somewhere in my bag...' Rambling, waffling. I didn't know why, but I felt I needed to justify why I hadn't picked up. He might otherwise think I was ignoring him, too busy having some form of a life instead.

'It's fine.' He coughed to clear his throat. No disguising how hard this call was for him. 'It was just to tell you I think Jack would like to talk to you now. I know you spoke with Matt, but it has been much harder for Jack. We've chatted now and I think he would be OK to talk to you.'

Feeling the relief, mixed with excitement. The weight of the emotion revealed by this statement rested on my chest. Breathing shallow, tears forming. My boys.

'Is it OK if I call him this evening?' I gently erred on the side of politeness, conscious of the situation we now found ourselves in.

'Yes, that should be fine. He won't be back until after 5.30 p.m. as he's got rugby train...'

'Yes, I know.' I felt rude. I'd interrupted, knew I had, but eager to demonstrate that I still knew something of my son's, our son's timetable. 'Sorry. I was just trying to say that I'll call after 6 p.m.' My voice went quiet, almost timid, and I regretted trying to get my way in with the acknowledgment. Words were now tumbling over, unable to speak clearly, think clearly. My baby.

'It's fine. I'll let him know.' He sounded as though he had finished. Had nothing more to add to our chat. More an exchange of information.

'I.' One word. Left hanging. One word. Might have led to so much.

'I was just wondering how you are...?' The piercing sharpness of those words in the air contradicted with the warmth and comfort within which I was taking part in this call. 'I'm...' Yet I wasn't. Not really. To be sorry implied regret. My soul questioned whether that was really within me.

Simon could tell where those words might go. But he avoided uttering that he did not want to hear it.

'OK, so I'll tell him to expect a call later, then.' He became hurried now in his desire to end the call.

'Yes, yes, that would be great. Thank you.'

'What for?' His voice low. A hint of anger, distrust. As I held the phone with a tightness in my palm, I could picture him. The pain of my actions etched in his face, in the lines that once contained laughter. Recalling how he had changed and how I only noticed it when I left. I did that. I know I did that to him.

'Talking to him, them. Helping them to agree to talk to me. I guess.' I softly gave over my gratitude and understood how tough a choice that all must have been.

'You are, after all, still their mum.' He was gone.

Chapter 50

Sat on the sofa, back in the cottage, running through all our mistakes. Decorating with the wrong paint. Spending hours poured over flat pack instructions, only to still put the wardrobe together wrong.

Simon and I had met at university, embarking on a journey together, becoming professional people. Adults. Our first home, excitedly looking over pregnancy tests, sharing news on promotions. Time spent with friends for no particular reason other than life.

As I sat listening, just to the waves, I felt fiercely faced with the reality that I had really and truly hurt him. Whatever state my mind had been in, whatever I was feeling, or going through, I had torn apart his hopes, his future. At no point had I sat down and decided 'this is over'. At no point had I explained how I felt about our marriage. I just wasn't sure it was really what I wanted anymore.

The wind was getting up. Flexing its muscles. The sound of the waves increased and barged its way through the open window. My chest hollow. The realisation that I had discarded all our adventures in favour of my own. An adventure unplanned. Or an unplanned adventure? To relieve the boredom? No, it was way more than that.

The conversation with Jack was trickier than with Matt. Not surprisingly. The two-year difference in age, coupled with the fact they were such different people was bound to impact how they each reacted. I endeavoured to keep it light, asking about school and friends. Mentioning so little, I steered clear of discussions on where I was, but he did question what the cottage was like.

I decide to tell him that it was OK. Comfortable. I made no mention of my plans. Fearing he would go on to ask when I would return.

Several hours later, the quiet was interrupted. Spread long on the sofa, I considered whether to answer the ringing phone or not. Decision made on seeing who it was.

'You finally spoke to Simon, then?' It was a forceful statement. Accusing me of doing yet more wrong.

'Yes. I guess he rang you then?' Chrissie might have rung Simon in fairness. I could imagine the two of them discussing my appalling behaviour.

'Did you not consider contacting Simon, or me, before now?' I could tell there was an air of exasperation about her question. Disbelief. No, I had not rung Simon. No, I had not rung her. In fairness, I didn't consider that either of them would have been happy to speak to me and so I had spared them the interruption.

'I thought you might have done sooner, that was all. Even just to say you were OK.' The reality was that Annie knew. Someone knew I had made it there in one piece.

'I'm not sure he would have cared to be honest. He didn't call me to check. In fact, he has barely spoken to me in the past few weeks and he wasn't even home when I left. Before you say anything, I know I have no reason for him to care. I'm just making the point.' I was endeavouring not to sound too confrontational, but it was fast becoming the least natural conversation.

An audible sigh came. For a moment, I wasn't sure which of us gave it.

Silence. I don't think either of us really knew what to say.

'Look, Georgia….' She tailed off. Another sigh. I waited. Something in the wait and the fact she was calling me highlighted the reality of the situation we found ourselves in. 'I'm sorry, Chrissie. I'm really sorry.' Fighting back the tears that had started to develop I carried on. 'I know I've hurt you all and I know you don't understand. All I can say is that I had to. My state of mind couldn't take anything else.'

Despite the sunshine outside, the cottage now felt cold. The atmosphere deep and heavy. Laden with words unsaid between close friends and an explanation not found.

'I'm not the monster you think I am. I really think I tried to avoid anything like this. I think I did, Chris.'

More silence.

'I know.' It was quiet, barely heard. 'I know.' She repeated.

Still more silence.

'Look, I don't want to go over all this again. It's not helpful for any of us and to be honest it gets me nowhere in trying to understand. I want to help, George, I really do. Sometimes, though, I want to shake you.' Her exasperation at risk of getting out of control.

'I don't wish you any harm, you know that. Let's stay in touch, yeah?'

I wasn't quite sure how to interpret all she was saying. Was that it? A friendship in tatters, scattered amongst the waves? Or was she throwing me hope? It was hard to hear those words, even though we had barely spoken since the day before I left. There was little doubt of the impact my actions had had.

'Of course.' I almost silently confirmed.

Shortly after that, and a sprinkling of small talk concerning whether the weather was as good as I'd hoped. She was gone.

Left once more, alone with my thoughts and the silence of my new home.

Chapter 51

Routine. That was what was undoubtedly needed. Something to keep the days full and occupied. A sense of purpose. My relatively informal interview escalated into a tea and cake morning. Tilly was incredibly easy to chat to, with a warmth that she gave without request.

Asking only a little about me, I could sense her sizing me up as she watched me, sat just across from her. She wasn't going to make any decision based on a paper CV. In fact, she didn't even require one. My answers carefully thought through before being released. Giving just enough information for her needs. I was careful not to leave myself open. 'Yes, I was staying for at least the summer, if not longer.' 'No, I didn't mind what hours I worked as I had plenty of free time.' 'Yes, I had children, two boys, all grown up and now left home.'

Only three days a week to begin with, most likely, but that would give me the right balance between free time and a commitment. From that point, I had a reason to get up and get out. A reason to look up.

The job began the following day and as the weeks passed, I found myself easily settling into the routine I had created or found for myself. The café made me speak to others. Forced me to ignore my phone and the rattling recollection of events that had led me to this point.

Sometimes the faces that streamed through for refreshments were those that had become familiar. An older gentleman popped in most days, around mid-morning, for a slice of cake and a tea. Bill loved the table right by the window, but he was gracious if it was taken before he arrived. I found something both lonely and yet warming in his demeanour. We shared only the smallest of conversations to begin with, then the initial hesitancy of strangers passed after a while. I still struggled to move myself outside of the spot where I could engage in lengthy chats. Yet Bill forced me to at least try.

The job itself was easy enough. Not particularly mentally taxing and while my feet weren't used to the hours of use, it worked well for me. It made me leave the cottage. I knew if I just sat in there day after day, I would start to wonder why I had done all this. Consider that maybe my own recent choices had been wrong. So instead, I worked, I chatted, and I tried to pick myself up.

I'd be lying if I said there weren't some days I really and truly enjoyed myself. A lightness of responsibility. A chance to stand still. Arms wide. The breeze coating me. I smiled. On occasions, I really and truly smiled.

After several weeks of having left them abandoned in the bottom of the case, I reached for the familiarity of my running shoes. Until that point, I hadn't had the courage to put them on. That sounded ridiculous. Running and music had been in my life for years. Both my solace and my saviour on many an occasion. Yet here I had found myself without the ability to reach for my stabling footwear. The fear of revealing too much of myself, maybe? Perhaps I was fearful of being reminded of my running routines from before.

Mentally heaving myself up, aware of a tiny element of excitement festering in the back of my head, I reached in to ease them out of the case. Putting them on felt like hugging an old friend you hadn't seen for far too long. I noticed the dark scuff marks, material slightly worn. Running my hands along, caressing the soles. I was reminded of the impact on me of run after run. Over concrete, paths, tracks alongside farm fields, faded splashes of mud from the days when the exercise and rain helped wash my anguish away (for a time).

I, for that brief moment, felt just like me. The relish of putting them back on, being alone and taking my journey wherever I felt. This time I would fill my lungs with the sea air, smell the hint of salt, and pound rhythmically along to the songs that had both lifted me and grounded me throughout my life.

My upper chest felt open, light, and I stood tall in front of the mirror, in my trainers. I could see my full self. Recognised some, maybe most, of what I saw. Still a little tired. More than a little tanned. Not quite as I felt inside, but it was definitely me.

Talking out loud to myself, I selected some of my favourite music to accompany my feet. All set, I allowed myself a smile before closing the cottage door behind me.

Chapter 52

Several more weeks passed and the routine of a job was really starting to do me some good. The space I had found for my head and my thoughts was a good one. Not always so negative. I would tell myself constantly 'it is going to be a good day today' and some days I almost felt it was.

The weather became pretty consistent with sun and breeze in not quite equal measure. The opportunity to lift into the warmth, feel the sea between my toes every single day became more solace than I think I ever anticipated it could be. Like a therapy, washing over my soul, it brought me comfort of the like I don't know I'd ever experienced, or even needed before.

I made sure I came down to the beach every single day, sometimes several times. The sea could be seen from the window out the back of the café, and the walk home provided me with a constant backdrop of subtle crashing sounds as the waves took charge.

Starting to become more familiar with some of the most regular customers gave me passing conversations and much more. I began to feel I'd become part of the place. Another artifact making itself at home on the walls. Even after many weeks, I seemed to still keep finding parts of the café I'd not noticed before. Bill gave me a smile every time I was in. The weather and cake, our constant conversation point as he sat himself in his usual spot (vacancy permitting).

The man with the son, who I'd come to know to be Sam and Freddie, came in now and then. Their visits were the only real times I found I needed to stop and catch myself. Concentrate on the present. The depiction of father and son, so comfortable, so content with each other, had become a harsh reminder.

Every week I made sure I rang the boys. Pushed away the urge I sometimes felt to call them every day. If I wanted to speak to them that often, why had I left? It wasn't always easy to pick up the phone sometimes, but I made sure I spoke to them, or at least tried. They were generally a little more reluctant to make the first step.

Sometimes I would ask them how their dad was. The response often hesitant, muted. To be honest, I was putting them in a difficult position by even asking. At no point had they pushed me for a lengthy explanation, not since I had left. I had tried to give them an indication of how I felt and what I was going to do when I first told them my plans. It was clear they didn't really understand. How on earth could they? Whatever words I used I knew it couldn't take away the feelings they must have had, that it was somehow their fault. A realisation that everything they had come to know as home was gone. I wanted them to understand that none of this was because of them. That they were the most amazing human beings, the two things I was most proud of in my life. However, that didn't change the fact that I had to do this. Do this for me.

Now, as we spoke in each phone call, or in each message sent, we made an effort and kept the conversation light. We all did. I think they just didn't really know what to say much of the time. Why would they?

If I knew how to phrase it all to make sure they knew it wasn't their fault, then I would, but what words could I possibly use for that? Before I left, I would kid myself that they were growing up and would need me less and less. Now I had come to realise that they would never not need me.

Chrissie and I had managed to send a few brief messages here and there. Casual chatter. She did once say that she hated me being far away. I missed her. I found myself missing so much of what we had.

Erica had apparently been struggling even more. Trying still to balance her dad's needs and her own home. Mark offering as much support and help as he always had. My finger had hovered over her name in my contacts list on several occasions. No courage found within me to do more than that.

Alice, on the other hand, had rung and I likewise. Keeping me up to date with the slow progress between her and her new man. She seemed happy. Cautious but happy.

She almost seemed joyful for me, and I think while she was honest enough to admit she didn't altogether understand, she was happy to see me doing something positive for myself. Actually, speaking to her helped build a bridge between the past and that present. It made me feel a little less as though that was all a previous life that I could never return to.

Leaving work one day, I decided to head out on to the sand, rather than straight back to the cottage. The sun was still comfortingly warm and while the beach was busy, there remained plenty of space to roam free. My shoes hung loosely from my hand. A flippant feeling that I was embracing a sense of freedom not commonly within my grasp.

Over amongst the rock pools I could hear the light screams of delight from finds over and above what was expected. The joy of small hands taking hold of crabs, jewelled stones, and shells found surprisingly still intact. With a small ache and a remembrance of my holidays gone by, I cast my eyes over to the side to follow the sounds of delight. The rays of sunlight draping across the rock pools and boulders. I recognised the voices as Sam and Freddie. While the love weaving between them both was unmistakably heart-warming, I was unable to quell rising sensations of remorse.

Maybe somehow sensing my stare, Sam looked up at the same time and waved in recognition. Mouthing 'Hi', he smiled broadly. I found myself smiling back, with a hesitant wave.

I continued strolling around the side of the rocks and passed where they were exploring, deciding to move deeper into the bay. A favourite place to be. As the tide was out, I took the decision to find refuge balanced on a solidly balanced rock, teetering out on the edge. The formation contained a handy flat space and so a seat of reflection had formed, and I took advantage. With my bag and shoes settled next to me, I could lean back and close my eyes. A hint of peace, edged with a tinge of sadness. I gave in to allow the sound of the waves to demand my full attention.

The voices became louder as they worked their way around the edge of the beach. I could hear discoveries and more shrieks of delight. They discussed which way to head and while I noted their voices; I concentrated on the sounds in the background.

After a time, I became aware that the two voices had faded. They must have carried on back up to the top in order to exit the beach. Taking home prizes found and sharing stories of the adventures had in the exploration. They were clearly a family of deep bonds. Holding each other up, following the unexpected loss of mum and wife. Sharing and supporting in their own grief.

I hadn't spoken in great depth with Sam, not really more than a few casual conversations over the weeks at the café. One day however, I'd bumped into him while he was out running, alone, as I was heading back from work. He made the time to stop and chat on the basis he was ending his run only a little further along, anyway. It began as a conversation over running and favourite routes – his recommendations I tried hard to note – and then a little bit of background. He explained briefly about having lost his wife and I...well I skirted around my own situation as best I could. I hadn't really thought it through my 'back story' as such. I furnished him with sketchy details of how I was there for a while to investigate. Mentioned vaguely possible plans to move there with my husband. Keeping details loose, enough to hopefully indicate I wasn't about to give much more away. He hadn't pushed hard for clarification, thankfully.

Chapter 53

It rang for what felt like an eternity. It seemed he wasn't about to pick up and I wondered if indeed he even should. I was almost at the end of the wine I'd bought on my way back to the cottage after work. That was a mistake. Little to eat, too much to drink. It was only ever going to go one way.

In my head, at that moment in time, it made sense. I just needed to try to, in some way, apologise. Seeking out my reflection in the bathroom mirror, I decided to ignore the streaks of mascara delicately hanging on to my cheeks. The cold-water splash would only make it worse, but I still found I searched for it.

I hung up.

Until I couldn't help but call again.

Still no answer. And still no real idea as to what I might even say if he should pick up. I could hardly open it with 'sorry I left you'.

Wondering, fleetingly, what Simon would actually make of the collection of missed calls, I continued. Like some crazed, obsessive woman, I rang and rang, in between using the back of my hand to further spread damp mascara over my face, using the back of my hand. Then finally he answered. It was 11.30 p.m.

'Hello?' The tone was unwelcoming. Unsurprisingly. He knew it was me. He knew it was late. Probably assumed I had stayed up just drinking.

'Er, hi.' I felt myself surprised at him picking up the call, even though it was me who had rung him. Constantly. Poised on the edge of the sofa, smoothing the edge of my dressing gown, an anxious motion being repeated.

'I'm, I'm sorry, I know it's late. I...'

'Yes, it is. What's wrong?' I knew the tone of agitation. Quite rightly too. Yet a part of me, brought about by the glasses consumed, wanted to hear the softness I had previously become accustomed to. Hear Simon ask how I was and maybe even actually care about the response. I edged back into the sofa some more. Hoping to refrain from the gentle rocking that had developed.

'I just wanted to say hi.' Feeble. Ridiculous. His sigh verbalised my own thoughts.

'I assume you've been drinking?' The tone relaxed only slightly. Just enough for me to sense a hint of the real him coming through, as opposed to the Simon I turned him into.

'I've had a couple of glasses, yes...' Should I apologise for that? 'I just wanted to check how you all were.' My courage dissipating, disrupted by the lack of focus I now had. The words continued to find the air. I was powerless to stop them. 'How are you?'

I don't think he knew what to say. I had very much caught him off guard. Late at night. Drunk.

'OK. How are you?' I became aware of shuffling. The sound of someone disturbed from sleep, getting more comfortable between sheets. Was he alone?

More, much more than I expected to, I became filled with gratitude for that moment. I could picture his face, maybe a hint of a smile. Imagining him sat in bed, maybe our bed, propping himself up as he always did, with as many pillows as he could find. Wondering if I could really, accurately, recall the details of his face, his eyes, his smile.

'OK.' That was it. I didn't know what else to say to him. How should I carry on this conversation I had so foolishly begun?

'Are the boys OK?' I tentatively continued. Feeling more than a little guilty for even asking and just a tiny bit sick.

A heavy intake of breath, clearly audible down the phone. Could I hear him shuffling some more? I could see the mid green sheets, the throw no doubt cast loosely over the end of the bed. If not discarded completely, maybe? Had our room changed? Was it just him there?

There was a delay in the response, but he still indicated that they were both doing OK. No change from when I last spoke to them a day or so ago. The boys let him know whenever I rang, pretty much. Open conversations as they all tried to deal with the situation they had been thrown in to.

There was too much silence. My brain rummaged around for something else to say, trying to keep the conversation light, not too awkward. The drink was doing anything but helping me to formulate the right words and I was now starting to worry I'd get it all wrong. Mess it up. Again.

'I guess I'd better go. Let you get some sleep.' My attempt at a light-hearted, natural sign off failed without a doubt.

'OK, thanks.' His response was brief. I'm not sure what else I expected.

Just as I sensed he was about to hang up…

'Simon?'

'Yes?'

What did I want to say? What could I possibly say as we found ourselves in this mess?

'Goodnight.'

He uttered a goodbye and while it all remained stilted, it became, for that split second, just a tiny bit less awkward.

The phone weighed heavy in my hand. The last of the final glass of wine waited for me. I placed the phone carefully on the coffee table. Leaving the glass by its side. My eyes ached. My chest contained a discomfort that I recognised. Resisting the urge to pick the phone back up and scroll through old photos, messages, I leant over to take the glass with both hands. My head bent forward, feeling light and yet weighted. My eyes closed.

Dispelling the compression within, the tears began.

Chapter 54

Looking back, the next day was actually a fairly good day. In fact, the week eventually turned out to be a pretty OK week, in the main.

I knew I couldn't just wallow and mull over the previous night's actions. I had done what I had done and would just have to move on. So, now Simon would think of me as some drunken runaway. So be it. But I would not wallow as a result. That would be even more selfish.

Tilly and I spent some time together outside of work for the first time that week. She and Isla had both, on occasions, invited me for a walk, coffee, or a drink after work. I'd always thanked them politely but firmly declined. It had felt wrong to go. Maybe I didn't deserve it? Or maybe they'd ask too many questions? That week, though, I took the plunge. Tilly and I walked out together, after the café had served it's last customer of the day, Isla heading off in the opposite direction, further away from the sounds drifting off the beach below. Repositioning my sunglasses, I followed Tilly as she headed further inland, a route I could explore, maybe use for a run another time.

Having mainly concentrated on the coastal edge, I hadn't investigated the areas much further inland. However, it didn't take long before we found ourselves stood at the top of a most incredible viewpoint. Further away from the sea's tempting edge. Out of the direct heat of the sun, shadows and shade draped over our beings.

I tried to keep the conversation focussed on Tilly and her life. Her boyfriend worked in a bar situated in the next bay, along the coast. They'd lived there for years. Tilly herself had grown up in the area and while her parents had hoped she'd maybe move out and head off to university, it wasn't to be.

'But I think your café is so unique, it's so you. Why would you want to do anything else? Are you pleased with it?' Genuine interest in my question. I really wanted to know if it was all she'd hoped it would be.

'I am to be honest.' Her smile reinforcing her answer. 'I'm sure for many it wouldn't be anywhere near enough, but it's perfect for me. I was never going to head off to the city and study for years. Hated school as it was. It's me and I'll manage it as I need to.' She motioned to turn right as we reached a junction. I dutifully followed her instructions as they came.

'What about you? Will you look for an accountancy role close to here, once the summer ends? Get back to what you used to do? Is your husband joining you?'

My background 'story' wasn't as solid as I probably should have ensured it was. I didn't come here for anyone else. I came here for me. So, to be honest I hadn't given much consideration to what I should, or wanted, to tell others as regards to my sudden appearance. Obviously, people asked questions occasionally. It's just human nature to be inquisitive and I couldn't be cross with anyone for doing so. I guess Tilly had asked the most, although she was noticeably careful to appear casual in her queries. Mary had never asked a great deal at all. Yet I always felt that for some strange reason, it was almost as if she already knew.

I tried desperately not to get too tangled up in detail.

'I'm not sure at the moment. If we do move here, there's a lot to organise so I'm here alone for a while and we'll perhaps make more plans later.' Hoping I had deflected the query.

'I can imagine your boys would love to come and visit. Have they been down at all or are they busy now with their own lives?'

I swallowed hard. Concentrated on the sensation of the light breeze draping across my being.

'They are busy to be honest, what with jobs and their own lives, but I'm sure they'll be down before long, if they can…'

I needed a distraction to prevent me from tripping myself up. The view.

As I commented on the hills to the left, enquiring on how far you could walk round, it occurred to me how much I missed these interactions. While I hadn't known her that long, she was easy enough to be with. The physical human company was welcome.

We followed a route which brought us back to where we started. I made mental notes to remember for a run another day. Idle chatter about the café and the cottage completed our trip. I was certain Tilly wanted to ask more, but she was thankfully kind enough to hold back.

Later that day, I called Annie. We were still regularly speaking, and I looked forward to those moments immensely. She was working on her jewellery and the kids were doing fine. I resisted the urge to ask about Simon, if she'd seen him or spoken much to him. She didn't deserve to be put in that position. I did ask after Chrissie and Erica, though. Just tentatively.

'Have you heard anything from Erica?' Annie asked.

'Nothing.'

'Oh, I'm sorry. I would have hoped she'd at least send a message or something?' Annie couldn't really justify her silence, but I think I probably could. Erica would never have walked away from everything I had. Her desperation for a better life would have been at such odds with my actions.

'No, I can completely understand, Annie. She won't be in touch, maybe ever. Do you know how she's doing?'

'Her dad's really not great. If I'm honest, I don't know he'll make it to the end of the year. I don't think Mark's any more helpful, either. We do chat, just not as often, I guess.' I can hear the sadness, regret in her voice. A regret that isn't hers to feel.

I missed Erica too. Despite this chasm of difference in our lives and ultimately our desires. The ripples of reaction from my decision did not stop at my home. Went far beyond my door. That was clear.

So, anyway, my good day began with the sunshine and ended with the sunset. After Tilly and I had taken a stroll, she'd invited me to join her and a few friends at a party at one of the restaurants the following week. My first inclination was to politely decline. Instead, I forced myself to actually accept.

Chapter 55

That weekend, I felt plagued by a burning need to run. And to run far.

A need to release, to breathe out, to just be.

Having run only a handful of times since I'd arrived, I now felt an excitement in this desire within. Previously, I would have been out several times a week without fail. Releasing the pressures from the week, exploring some space, and allowing my head to clear. For whatever reason, my kit had rarely made it out of the suitcase in recent months.

Standing. Looking at myself in the mirror, preparing, ready to take to those streets. I took a second to force myself to really observe the reflection facing me, as uncomfortable as it was. Taking a moment in time to stop, to acknowledge who I was. This was me now. Did I look any different? I wasn't sure. My hair still hung down, teetering on the edge of my shoulders. My shape hadn't altered much. How long had I been there now? A couple of months? Longer? I struggled to work it out.

Leaning down, I tied up my trainers, arranged my phone holder and stood straight. Found myself focussing on the smears I noted on the glass. Avoiding having to focus on the detail of my own face. On me. But before long, I couldn't help but do so. In some sort of self-torture fashion, I made myself. I made myself really take in all that I was. Had become.

The sea breeze had turned out to be a therapy much under-prescribed. The drifting hint of salt in the air. That moment you closed your eyes, and the sounds entered every fibre of your body. Taking you with it as it rhythmically washed over everything that heard it.

My face did not truthfully appear to be one I recalled wearing. The sun had coloured my skin beyond its usual pale hue. Make-up a less used commodity. Leaving my natural look to bear all. Hidden from obvious view, I wondered if there was a hint at a freshness. Maybe a renewed layer? Maybe the start of something I'd long been looking for?

I located my favourite running playlist and made sure it was loud enough to wrap around my head without being so much as to drown out the sounds of the waves. I'd become a little more familiar with the roads and pathways from the cottage, so I decided to run back inland first, before heading to where the drop towards the beach wouldn't be too steep.

It didn't take long before I realised how much I needed it. I needed the release. To let go of my feelings. Just to live in that moment, at that time, with that body. My body, with its rapidly changing exterior. The run was noticeably harder than it might previously have been, but I relished every move, every step. I was taken to a place of comfort, long familiarity. Home.

As I returned to the cottage, I decided to take a shower and then call. Matt first. He would be able to let me know how Jack was that day and whether a conversation with him would be entertained. Sometimes it had been too upsetting for Jack to talk much, so we had agreed that if he didn't want to speak with me, he didn't have to. Despite my own hurt at the arrangement, I needed to keep our communication flowing in a way that worked for them both. Not for me.

I did sometimes ask how Simon was. It seemed almost better to do that than ignore his very existence.

'He's OK, he's at work right now, but back later. Tom's mum is taking me to rugby in a bit instead.'

It was Saturday.

'Oh. Why is he working today?' I enquired, more than a little surprised.

'He sometimes does some extra time. A different role, I think. He's home most days, not long after us, though.'

Working hard to disguise my surprise and desire to ask more questions, I moved the topic on.

'Who are you playing today, then?' Distracted, but attempting to focus on the response received.

'It's training, a bit of fun to be honest, as the season is almost over. Anyway, I'd better go, Mum, sorry. Tom will be here soon. Do you want me to let Jack know you'll call him later?'

Of course it is. I should know that really, remember it. I'd seen enough years of rugby seasons now.

'Oh yes, of course. OK. Well, enjoy it and yes, by all means let Jack know. Look, if he doesn't want to talk it's no problem yeah?'

'Yeah, I'll tell him. See you later.' He disappeared.

I should have let it go. I should have just acknowledged that Simon was apparently out working more and left it at that.

My text to him left my phone not ten minutes later.

The response came three hours later.

'Yes. I'm working more now. I have to.'

I should have accepted that. Moved on. But I rang him instead.

'Oh. I didn't realise.'

'Well, you wouldn't know, would you?' Could I detect a hint of venom passing from his lips?

'I'm sorry I wasn't aware.' I was desperately trying to keep it light, careful. 'What made you do that?' For goodness' sake! Why did I even ask?

I could almost hear him thinking hard about his response before it fell from his lips.

'Because I need to keep our boys fed and watered, amongst other things. You know how much they eat. Or you did.' No mistaking the bitterness.

'But I left you the majority of the savings. I thought that would be enough for you all?'

He wasn't going to hold back, I could sense it.

'Well, it isn't. So, I'm doing what I need to do as a parent.' The volume increased. I suddenly wondered whether he was at home or work. Could the boys hear this?

'I was just surprised. I did think I'd left enough for you to all manage while I was away. Honestly.' I needed to stop. Why didn't I just stop?

'While you are away? Coming back are you? Nice of you to let us know.

Just give me a head's up once you're done with your holiday would you?'

'Come on, I don't mean it like that. I was just trying to say I didn't leave you with nothing!'

Pause. The sound of waves crashing forcefully against the rocks filled the interlude.

'No. That is right, George. I will give you that. You certainly didn't leave me with nothing. You left me with two distraught kids, an obligation to work more than full time now, and a realisation that I have no idea who the hell I bloody married!'

I thought he'd finished.

'How could you think that you pissing off wouldn't have an impact on everything? Of course, I have to work more! You just don't see the bigger picture, do you? All you ever see is you!'

My heart was thundering. How should I respond to this? What had we both become?

'I'm…'

'Don't even say it, George. Don't even say those fucking words! I'm just, in some ways at least, grateful your mum isn't here to witness this bloody mess.'

The line went dead.

Chapter 56

The positivity granted by my recent run, and the time spent with Tilly, had all evaporated. Even having made myself go out for a few more adventures with trainers couldn't mask the way I felt.

Sat in the shower, the water tumbling over me as I hugged my legs towards my chest and just sat. Wishing, hoping the water would wash away the stabbing pain I felt. I let it move over my head, finding the easiest way to reach the bottom of the bath. The end of my nose became the edge of a cliff where the tiny droplets slowly fell. Drip…Drip…Drip.

Eyes closed, head tilted down. I hugged my legs just a little harder and noted how hot the water had become. It seemed determined to hit my back and head with force. I had no idea how long I'd been sitting there, enveloped by the steam the shower created. Burying my head some more, I squashed my nose against the top of my knees and between my thighs. Before long, there was the realisation that the water hitting my legs was no longer solely from the shower. My body heaved uncontrollably, the motion mimicking the relentless forward and backwardness of the waves on the beach. I gave it no force. It was a release I did not expect to come.

Great sobs filled the bathroom. My whole body gave in. I was letting go. Cry after cry. Heave after heave. Each time, hugging my legs just a bit more. Compensating for the fact that there was no one else there to hug me. I hugged myself. I was all I had.

The water started to burn my back, and as I slowly opened my eyes, I could barely see through the steam. How long had I been there? My eyes and nose felt puffy. Exhausted.

Using the sides of the bath, I hoisted myself up slowly and turned around to face the taps. Turning them off, I paused for a moment to get my breath. I must have looked like someone twice my age, as I turned myself around gently, to move over the side.

The rest of the bathroom felt cold, even though the steam had yet to disappear. Grabbing the towel, wrapping it around myself, trying to find some comfort from that small movement. Blood. Lots of it. I had no idea when the last time was. Was it before I left? Or more recently? I couldn't recall.

Grateful the mirror was now out of action. I would only be faced with a mess otherwise. While I was able to clean myself up, the image of my face could not be altered so easily. I no longer knew the person I displayed, the things that I did, decisions I had made. I was out of control.

Locating my grey hoodie and loose joggers, I dressed myself carefully. My injured body wouldn't cope with sudden movements. Once dressed, I moved through to make a cuppa. It was no doubt a better option than opening a bottle. I was cold. So cold.

The kettle was on. I stood with hands in my pockets. The expanse of hills and fields I could see from the cottage made me feel so small and insignificant. I didn't really matter. My feelings didn't matter. However, what I had done to those I loved, to those I needed, was show them that they didn't matter either. I realised that then. I realised I had failed us all.

The kettle boiling disturbed my thoughts, and I made the tea. There was only just enough milk in the fridge. Mental note to head out sometime soon and grab some more. Once ready, I found my way to the sofa, sat down, pulled the throw over me and rested my head back on the cushions.

My head became filled with one all-consuming thought. I was a mum, and I had abandoned my children. I had consciously done so.

Simon was right. My mum would have been horrified. Ashamed that I put myself first. That I had made my boys believe that I was more important than they were.

I became so disgusted with my choice. The tears continued. "I'm sorry...

I'm sorry," I muttered, over and over again through the floods. "I am so very sorry."

The tea had spilt, and I put the cup on the table. Drowning myself under the throw, I pushed myself back into the sofa like a frightened dog, wishing to become completely cocooned. After a time, I ran my hand through my thinning hair and wiped my sore eyes with my sleeve.

I restrained from the burning desire I had to call my boys, to try to tell them I was sorry. I knew I couldn't just say sorry and go back. There was no quick fix.

I brought two lives into the world. Two lives that I was to nurture and love and care for. I'd lost it all. All because I had let myself become a mess. How had any of this even started? Mourning the memories of what we had. When I was me, when I was well…when I was together.

Chapter 57

I never made it to the party.

I wasn't even going to take up Sam's invitation for a bite to eat, either. It felt just wrong. I was still wrong. It would have been kind of odd and awkward, I was sure. But I bumped into him a few days after the missed party and accepted I was doing myself no favours, having run away to just then shut myself up in a cottage. So, I pulled myself up. We'd bumped into each other a few times while both out running and had sometimes ended up joining forces for the last stretch. He became easy enough company and took me on some more varied routes. Places I would probably never have found otherwise.

He seemed to be out often when I was. Trainers on. Idle chat in between breaths turned into a walk to talk more. I appreciated the fact he didn't pry. Not too much, anyway. Then, after a time, we'd pick up the pace again and fall into a rhythm. He was adept at running a greater distance than I and clearly more used to the undulations that the cliffs and roads provided. But he held back a bit. For me.

I tried to avoid excessive conversation about myself. Fearful I would become further entangled in a web of deceit and stories that I would lose track of. So, I had my background and did my utmost to stick to that. I tried to lead conversations to the present instead.

It was just a meal. That is what I told myself. We had agreed on lunch too, (so less like a proper dinner out, an evening date). Just lunch. In a café. Not a date.

We chatted. We talked about the sea, about our favourite films. The conversation was relatively easy. Although I was still a little on edge. I could feel it. Considered responses. Pauses for thought.

I continued to be relatively vague, gearing the conversation more towards him. Hoped I wasn't probing too much.

'It must help having your parents nearby to be able to have Freddie sometimes?' Found myself moving my salad around a little more than actually eating it. Nerves, most probably.

'I couldn't do what I do without them to be honest.' He looked directly at me while tucking into his sandwich. 'People to share the pain with too…I guess.'

Clearly still quite raw, even two years down the line.

'How about you? Do you have your parents close by? Close to your home?' A completely innocent question. Even over twenty years later, I still needed to pause and take a breath before responding.

'My mum, well, she's no longer with us.'

'Oh, I'm so sorry. I shouldn't have asked.'

'No. No, it's fine. She died many years ago. It's fine.' It wasn't, but I took a drink and carried on.

'My dad and I, we have a distant relationship I guess you'd say. We do speak occasionally, very occasionally but that's about it.'

I contemplated it all for just a moment.

'That must be hard. Then being here on your own, without family.' He concentrated on his food while the words were uttered. There was a change. He was now starting to probe.

I stopped eating, carefully laid down my cutlery, and looked at him as he carried on.

'It's none of my business. It really isn't. So, feel free to tell me to butt out. But I couldn't help notice the pale line on your left hand, where a ring would have been, once?'

There was a silence. It was mainly my own.

'I really should mind my own business. I'm sorry.' As if trying to gauge whether he'd taken an unwelcome road. There was a stillness.

He softly tried to explain himself further.

'I just know how much I've relied upon parents and friends for support, just generally in life, and to be here, on your own, would be really brave.'

Where should I go from there? He was being particularly kind. How honest did I really want to be?

'I don't think others would say I'm brave, least of all me.' I tried to give a light smile, maybe diffuse the situation a little and provide a distraction, while I decided what more to say. How much to give.

Reaching for the glass.

'I am here – yes. Alone, yes. My husband, ex-husband, I really don't know. But anyway, he's back home.' Even making that statement felt odd, wrong, left me with an emptiness and an unfamiliarity with myself.

'I see.'

I went on to tell Sam how I needed some time and that I really knew very little about what I'd do in the coming months. I reassured him and also myself that it was OK and I'd no doubt figure it all out.

He seemed to accept I was unlikely to provide any more information at that point. I wondered if he, in fact, regretted having asked so much.

'Why would you say I'm brave?' I couldn't help but enquire of him. I didn't believe anyone would consider me to be so. When is it considered brave to hurt all those people?

He took a moment. Considered. Placed his glass down.

'It's easy, and some might say cowardly, to stay in the same place, the same situation, when you know you're deeply unhappy. It is way harder and incredibly courageous, to do something about it.' He goes to resume drinking and then decides to place his glass down again.

'How long had you been feeling that unhappy?'

He caught me off guard a bit. I needed to consider my reply.

'Erm…I guess maybe I knew things weren't right for me for a couple of years. It's hard to remember, though.' I took a drink to mask the uncomfortable feeling creeping over me, as I found myself opening up to someone. Someone I didn't really know all that well.

Cutlery down, glass in hand as a crutch.

'I never thought of it really as being unhappy. It just felt wrong. I guess I felt wrong. Different. I wasn't myself.' This was becoming way too hard. Too honest.

There was an uneasy silence as Sam seemed to realise that this conversation was going too far. He appeared to sense I wouldn't be able to continue.

He looked away. Concentrated on eating.

'That is a long time in your life to feel that way.' He didn't even look up.

'Yes. I guess it is.' Neither did I.

We somehow managed to move on. I think he just blatantly changed the subject onto alternative running routes a bit further along the coast, a short drive away. He asked if I fancied trying one together, maybe the following week? I said I would see.

Chapter 58

I'd not run for well over a week. Maybe consciously not going out in order to avoid bumping into Sam again. Instead, I'd spent some days, when I wasn't working, just lying on the sofa, not exactly sure what to do with myself.

I knew that would be no long-term solution. So, I forced myself up and out once again. Changing course.

My run took me up through the winding roads, in an attempt to clear my head of doubts that kept creeping in. The road heading east journeyed from the furthest point of the busy area. A section filled with shops, arcades, and ice-cream parlours. In a car, it was tricky to navigate around the curves and drops of the road. Luckily for me and my feet, there was a pathway set just back from the road, enabling me to avoid the challenges.

The trees spread and formed protective archways over much of the road. They seemed to clasp together as each vehicle got closer to them. I often wondered, if you stopped the car and turned around, would you see the branches part again, as if to have coupled you before sending you on your way? There was however no opportunity, when driving, to spend too long looking behind you. The passing places and clear views were few and far between.

Doubtful on my legs' ability to carry me with ease over this hilly terrain, I decided I wouldn't go so far as to reach the next bay. I would limit myself as far as I thought I could manage and then return. From halfway along the path, the view was of the entire expanse of beach in the bay where I then lived. The edges were clear; the time beaten rocks denoting the boundary.

The shore felt almost within reach, despite the depth of the drop required. If I just held out my arm as far as it could go, maybe I could feel the tide washing over my hand, cleansing it. Smoothing it. I paused to take my breath. Take in the sight. Finding a bench, set back a bit, I took a seat to absorb the view some more.

Closing my eyes, I focussed on the warmth of the sun, gently tracing over my face. I could hear the sea, not touch it really, but hear it, feel it. The waves caressing sand undisturbed at that time by small noisy footprints and giggles. Some of the shops and restaurants would be preparing to enter the busiest time of the year. In many ways, I was looking forward to the distraction of more hours and more people to meet in the café. Yet a little nervous and apprehensive about what life after the summer would bring. If there was to be less life in this seaside town, how would I ever find my own? I expected that I would then just feel the same as I did before but set in a different place.

Opening my eyes, I glanced up and could see further along the path. Other runners were also out to challenge the stamina of their limbs. I realised that if I stayed seated, I might lose my focus. On that day, it was to challenge myself. Really push myself forward and not allow my body to fall.

I made it. Back in the cottage I found a sense of both pride and relief that I had done it. I had taken myself out and away from the perceived comfort of wallow.

Busying with getting ready to head for a shower, I was disturbed by the shrill ringing of the phone. Grabbing it in my hand, I couldn't initially decide whether to answer it or not. Ring after ring, time was running out to decide.

'Hello.'

I could hear him, maybe shuffling, the hint of his breath.

'Hello?'

Not wanting to get agitated, but not planning on waiting forever.

'Hello, Simon?'

'Sorry…Hi.' Not convinced he even knew what he was calling for. While I waited for him to decide, I grabbed a water and headed to the bathroom to start to get ready.

'Sorry to bother you.'

'No, it's fine. Is everything OK? Boys OK?' Guarded after our last conversation ended so badly, but I did still want to know if anything was the matter with the boys. I assumed that was probably the only reason he would call.

'No, I mean yes, all is fine. Boys are OK. Have you spoken to them recently?' He really couldn't have just rung to ask that.

'Erm…a couple of days ago I chatted to Jack and yesterday Matt and I were messaging. It's been really nice.'

'Good, oh good.'

Grabbing the bottles for the shower and some clean clothes, I awaited his next statement.

'I'm sorry. I just rang to say I'm sorry for what I said about your mum. That was way too far. I know that.'

Taken aback, I sat down on the bed for a moment. I knew exactly the words he was referring to. They'd played over and over in my head. It wasn't an unfamiliar sentiment. I had told myself almost those exact words, several times, over the last year.

'Thank you.'

'I was caught in the moment. Frustrated, upset, and angry. But I wanted you to know that I didn't mean it.' Was that a sigh of relief I could hear?

That was probably the most civilised conversation we'd had for some time. Settling on the bed, putting down the clean clothes, I engaged with Simon, and forgave him for those words he had uttered in a moment of despair.

I had spent many evenings over the previous months inwardly asking him for forgiveness. This moment was relatively straightforward.

Chapter 59

'You have to come along. I'm not going to let you miss out and spend the night alone in that cottage. Meet me here at seven and be ready for some fun.'

Tilly stepped out the door, passing the final customers, while Isla and I cleared down the last of the tables. I accepted the order.

'Sounds as though you don't have a choice there.' Recognising the voice, I looked up and saw Sam looking over at me.

'I don't think I do.' Carrying the pile of plates and cutlery, while directing my reply to both Sam and Freddie, as they grabbed the last of the sausage rolls.

'How are you? Not seen you out running for a while?'

Determined to reply flippantly, as though I hadn't purposefully looked out to avoid him.

'I have been out, but just a little. I really need to get back into the swing of it a bit more.' Passing the food to them both, I smiled, hopefully with a conviction.

'Might see you later, then?' He turned to catch my eye as he moved out the door. Not knowing how to really reply, I smiled and give Freddie a wave.

'You will go, won't you?' Isla finished putting all the chairs on the tables as I cleared down the work surface. "It's a lot of fun. You'll enjoy it, I promise."

'In which case I will, but I'll hold you to that promise.'

Finishing up getting the café ready for the morning, we chatted lightly about what the evening might bring. Leaving work together, we walked around the top of the bay before we each disappeared in different directions. I could see groups setting up for the festivities on the beach. A little nervous. Socialising on mass seemed to take me very much out of my comfort zone, but I was determined to push myself. To see what life might bring me as a result.

The evening entertainment was just as promised. Bands continued to play as the sun ended its work for the day. People filled the beach, the bars, waiting for the fireworks later in the evening. I ate, I drank, and felt more a part of the occasion than I thought I would. Tilly was more than welcoming, and I spent some time with her and her friends. It was easy. Well, easier, anyway.

Sam caught me at one point. I'd been dreading seeing him. He knew too much and had caused me to open up when I really wanted to just close down. He'd been really kind, but I still felt the desire to put some distance between us.

Insistent upon buying me a drink, I gave in to his relaxed persona. Freddie being looked after by family. His opportunity for adult time was not going to go to waste.

Parting from his group of friends for a time, he gently took my arm and lead me to one side of the cove, where words might be heard and understood.

'I just wanted to apologise if I sounded as though I were probing when we went out the other week? I really didn't mean to make you feel uncomfortable. That's it really, I've just been trying to find the right time and way to apologise for ages.'

'Genuinely, it's fine. Don't worry.' Taken aback by his thoughtfulness. Fuelled by alcohol, I guessed.

'But I didn't want you to feel you had to avoid me as a result. I'd love to go for a run with you again. I promise no awkward questions.'

Our relief-filled smiles broke the moment. I could see he really meant what he had said. In fairness, it was only my paranoia I guess, at what people would think if they knew the truth, that had kept me withdrawn. We agreed to meet the following week, and I'd get some practice in, in the meantime. I'd try to keep up.

Heading up from the beach, over to what was my favourite bench for a break from the noise and chatter, I was stopped part way by Tilly.

'You OK? It's worth the trip out, isn't it?' She was almost shouting, even though it wasn't really necessary so far up.

The view from there was, in my opinion, the clearest, most undisturbed view of the beach below. It was a popular one for certain, and I was surprised to see an empty spot when the beach was so full of bodies. Tilly and I had, on occasions, taken some time to catch up on that bench. Chat about the day, locals, other areas to explore. As weeks passed, I had shared a few more details with her. Still guarded over the most important parts, of course. She knew I had only a few plans and that none of them included Simon.

As we took our respective seats, each of us with a drink in hand, I agreed that it had been worth the effort. The atmosphere that evening completely brought the place to life in such a different way to the daytime. The beach had a beat, it was alive, it roared with people, with existence.

A comfortable silence appeared between us. Relaxed by the setting sun, the several drinks consumed, and the ease of the late evening.

'Will your boys come and visit during the school summer holidays, do you think?'

'I hope so, but I don't really know yet.'

Then I realised. I realised how much she knew already. How much she had worked out from the pockets of truth I had given her.

I turned and looked at her. She took my arm.

'It's OK.'

'How did you know?' I could feel my heartbeat quicken as I wondered what this might do. How this reality might change the shape of this comfort.

'I just did. I guess picking up on little things you said, the points that seemed to really bother you. Just wasn't convinced they were as old as you said they were.'

I swallowed the rest of my drink down. This would change everything. Ruin it all.

'I'm sorry.' My eyes cast downwards. I no longer felt able to even look at her.

Tilly increased the hold on my arm. She moved in close and told me clearly and slowly that it was OK.

'Don't be sorry. You have no need to be. But why lie?'

Thinking about my response.

'Why would a mum ever leave her children, while they are still children? Who is ever going to understand what I did?' My gaze focused on the cup in hand. I could feel her gazing directly at me, but I was unable to reciprocate.

'I think people will understand far more than you realise. Anyone is capable of doing anything, if pushed. I can only assume that you felt you had no other choice than to do it.' Her words contained nothing but care.

'I didn't know what else to do. You'd think at my age I'd have it all together. But I'd got myself into a place I saw no escape from unless I physically escaped.'

We sat watching the fireworks as they got going. The colours and sounds a welcome distraction from the conversation. Yet in many ways a weight had at that moment been removed, almost. Tilly had helped me to ease it a little from my shoulders.

'Do you regret it?' I looked at her but gave no words.

'You know you could have stayed, don't you? There are so many people and organisations that can help anyone and everyone who is struggling. You never needed to go to the lengths of leaving everything behind. Everything was probably just where you needed it to be. Life can be really tough. Regardless of what you have or don't.'

I smiled in a way in which I hoped would let her know that I understood but didn't necessarily completely agree with.

'Has this helped?' She casts her hand to motion to the beach. 'Coming here?' I don't know how long I paused before answering.

'It has given me space. I still don't have a plan or a future. I still find myself a little lost. But I have had space.'

'I'm convinced it's actually quite normal to feel lost. Many more people than you probably realise, than any of us realise, feel lost. The trick is to know that you don't have to do anything drastic. That you can be found.'

Tilly gently put her hand on my arm as if to apologise for asking such questions. I smiled at that. Turned my head just slightly to catch her face. Aware that trickles of water would be ruining the make-up I'd taken time to carefully apply.

Her arm around the back of my shoulders tightened, and I wiped at the liquid.

Time passed, and we sat and talked, long after the fireworks, mainly about random things. Almost anything other than the facts she now knew.

Sat above the expanse of beach, I recalled the boys' excitement even at their older ages, in spending time on the sand. For me, the comfort and cocoon of the rocks as they formed in the age-old cove was far more invigorating. Many times, over the last months, I had clambered down to the base of the cove, discarded my flip-flops and felt the sand and the stones mixing together, massaging over the base of my feet. I had walked with confidence, through to where the sea came in, not wanting to stop.

Chapter 60

What time was it?

Knocking continued.

For god's sake, it wasn't even 9 a.m. Who would be so physical with the cottage door at that time?

Scrambling for something to cover my exhausted and slightly hungover body, I padded through the rooms to answer the inconvenience.

'I know, I know, but we're going out.'

'What the…' I could barely focus enough to see who it was but recognised the voice instantly. It could only have been about six hours since I'd last been sat out with her.

'Tilly, I don't mean to be rude but what the actual hell are you doing here?' Tying my dressing gown belt, running weary hands through locks, I covered a yawn as she replied.

'OK, I know what you're going to say, but genuinely we have to go. My friend James is picking us up in about half an hour. You need to be dressed for a temperature colder than it is outside. Now you go get dressed, I'm going to track down your kettle….'

And then she was off. Leaving me to close the front door, she found with ease the object of her desire and I was left to process the last three minutes.

Eyes rubbed, made no difference. I was still far from awake.

'Tilly, it's really lovely to see you again. It's been so long…'

'You need more milk.'

'I'm sorry, but if I'd known you were going to descend, I'd have been prepared...'

Still more than a little confused, I followed Tilly's path to the kitchen.

'Can you please enlighten me before you take all my nourishment?' I pleaded. Grabbing another cup, so as to not miss out.

'Look, if I tell you what we're doing, you'll back out, but I need you to come. I really do. So just go get dressed and leave the rest to me. We have twenty-five minutes.' Rummaging for spoons, sugar, she made herself more than a little at home.

I gave up. Headed back to the bedroom, casting a longing look at the bed I'd been so rudely turfed out of. The open wardrobe gave me no real assistance in finding what would be suitable attire for a day I had no clues on. Something, anything, would have to do.

James arrived. Tilly bundled into the front seat, leaving me alone with my guesses in the back. James gave nothing away. Even mentions of how it looked as though the conditions would be perfect for it served not to enlighten me.

The drive took no more than half an hour and the views along the way made me forget the mystery. For a time.

As we pulled into the car park, floating above the bay below, the abundance of cars gave no clues. A walk maybe? Explore somewhere further afield?

'Head over the left and David will be waiting for you. I'm off to catch up with a few people, but I'll see you shortly. He knows to expect you.' James secured the car and walked briskly in the opposite direction to our instructions.

'Come on, this way, he said.' My hand was grabbed. Still dazed and a little concerned I followed her towards a group of people who looked to be setting up various forms of equipment and sheets of some material. Confusion was abound, but it seemed I was just required to follow.

Tilly located David and motioned to him that we were a two. Two participants, it seemed. I'd not had the chance to pin her down. Obtain an answer of any sort.

A cheer went up. I looked over in the direction of the sound and could make out a group of people motioning towards something further out, over the cliff edge. Some success by all accounts.

'OK, so, we'll get you both kitted out. Your partners are just getting the gliders ready and they'll go through a briefing with you before you head out. Enjoy.'

I stared at her. Her grin clearly marking her excitement at the adventure she'd dragged me to.

Lost for words.

'Come on. Over this way.'

A complete lack of appreciation of my expression. Gliding?

I couldn't quite decide what I should do. Or even what I felt. I was going gliding?

Unable to even formulate a sentence, Tilly's forceful grip lead me over to where our 'partners' appeared to be preparing everything for our experience.

I could hear her chatting happily to her 'flying friend' as they got themselves ready. Turning to try to take in all my instructor was saying, still not completely sure how I felt about this.

We were ready, lined up alongside each other. Tilly's smile and thumbs up became infectious. What was I doing there? Complete and utter madness, with a hangover!

'I'm going to show you it's never too late to fly,' she practically screamed at me as they got ready to go. Her squeals of delight and life lingered long after they had taken hold of the light winds and made it over the edge.

Her words remained strong within my head as we soared over the bay below. The determined breeze caressing my face, planting a sense of freedom over every limb. Eventually, I became brave enough to open my eyes. Seize the view. The sky. The sun.

My spontaneous smile accompanied by a light laugh. Laughter at what Tilly had coerced me into doing. Damp cheeks but for once, for that moment, not as a result of sadness.

Chapter 61

Lying on the beach, my shoulders propped up with palms spread out behind. I was on the edge. On the edge of where the sea engulfed the sand. Smothered it in its own being and washed over it without a care.

This reminded me of childhood holidays, seeing my mum do exactly the same. Arms outstretched to keep her stable. Even in her last year, she loved to spend time by the sea, on the coast. Anywhere the land ended. Before she left this island too soon.

It was late in the evening. The sea gently rippled in the calm. This was the time of day when the sea gave thanks for your company but claimed that this was now 'my time'. It no longer existed for others. The gentle ripples became the product of the waves, doing as they pleased, in the quiet of the later day. The sea said, 'I have entertained you all this this day. I have comforted you and now I just need to be.' So, I came to the edge and I lay with it. And we could both just be.

After a time, I stood, hoisting myself up with leverage found within. The sun sat gently on the horizon as if it was about to dip into the sea without making a splash. Mesmerised by the soft glow coming from the light, it became hard to notice anything else. Hard to not to be drawn in, not to follow a route to the sun. Wondering if some form of salvation, some feeling of peace might be available at the end.

People before me had disappeared. I imagined they too must have been taken in by the quiet beauty and glow from that part of the day. For some there will have been a pull so great that they felt they had no choice. A promise of a better existence beyond all that they left behind. Or the desire for an existence no more. For the pain, anguish, and sheer despair to be over. It took so little. One foot first and then the other and a persistence to keep walking forward. To then keep going until the warmth and glow existed all around you. People before me will not have stopped. The pull would be too great. The desperate desire for some form of inner peace that this gentle glow promised to give. Only when it was too late did those people realise that the promised comfort was always out of reach.

How many lives were lost to a desire for more? For the feeling that there was no hope of ever finding what really fitted? As a result of realising they were not enough?

My mum's life wasn't lost because she couldn't find herself. Illness found her and it took hold like some twisted demon before she gave up. That sounds wrong. She didn't give up. She wasn't weak. Weaker than others who came out the other side. IT just didn't give in.

She would have loved this. This place, this time.

I wondered what she would have made of me being here, alone. I had thought about it often. Would she have understood? In part, I think she would have wanted me to find what was missing. As a parent herself, a committed parent, I don't know that she could have wholly understood my reasons for leaving everything behind. Including my children.

That was probably the first time I'd really considered what impact my actions would have had on my mum. I was an only child, and I felt the full force of her love and encouragement throughout my childhood. Not once did she ever say I wasn't capable of something. Not once did she try to put me off whatever dream I had that week. Every little win was celebrated like an Olympic gold medal. Dad quietly smiled at the back, while Mum whooped and cheered at every little accomplishment.

I was heading towards twenty-eight when my mum left. When she was taken. Terminology can be so important to get right.

Dad became distant afterwards. So much so, he set up life with someone else who just wanted to care for him and as a result we hadn't had much contact afterwards. I tried, but the connection felt forced and lost, all at the same time.

A rogue dog scampered over to the right as I continued to stand in the sea. Owners keeping watch from a distance. Living life to the full, making his, or her, own waves. Such joy clearly etched on its face. The dog grabbed my attention for a time and I found myself smiling, somewhat unwillingly. The owners managed to catch up with the freedom on four legs and cast an eye over to where I stood. We casually smiled, a light-hearted greeting between strangers.

They passed in front and moved across the bay. My focus returned to the view ahead and the sun that had dropped just a little more into the sea, as gracefully as some experienced diver, barely breaking the seal.

Gazing down at the sea, my feet became unable to resist the sinking element of the sand. I started to walk further forward, the sea beginning to reach my knees. Before long, I realised I carried with me a heaviness of guilt, not of a weight I recalled ever having held before. Of having failed at the duty of parenthood that my own mother so embraced. I had let her down. My chest carried this load as I continued to walk forward. My head filled with the words *I'm sorry, Mum.*

Chapter 62

I couldn't recall ever having called in sick before. Not unless I'd been genuinely really ill.

The day broke, and I knew. Despite my recent adventure, I knew I couldn't make it in. I couldn't keep the pretence up any longer and the call from Annie the previous day cemented that feeling.

'Hi.' I'd opened the conversation with a lightness and a feeling of joy at having had a call from her. Annie and I had spoken most weeks and every time, I felt the same.

'Hi, how are you doing?' There was a muteness to her voice. Something was different.

'I'm fine thanks, hon. How are you? You sound low, all OK?' Settled myself down for a comfortable chat after getting in from work.

'I'm fine. I've just come off the phone from Chrissie, though. Erica isn't great. Her dad died yesterday. I thought you probably ought to know.'

Despite not having spoken to Erica since I left, I felt a level of concern unaltered since our distance. I knew where she would be.

Annie and I chatted about it all, as much as she was aware, at that point. Not unexpected, but too much for Erica to really cope with. Chrissie had been to take the place of her husband, who by all accounts was clearly relieved.

As I came off the call, I knew I wasn't going anywhere.

This whole adventure was clearly becoming a failure. Moments of insight not enough to make it feel a success.

I rang Tilly and then pulled the quilt further up, tucking it under my chin as if relying upon it to hold me together. The sun was softly beaming through the thin curtains and I rolled over to face the other way, as if turning my back on any form of light that might want to shine over me.

I didn't deserve it.

I'd dreamt of my mum, after my thoughts of yesterday. Feeling her soft fingers as we held hands walking along the beach. Something we'd done so often. I could touch her fingers. Feel them as if she were still right there.

Aware that at some point in the night, I was crying. So hard my chest heaved and convulsed as if under the pressure of a large weight. I woke briefly, not sure for a moment as to what was real and what was not. I wiped my eyes, lay on my back, breathing hard. Wondering if I would make it back to sleep.

I clearly did and there I was, trying to find comfort in the weight of the quilt and the tightness with which I wrapped it around.

I no longer knew what to do.

Had I gone too far to ever go back? Did I even want to go back? Surely, I'd still feel the same way, even if I did? Nothing had changed, had it? I really wasn't sure. But I knew I just felt more guilt, more uncertainty. I'd come here to find myself, to work out what was missing, and I felt no further forward.

If I could think rationally, I might accept that I had gone there with no plan. All I had known was that things weren't right for me where I was before and I needed to remove myself from it. It had gone on for too long and I needed out. I had no idea, beyond that.

Annie had, in one of our conversations before I left, said if I really looked hard, I could find what I was looking for right where I was. I didn't need to disappear for good. I just needed some space, maybe some time. That life was changing. I was changing. But that this just might not be the start of the end. This might actually be just the beginning.

Maybe she was right. Maybe I should have sought more help where I was. My mind behaved like a swirling fog, a mist of dread and despair that enveloped me and refused to release a single part of my very being.

The sound of the waves filtered lightly through the open window. Panic set in and I pulled the quilt over my head in the hope of being able to drown it all out.

Chapter 63

The next few weeks passed by. I went back to work after a couple of days, claiming a migraine. Whether Tilly fully bought into that or not, I couldn't tell. The sunshine season started to wane, and the beach took on a different projection, which I'm sure added to my mood. The damage was however already done.

Fortunately, Tilly kept me on until the very end of the season. She kept the café open beyond, but she and Isla needed no more hands. As the end approached, as the weeks became quieter, and the weather started to feel a little less settled, I was acutely aware that I still had no decided course of action.

I could ride it out for a few more months from a financial point of view. However, that was probably the least of my considerations.

Feeling positive about where I was, quickly became much harder. Missing family and friends was, however, much easier. Thoughts of them all took up more of my days. Simon and I spoke now and then and I was relishing the regular contact with both Jack and Matt. They hadn't visited during the summer. Their choice, not mine.

My walks along the seafront became a little less, my time sinking my feet into the sand also.

'You've really lost yourself, haven't you?' Tilly probed during a break on a busy day.

I looked over at her, pausing from clearing the counter.

'I don't mean to pry, you know I don't, but I can't help but notice you're not as you were. Can I help?' She stopped to grab my eye. It appeared a little confrontational, but I knew enough about Tilly by then, to appreciate it was not meant in that way.

Trying to think how to reply, what words to use, how honest to be...

'I am struggling currently. I think that would be a fair statement,' I answered.

'Have you thought about going back?' Her eyes looked towards me, gentle yet probing.

'I really don't think I can.' I barely looked up at her. She was forcing me to give attention to the specific questions I might wrestle with alone, but had given no external volume to.

Tilly walked over to me. Wanting me to be part of this conversation; forcing the point.

'I don't think I have ever had the full story from you, but to be honest, I don't care. That doesn't matter. What matters is what you do now. You came here for a reason, and I don't know if you found any of what you were looking for, but you need to do something. Something to make whatever it is you want to happen or change. Do exactly that. If you hang around here throughout the winter, you will feel no better. No different.'

Her hand rested on mine, giving a level of comfort I'd not felt from others since I arrived. How could they? They didn't know me.

I met her gaze and continued to forbid the tears from flowing. Feeling the nails in my other hand dig into my palm to keep it together. My toes in my shoes scrunched hard, curled under to hold on, hold it in.

'How do I go back?' I pleaded. 'Even if I wanted to? I just don't think I could. And what if the answer really isn't there?'

'What else are you going to do? Stay here? Wait for the gloomy mornings, the cold, isolating winds that cause the waves to cover the beach, forbidding access? Work for me again next year, meet a few more people, go gliding? All this is fine if you're in it for the long haul. You know yourself you don't make a new life overnight. You've left a steady and lucrative job and lifestyle, husband, and children. You cannot get to that point, in whatever form it takes, quickly. Are you going to stay here for the long haul? Is this where your answer is?'

Standing back up straight, we parted hands.

I paused.

'I wish I could tell you. Genuinely I do.'

'It was a drastic and brave, if somewhat selfish manoeuvre...' She treads carefully.

'I know, I know. I'd got to the point I didn't really know what else to try. I am very aware now of how selfish it was, but I still stand by the fact that I deserve to be happy. I, like everyone else, should not be afraid to put myself first. Surely?'

I was looking for back-up, some confirmation that I was right, that I was OK to put myself first.

'I don't think anyone would deny that, hon. It's, I guess, what you do in order to achieve that. The people you leave on the way, the things you give up.'

'I know. I get that.' I started putting cups away and clearing the area behind the counter. It was a distraction.

Tilly continued.

'Yet I can see that if you didn't, you might feel that you'd given up on yourself.' She stopped what she was doing. Looked at me and I met her gaze across the deserted café.

'I can see that, George. I get that part.' She smiled. A soft smile of understanding, some understanding anyway.

We finished clearing the café, keen to get finished and out. Tilly locked up and then decided she was taking me for a walk along the cliff top for a good bit of 'problem solving' sea air.

We walked along a now familiar stretch of cliff, around the cove where the couples often gather, away from the families enjoying the wide expanse of beach on the other side. Where at certain times you can buy an amazing meal from a small hut directly on the beach. Where the rocks almost cocoon you, giving you shelter from the force of the sea. Instead, it contains it, in a way that lessens the force, the sea only able to gently head inland, buffered each side.

We linked arms. There had become a beauty in this friendship I had found. Had been gifted. A newness of interest and a lightness of having not lived through all those life events together. We met, we laughed, we chatted. There was support. Tilly had been a source of strength, even through this short period of time.

We grabbed a seat at the edge of the cliff top, looking down at those waiting for food. The hut would be closing soon I'd heard, hibernating in readiness for the next season.

'Thank you,' I said to Tilly. Looking down as I did so.

'Thank you for listening.'

I turned and smiled.

'Seriously, you're welcome. I just want you to find whatever it is you need. Wherever that may be. Although obviously I'd love you to stick around here, of course.' She nudged me and there I found a moment of bright sun.

We parted ways, and I headed back up to the cottage. The walks back had felt so heavy in recent days. I recalled the ease with which I made them when I first arrived, full of hope and possibility. A new start, a change of situation. Now that seemed to have dwindled and, in many ways, it had not provided the answer that I thought it might.

I spent the evening in the cottage, wrapped up in a now well-worn hoodie and joggers. Still finding comfort in the old but welcoming sofa. I never tired of the fact that it sat side on to the window and allowed an easy viewpoint for the hills. When the tide started to draw in, I could see the waves and watch them approach with anticipation.

Putting on some music, pouring the wine, had become a regular evening for me. Thoughts running through my head focussed on the conversations with Tilly. A culmination of many weeks of small passing's of information, feelings, discussion. I drank the wine in large gulps, somehow thinking I might suddenly find the answer.

Feeling the need desperately, I called both Matthew and Jack. We chatted. I was guarded to ensure they were not aware I was drinking and also to ensure they didn't pick up on my low mood. Ended each call telling them that they meant the world to me. That I was proud to be their mum and would always be.

Chapter 64

Two days later, I am here. On the edge.

My eyes are now fully open. Not just to the sea, the clouds, those seagulls soaring along the seafront. My eyes are actually open. I feel my heartbeat accelerating and hear a trickle of stones fall from the edge of the cliff top. A reminder of where I really am. My toes very much aware of my location. The pain, the throbbing increasing with every minute. My arms previously held out wide for balance and, as if to signify myself to be some form of sacrifice, come down to my sides almost too quickly. I take a small stumble. My damaged toes are struggling to keep me stable. The smallest of moves, but enough to jolt me into the present. Heart pounding, I cannot help but look down again. The thunder in my heart, my head, mixes with the crash of the waves below. I can barely hear anything, just loud noise.

I regain balance and quickly but firmly step back. My heart racing, my breath having become laboured, chest tight. The heaving sensation continues, but I have stepped back. Sitting down, almost clinging onto the dry grass and closing my eyes as I try to calm my breath. I realise I did not want that. I really thought I might. I thought it might help, might free me from the pain, the confusion, the upset. Lying back on the bank, my feet feeling the certainty of the grass, my arms spreading to give me grip to the earth. I accept that that will not be the answer.

Epilogue

Hoodies and short folded. Newly acquired attire that is likely to be shut away for a time to come. The suitcase is straining under its additional cargo and using my weight I force the two sides to meet and the zip to close.

Everything else is packed.

Taking one last look around the cottage, I find myself with a subtle smile and inwardly giving thanks to what was my home for a time. It gave me space and comfort despite the fact it was never really mine.

The view from the window graces my sight for what I think may be the last time. I breathe it in. Try to imprint the hills and coast to my memory for fear I may not return to absorb them.

The door pulls to, keys left inside. I walk to the car.

The End

About the Author

Broken Toes is my debut novel. Yet whilst growing up, and even into my forties, I have never felt an ingrained desire to become an author.

Elizabeth Gilbert made me do it!

The inspiration for Broken Toes came whilst sat on a beach, enjoying a family holiday in 2019. It was one of those times where the clearest of thoughts appear, once we actually find time to just stop and be. The ideas from that week away never left me, and after delving into the advice and insight given by Elizabeth Gilbert in her book - 'Big Magic', I decided to share it all.

And so the 'project' began.

I have always had a deep rooted interest in the human condition. What makes us do what we do? What impact do single, individual moments have upon our lives and those of others? How much is actually completely out of our control?

I am drawn to reading stories that are real, gritty, and shed light on what makes people who they are. Stories that make us realise we are not alone. Books by Rachel Joyce, Gail Honeyman and Ruby Wax are amongst many others found on my bookshelves.

I live in Cambridgeshire with my husband, two teenagers and two dogs. My passion for dungarees, boots, and 1980's music, a regular source of embarrassment for my children. I'm sure they'll forgive me some day....

How to get hold of a free copy of my short story 'All That is not Mine'....

I am already working on my next novel and whilst I'm doing so, I'll be sending out regular emails to those interested in hearing how the process is going. I'll also be chatting about where I find my inspiration, how disruptive my dogs are to my working day and anything else that might be relevant or hopefully interesting. I promise I won't be bombarding you with my ramblings and as a thank you to all who join my mailing list, I'll be sending a free copy of my short story, 'All That is not Mine'.

If you would like to receive this FREE book, check out my website or use the direct link, below, where you can add your details to my mailing list and bag yourself a freebie along the way!

If you enjoyed this book, I have a favour to ask.....

If you enjoyed reading Broken Toes, I would be incredibly grateful if you could leave a review on Amazon. As a new author, reviews go a long way to helping me develop my career and nudge me along to get the next book finished!

Thank you very much for your interest and your help!

You can connect with me on:
- https://lisa-richardson.co.uk
- https://www.facebook.com/LisaRichardsonAuthor
- https://www.instagram.com/lisarichardsonauthor

Subscribe to my newsletter:

✉ https://preview.mailerlite.io/preview/482577/sites/94122305345554098/allthatisnotmine

Also by Lisa Richardson

All That is not Mine

Envy. The destroyer of self. 'All that is not mine' is set several years prior to 'Broken Toes'. It features Erica's introduction into Georgia's life and the beginning of the friendships that become so important. Yet before Erica has a chance to seek to fit in, she creates a situation that might just bring everything to an end before it has even begun.

Printed in Great Britain
by Amazon

32207378R00142

BAD GAMES:
MALEVOLENT

BAD GAMES: MALEVOLENT

JEFF MENAPACE

MIND MESS PRESS

2017

CHAPTER 1

Bucks County, Pennsylvania

November 2003

Kelly Blaine, nine years old, went for her favorite book in the classroom's bookcase. She'd made it very clear in the cafeteria during lunch that this was her favorite book; no one was to touch it when the time came.

That time was now. SSR—sustained silent reading. The book was about firefighters and the heroes they were. The sacrifices they made. How they put their lives on the line each and every time they battled a fire.

Kelly didn't care about any of that.

What Kelly liked was that there were a few real-life aftermath photos of major fires and pictures of burns, some of them horrific. How the book, despite its message on the bravery of firemen, remained in Miss Riley's third-grade classroom with such pictures was a mystery. Or perhaps it wasn't. Much like her daily warning at lunch for everyone to steer clear of the book during SSR, so too had she warned others to never tell Miss Riley of the pictures in the book.

And no one ever did.

But as far as leaving the book alone come SSR time? Becky Sole wouldn't hear of it. Becky didn't want the book, didn't even like the book, but to be told "hands off" by a fellow student? She wouldn't hear of it.

Becky Sole was new.

.   .   .

"What are you doing?" Kelly asked.

Becky Sole had hurried to the bookshelf before Kelly could get there, snatching up the book. "I'm reading this book for SSR," she said.

"Didn't you hear me at lunch?"

"This is the *classroom's* book," Becky proclaimed defiantly. "You don't *own* it."

Kelly took a deep breath through her nose and let it out slowly. "Give me the book."

"*No!*" Becky slammed the book flat to her chest as though she'd sooner die than part with it.

Miss Riley, alerted by Becky's shout, approached. "Kelly? Becky? Is something wrong?"

"She says this is *her* book," Becky said. "I told her it was the *classroom's* book, not *hers.*"

Miss Riley looked down at Kelly. "Kelly, there are plenty of other books for you to read. Why don't you grab one of those?"

Kelly looked up at Miss Riley and smiled. "Okay."

Becky strode off triumphantly with the book and took a seat at her desk.

.   .   .

Kelly watched her the entire time during SSR. It was apparent Becky did not care about the book at all. She flipped lazily through the pages with barely a glance for each. When she arrived on the pages with the burn victims, a sudden look of fright came over her, and she quickly flipped past them.

It was now blatantly obvious to Kelly that Becky's need to have the book was simply to show her up. Nothing more. Worse still, when SSR ended, Becky did not return the book to its spot on the shelf, but instead tucked it away in her desk and then glanced back at Kelly with a condescending little smile.

Any other child would have immediately gone running to the teacher.

Kelly didn't say a word.

. . .

Show and tell.

Becky Sole's mother had entered the classroom five minutes prior, carrying the unmistakable wire cage of a hamster—the wood chips, the hanging water bottle, the exercise wheel.

"This is Roger," Becky said proudly, lifting the small cage high for all to see.

Boys smiled; girls cooed and begged to hold it. Becky refused, of course, but did strut from desk to desk with the cage, allowing everyone to see Roger up close.

When she arrived at Kelly's desk, she looked down at Kelly with a wary eye.

"He's cute," Kelly said. She stuck her index finger through the thin metal bars.

"*Don't!*" Becky jerked the cage away.

"What's wrong?" Miss Riley asked from her desk.

Becky spun around. "She tried to touch him."

"Look but don't touch, Kelly."

Kelly nodded toward Miss Riley. "I'm sorry." Then to Becky with a smile: "I'm sorry."

. . .

Becky Sole had asthma. The classroom had gotten firsthand experience with this fact on Becky's very first day. She'd had an attack. Anxiety of being the new kid and all. The scene had been a frightening one: Becky crying, struggling to breathe; Miss Riley desperately fiddling in Becky's desk for her inhaler and then cradling Becky in her arms while the girl used the device; Miss Riley gently stroking Becky's brow and consoling her.

Not a single child in the classroom could tear their eyes away from the scene. A few had even started crying themselves out of empathy or fear. Kelly Blaine had been no less transfixed than the others, but she did not look on with fear or empathy for the new girl. She looked on, though unable to articulate it so at only nine years old, as someone with a keen understanding of natural selection: Becky's affliction made her a weak member of the herd. A disgusting thing that would never thrive.

Kelly took note.

And so today when the kids returned from afternoon recess, the boys lining up at the sink in the back of the classroom to tilt their heads to the side of the faucet to crudely gulp water, the girls chattering and laughing, Miss Riley standing patiently at the head of the class for everyone to eventually take their seat, Becky Sole made an even greater scene than she'd done on her first day.

Her hamster lay dead in his cage. Becky did not scream; she *shrieked*. An ear-splitting cry that spun, then froze, everyone.

Miss Riley rushed over to confirm Becky's discovery. The hamster was indeed dead, though the cause was not immediately evident. It simply lay on its side, lifeless.

Becky's hysteria quickly prompted another asthma attack. Miss Riley, as she'd done just one week prior, hurried toward Becky's desk for her inhaler—only to discover it missing.

Miss Riley tore through the desk, tossing its contents to the floor without a care.

Still no inhaler.

Becky's condition worsened. She was on all fours now, her sobbing becoming less and less without the oxygen to fuel it. The classroom, previously stunned into silence, had now erupted. Those who'd cried at the scene one week ago were in hysterics, as if they too were in the throes of an attack. A few of the braver students had darted from the classroom for help. By the time that help—in the form of Mrs. Mills from across the hall—arrived, Miss Riley was a woman possessed, rifling through Becky's desk as though it contained some sort of hidden bomb quickly ticking its way down to zero.

When Mrs. Mills rushed toward a crumpled Becky, she called over to Miss Riley in desperate tones, insisting that she needed to leave the desk alone and help her get Becky to the nurse's office immediately. Miss Riley appeared deaf to Mrs. Mills' cries. Her only response, fueled by what had now seemingly become her obsession, was: "*WHERE THE HELL IS IT?!*"

More teachers arrived on the scene; Miss Riley eventually came to her senses and left the desk, rushing toward the aid of her student; and Becky Sole was carried off toward the nurse's office, where several emergency inhalers were kept.

.   .   .

Two things had hit Kelly Blaine during the whole ordeal. Again, being only nine, she might have been hard-pressed to articulate them, but she felt them just as sure as she felt her own skin.

One of those things was irony. The other was shame.

The irony came when Miss Riley was tossing the contents of Becky's desk all over the place. The book Kelly treasured so much, the one Becky had not returned to the bookshelf but kept in her desk to spite Kelly, had landed mere inches from Kelly's feet.

The shame came from not having the foresight to take the emergency inhalers from the nurse's office as well.

Still, suffocating the hamster during recess had been amusing. And of course she had her book now.

.   .   .

Becky Sole was sent home. Miss Riley, still visibly shaken, announced that the remainder of the day was to be SSR.

Make that two for irony.

CHAPTER 2

Autumn 2012

Joan Parsons had the biggest daytime talk show on television. All the top celebrities. Unlike most daytime talk-show hosts, however, Joan Parsons also had a knack for news. Real news. Well, as real as news could get on daytime TV without entirely succumbing to bad taste. Still, she was a magician at getting exclusives—one-on-ones with those smack in the middle of whatever drama was sweeping the nation.

Her guest today was Kelly Blaine, the eighteen-year-old girl who'd recently been acquitted on several counts of murder along with aiding and abetting known serial killer Monica Kemp, sister to mass murderers Arthur and James Fannelli. The trial had been big news. *Any* legitimate connection to the infamous Fannelli brothers over the years was big news.

And so, finally breaking her silence months after her acquittal, Kelly Blaine agreed to one—and only one—interview. She chose *The Joan Parsons Show*. Every single American would be watching. Perhaps none with more vested interest than Amy Lambert and Domino Taylor.

Montgomery County, Pennsylvania

Cell phone balanced between her chin and shoulder, Amy Lambert uncorked the bottle of Chardonnay and poured herself a glass. "You're not going to make me drink alone for this, are you?" she said into her cell.

"Not a chance," Domino Taylor replied on the other end. "Got a bottle of Belvedere in the freezer just begging to be cracked."

Amy looked at the digital clock on her microwave. 2:45. *The Joan Parsons Show* began at 3:00. "Better get cracking then. I don't know about you, but I'd like to have a buzz going before it starts."

Domino chuckled. "Twist my arm."

Amy heard him begin to busy himself on the other end. The clink of ice cubes in a glass. The satisfied gasp after the first sip.

"Atta boy," she said.

"Where are the kids?" he asked.

"After-school playdates. Figured it was best if they were out of the house when I watched. Caleb would have probably been oblivious to it, but you know Carrie—little pitchers and then some."

Domino chuckled again. Then another little gasp after a sip followed by a grunt and a long sigh, the unmistakable sounds of a man Domino's size taking a seat on the sofa.

Amy did the same, took the remote from the coffee table and turned to the proper channel. On the screen was a less-than-reputable daytime talk show, where a young woman sat between two young men, the caption at the bottom of the screen reading something about waiting on the results of a paternity test to see who was the real father. Amy hit mute but still kept a shameless eye on it as she spoke.

"Think you'll recognize her?" she asked.

"Kelly? Of course."

"You know they're gonna have her done up like a victim, right? An angel even?"

"And that's why we're drinking."

Amy smiled. "Call you when it's over."

.   .   .

Amy was on her second glass of Chardonnay when the show began. The hour-long segment was to be devoted entirely to Kelly Blaine, though Amy would have bet the remaining bottle of wine (and she did *not* like to part with her wine, thank you) that she—along with Domino, Monica, and those delightful douchebags, the Fannelli brothers—would be getting a few shout-outs too. Maybe even Monica's psycho dad, John Brooks. Hooray.

Commercial over, and here we go. Close-up of Joan Parsons first, dressed in her classiest no-nonsense garb, her straight blonde hair healthy and vibrant, teeth impossibly white and impossibly straight, fifty-year-old skin looking closer to thirty (something that Joan had always laughably credited to nothing but clean living and consistent hydration).

"She was a troubled little girl that bad luck seemed to follow her entire life. That bad luck would come to a terrifying head when, at only sixteen years of age, Kelly Blaine would meet serial killer Monica Kemp, sister to the infamous mass murderers Arthur and James Fannelli. What would transpire after that for Kelly Blaine was, quite simply, the things of nightmares. Kelly, thank you for being here with us today."

Quick cut and there she was. Kelly Blaine. Amy's first reaction was shock, specifically at her attractive yet modest girl-next-door appearance. Deliberate, no doubt. She was playing the victim, after all, but…

But what, Amy? Were you expecting a confident knockout like Monica? Amy's knowledge of Kelly came from Domino and what she'd read in the news or what she'd seen in court. She had not spent the "quality time" with Kelly that she had with Monica and the Fannelli brothers. Thus today it was as though Amy were seeing Kelly Blaine for the first time, and the innocence the girl was projecting threw her.

Yes, she *had* been expecting a Monica Junior—gorgeous, arrogant, looking like the cunning assassin she was. Kelly Blaine (again, no doubt deliberate on the part of the producers) looked every bit the antithesis of Monica. She *did* look like a victim.

But isn't that what Domino had told Amy on more than one occasion? That what made Kelly so dangerous was how innocuous she appeared? Those big brown eyes? That long brown hair that occasionally (deliberately?) fell over those big brown eyes to mask what truly lay within? That diminutive stature (she couldn't have been more than five-two and a hundred and ten pounds)? That seemingly docile way she carried herself, almost as though she were incapable of even a modest shout?

"Thank you," Kelly said.

"What made you decide to finally break your silence so long after the trial, Kelly?"

Kelly shifted in her seat, looking uncomfortable. *Real or an act?* Amy wondered.

"I wanted to tell my side of the story, I suppose," Kelly said.

Joan Parsons nodded with an understanding and nurturing face. No mystery to that bullshit display. If you asked Amy, Joan Parsons was just as much a psychopath as little Kelly there, each about as equipped with compassion for anyone but themselves as they were equipped with a penis.

"You feel that despite being acquitted on all counts, there are still many who believe you are guilty," Joan said.

"To an extent, I *am* guilty," Kelly said. "I *did* do many of those terrible things I was accused of."

"And you've never claimed otherwise, have you?"

"No. But I have always claimed that I wasn't myself at the time. Monica Kemp's influence was very strong. She abused me both physically and mentally on a daily basis. When I disobeyed, the punishment was…" She paused, head down, long dark hair hanging over her eyes. Her mask.

Joan Parsons handed Kelly a tissue. Kelly took it and dabbed at her eyes, raised her head, and took a deep, steadying breath.

"Are you okay?" Joan asked.

"Yes." She cleared her throat. "When I disobeyed, I was severely punished. She burned my parents alive and made me watch."

The audience gasped. One woman could be heard crying out.

"After that, I don't know, I guess I just broke. I became numb… like a zombie."

Joan put a hand to her chest and shook her head.

"All the things I did after that," Kelly continued, "helping Monica abduct Ben Jane and Domino Taylor, assisting in their torture in the Pine Barrens…I never denied doing any of that. I just pleaded my case and hoped that the jury would understand that I was a sixteen-year-old girl who was brainwashed by a psychopath."

Joan Parsons leaned in and put a hand on Kelly's knee. "Well, the jury *did* understand." Hand still on Kelly's knee, Joan then turned her head toward the audience. "Kelly was acquitted on all charges."

The crowd applauded as though they were hearing this news for the first time.

Kelly smiled. It lingered too long. A cat with the canary if there ever was one. "Better reel that in, girl," Amy said.

As if hearing Amy, Kelly immediately dropped her head and let her long brown hair fall over her eyes again.

Amy downed the last of her wine in a gulp. "Good kitty."

·   ·   ·

The middle of the show was surprisingly tame for a Joan Parsons gig. Kelly kept playing the woe-is-me card, the it-was-all-mean-old-Monica's-fault card.

The murder of seventeen-year-old Devon Haye in the Hamptons?

Monica did it.

The murder of Stephanie Sands, Vice Chairman of the Board of Directors at Stratton Grove Youth Ranch for Girls?

Monica did it, then framed me for it. It's how she initially blackmailed me to obey her. Woe is me.

The charred remains of the three Russian men found in the ruins of Monica's "House of Horrors" in the Pine Barrens?

Monica did it. Well, Domino Taylor killed them, but he had no choice. They were trying to kill him on Monica's orders. It was self-defense.

And speaking of that "House of Horrors," why did you burn it down, Kelly?

I finally came to my senses. I was trying to save Domino and Ben. Setting it on fire was all I could think of in my addled state.

When Monica left the blazing scene in the Pine Barrens and sped toward Amy Lambert's home with the intention of killing her?

I knew absolutely nothing about that. I was busy hiding in the freezing cold woods, praying Monica wouldn't find me. I was so relieved to hear that Amy Lambert had survived and actually managed to kill Monica instead.

("Fucking right I did," Amy had muttered during that segment).

And when Domino Taylor tracked you down six months later, only to bring you into custody, despite you trying to save his life?

He was trying to do the right thing, I guess. I don't know. I only wished he realized I was trying to save him.

Amy had groaned during that one. She bet her remaining bottle of wine she had chilling in the fridge that Domino had groaned too.

More and more of the same. Monica did it. Woe is me.

Then it got good.

Joan Parsons finally unsheathed her claws for what was to be the final segment: someone from Kelly Blaine's past was about to make a guest appearance.

CHAPTER 3

Philadelphia, Pennsylvania

Domino sipped his Belvedere Vodka and ice, equally as unamused as Amy had been during most of the show thus far. Kelly was playing the martyr. Not surprising, really. He'd expected it. The bullshit about setting the "House of Horrors" on fire in order to save him and Ben Jane had made him laugh out loud. At least that was amusing. Domino knew better. Kelly Blaine was a murderous psychopath. Monica Kemp was a murderous psychopath. People like that, despite any similarities they may share in horrific needs and desires, will ultimately clash. Too many cooks in the kitchen and all that.

Except Monica was a badass.

Kelly was, for lack of a better term…what? A junior badass? No. He and Amy had often talked about Kelly and Monica in the same breath. Was Kelly a Monica Junior? No. Monica was highly trained. A lethal assassin in addition to being a raving whacko. But Kelly? Amy had once asked whether Kelly had the potential of Monica. Sure, Domino had replied without much thought. Not the training, but the potential? Sure. The desire—that impulse that drives the sick minds of the world—was there. Perhaps Kelly even had the potential to *surpass* Monica. Doubtful, but possible. The urge for atrocity was certainly not in short supply. And the need for self-gratification at all costs was paramount.

Still, Domino could do nothing but laugh at her claims of innocence, of being under bad old Monica's influence—he'd had a front-row seat to it all back in the Pine Barrens. Had seen it in the girl's eyes. Yes, Monica had manipulated her, abused her, and turned her into a marionette, but hadn't he seen satisfaction in the puppet's eyes when she was carrying out those terrible deeds on him and Ben Jane back in the Pines? Satisfaction and *delight*? Kelly would never be content to dangle beneath the strings of Monica forever, this Domino knew surer than his pulse, and so the fire Kelly set—their ironic savior—had certainly not been an attempt to save him and Ben, but a big middle finger to Monica. A *fuck you, lady; think you can out-crazy me? I'll show you crazy.*

And she had, hadn't she? Pound for pound, Monica beats Kelly a million times out of a million, but that night Kelly had pulled the upset. How?

By being Kelly, a voice inside his head whispered, sending a finger of ice down his back. Wasn't that Kelly's way? The beautiful little flower somewhere deep in the remote jungles of the Amazon, so harmless and unobtrusive, until it brushes against you unnoticed, getting its venom deep inside you. And then what? Two days later you're dead. But how? And when and where? Certainly it wasn't the harmless flower. Never the flower.

Christ.

Domino shook the thought away, actually said "fuck you" out loud, and took a deep pull from his glass of vodka. "You were Monica's bitch, kid," he said to the TV. "Nothing more."

Joan Parsons readied her bombshell.

"Kelly, one of your most outspoken critics, perhaps *the* most outspoken critic, has been Kevin Lane, a former employee at Stratton Grove." Joan turned toward the audience. "For those who don't know, Kelly had been under Kevin Lane's watchful eye at Stratton Grove for the five years she was there." Back to Kelly. "Kelly, during the trial, you, along with a few other girls from Stratton Grove, testified that Kevin Lane demonstrated multiple acts of sexual misconduct during your tenure there."

"That's right."

"Yet, in a somewhat unprecedented series of events, these facts only came to light *after* Mr. Lane had taken the stand on behalf of the prosecution, testifying to what he believed to be your guilt after spending such an extended period of time as one of your primary counselors."

Ah! Domino thought. *Was that a slight curl of disgust I just saw flash on your upper lip, Kelly? The world probably missed it, but not me.*

"Are you asking me a question?" Kelly asked.

"Why weren't the allegations of sexual abuse brought forth at the beginning of the trial?"

"What does it matter?"

Domino grinned. *Keep chopping away, Joan baby.*

"Mr. Lane has since claimed that the allegations were brought forth simply out of spite after his testimony. An attempt to ruin his career."

"It did ruin his career." Quick flash of satisfaction from Kelly. Again, likely missed by all, but Domino was trained to spot micro-expressions on a mannequin. He shook his head with a dry chuckle. Evil little bitch.

"Why do you suppose the judge allowed your newfound accusation in the middle of the trial?" Joan asked. "It's my understanding the prosecution went berserk over it."

Kelly shrugged.

And there's that quick flash of satisfaction again. If Kevin Lane is watching this—and Kevin Lane IS watching this—he must be spitting up bile by now.

"I don't know. I'm not a judge," Kelly said.

Joan sat upright in her seat. Adjusted her attire. Addressed Kelly but kept her eyes on the audience. "Well, Kelly, we have Kevin Lane standing by on live feed right now…"

Domino nearly choked on his vodka, leaned forward with a grin, and blurted: "*Oh shit!*"

"…He would very much like to tell his side of the story and has promised to keep things civil. You have *every right* to decline, but if your goal here today is to tell your story and clear your name, this might be something you might want to consider. Are you willing to have Mr. Lane join us?"

She'll say yes. With her ego? It would be too damn fun to pass up.

Kelly actually smiled. Small and short but ever present.

And that, Domino thought, *was as genuine a smile as they come.*

Kelly was finally going to get a little action. Her psychopathic impulses had been under lock and key with the trial and media all over her these past two years. An ungodly itch she'd been desperate to scratch. Seeing poor Kevin Lane—long since fired from the job he loved, long since a pariah in his once harmonious community—plead his case would be more than enough temporary freedom to have a go at that itch. And on nationwide TV no less.

She'll say yes.

"Yes," Kelly said.

CHAPTER 4

The second the commercial break started, Amy phoned Domino.

"*Are you watching this?*" she blurted.

"I knew she'd say yes."

Amy frowned. "It's gonna turn into a shit show. She's got that whole audience sympathizing with her, and now she's going to risk blowing it by allowing them to bring on some guy with a vendetta against her? It makes no sense."

"She couldn't resist. A chance to see this man rant and cry and plead, no, scratch that, a chance for the *world* to see this man rant and cry and plead? She couldn't pass that up."

"I never followed up on this Kevin Lane guy after the trial," Amy said. "Was Kelly right? Was his career ruined?"

"Yep. Lost his job at Stratton Grove and hasn't been able to find work in his field since."

"But it's *alleged*," Amy said. "All the things Kelly and her classmates claimed. That hasn't gone to court yet."

"It doesn't matter what any future trial is going to say, Ames. In today's society, simply being *accused* of something like that is as good as any guilty verdict. Enough to ruin any man."

Amy thought about it for a second. Domino was right. Society can forgive all kinds of things in time, even alleged murder. But a sex offense? That was something altogether different. Whether you were found guilty or not, once the accusation was out there, it became a stain, impossible to scrub away. Kelly Blaine knew how to destroy this man without ever laying a finger on him. Had she once thought herself wrong for expecting Kelly to look like Monica? Yes. And she *was* wrong. Outwardly, the two appeared very different. *But if we cracked the shells, took a look inside...* "They could be twins," she whispered.

"Huh?"

Amy came to and shook the thought away. "Nothing. Sorry."

"It's about to come back on," Domino said. "Call you after?"

"Wanna stay on and watch together?"

"You mean like high school sweethearts do?"

"Forget it."

Domino laughed. "You need more wine."

"I wish. Figured it best Mommy wasn't slurry when the kids came home."

The show came back on.

"You staying on or not, dreamboat?" Amy asked.

"I'm staying, Peggy Sue."

•　　　•　　　•

"We're joined now by Kevin Lane, former head counselor and teacher at Stratton Grove Youth Ranch for Girls. Kevin, thank you for joining us."

Kevin Lane appeared on the studio's giant screen for all to see. Once a fit and attractive man, Kevin Lane now looked exceptionally thin and tired.

Amy: "He looks awful."

Domino: "Probably hasn't been able to eat or sleep since Kelly ruined him."

"Believe me," Kevin Lane said, "it's my pleasure."

"Are you surprised Kelly gave her approval for you to be joining us today?" Joan asked.

"Curious, not surprised."

"Curious, how?"

"Kelly *always* has an ulterior motive. I just can't figure out what this one is yet."

A murmur from the audience. Kelly remained stoic.

Domino: "Smart dude."

Amy: "He spent five years watching her. Probably knows her better than anyone."

Domino grunted in agreement.

"Kevin, what have you been doing since the trial? Are you teaching again?"

"No, I am not. I haven't been able to find work in the field I love since Kelly's accusations."

Joan gave a theatric shift in her chair. "Well, it wasn't just Kelly's accusations, though, was it? Three more girls from Stratton Grove eventually came forward."

Kevin Lane laughed. "If the jury knew Kelly Blaine like I did, you'd know the testimonies from those three girls held about as much water as a colander."

Domino chuckled.

"Care to elaborate?" Joan said.

"It's simple. The testimonies of the three girls were coerced."

"By Kelly?"

"She was certainly behind it. I'm not sure how she did it, but she did."

Murmurs from the audience again.

"You're saying Kelly tracked down three former students from Stratton Grove and…what? Strong-armed them into giving false testimonies under oath?"

"That's exactly what I'm saying."

"I'm sorry, Mr. Lane, I hope you'll forgive me when I say that this accusation seems far more fitting for your colander analogy."

Kevin Lane leaned in closer to the screen, the bags under his eyes more pronounced. It was evident he hadn't shaved today.

"No apology necessary. Why should you think differently than anyone else? This is who Kelly Blaine is; this is what she does. Everyone at Stratton Grove was terrified of that girl. And these were tough kids, street kids. Stratton Grove was their last shot at flying straight. They did *not* scare easy."

Domino: "She's loving this."

"Be that as it may," Joan said, "I still don't see how she could have gotten three girls, long since left Stratton Grove, to give those testimonies."

"Of course you don't. No one does. Including me. But she did it. She got to those girls somehow and told them what to say or else. And they did. Those girls were so frightened of Kelly Blaine that they were willing to lie under oath. Destroy my career—"

"You destroyed your own career." Kelly's first words since Kevin Lane came on. She spoke them calmly and succinctly.

Amy: "Oh shit."

Domino: "It was killing her to keep quiet."

"You *know* I didn't," Kevin Lane said. "*You know it!*"

"Mr. Lane," Joan said, "please lower your voice. I would like to conduct the remainder of our show with as much civility as—"

"Accidentally walking in on us during the precise time we were undressing?" Kelly said. "Groping us in those oh-so-subtle ways you pawned off as being nothing but friendly and harmless whenever we complained? Spying on us as we showered?" She turned toward the audience. "Do you know he actually drilled a hole in the communal shower's outer wall?"

The audience gasped.

"You have no proof," Kevin Lane said. "None. *Zero.* All you have is conjecture. This hole you said I drilled? Where is it? My attorney has since been to Stratton Grove. He found no such makeshift hole in the communal shower's outer wall."

Kelly shrugged. Gave a subtle scratch of her nose with her middle finger.

Domino: "Ha. She just flipped him off."

Amy: "Huh?"

"*Do you know she killed her older brother?*" Kevin Lane's blurt had the impact of a train. For a brief moment, it was as though the entire audience had been muted. Never at a loss for words, even Joan Parsons herself could only stare and watch.

Domino and Amy together: "*Oh shit.*"

"I did not kill my brother."

"You burned him alive. It's why you were sent to Stratton Grove. Even your own parents thought you did it. We could ask them, but you know, they're dead too. Also burned alive. Quite a coincidence, wouldn't you say?"

Joan Parsons finally found her voice. "Mr. Lane, I think—"

"Do you know *why* she killed her brother? Because he caught her smoking and told on her. That's it. That's all he did to warrant being burned to death. Her own brother."

"My brother was the one smoking," Kelly said. Her voice began to crack. "I would never..." She dropped her head, long brown hair falling forward. "I loved my brother so much." She wiped at her eyes. Joan Parsons handed her a tissue. Kelly took it. "I would never..." Her voice cracked again.

Joan Parsons leaned in and put a hand on Kelly's shoulder. "It's okay," she said.

"Cry me a river," Kevin Lane said on the big screen.

Joan flashed a look of contempt his way. "I think we're done here today, Mr. Lane. Thank you for your time."

"You'll see," Kevin said. "One day, you'll all see that I was right. How about you have me back on the show when that crazy little bitch is behind bars, Joan? What do you say to—"

The screen went black. The audience whispered nervously to one another.

Kelly eventually raised her head, sniffling and dabbing at her eyes with the tissue.

"Are you okay?" Joan asked.

Kelly nodded. Took a deep breath. "I just—he knew it would get to me."

"Mentioning your brother?"

Kelly nodded again. "He knew how much my brother's death upset me from our time back at Stratton Grove. He said it deliberately, just to upset me. He did it all the time back at Stratton Grove."

Joan gave a practiced tilt of the head to project deep sympathy. "There are always going to be detractors, Kelly. Those who will always believe you are guilty, no matter what. But *you* know the truth, and the jury *saw* that truth. Monica Kemp, you are *not*."

The audience applauded.

Kelly did not seem grateful.

Domino: "*Ooh*—she didn't like that."

Amy: "What?"

Domino: "That comment about Monica."

Amy: "Why?"

Domino: "Ego. I promise you, what Kelly just heard was 'Monica Kemp is better than you.'"

Amy: "You think?"

Domino: "I know. Still, the show couldn't have gone any better for her. Kelly let the world see Kevin Lane for the man he isn't. Poor guy didn't stand a chance."

Amy: "Think she really killed her brother?"

CHAPTER 5

Kelly Blaine asked for a treehouse when she was eight. She got a dollhouse instead. Earlier that year, her ten-year-old brother Kyle had asked for a treehouse, and their father promptly went to work, not building one himself, no—the only dirt the Blaines got on their hands came from money—but calling contractors to come and build an impressive little dwelling, high up on a massive oak within their vast wooded property.

Kelly's response to this had been to remove the small glass panes that were the tiny windows in her dollhouse, grind them into a near dust, and then mix them in with her father's tapioca he ritually had every evening following dinner. Conrad Blaine was later rushed to the ER with intense stomach pains. The culprit was soon found—the pulverized glass—and a lawsuit against the tapioca company was instantly filed. The result was a tidy sum, a lifetime supply of tapioca, and the beginnings of Kelly Blaine's realization, at the ripe age of eight, that God either didn't exist, or He simply didn't care what she got up to.

Either way was fine with her.

.   .   .

Kelly first tried smoking when she was ten, liked it, and habitually used her brother's beloved treehouse to indulge her habit when he was due home late from basketball practice.

Today practice had been cancelled, and Kyle Blaine ascended the long wooden ladder to his treehouse to discover his eleven-year-old sister smoking a cigarette and drinking a soda.

"*What are you doing?*"

Kelly immediately dropped the cigarette butt into her soda can and fanned the smoke away. "What's the big deal?"

"You're *smoking?*"

Kelly rolled her eyes. "I was just trying it."

"Do you know how bad smoking is for you?"

"So?"

"I'm telling Mom and Dad."

Kelly stood. "Big fucking surprise."

"I'm telling them you swore too."

"You are such a baby. I guess that's why you're so little."

Kyle Blaine, thirteen, had yet to hit puberty. His size had become a sore spot when the friends around him seemingly grew inches by the day, started growing hair where there hadn't previously been, and spoke with deeper voices. Kyle was often mistaken for Kelly when he answered the telephone.

Kyle stomped forward, boards beneath them creaking. "Look who's talking!" He placed a hand on his sister's head.

Kelly swatted his hand away. "I'm a girl, I'm supposed to be small. But you...you're going to be a little fucking pussy the rest of your life."

Tears welled up in Kyle's eyes. He began to stammer, a habit that happened to him under times of stress. "*I-I-I-I'm telling M-M-Mom and D-Dad.*"

Kelly grinned, steepling her hands beneath her chin as though praying in fear. "*Oh, puh-puh-puh-please don't t-t-t-tell.*"

Kyle lunged forward and shoved her. Kelly flew back and hit the wall of the treehouse, stumbled, and fell into the wooden table of books next to her, one of two stone gargoyle bookends dropping to the floor with a heavy thud.

Kyle turned to leave. Kelly rose behind him. Hoisted the stone gargoyle overhead with both hands…

.   .   .

Her older brother unconscious at her feet, Kelly knew she had to work fast. Fortunately, she knew what worked and what didn't when it came to starting a good quick fire. She had no gasoline or other extreme accelerants, but then she wouldn't have used them if she did have them. She'd read in her favorite book at school that fires caused by such extreme accelerants were not difficult to detect in the ensuing investigation. It needed to look as though Kyle died from trying to smoke cigarettes in his treehouse, the careless boy.

So what to do? Kelly had found over the years that the minimal amount of lighter fluid in a cheap lighter was more than enough to get a good blaze going under the right conditions. And a wooden treehouse containing plenty of books and magazines was *ideal*.

Kelly snapped off the top of her plastic lighter and sprinkled the fluid evenly over her brother's unconscious body. She placed her pack of cigarettes next to him along with her soda can filled with cigarette butts. Took a step back and pulled a pack of matches from her pocket.

Common sense told her to run the moment her brother went up. She needed an alibi. But she could not resist watching, if just for a short while. Not to mention the prospect of her brother regaining consciousness to find himself burning alive was far too enticing to pass up. Besides, he might somehow manage to escape his predicament, in which case she would need to whack him another one with the stone gargoyle bookend.

And she was right.

With the match lit and dropped, her brother was soon engulfed in flames, the flames then waking him. He began screeching wildly, slapping frantically at the growing blaze that was cooking his skin.

So Kelly whacked him another one. And he went out. And Kyle Blaine lay there on his treehouse floor and burned to death.

.   .   .

Kelly Blaine's neighbor three doors down was more a convenience than a friend. Jenny Hayward, though twelve years old, read at a first-grade level, and it was not for lack of trying. She was simply not equipped with the ability to process or comprehend the way other kids were at her age. She made up for this in spirit and compassion and was considerably well-liked among her peers, but to Kelly Blaine, Jenny Hayward was a sometimes-useful tool, nothing more.

Today her tool would be playing the role of alibi-confirmer.

"What are we watching?" Kelly said as she strolled into Jenny's living room with a big smile.

Jenny sat bolt upright on the sofa, eyes wide and fixed on Kelly. "What are you doing here?"

Kelly gave a silly little frown. "You *told* me to come."

Jenny's brow scrunched, trying to make sense of it. "I did?"

Both of Jenny Hayward's parents worked. After school, her seventeen-year-old brother watched her. Her seventeen-year-old brother who hardly ever left his bedroom. Kelly had counted on this.

Kelly laughed. "Are you okay?"

Jenny nodded, though her dazed expression suggested she was still trying to process it all. "I don't remember…"

"You told me to come over right after school so we could hang out. You really don't remember?"

Jenny gave an uncertain nod. "Yeah, I guess I do. How did you get in?"

"Your brother let me in. If you don't believe me, we can go ask him."

"*No.* No, that's okay." Perhaps the one person who did *not* share an affinity for Jenny Hayward was her own brother. Kelly had counted on this too. That and the kid smoked a mountain of marijuana, immediately casting speculation on anything that might come out of his mouth in the near future.

"So, if anyone were to ask, you would tell them I came over right after school, right, Jenny?"

Jenny nodded.

Kelly smiled and took a seat next to her. Sirens sounded in the distance. Kelly took the remote from the coffee table and turned up the volume.

The back lot of the Joan Parsons Show, Burbank, California

Autumn 2012

"Miss Blaine?" the chauffeur driver called, holding the limo's door open for her.

Kelly, smoking a cigarette near the back door of the studio, lost in the pleasant memory of her brother's death, snapped from her daze and nodded toward the chauffeur. She took a hard and final drag on her cigarette, turned, and flicked it towards the studio. The pleasant recall of her brother was now completely gone, replaced with something that had been needling her since the moment it was spoken.

Monica Kemp, you are not.

CHAPTER 6

Allan Brown could make eggs, all kinds. He could flip a mean pancake. Cook bacon and sausage blindfolded. Toast? Please. He even knew to cut it at angles to make it somehow taste better. He was a master at the breakfast arts.

When it was just him and the girls.

Him and the girls and four of their friends the morning after a sleepover? He was a day-one white belt in the breakfast dojo.

Not that he didn't try. The trick wasn't cooking the food itself; the trick was cooking the food and having all of it ready at the same time. Pancakes went cold. Toast got burnt. The forecast for eggs sunny-side-up was way off. He never even made it to bacon and sausage.

Turning his back on a kitchen countertop littered with culinary atrocities, he smiled apologetically at the table of hungry little faces and threw a Hail Mary.

"Who wants McDonald's?" he asked.

The table cheered, and relief nearly buckled Allan's knees. And then just as fast, never once giving him a moment without painful reflection, grief slowly dissolved his smile and reminded him that his wife, Samantha, would have handled this morning effortlessly—and happily.

.   .   .

The last of the sleepover girls finally dropped off, Allan would have sold a toe for a nap.

"Daddy?"

Allan looked in the rearview mirror and caught his daughter Jamie's eye. "What's up, honey?"

"Are we still sleeping at Aunt Kat's tonight?"

"Yup—Daddy's hosting that thing tonight, remember?"

Jamie's twin sister, Janine, chimed in. "Why can't we come?"

"Because it's for grownups only, kiddos. Sorry."

"We'll stay in our room," Jamie said.

"What's going on with you guys? I thought you loved sleeping over at Aunt Kat's."

A unanimous but hardly enthusiastic: "We do."

"Would you rather stay with Mr. and Mrs. Rolston next door?"

"No."

"So then what's going on?"

Neither sister responded.

Allan came upon a residential area and rolled his SUV to a stop. He turned in his seat. Both kids looked as if they were on the way to the dentist. "Okay, what's going on with you two?"

Jamie asked: "Is tonight's thing about Mommy again?"

Allan felt the familiar burn in his chest. It would have been nice to blame it on the McDonald's he'd just eaten; that could be fixed quickly with a few TUMS. No TUMS were quick-fixing this.

"It's not really about Mommy," he said. "It's about the thing that made Mommy pass away."

"Cancer?" Janine said.

Allan nodded.

"Did all the people going tonight know someone who died from cancer?"

Allan nodded again. "It helps us to all get together and talk like we do. It's therapeutic."

"What's that?" Jamie asked.

"Therapeutic? It means something that helps you heal. The more Daddy can talk about Mommy, the less sad he'll be."

Jamie pulled a face, a confused, frowny expression. The same expression he'd seen countless times on his wife when trying to convince her the appeal of Western movies or a man's need for a cave in his home. Parallels like this between his girls and his late wife were frequent, their impact always forcing him to take a moment to regroup. His therapist said the frequencies of these parallels would increase as the girls aged, as their personalities and nuances (those were the toughest, the nuances; the little things like the confused, frowny face now) were unavoidably cultivated with his wife's DNA.

His therapist had said the parallels would increase yet his ability to cope would grow stronger, his ultimate goal being the ability to, one day, recognize a trait of his wife in one of his girls and experience a pleasant nostalgia for what he'd once had. Stark, stark contrast to what he experienced now: the desire to break down and sob in front of his girls, share their excusable naivety in asking *why?* over and over until his voice quit.

"Talking about Mommy makes you feel *better*?" Jamie said. "I get *sad* when I talk about Mommy."

"Me too," Janine added.

"I know you do. That's why Daddy's thing tonight is just for grownups. Someday you'll understand that sharing your sadness with others can sometimes help."

"Therapeutic," Jamie said.

Allan smiled and tapped her knee. "Bingo," he said, feeling an odd mix of pride and sorrow at his daughter's retention at the expense of her mother's passing.

"So my Deejays all good in the 'hood then?" he asked in a painfully lame attempt at sounding like one of the many teen hip-hop idols they worshipped.

"Eww, Dad, stop," Janine said.

"I will *never* stop calling you my Deejays." His Deejays, short for "double-J's," itself short for "Janine and Jamie," had been proudly branded as such (at least from Allan; Samantha could only roll her eyes and smile helplessly) the moment he and Samantha had chosen the names for their twin girls.

"No," Janine said, "you need to stop talking like you think you're cool."

"Ouch." Allan turned back in his seat and started up the car again. "Don't be player hatin', girlfriends." Was that a thing? *Player hatin'? Girlfriends?* It sounded like something. His lameness was embarrassing even to him. But he had ulterior motives. And as soon as his Deejays started to giggle and mock their dorky dad, his ulterior motive for some serious levity at his own expense had come to fruition.

Allan pulled up to a stop sign and locked eyes with his girls in the rearview. After a quick huddle of whispers and giggles, both sisters made the letter *L* with their thumbs and index fingers and slapped them on their foreheads for their father to see—the classic "loser" gesture that even Allan knew.

"*What?!*" he cried playfully.

Janine and Jamie started laughing hysterically. Allan managed to maintain his flabbergasted expression even though he was grinning inside. He hit the accelerator and started through the stop sign, only to jam on the brakes as the car to his right blew right through its own sign.

"*FUCK!*"

Everyone sat frozen in the big SUV for a moment: Allan's right arm extended across the passenger seat, instinctively bracing what would have been his wife; the girls in the back seat, wide eyed and open mouthed.

Everyone slowly thawed, and Allan turned in his seat again. "You girls okay?"

Both girls nodded, but were now clearly stifling giggles.

"Oh, that was funny to you, was it? Another car nearly smashes into us and—*ohhh*…it was because Daddy said a bad word, wasn't it?"

The girls could no longer contain their giggles. Allan shook his head and started for home again. "You girls know you should never use that word, right?"

"Not until we're older," Janine said.

"Not ever."

There was no intersection at the next stop sign for assholes to blow through, so when Allan saw the police car with its flashing blue and red in his rearview shortly after, his initial thought was that the cop was pulling him over to get details on the jerk who'd all but killed them. Make of the car, what he looked like. Perhaps the guy outran the police and now they were stuck with Allan's eyewitness account to catch the bastard.

Nope.

"License and registration, please."

Allan did as such. "What's the problem, Officer?" he asked. It felt weird out of his mouth. Like a line in a movie.

The officer took his registration and license without a word and went back to his cruiser.

"Daddy, what happened?" Janine asked.

Allan, without a sprinkle of sugarcoating because he too was in the dark, answered honestly: "I have no idea."

The cop returned and handed Allan his license and registration back.

"Do you know why I pulled you over?" the cop asked.

"Honestly?" Allan began. "I figured it was because of that guy before me. The guy who blew through the stop sign at the intersection back there."

The cop carried on as if Allan had said nothing. "I pulled you over because you didn't bring your vehicle to a complete stop at that last stop sign."

It was out of Allan's mouth before he could leash it. "Are you *kidding* me?"

"No, sir, I'm not. You should always bring your vehicle to a complete three-second halt at a stop sign before proceeding. You rolled right on through in less than one."

"And what about the guy who almost killed us a few minutes ago?"

"I'm sorry?"

Allan relayed the tale.

"Well, I'm sorry, sir, I didn't spot him. Only you."

Allan forced a smile. "All right, all right—I'm sorry, Officer. It won't happen again."

The cop handed Allan a ticket. "Please be more careful next time, sir—" He gestured in back toward the girls. "You're driving for three, you know."

Allan's anger was all but cartoon steam shooting from his ears. The sarcastic contempt in his reply was unavoidable. "Yes, Officer, I am well aware of my children, thank you. That's why I was telling you about the guy who—"

The officer turned his back on Allan and returned to his cruiser.

"*Asshole*," Allan said through clenched teeth before realizing it would result in another round of giggles from the back.

Except it didn't. The girls seemed to realize the unfairness of the situation too and, if given permission, would have happily labeled the officer and the situation an asshole as well. Maybe even a *fucking* asshole now that Daddy had increased their vocabulary. And at this stage in the game, Daddy might have even applauded them for it.

The process over, Allan all but tiptoed his SUV back home. Each stop sign and light was met with a good *five*-second pause, despite a honk or two from behind. The scales of justice were anything but horizontal today. Every day. Every damn day for the past two years.

Vertical, they were. The bastards were vertical.

CHAPTER 7

Allan pulled the SUV into his garage, killed the engine, and caught the girls just as they were ready to dart from the car. "Wait!"

Both girls froze, each with a foot already out their passenger door.

"Daddy said two bad words back there. He was wrong."

"Tell it to the swear jar," Janine said.

Allan chuckled. "I will." He then raised the ticket the cop had given him. "But we may just need to empty it in order to pay for this."

"You said we could use that money for bowling!" Jamie whined.

Landmark Lanes, a nearby spot that was a waking dream for every kid (bowling, laser tag, arcade games, good junk food) and equally so for every honest adult (bowling, laser tag, arcade games, good junk food), was not something he was about to deny his kids (or himself; the blessed place had a bar too).

"Don't worry, we're still going to Landmark."

The girls, pleased with their father's flip-flop, went to dash away again.

"Wait!"

They returned, both simultaneously huffing their impatience.

He had nothing to say. Well, that wasn't true; he had lots to say, but at that precise moment he didn't know how. Sometimes it was easier to look and love and hope they felt it.

"Daddy?" Janine said.

"Yeah?"

"You're getting that weird look again."

"What weird look?"

"Like you're going to ask us for a hug or a kiss or something."

He laughed. "I'll get my fill tonight while you're asleep."

"Can't," Janine proclaimed triumphantly, "we'll be at Aunt Kat's!"

Allan looked away for a moment, suddenly remembering something. "That reminds me; I need to call her and—"

The sound of two car doors slamming shut cut him off. The girls were already entering the house through the garage entrance.

He laughed again and followed them in.

•   •   •

When Allan entered, both girls were already stationed in front of the TV. Bellies down, hands under chins, lower legs wagging back and forth like cats' tails, concentrations unbreakable from their latest teen heartthrob, whom Allan couldn't even identify because they changed so often (in name only; to Allan, they were all skinny hair helmets that he would snap in two if they came near his daughters). Of course, the girls being only nine years old, this had yet to be an issue. But the day *would* come when a kid like that would be ringing his doorbell, wanting to take one of his babies out. And he'd answer that door wearing a not-quite-right smile and a red-spackled "NRA for Life" T-shirt.

Oh, how he loathed ruminating over stuff like this. He didn't even want to *think* about the day when it was time to have "The Talk." He shuddered. *Best leave that one to Aunt Kat*, he thought.

Aunt Kat. Gotta give her a buzz.

He gave one final look at his oblivious girls, silently warning them to never grow up, and then headed into the kitchen. He took the traffic violation and pinned it to the fridge with a magnet Aunt

Kat herself had given Jamie and Janine. The magnet was a square that held a photo from a few years back

(*when Sam was still alive, had just started chemo*)

with both girls on either side of Aunt Kat, hugging, grinning for the camera,

(*ignorance truly* can *be bliss*)

the frame reading "Aunt Kat and Her Kittens."

And aren't they still *ignorant to a degree, Allan? Much like the dreaded "Talk," would there not come a time when the realization that their mother was gone for good truly hit home and make "The Talk" a cakewalk in comparison?*

He touched a second square magnet that framed a photo, this one of both his girls and himself, a year after Sam was gone. The message on the frame of the magnet was not unlike his sister's. "Dad and His Deejays," it read, the girls grinning and hugging like they did in Kat's picture. But wasn't there a difference? The grins not as broad, the hugs not as tight? Certainly it was no slight on their father. Likely,

(*likely? Almost assuredly*)

the acceptance and understanding of their mother's absence may not have been fully absorbed into the girls then, but the unforgiving process had no doubt begun. And with each passing day, the more they absorbed, the more their ignorance would become diluted, allowing for comprehension and realization and all those super-duper things that would make "The Talk" a cakewalk by comparison. *So much to look forward to.*

Allan kissed his first two fingers and touched the magnet a final time before pulling out his cell phone. He scrolled through his contacts on his cell until he arrived at "Kat," hit send, and waited.

"Hey, bro."

"How's it going?"

"It's going. Yourself?"

"Like an addict: one day at a time."

She laughed. A raspy voice given to her from birth and not bad habits. "Always hold on to the humor, little brother."

"I'm trying. We still good for tonight?"

"Of course. Me and my Kittens are gonna be on the prowl."

"Don't get too crazy, all right? No hard stuff."

"Beer and wine okay?"

"Yeah, they can have beer and wine."

"*What did you say?!*" Janine called from the den.

"Nothing. Go back to your show."

She did.

"It's amazing how selective their hearing is," Allan said.

His sister laughed her raspy laugh.

"Listen, I'm calling because I'm wondering if I can drop them off a little early tonight," he said.

"Of course," she said. "Everything okay?"

"Yeah, absolutely. But you know they had that sleepover last night and the place is still a mess. I need time to tidy without them getting in the way."

"*We won't get in the way!*" Jamie called from the den.

Kat heard Jamie's response and started laughing again.

"Told ya," Allan said. "It's downright creepy. Now watch me tell them to go clean their rooms. I'll bet you a million bucks it takes at *least* three tries before they even blink."

Again the raspy laugh. "Drop them off whenever you want. I'll be here."

"And you're sure you're cool with taking them to school in the morning?"

"Not a problem."

"Thanks, Kat. I'll give you a call from the road to let you know we're on our way."

"Sounds good. Love you."

"Love you too."

Allan hung up. Then, his hypothesis demanding testing, he called into the den: "You guys mind cleaning your rooms?"

Not even the slightest twitch of acknowledgment.

He smiled to himself and headed upstairs.

CHAPTER 8

Montgomery County, Pennsylvania

The landline in the Lambert house rang. Caleb Lambert, nine years old, answered.

"Hello?"

"Who's this?" A deep male voice.

"Who's *this*?" Caleb replied.

"*Caleb!*" Amy Lambert yelled from the kitchen.

Deep, genuine laughter in Caleb's ear now. The boy smiled. He knew the laugh well.

"How's my man?" Domino Taylor asked Caleb.

Amy hurried to the phone and snatched it from Caleb's hand before he could answer. "*Hello?*"

"Good evening, madam," Domino said in playful tones.

Amy's shoulders dropped. She sighed and said: "Okay, it's just you."

"Nice to hear from you too."

Amy shook her head into the phone. "No, no, I'm sorry. I thought Caleb might have been parroting something he heard me say on the phone earlier."

"I don't follow," Domino said.

Amy took a seat at the kitchen table. "Our phone's been blowing up for over a week now. Apparently the scum at *First Peek* want to do a story on the 'five-year anniversary' of what happened at Crescent Lake. They want an exclusive with me. Having an unlisted number in this day and age doesn't amount to shit."

"Caleb wasn't parroting you—I asked 'who's this?' first. We were just playing."

"I know that now. It's just—" Amy made a frustrated little strangled noise. "Do you know they caught me coming out of the supermarket this morning?"

"What?"

"Yep, assholes shoved a camera right in my face. My arms were tied up with groceries, so I was torn between a headbutt or a kick to the nuts."

Domino chuckled, played along. "What did you choose?"

"Sadly, neither—common sense got the better of me. Still, I thought you'd be proud to know your training still syncs nicely with my instincts."

"Indeed I am. How's my little Carrie doing?"

"Not so little. She's getting taller every day. Got her dad's genes."

A pause, as was common between them whenever Patrick was mentioned.

Amy eventually broke it with: "She's got my smart mouth, though, that's for sure. She's going through this 'tween' phase. Everything is 'lame'—Mom being chief of them. If she rolls her eyes or clucks her tongue at me one more time..."

Domino laughed. "And I'm sure you were nothing like that at her age."

"I was an angel."

"So was Satan."

They laughed together now. Good laughter.

"How's the counseling going?" Domino asked. "You still doing the support group thing?"

"Yeah. Got one tonight."

"Where at?"

"Not far."

"Where at?" Domino insisted.

Amy sighed at his overprotectiveness, stood, grabbed the address from her countertop, and read it to him.

"Okay, got it," he said. "Who's watching the kids?"

"Mrs. Flannigan from across the street. You've met her. Nice old Irish lady? Still has a bit of an accent?"

"I remember."

Another brief pause.

"You still telling them Patrick died of cancer?" Domino eventually asked.

"I am, yes. It's a support group for the loss of a loved one. I didn't think the cause was too relevant. I've been able to maintain a decent amount of anonymity these past few years, and I'd like to hold on to it. Although, if the assholes at *First Peek* had their say, my streak would come to an abrupt end."

"It'll die down. Just keep doing your thing."

"I'm trying. When are we going to see you again? Caleb misses his idol."

"Ah hell…"

Amy smiled into the phone. She knew he was blushing. Though the black skin God gave him would have hidden the fact, she knew that, if they were together, she need only press her hand to his cheek and feel its warmth.

"Well?" she said.

"You tell my little man that next weekend we're gonna tear it up at—what's that bowling place y'all go to?"

"Landmark Lanes."

"You tell my little man that next weekend we're gonna tear it up at Landmark Lanes. Carrie too if it's not too 'lame' for her."

"Oh, she loves it there. She pretends she doesn't, but she does."

"Well, then, it's on. I'll be in touch soon. Love you, Ames."

"Love you too."

.   .   .

Domino hung up and stuffed the address Amy had given him into his pocket. He then went into his kitchen and immediately smiled at the photo stuck high and firm to one of his refrigerator doors with a Semper Fi magnet. The photo was a shot of him and Caleb at Dorney Park two summers ago. Caleb perched high on Domino's massive shoulders, grinning, an orange Popsicle dangling in his little hand, Domino's head turned towards the Popsicle, pretending to sneak a huge bite out of it. He remembered right after the shot when Caleb squeaked out a "*Hey!*" and yanked the Popsicle away, and Domino laughing hard enough to shake Caleb on his shoulders, which in turn made Caleb clamp onto Domino's neck for dear life, giggling all the while.

Domino loved Amy and Carrie, would die for them (and very nearly had). But damn if he didn't have a special bond with Caleb, the little bugger.

Domino opened the freezer door and withdrew a frosty bottle of Belvedere. Today was Sunday. Sunday was his drinking day (excluding special occasions like watching crazy Kelly Blaine on *The Joan Parsons Show*, of course). He touched not a drop the remaining six days of the week, but ever since retirement, his routine on Sundays was ironclad. Church. Then the liquor store in neighboring Camden. Then to the sofa where he would plop himself down with a good bottle of vodka, throw on some of his favorite old-school films, start drinking, and then, when he was drunk enough, start talking to Patrick.

CHAPTER 9

Philadelphia, Pennsylvania

Half the bottle of Belvedere was gone. He was buzzed hard, but not drunk. A man Domino's size was not easy to topple with booze. He filled his glass with more vodka and turned off *The Deer Hunter*, one of the current old-school favs of his he'd been watching. He'd clicked it off during the classic Russian roulette scene where the Viet Cong are forcing the captured De Niro and Walken and other U.S. soldiers to play the deadly game against one another. A scene that Domino believed was easily one of the greatest and most intense scenes in cinematic history.

But Patrick deserved his complete attention.

"Spoke to Amy today," Domino said to his empty den. "She's doing good, brother. Healing."

Domino took a healthy sip.

"She's still doing the support group thing. Still telling everyone you died of cancer." He chuckled dryly. "Can't blame her, I guess. She's had decent solitude since moving your brood out there to Montgomery County. I'm sure you've been out that way before. Beautiful in spots. Rural. You'd have loved it, man."

Domino immediately thought of Patrick's love for the rustic outdoors—the very reason Patrick had brought his family to

Crescent Lake some five years ago—and grimaced, taking down the remainder of his vodka in a single gulp. Alcohol allowed him to talk to Patrick, but it also loosened the cap on his tank of guilt. His talks with Patrick were meant to be cathartic, to let him remember the good, not to drown him in fault and sorrow.

He went to his freezer and poured himself another glass. Most Sundays he never finished the whole bottle. Now it was seeming likely.

He flopped back onto the sofa, spilling some vodka on his lap and not caring. "Spoke to Caleb today. Amy called me his idol. I all but cried, man. A good cry, but a bad one, you know? Good because I can be there for him as a male role model throughout his life, but…you know…bad because…" Tears started. His throat began to tighten. He cleared it loudly and wiped his eyes. "Bad because that role model should be you."

His landline rang. Very few had this number. Amy again?

He stood, swayed a little, and made it to the kitchen. Caller ID said it was an unknown number. His drunkenness egged on his curiosity.

"Hello?"

"Is Monica there?" An odd, sexless voice. As if they were using a voice changer.

"What?" Domino's tone was not polite.

"Is Monica there?"

"Who is this?" Like Amy in Montgomery County, Domino had decent solitude in Philadelphia after retirement. Still, what was it Amy had said earlier? Having an unlisted number in this day and age didn't mean shit? Sad but true. But then that would mean this person calling his home knew exactly whom they were calling and, more unsettling, whom they were asking for.

Monica.

Had to be a wrong number.

"I think I've got the wrong number," the caller said.

Domino forced a civil tone. "It's all right."

The caller hung up.

Now his cell phone rang in the den.

Though not as private as his landline, only a small handful of people had his cell number. When it rang, he only expected the odd telemarketer (who rarely phoned back after Domino told them exactly what they could do with whatever they were selling) or someone he knew and trusted.

He went to his den. Like the caller ID for his landline, the one for his cell read it was an unknown number.

"Hello?"

"Is Monica there?" Same odd voice again.

Domino believed in coincidence as much as he did Bigfoot. "What kind of fucking game are you playing?"

They hung up.

His landline rang again. He rushed for it, banging his shin on the coffee table in the process, edging his mood into powder keg territory.

He did not bother to check the caller ID this time. Just snatched the phone from its receiver. "*Who is this?*"

"Is Patrick there?"

Domino's rage nearly flew off its leash at the mere mention of Patrick's name. He found it impossible to reply right away; could only breathe into the phone as he tried to steady himself.

"Why won't you talk to me?" the voice asked.

"Tell me who you are first," he managed.

"Guess."

"Fuck you."

"We can make it fun. Ever play hot and cold?"

Domino took a single deep breath through his nose and let it out slowly, still struggling to control his rage. "I guess who you are, and you say 'hot' or 'cold' depending on how close I am," he eventually said.

"Exactly. Only I don't want you to guess who I am, I want you to guess *where* I am, Mr. Belvedere."

An instant surge of adrenaline raised the flesh on Domino's arms. He hung up, hurried back to his den, and opened his wall safe. Withdrew his Glock 9mm, popped the clip, checked the ammo, then slammed the clip back home. He then unlocked his sliding glass door and stepped outside onto the back porch.

His cell rang again. He hit answer but said nothing.

"Cold," the voice said.

Domino inched towards the edge of his porch. Leaned over the railing and scanned his backyard in all directions.

"Colder."

"You can see me, huh?" he asked.

"Unfortunately. You haven't aged well."

Something started to gel. He might have gotten there sooner after the mere mention of Patrick's name, but alcohol and rage had blurred his reasoning.

He stepped back inside and locked the sliding glass door.

"Warmer."

Domino tossed some bait. "Playing a kid's game like the amateur you are. Why am I not surprised?"

A pause, and then: "This 'amateur' is going to pull off what your 'professional' never could."

Domino could not help but smile. More bait: "Oh, that Joan Parsons really got to you last year, didn't she, Kelly?"

No reply.

Domino started down his hallway towards the front door to double-check the locks. "I don't know how the hell you did it, but simply locating one's phone number is hardly cause for a pat on the back." Then, saving the best bait for last: "*Monica Kemp, you are NOT.*"

Kelly Blaine responded without the voice changer. "You're right. I'm not Monica. I'm better. And you're red hot."

Domino's front door burst open, the impact splintering the frame, catching Domino in the chest and knocking him clean off his feet, head ricocheting back against the hardwood floor, gun and phone flying.

Two enormous men came through his doorway, one bald, one not. Both ugly and scarred. The one with hair wielded an aluminum baseball bat, the bald one a weighted battering ram that hung in both his hands like a small cannon with handles.

The bald one set the battering ram to the floor and closed the door behind them. He then pulled a thick length of pipe from his waistband and tested its weight with a solid whack into his palm.

Both men loomed over a dazed Domino.

"This is the Negro who kill Ivan?" the one with the hair asked in a thick Russian accent.

"That's what the girl said," the bald one replied, his accent no less thick and Russian.

"I thought he was supposed to be sick."

Sick? Domino managed to process. *What the hell is that supposed to mean?*

The bald one shrugged. "That's what she tell me."

"He look drunk, not sick."

Slowly, and with no sudden movements, Domino began scooting back along his hardwood floor, trying to buy himself time until his head cleared. If he had to guess, he'd wager "Ivan" was one of the three Russian men he was forced to kill when Monica had hold of him back in the Pine Barrens, and these lumps standing over him now were somehow related, seeking vengeance.

As for "the girl" the lumps mentioned? Well, that had to be Kelly, didn't it? Amateur indeed. If she was looking to one-up Monica, she was not only on the wrong track by trying the same exact thing Monica had, but she was only sending two men to the party instead of three.

"You're right, I am drunk," Domino began, still casually scooting backwards, still looking to buy time. "Why do you think she told you I was sick?"

Neither man replied. And they were not ignorant of Domino's movement; they followed him, step for scoot, unnervingly patient, as though they were in no rush to do the job.

Domino went on. "The girl who sent you…she can't be trusted. If she paid you and told you I was going to be an easy target because I was sick, she was lying."

The two men exchanged a look.

Bald placed his gaze back on Domino and said: "She is paying us nothing. She only tell us you kill Ivan and where we find you." Bald slapped the heavy pipe into his palm again. "This is personal."

Hair grinned and brandished the bat. "She tell us you being sick is just bonus. Allows us to take our time and have fun."

Domino had managed to scoot into his den without incident. His head was somewhat clear now. Still buzzed good from the alcohol, yes, but the cobwebs from banging the back of his head on the hallway floor were gone.

"Well, I'm sorry to ruin your fun, boys," he said. "But I'm not sick…" Then, in fluent Russian: *"And I'm no easy target."*

The two men paused, Domino's Russian throwing them as he'd hoped it would, buying him precious seconds.

Domino rolled and dove at Hair's waist, hitting him with a diving tackle that would have cut a smaller man in two. The two big men crashed hard to the floor, Domino on top. Hair fought to regain his consciousness. Bald lunged forward with the pipe, swung it for all he was worth at Domino's head. Domino rolled away at the last second, and the pipe came down onto Hair's skull instead, knocking him cold.

"B'lyad'!" Bald cried.

Domino hopped to his feet. "'Fuck' indeed, dumbass." He started laughing. "I'm dealing with two-thirds of the Russian Three Stooges here. I guess that would make you Curly with your bald ass, *da*?"

Bald growled and charged forward, pipe high. Domino caught his charge with a thrusting kick to the gut, folding Bald in half, the pipe leaving his grip and clanging to the floor.

Bald writhed at Domino's feet, wide eyed and gasping, desperate to find air. Domino immediately stomped on his face and put him to sleep. He then hurried toward his wall safe, unlocked it, withdrew four pairs of plastic flex cuffs, and went to work on cuffing both men by the wrists and ankles as they slept.

.　　.　　.

Finished, Domino went towards the front door to look for his gun and cell phone. He swayed then stumbled along the way, dropping to his knees. He shook his head once and hard. Surely the adrenaline of the fight had helped sober him up. So why did he suddenly feel even drunker than before?

He got to his feet and resumed his search, eventually spotting his gun in the kitchen and his cell phone by the front door.

Heading back towards the two men, he swayed again, slapping a heavy hand against the wall to steady himself.

"*The hell is wrong with me?*" he muttered.

Hair started to come to. Domino stood over him, gun in his face.

"Where is she?" Domino asked.

Hair blinked several times, dazed, perhaps forgetting where he was.

Domino slapped him. "Where is she?"

Hair flashed disgust, Domino's slap bringing him all the way back into the world. "I don't speak English," he said.

Domino slapped him again. "I know you speak English, dick hole. Where is she?"

Hair looked away.

Domino struck him in the throat with his fingers, in and out like a snake. Hair gasped, and Domino jammed the gun barrel into his mouth.

"I only need one of you to talk," he said. "Maybe your buddy is more reasonable." Domino cocked the trigger and raised his free hand over Hair's face to shield the inevitable blood spatter after he blew his brains out.

The bluff worked. Hair's eyes bugged out of his head and he began a frantic string of garbled pleas (in English) around the barrel of the gun.

Domino pulled the gun from his mouth. "Where is she?"

"I don't know where she is. I swear to you."

"Bullshit. She was watching me. She even knew the brand of vodka I was drinking."

"She do that all before."

Domino frowned. "*What?* What the hell does that mean?"

Bald began to stir. Came to and started fighting his binds. Plastic cuffs are quick and easy, but they aren't perfect. An exceptionally strong man could snap them—and Bald was a big boy.

Domino left Hair, walked over to Bald, and stomped on his face again. Back to bed.

He returned to Hair, stumbled and fell to his knees at Hair's side. He shook his head hard again. Something was definitely wrong. His buzz should be receding, not growing.

Domino wrapped his hand around Hair's throat and pointed the gun between his eyes. "Why did you think I would be sick? Tell me now or you're dead."

"I already tell you everything. I know nothing else. She tell us you kill Ivan and where you live and that you will be sick and easy to hurt."

"*Hurt?* Not *kill?*"

"Yes. We were not supposed to kill you."

"Because she wanted to be the one, right?"

Hair shrugged. "I guess. I don't know."

"How would she know when to show? You supposed to call her? No, of course not—she can see, right?"

Domino stood, swayed and stumbled all the way to the right, his big body hitting and cracking the drywall before dropping to his knees once again. He raised his head and looked at Hair. Hair looked back, his eager expression akin to a hunter waiting for an animal to succumb to the wound he'd inflicted.

Only he's not the hunter. She is. She inflicted the wound. But how?

(*Mr. Belvedere.*)

Domino's last thought before he blacked out was both a question and an answer: *How the hell did she get to the vodka?*

CHAPTER 10

Domino woke in a fetal position on his den floor. He was bound by the ankles and wrists with the same type of plastic flex cuffs he'd used on the two Russian men, who, curiously, were in the same predicament he'd left them, fetal and bound on the floor as well, facing him—whoever had bound Domino while he was unconscious

(*you know it was Kelly*)

had not bothered to free the two Russian men yet. And the Russian men, big as they were, had either not yet attempted to break free of their plastic binds, or were simply unable to.

Domino, however, was able. Or was *once* able; he quickly found out, after his first attempt, that his entire body was useless. Every damn thing useless. Except for his mind. A dreadfully ironic

(*deliberate?*)

predicament when he recalled its woozy condition only moments ago.

But *was* it moments ago? How long had he been out?

Everything but his mind, paralyzed. He couldn't even speak. Just blink, breathe, listen, and think.

Deliberate.

What the hell had she given him? And was she here now? In his den? If he could turn his head, he'd look for her. If he could talk, he'd call for her. The best he could manage was a weak moan that never left his mouth, just reverberated in his throat.

He heard footsteps approaching from behind, a soft tread on his hardwood floor. Now the sense of someone standing over him. And very close. Domino was forced to watch the Russian men's reaction to gauge the scene behind him. He saw no initial alarm or panic in their eyes. This told him it was someone they knew. This told him Kelly Blaine was here.

"Cut us free," Bald said.

"You failed me," she said. Her tone was cavalier, unsettling.

"You said he'd be sick."

Domino sensed her squatting behind him now. Felt gloved hands working on the flex cuffs binding his wrists and ankles, cutting them free. Finished, Kelly took hold of his right wrist, raised his heavy arm in the air, and then let it slap uselessly to the floor in front of him.

"Does he look well to you?" she asked after her display.

"He was not like that before," Bald said. "He was still strong. *Too* strong."

"It's okay," she said coolly. "You were supposed to fail."

"*What?*"

Domino felt a gloved hand on his cheek now. She caressed his face as she spoke. "Well, I *did* happen to watch him kill your pal Ivan and two other men with his bare hands, you know. I'd have to be a fool to think the two of you alone could get the job done."

A setup. A goddamn setup. She wasn't being careless in attempting to mimic what Monica had tried; she was using these two unwitting lumps to play interference for her.

As if reading Domino's mind, Kelly confirmed his thought for him. "You were a distraction," she said to Bald. "Allowed me to enter unnoticed while he beat the shit out of you. That's all."

"Okay, so we did our job," Hair spoke up. "Cut us free now."

Kelly stopped caressing Domino's cheek and stood. She approached the two men, and Domino got a look at Kelly Blaine for the first time since her appearance on *The Joan Parsons Show.*

Her hair was long and dark as he remembered. She was small as he remembered. She wore a black wool overcoat and gloves.

What Domino did not see was the mask she frequently wore. The mask that she wore in court. The mask that she wore on *The Joan Parsons Show*. That she wore when she needed to be on stage before a public that could not know she was a baleful psychopath.

She was not wearing the mask because she had no need for it. No secrets to hide, no performances to give. The mask was off, and the terrifying potential of what lay beneath was on full display.

"I can't cut you free just yet. This is a home invasion gone awry, after all." Then, in a mock Russian accent: "*Revenge for your fallen comrade.*"

She laughed, produced Domino's gun from inside her coat, grabbed a pillow from the sofa, placed it over Hair's face to muffle the sound, and pulled the trigger.

There was a pop, and Hair's bound legs momentarily convulsed as one before coming to a dead stop.

Kelly removed the pillow, and peeked at her work beneath. "Eww," she said. She turned and made a silly yuck face at Domino. "I got him in the eyeball. So gross."

Bald started screaming for help. Kelly tossed the gun on the sofa and picked the lead pipe that Bald had brought with him up off the floor. Without hesitation, she brought it down onto Bald's skull.

The first blow stunned him. The second knocked him out. The third, fourth, fifth, and sixth made sure he was dead.

Domino could only look on, sickened with himself that one of his first thoughts was that the Russian's once shiny bald head was the perfect canvas to accentuate the excessive damage Kelly had done.

Panting, Kelly strode towards Domino, placed the pipe in his limp hand, curled his fist around it to ensure his prints took, then tossed it aside, metal clanging on wood wherever it landed.

She squatted next to Domino again, this time facing him, looking him in the eye. "No need to do that for the gun, right? I imagine your prints are already all over it."

Done with the pipe. Is she done with the gun now too? What does that leave? The bat? The aluminum bat Hair brought?

Domino willed every muscle in his body to move. Felt as if he was tapping into his very soul, willing something, *anything* to move.

He zeroed in on her supple throat. If he could just get his hand around her neck, he could rip her throat clean out. *Just move, goddammit. Please move.*

"Do you remember anything unusual at the liquor store today, Domino?"

Domino quickly thought back. He remembered nothing out of the ordinary, no strange faces, no odd behavior from employees; quite the contrary, Karl the shop clerk had greeted him with a friendly hello as he did every Sunday, even remarked how lucky Domino was to grab the last bottle of Belvedere, that a couple of guys came in not long ago and nearly cleaned him out...of...the...stuff...

Ah, shit. Did they happen to be two big Russian fellas, Karl? One bald, one not? Of course they did. And that one bottle they left on the shelf. Did they happen to bring it in with *them and place it on the shelf when you weren't looking, by chance? After spiking it with God knows what? Pull the security tape, Karl; I'll bet you all the fucking Belvedere in Poland I'm spot on.*

Kelly smiled. "Yes, that's right. The *same* liquor store you go to *every single Sunday* at the *exact same time* after church. It's hard to tell, you practically being a zombie right now and all, but I'm willing to bet you just figured it out. Retirement got you complacent, didn't it, big fella? Started developing routines?" She shook her head. "Tsk, tsk..."

She's so damn close. Move, goddammit...

Domino focused all of his will on his right arm. He didn't need the rest of his body to move. If he could just move his right arm, get his hand around that supple neck. Even at twenty percent strength, he was sure he could crush it.

"I don't want to be Monica, Domino. I never *wanted* to be Monica. Monica's a failure. She failed in killing you, and she failed in killing Amy." She caressed his face again. "But I won't fail. And I am going to do what Monica never could—because I can."

Oh, Christ, no, please no...

"Do you know what Amy is doing tonight?" she asked him. "She's going to some support group out in Montgomery County. It's at some guy's home. Apparently, the members take turns as hosts.

She's been doing it for a while now, you know." She smiled and patted his arm. "Of *course* you know. You're pretty chummy with her, huh? Her kids too. I love the photo on the fridge. The one of you and Caleb. Yes, I know their names. I know a lot, don't I? I always was good at homework—well, when it benefitted me directly, that is. Hated algebra." She laughed at her own wit.

If you go near that family, I'll kill you. I will kill you stone fucking dead, you crazy bitch.

"I could never go after Amy directly, of course. Well, I could, but I'd probably end up being a person of interest after they found the mess, wouldn't I? I mean, I never *did* have a beef with Amy; we've never even really spoken. But I would almost certainly be a person of interest—at least initially. Definitely don't want that hassle."

She stood, continued talking as she approached the two Russians.

"So yeah, I've got no beef with Amy, or even *you* for that matter. Sure, you did catch me a few years ago, but that's just your bullshit Superman code you live by; I didn't take it personally."

She pulled a straight razor from her coat pocket, bent and started cutting the Russians' binds and then pocketing the plastic strips after.

"Anyway, I can't go after Amy directly, so I thought, why not Amy and a host of others? The support group tonight in a private residence is the *perfect* place. All those people—who would ever know who the prime target was supposed to be? *Especially* after what I have planned comes to light. In a weird way, I kind of wish you were going to be alive to see it. It's going to be so much fun, and more than a little brilliant, if I do say so myself."

Domino wiggled a finger.

"You were right when you said Joan Parsons got to me. She did." She cut the last of the flex cuffs, pocketed them, and turned back to Domino. "Oh, sure, I know I was playing it up as the victim and all—and doing my usual stellar job—but still, it got to me." She knelt beside him again, started tracing the blade of the straight razor lightly across his face.

Domino wiggled a second finger.

"The moment that pretentious cunt said what she did on national television, I knew what I had to do. I needed to prove it to myself. No one else. Me. I needed to prove that Monica Kemp wasn't just my peer, but that I was better. Much, much better. Because I am. Hell, when you think about it, *I* was the actual catalyst to her death. If it wasn't for my setting that funhouse of hers in the Pine Barrens on fire, she never would have left and gotten herself killed by Amy."

She traced the blade down his cheek and stopped at his throat.

"A home invasion gone awry. Two Russian men seeking vengeance against Domino Taylor for the murder of their—what the hell was he to them again? Cousin? Friend?" She shrugged uncaringly. "Anyway, Mr. Taylor, Marine and trained security specialist, thwarted their attempts, however, killing both men in a heroic act of self-defense." She smiled and took the blade off his throat so she could give tiny little claps and applause. "*Yaaay.*"

Three fingers. He felt blood returning to his forearm.

Kelly placed the blade back on Domino's neck. "Unfortunately, Mr. Taylor suffered substantial injuries during the assault—"

Twenty percent strength is all I need! Fifteen! I'll take fifteen!!!

"—and ultimately succumbed to those injuries."

She began a slow, deliberate cut into Domino's neck.

MOVE, GODDAMMIT! MOVE!!!!!

Domino's right arm sprang to life and flew toward Kelly, his hand going straight for her throat.

Kelly flinched, fell back onto her butt and quickly scooted away.

Domino continued to flail wildly with his right arm like a man groping in the dark.

Kelly hopped to her feet. Momentarily startled, she was now smiling as she regained her composure and breathed out a sigh of relief.

"Serves me right for going on and on," she said. "*I'm going to kill you, Mr. Bond,*" she began in playful, sinister tones, "*but first let me take considerable time in telling you the intricate details of my master plan so that you may thwart them later.*" She laughed hard. "I almost became a cliché casualty!"

Kelly positioned herself just out of Domino's reach, bent over him, and continued slitting his throat, careful to avoid the arterial spray.

Finished, she took a selfie with Domino's cell phone—her grinning; him dying—and then pocketed it.

.　　.　　.

Domino's final image of Kelly Blaine was a slanted view of her strolling down the hallway toward his front door, carrying the pillow she'd used to muffle the gun, and speaking over her shoulder as she left him to die:

"In other news, Amy Lambert, survivor of the infamous Crescent Lake Massacre, was found dead..."

.　　.　　.

Amy's cell rang. The screen displayed Domino's landline number.

She'd kind of expected this. Expected it nearly every Sunday, actually. She knew about Domino's Sunday ritual of drinking and mourning Patrick. Knew that he often phoned her after strapping on a healthy buzz, wanting to talk, if only for a minute or two, and often about nothing at all. Amy had her support group sessions; Domino had this.

"Hey, big guy," Amy answered. "How's that Belvedere treating you?"

No reply.

"Domino? You there?"

No reply.

"Did you drunk dial me, mister?" she said with a smile. "*Hellooo?*"

Still nothing.

She hung up, tempted to phone him back. Except this was not the first time he'd called her and hung up without saying hello. It had happened a few times before, in fact. He'd later confessed that he'd been too drunk to talk, but needed to hear her voice. Needed to hear that she was safe so he could relay the message to Patrick at the time. Amy never once questioned it. Just smiled and took his hand

and said, "*You can hang up on me anytime,*" to which Domino let loose his trademark laugh that shook the house.

Amy smiled at the memory and decided not to call him back.

. . .

Domino flopping, bleeding profusely, feeling as though his body belonged to someone else, found his cordless phone. He tried and failed three times at first, fingers too slick with blood, hands too weak and uncooperative with whatever drug Kelly had given him.

Please, he begged his body.

On the fourth try, he got Amy.

"Hey, big guy. How's that Belvedere treating you?"

Domino opened his mouth to speak. Only blood escaped. He could not even manage a moan this time.

"Domino? You there?"

He tried to speak again and had even less success than before. His vision was a narrowing tunnel.

"Did you drunk dial me, mister?"

Domino started crying. No sound, just steady streams of tears down his cheeks.

"*Hellooo?*"

Patrick…I'm sorry…

Amy hung up.

CHAPTER 11

Kathy Brown, aka Kat, aka Aunt Kat, was waiting outside on the front steps of her cozy suburban home when her brother, Allan, pulled up. Her smile was bright and true, and when she stood she performed tiny jumps in place with little claps of her hands. Whether it was strictly a show for the girls in the back seat or genuine excitement at their arrival, Allan couldn't have loved his sister any more because the girls started laughing and giggling at once, easing any misgivings he'd had about dropping them off for the night after their asking to stay home earlier that day.

The second Allan rolled the SUV to a stop out front, Jamie and Janine darted from the car and raced toward an open-armed Aunt Kat. Any other woman might have toppled from the impact of the twins' charging embrace, but Kathy Brown was no stranger to fitness. Long brown hair eternally in a ponytail (Allan could not, for the life of him, recall the last time he'd seen her with it down) and always donning some sort of attire that would do in a pinch if a workout fix beckoned (tonight's was black sweats and a black tee that showed off her sinewy arms), Kathy clearly had made exercise her stress-buster of choice. And although Allan was grateful it was something healthy, unlike his preferred method of scotch and saturated fats, such a thing could be overdone. And judging by the increasing vascularity and weight loss he noticed every subsequent time he saw his sister, his concerns were not without merit. Not so much for the fact that she may injure herself, but for the underlining cause of such excessiveness.

Never one to discuss her problems (depression, generalized anxiety disorder, and an ugly divorce from a douchebag of the highest order), Kathy was always the type to smile, pat your arm a little too hard, and insist "*I'm fine, I'm fine*" whenever you tried to get too deep. She was a world-class shrink when it came to talking about Allan, but when it came to herself, not a chance. It simply wasn't her way. The gym was her way. And Allan had noticed once again, as he had each successive time prior, that she looked even thinner than before, more veiny than before. Ironically, unhealthy. He would file this away for another time. Although he supposed he might as well file it in the trash for all the success he would likely end up having in getting anywhere with her when the time came.

Aunt Kat held and squeezed her "Kittens," firing off a million things at once: *Tell me about school. How was your sleepover? You're getting taller every day. Any boyfriends yet?* And so on.

Allan, whose chauffeur duties apparently now extended to those of bellhop, reached into the back seat and pulled out both girls' overnight bags, slinging them over one shoulder with a grunt.

"Yeah, no worries, girls; I've got everything," he called to them.

The twins spun and ran to their father to retrieve their things. Kathy laughed her raspy laugh.

"Go on inside, there's a surprise waiting for you," Kathy said to her nieces when they returned with their overnight bags.

"What is it?" Janine asked.

"Go in and see," Kathy replied.

The girls started to bolt for the front door.

"*WAIT!*" Allan called. Christ, how many times had he said that to them today? He marveled at the resiliency of children. Every emotion he'd experienced today still clung to him like something sticky he couldn't quite wash off. The girls had had their share of emotion too—the talk of their mother and cancer in the car; the wanting to attend tonight; watching their father lose it when getting a ticket—but right now their whole world resided in the mystery surprise from Aunt Kat lying in wait behind her front door. Nothing else existed. Allan wanted to bottle this resiliency for use with his girls at a later date. For when that moment he was ruminating over earlier, about discussing the death of their mother, finally hit. The one that would make "The Talk" seem like a cakewalk.

And for himself.

Allan would love to bottle the stuff for himself. Hell, he'd walk around with it in a paper bag, taking pulls from it every ten minutes like some kind of drunk.

The girls, hearing their father's cry, turned and froze a few feet from their aunt Kat's front door.

"There is no *way* you are going inside that house without saying goodbye to your father," he said to them.

Kathy smiled at the scene.

The girls immediately spun and ran back toward their father, hugging him simultaneously. Allan's throat tightened. His heart swelled.

"I love my Deejays," he said.

"We love you too," they returned somewhat robotically, though Allan took zero offense. Nothing else existed except for the mystery surprise waiting for them behind Aunt Kat's door, he reminded himself. And he would sacrifice a thousand *love you too*'s to give them this moment time and time again. A moment free of everything and anything but the here and now.

He then wondered about himself. What would it take for *him* to be momentarily free of everything and anything? To bask in the here and now? A hell of a lot more than a little surprise from his sister; that was for damn sure.

"Gimme a kiss," he said, bending and kissing his girls one at a time. He then patted them on their butts and said: "Okay, go."

They dashed for their aunt Kat's front door once again, not to be denied by their father's increasingly habitual *wait!* this time.

Kathy turned to Allan after watching the girls disappear through her front door and said: "So how's things, ding-a-ling?"

Allan smiled. "Like I said on the phone, one day at a time. What's the surprise you got them?"

Kathy waved a hand at her brother. "Just junk. Candy, toys. So, what's happening tonight?"

Allan shrugged. "The usual. Grief-stricken people sharing grief. Catharsis has a weird sense of humor."

He expected a chuckle from his sister, but got a concerned face in return. "You look tired," she said.

"I am tired. I just had half the girls from my daughters' elementary school stay the night at my house."

Still no chuckle, but she did smile. "What kind of turnout are you expecting tonight?" she asked.

He shrugged again. "It fluctuates. Some people go once and can't handle it, never show up again. Others show and get hooked, become regulars."

He paused there for a moment, thought about telling his sister the conversation he'd had with the girls earlier that day, but decided against it. The devil in him was all too keen to let the filterless mouths of his daughters bombard his sister with such queries about the content of the evening's meeting and why they weren't allowed to attend, see whether she could exercise her way out of that one. But of course he knew she'd be just fine. It was about someone else, after all, not her.

"*Aaannnd...?*" Kathy crooned, waiting on her brother like the dog-eared paperback he was to her.

"And nothing," he said, wanting to punch her in the gut like they were kids again for her knowing him so well, although truth be told, she had delivered most of the gut-punching growing up.

"Well, it's good that *you're* a regular," she said. "It must help."

"It doesn't hurt. Commiserating doesn't have to be a one-way street, you know," he said, bracing himself after such a passive-aggressive dig, memories of childhood gut-punches being mere moments ago and all.

"There's that humor again, little brother," she said, patting his face gently, each pat becoming increasingly harder until she whacked him a good, albeit harmless, one. "Remember to never lose it."

Allan laughed and rubbed his cheek. "Make sure they do their homework. You sure you don't mind taking them tomorrow?"

"Would you shut up?"

He smiled and started for his car. "Take care of my girls."

"My Kittens are *always* safe with me," she said. Then: "I hope tonight goes well. I hope you get some new faces."

"We'll see."

CHAPTER 12

Philadelphia, Pennsylvania

Kensington Avenue

Only Jennifer paced the room of the apartment. Tim and Michael were far too sick, lying back to back in fetal balls on the room's solitary mattress, sweating, shivering, moaning. No less sick, Jennifer's violent tendencies did not allow her to just lie and moan, waiting for their fix to arrive. She was more apt to stomp around the decrepit apartment, kicking and smashing what few items they had. Or what few items the true residents had. No one knew who the house truly belonged to. They'd managed to squat here for over a week now, undisturbed. The small girl with the long dark hair had found it for them. Told them to hole up there and wait for her arrival each day as opposed to going on the street for it.

Except now she was late. She was late, and Jennifer, periodically pulling long swaths of black hair from the self-inflicted thinning patch on the side of her head, was not pleased.

"Fuck this. Fuck this, man. She said three. Didn't she say three? She said three, right?"

"What time is it?" Tim said in a weak voice from the mattress.

"I don't know. Do you know? I don't fucking know. It's gotta be close to three though, right?" She kicked the mattress. Both men moaned in protest. "*Right?*"

Michael rolled his head over the side of the mattress and vomited. Rolled back and assumed the same fetal position as though he'd done nothing. Neither Jennifer nor Tim seemed to care.

"If she wants us to do this thing for her tonight, no fucking way am I doing it sick," Jennifer said. "No fucking way. She can't expect us to do it sick. She can't. She wants us to be right for this? She wants us to be right? We can't be sick. She can't expect us to be sick. No way. No fucking way." She pulled more hair from the side of her head and then absently flicked her fingers back and forth, the long strands falling to the floor.

An agonizing moment passed. Shivering, sweating, vomiting.

Jennifer picked up one of their only two chairs and threw it across the room. "She's got five minutes," she said. "Five minutes or I'm going on the street for it."

"Don't be stupid," Michael said. He had vomit on his cheek. "Any shit you get out there will pale to what she's been bringing us."

Jennifer approached the mattress. "I'm saying for now. Just for now. Until she arrives. We get something just for now to hold us over. Just for now."

Neither guy responded. Jennifer kicked the mattress again. Both men moaned in protest again.

"Look at you two, laying there like a couple of pussies. Big tough guys when you're all fixed up, aren't you? Look at you now." She kicked the mattress. "Look at you now." Kick. "Look at you now." Kick.

"*Fucking stop!*" Tim yelled.

There was a knock at the door. Tim and Michael sat up.

Jennifer rushed for the door and opened it.

Kelly Blaine walked in. She was not alone.

"Who's this?" Jennifer demanded, gesturing to the disheveled man standing beside Kelly. The man looked as if he hadn't slept in days, eaten in weeks, bathed in months.

Kelly said nothing, just stepped deeper into the apartment with the disheveled man at her heels like a puppy.

"Boys," Kelly said, gesturing to Tim and Michael on the mattress. "You're looking well."

"Fuck you, man," Tim said. "We've been waiting forever."

Kelly's eyebrows bounced. "Fuck me? Maybe I should come back when you're feeling more polite."

"*No!*" Michael rolled off the mattress and found his feet. He stood hunched over, clutching his stomach, his dark hair soaked with sweat, complexion a ghostly white. He spun toward Tim. "*Tim, shut the fuck up!*" Spun back to Kelly. "He didn't mean it. Seriously, we just need a little something, is all. He didn't mean it, right, Tim?"

Tim was on his feet now, his sickly posture and appearance identical to that of Michael's minus the dark hair. Tim's hair was blond and thinning, the abundance of sweat accentuating the diffuse loss throughout his scalp. He began nodding vehemently, forcing a smile that appeared like a grimace.

"Yeah, totally," Tim said. "I'm sorry, I'm sorry."

Kelly pulled a cigarette from her long black overcoat and lit it with a black Zippo. She kept the tiny lid of the lighter open for a moment and exhaled a long, thin stream of smoke into the Zippo's trademark windproof flame, watching it flicker and shrink before it stood tall again. She finally glanced back at the two men before her. "You guys really don't look so hot," she said. "I'm beginning to have doubts about tonight."

"We'll be fine," Michael said. "Hook us up and we'll be fine."

"*Guaranteed*," Tim added.

Jennifer stepped in front of Tim and Michael and faced Kelly. "You've seen us when we're fixed up. We're good as gold, and you know it. You just gotta keep us fixed up is all. Just keep us fixed up."

Kelly took a deep drag of her cigarette and looked away in thought. "I don't know—I'm not sure how long this thing is going to run tonight. Could last well into the morning."

"That's fine," Jennifer said. "It can last a week. We don't give a shit. As long as we have enough to keep us good, we'll go until you say when."

Kelly gave a theatrical and pensive purse of the lips. "Yeah, I'm just—I don't know..."

"*What?*" Michael said, running a shaking hand through his hair.

"I question that extra mile," Kelly said.

"Huh?" Jennifer said.

"I question if you're *truly* willing to go that extra mile for me like you promised you would." She turned and looked at the unkempt man she'd arrived with. "I know Winston would. Isn't that right, Winston?"

Winston nodded quickly, scratching his scalp hard enough to look as though he meant to draw blood.

"*What?!*" Jennifer said. "You can't back out! You gave us your word! You promised we'd be fixed for months after it was over. You gave us your word!"

Kelly exhaled smoke and again donned the pensive purse of the lips. "Yeah, but...I guess I just feel like I need more convincing."

"*Anything*," Tim said. "We will do *absolutely anything* you ask us to."

"Anything," Jennifer echoed.

Kelly laughed. "And a junkie's word is always so reliable. Especially when they need a fix."

Michael spit on the floor. "We could rush you and take it," he said. "You've got it on you now, right? What's stopping us from rushing you and taking it?"

Kelly laughed again. "You could do that. But what about tomorrow? You wanna go on the street for stuff that's one-tenth as good as what I've been giving you?"

"No, we don't," Tim said. "Michael, *shut the FUCK up*. He's not speaking for me, Kelly."

"Or me," Jennifer said.

Michael spit again, spun, and went toward the window, a dirty cracked pane that looked down on a dirty cracked street.

"*Anything*," Jennifer reiterated.

"*Please*," Tim said.

Kelly looked over toward Michael, who was still staring out the window, down into the lawless and unreliable streets below. "Michael?" she said.

Michael faced the group. "I'm sorry. My head's fucked. I don't feel right. Anything you want. Anything."

Kelly nodded. "I brought Winston up here with the promise of a fix," she said. "And he may get it too. He may get what I'd intended to give *all three of you*. Enough to last him days." Kelly dropped her cigarette to the floor and stubbed it out with her toe. "That is, unless you beat him to death first."

All four addicts exchanged twitchy looks.

"Beat him with what?" Jennifer asked.

"Beat him to *death*," Kelly corrected.

"Beat him to death with what?"

Kelly surveyed the room. "I see a chair, a table, ash trays, needles…" She gave a little shrug. "Surprise me."

All four stood frozen.

Kelly smiled, went into her overcoat and brandished a generous bag of heroin. "Convince me how serious you are," she said to Jennifer, Tim, and Michael. Then to Winston: "You too, Winston, old boy." Then to all of them: "Winner gets to chase one hell of a dragon."

CHAPTER 13

As big as the bag of heroin was, Winston wanted no part of this game. He was a transient, a survivor. He hadn't lasted this long on the streets by courting danger. He ran from it. As he did now.

Winston spun, went for the door, jerked it open, and the chain caught, Kelly having quietly slid it home when Winston's attention was on Jennifer, Tim, and Michael.

Winston cried out and fumbled with the chain, eventually having to close the door first in order to provide the slack he needed to slide the chain free.

Kelly looked over at Jennifer, Tim, and Michael. "He's going to get away."

Michael lunged first, snatching Winston around the neck and dragging him away from the door. Winston fought back. Not with his fists, no; Winston's fighting ability was more akin to that of a feral animal's. He clawed, bit, gouged, spat. The savagery of his attack deterred Michael's own assault, and he backed off as if he *had* provoked a wild animal.

"*Fucking crazy!*" Michael yelled.

Winston went for the door again. Michael changed tactics and dove for Winston's legs, wrapping them up at the knee. Tim immediately dove at Winston's torso, Michael's grip on Winston's legs allowing both men to topple Winston like a plank. All three men hit the floor together. Winston continued to fight like an animal, looking to bite any nose, any digit that came near his mouth, gouge any eyes that came near his thumbs.

Jennifer appeared with the heavy wooden chair raised high overhead, thick veins bulging from her malnourished neck. "*Hold him still! Fucking hold him!*"

Michael kept a firm hold on Winston's legs. Tim managed to pin both arms but was clearly struggling from the effort.

"*HIT HIM!*" Tim yelled.

Jennifer brought the wooden chair down onto Winston's head. There was a thick crack, like kindling over one's knee.

Winston barely flinched. Fought harder still.

"*Jesus Chr—AGAIN!*" Tim yelled. "*Hit him again!*"

Jennifer did. Seven times total. The only thing stopping her was the chair giving before Winston's skull. She stood panting over Winston's body with only a solitary chair leg in her hand, the remainder of the chair spread around them, looking not unlike the aforementioned kindling.

Winston's face was a mess.

Michael slowly rolled off of Winston's knees and lay on his back, gasping. Tim let go of Winston's arms and scooted backward before doing the same as Michael, flopping onto his back, desperate to find air.

Jennifer, no less panting than the others, still appeared to have something left in the tank. A more astute eye might have even suggested she was stimulated by the effort, that her labored breathing was more the result of excitement than exertion.

"Is he dead?" Michael asked from his sprawled position on the floor.

Kelly bent and checked Winston's pulse. Stood and wiped her hands on her coat. "Nope."

Tim sat up. "*What?*"

"He's still got a pulse," Kelly said.

Now Michael sat up. "Christ, look at him. He's as good as dead. Just give it a minute."

Kelly shook her head, disappointed. "You see, this is just the kind of thing I was talking about when it came to going that extra mile. You seem content with mediocrity, Michael. I can't have that."

Winston suddenly screamed, eyes popping to life, shockingly white and enormous in his bloodied face. His body seemed to defy physics, springing from the floor in one convulsive jerk without the use of his limbs, as though jolted with electricity.

Even Kelly appeared stunned.

A mad scramble and Winston was on his feet and at the door again. This time he ripped it open with frenzied strength, popping the chain, reaching the stairwell and taking the steps two, three at a time as he descended levels.

Jennifer brandished the dense chair leg and went to go after him, but Kelly placed a firm arm in front of her and shook her head. She looked at Tim and Michael. "You two go," she said.

Tim sprinted toward the open door and was gone. Michael stayed behind.

Kelly tilted her head. "Something wrong, Michael?"

"There's no point," Michael said. "Guy's got too much of a head start. Knows the area too well. We'd never find him."

"And if he goes to the police?" Kelly said.

Michael laughed. "Guy like that isn't going to the police."

Tim appeared a moment later, panting and dejected. "He's fucking gone." He glanced over at Kelly and dropped his head. "I'm sorry. I tried to catch him, I really did."

Kelly gave an accepting nod and then gestured towards Michael. "Michael here thought you were wasting your time," she said.

The realization that Michael had not followed Tim in the chase for Winston obviously hit Tim for the first time. His dejected face became a furious one. "Yeah...where the fuck were you, man?!"

"He had too much of a head start, man," Michael said. "He knows these streets better than us. We were never gonna catch him."

"Maybe if you'd helped, we would have!" Jennifer said.

"*Fuckin' A*," Tim said. "His head was all bashed in—he could have dropped after the first flight of stairs, and we could have dragged him back up."

"Did he?" Michael asked, a trifle smugly.

Tim got in his face. "Man, fuck you, you pussy. '*He's as good as dead, just give it a minute,*'" he said, mocking Michael's earlier words. "And then you don't even give chase when the fucker *isn't* dead?!" He spun toward Kelly, splayed his arms, and let them flop hopelessly against his legs, an exasperated gesture of apology for Michael's behavior.

Kelly lit another cigarette. "What to do, what to do..."

Jennifer stepped forward. "I say no way Michael gets equal shares after tonight."

"*What?*" Michael blurted. "Why the fuck not?"

"Are you *kidding* me?" Jennifer said.

Michael threw up his hands. "What? Because I didn't chase after the fucking guy? I held him down just the same as Tim while you beat on him. If anything, it was your shit job beating on him that allowed him to get away."

"And yet she was ready to go right after him the moment he popped up," Tim said. "Only reason she didn't was because Kelly stopped her."

All eyes fell on Kelly.

"Why *did* you stop her?" Tim asked.

Kelly dragged on her cigarette and smirked back at them. "It was beginning to look like three was a crowd."

Michael frowned. "What's that supposed to mean?"

"It means *you're* the crowd, dipshit," Jennifer said.

Kelly smiled.

Michael threw up his hands again. "Oh, so I'm out? Just like that? You know what? Fuck this. And fuck you, you crazy little bitch—I'm getting what's mine." Michael lunged for Kelly, began tearing at her overcoat for the heroin within.

Tim immediately punched Michael on the side of the jaw, dropping him to his knees. Jennifer followed it up with three solid whacks from the chair leg, the final whack pitching Michael onto his side into a fetal, protective ball. Tim snatched the chair leg from Jennifer and continued the attack, the first few cracks uncurling Michael's fetal ball as he went rigid, the final few cracks sending those rigid legs into convulsion as he seized.

When the chair leg eventually split from impact, Jennifer rushed towards the mattress-side table, snatched one of the syringes, and rushed back with a battle cry, seemingly keen on plunging the needle into Michael, and with none too much prejudice as to where it landed.

Of all people, it was Kelly who stopped her.

Jennifer, wide eyed, nearly frothing, stared hard into Kelly's eyes as though being woken from a nightmare. "*What?*" she panted out.

Kelly dropped her cigarette next to Michael's head, stubbed it out, then bent and checked his pulse. She rose and said: "This one is *very* dead."

Tim and Jennifer, both wheezing from the assault, exchanged a glance.

"This is excellent," Kelly said. "Truly, I couldn't have asked for a greater demonstration of going that extra mile. I now have every bit of confidence that tonight will be a great success."

Kelly withdrew the bag of heroin from her coat and tossed it on the mattress.

"Go do your thing," she told them.

CHAPTER 14

Amy cinched up her jeans, pulled her gray Penn State sweatshirt over her head, and then snapped her long brown hair into a pony-tail. Boom—ready for therapy.

She made her way downstairs and into the kitchen. Thought about pouring herself a glass of wine before leaving (desert dry, these things always were), and then remembered the last time Allan Brown had hosted a session. How the two had happened upon one another in his kitchen during a break. Or more appropriately, how Amy had been caught snooping in Allan Brown's fridge during a break.

She'd muttered a quick apology, only to have Allan smile, take a quick peek into the den to make sure no one was around, and then pull a bottle of good whiskey from the cupboard. They each took a long pull straight from the bottle, ending with Allan smiling and holding an index finger up to his shushed lips, as if to say, *our secret*.

It had been a thoughtful gesture, and though the whiskey had burned going down, it did the trick of giving her a quick shot of the mellows. Shame he didn't drink white wine. But then did most men drink white wine? She didn't know. Patrick certainly didn't. Patrick loved beer. One of the reasons Amy still struggled to keep beer in the house. Perhaps Allan Brown's wife had liked white wine as Amy did. One of the possible reasons she'd spotted none in his fridge when she went snooping.

Amy derailed her depressive train of thought before it descended further. Plenty of time for that later tonight. She would try to catch Allan in the kitchen like last time and be grateful if he offered the whiskey again.

· · ·

Amy went into the den. Caleb was sprawled out on the sofa in boxer shorts and a white undershirt, watching television. If Amy had convinced herself that the depressive train had been successfully derailed in the kitchen, she was woefully mistaken. Tack on thirty years to her son and she was looking at Patrick. The boxers, the white tee, the precise way they sat slumped on the sofa, lost in the haze of the television. Even the occasional dig in the ear with the pinky finger followed by a close inspection for anything good before absently wiping the finger on the sofa.

A few years ago, Amy would have rushed from the room in tears. But she could cope now. Constantly reminding herself to celebrate Patrick's life as opposed to constantly mourning his death. And slumped before her on the sofa, watching TV with his little finger in his ear, was the perfect example of that practice.

She bent over the back of the sofa, gripped Caleb's head with both hands, and planted a big smooch on the side of his face.

Caleb wriggled out of his mother's grip. An eternal mama's boy, he nevertheless didn't like being caught off guard.

"What?" he said, leaning his head back against the sofa, looking up at her.

"Go get ready," she said. "I told Mrs. Flannigan we'd be there early."

Caleb rolled off the sofa and headed upstairs.

"And don't think I didn't see you wipe your ear gunk on the sofa either, Mr. Gross," she called after him.

She heard him giggle as he went into his room.

Ah, screw it, she thought. *I'm having a glass of wine.*

· · ·

As far as Amy Lambert was concerned, the old axiom that taxes and death were the only two certainties in life everyone must abide by applied to 99.9 percent of the population. The remaining 0.01—Amy—abided by an equally potent third: Her daughter, Carrie Lambert, would never *ever* be ready on time. Ever. It had been true on her first day in nursery school, when Carrie had decided she did not like her new shoes and locked herself in the closet, thus forcing Amy to break the lock and drag her daughter to her first day fifteen minutes late; and it was true right now, when, having been told she needed to be ready in twenty minutes, Carrie was still in the precise spot Amy had left her those twenty minutes ago, doing precisely the same thing—yapping away on the telephone.

"*Are you kidding me?*"

Carrie, belly down on her bed and still wearing the same pajama bottoms and T-shirt she'd woken in, looked up at her mother with that mild look of annoyance only an eleven-year-old daughter can give her mother. "What?"

Amy marched into the room and snatched the phone from her daughter. "Goodbye, Carly," she said into the receiver, and hung up.

"*Mom!*"

Amy got in her daughter's face. "No—no '*Mom.*' I told you to be ready in twenty minutes. You haven't done anything yet."

"I *am* ready."

"You are *not* going over to Mrs. Flannigan's looking like that."

"Why not? It's not like we're going out or anything. What does she care how I look?"

"Carrie, get up, get dressed, and be downstairs in five minutes. If you're not ready by then, I am going to show up at school tomorrow and embarrass the living hell out of you in front of all your friends."

This was no idle threat. Amy had done it before.

"*Fine,*" Carrie groaned and started getting ready.

．　　　．　　　．

"You don't have to always walk us over," Carrie told her mother at the front door. "She lives like two feet away."

"And what if I want to come in and say hello?" Amy asked.

Carrie rolled her eyes. "Whatever."

Yes, the glass of wine had definitely been a good idea. Blunted her urges to drop-kick her daughter onto Mrs. Flannigan's front step.

"Can we FaceTime you tonight?" Caleb asked.

"I'm only going to be gone a few hours."

"So?"

"So Mrs. Flannigan uses her FaceTime to talk to her family back in Ireland."

"She's not going to be talking to them while we're there," Carrie said.

"I don't care. You don't need to FaceTime me."

"Can we FaceTime Domino?" Caleb asked.

"*No*," Amy said quickly, even though she knew Domino would have never answered her kids' call while drunk.

"Why not?" Carrie said. "We've done it before."

Because he's probably flat on his back right about now. "Because I spoke to him earlier and he said he didn't feel well."

Caleb looked suddenly concerned. "What's wrong?"

"Nothing, honey, he's just got a little cold is all. Can we go, please?"

* * *

Irene Flannigan opened the door just as Amy was prepared to knock. Though Amy knew it meant she was waiting on their arrival, likely watching from the window, she did the whole surprise thing anyway.

"*Oh!*" Amy said. "Perfect timing."

Irene Flannigan displayed every characteristic of the classic old Irish woman she was, right down to the red hair, the pale and freckled skin, and of course the accent that had never waned since her arrival in this country many years ago.

With a cautious, melodramatic face, Irene placed an index finger below one of her green eyes, bent to look at Carrie and Caleb, and said: "*I'm always watchin'.*"

They all laughed, even Carrie.

Irene invited them in. The kids immediately went for Irene's computer in the den. It contained one and only one video game: Tetris. And while Irene proclaimed she'd downloaded the game solely for Carrie and Caleb, many a night had passed with her clacking away on her keyboard in a bid to organize the little colored shapes floating downward on the screen, cup after cup of tea at her side, cursing in her thick brogue when the colored pieces grew increasingly jumbled and piled up too fast.

Amy went to reprimand her kids—darting for the computer as quickly as they had without first asking permission—but Irene smiled and waved a hand. "It's all right, love." She then leaned in and whispered: "Have you played the game? Like a drug, the bastard is."

Amy laughed.

"Cup of tea?" Irene offered.

"No thanks, Irene, I really have to get going. Their homework's all done—all you have to do is tolerate them for a few hours."

Irene gave a playful gasp and slapped a hand over her chest. "Such a thing to say about two adorable babies as these!"

"Shall I let you keep these babies for the week then?"

Switchblade quick, Irene changed characters. This time to one who had just heard the most absurd question ever posed. "I should think not. I've done my time, I'll have you know."

Amy laughed again. "How are they doing?"

"Ah, they're doing just fine. Tommy came round to see me not long ago. Caitlin is expecting her fifth."

"*Fifth?*"

"We're Irish Catholic, love."

Amy laughed again. It was tough to remember a time they were together when Irene didn't make her laugh. "Okay, well, you have my number and everything, and you have the address of where I'll be, yes?"

Irene smiled, closed her eyes, and gave one reassuring nod.

"Great." Amy then called to her children in the den: "I'm leaving, guys. I love you."

Carrie and Caleb, eyes stuck on the computer screen, mumbled something simultaneously over their shoulders that sounded like "love you too."

Amy turned to Irene. "Such sincerity."

Irene smiled.

Amy turned back to the den. "Password, please," she said to them.

Carrie elbowed Caleb and yelled at him for missing an important piece in the game. Caleb elbowed back and told her to shut up.

"*Password, please*," Amy reiterated firmly.

Both kids spun in their seats, faced their mother, and said "unicorn," then quickly spun back and resumed playing.

"Thank you. Be good for Mrs. Flannigan now."

"Oh, they're always good," Irene said.

"Yeah? My offer for the week still stands," Amy said.

Irene put a hand on Amy's shoulder and gestured toward the front door. "You're going to be late, love."

Amy laughed yet again and left.

CHAPTER 15

Hosting a support group session wasn't too difficult. As long as you had chairs, coffee, and pastries, things seemed to run smoothly. And typically, not many chairs, coffee, and pastries were needed. Attendance was spotty at support group sessions in one's home. Certainly nothing like group therapy at one of the clinics where it was usually a packed house.

But then that was therapy. A therapist was present and running the show.

This was support group. No therapy offered, none asked. Just a social gathering run by whomever the host might be, where attendees were free to open up about any and all things. No sign-up sheet, no last names. Just a smile, a welcome, and a *please help yourself and have a seat.*

•   •   •

All traces of his daughters' sleepover gone, a semicircle of folding chairs now center stage in his den, and refreshments spread out on a table in back, Allan checked his cell. 6:50. Ten minutes until showtime. He wondered whether that was enough time to sneak a quick drink. Booze was forbidden in support group. The reason was fairly simple. Booze made it easier to talk. Easier to open up and share. The goal of support group was to open up and share *without* any substance crutch. A somewhat amusing prospect to Allan when odds were better than good that every single attendee was on some type of medication to deal with their grief.

Still, it wasn't booze. Unlike the myriad antidepressants that attendees were likely on, they were just that—antidepressants. Booze was a depressant. A sinister little devil who promised the goods at a price. Working faster and more efficiently than anything from the pharmacy, it caught you smack in the ass with its pitchfork before too long, reminding you that you knew the deal coming in, buddy.

Allan had managed to steer very clear from the bottle immediately following Samantha's death, focusing all of his attention on his girls and the support they needed. But "slippery slope" was a saying for a reason. Soon, a small nighttime scotch became a large nighttime scotch became two or three or four large nighttime scotches.

The end came one day when he was supposed to drop off Jamie's science fair project at noon. The night before, the number of large nighttime scotches had hit a record high, and he'd been horrifically hungover all morning. Promising himself a short nap around ten, he then proceeded to sleep straight through his alarm and didn't arrive at Jamie's school until almost two, begging the teacher to forgive his tardiness, imagining what a hungover fright he must seem—once discovering he'd overslept, he'd bolted from the house without so much as a brush through the hair or across the teeth—and then having to shuffle on over to his daughter's desk where she sat crying as he apologized repeatedly, only to have her look up at him with eyes that seemed to scold Allan with the very real truth that Mommy would have never let this happen.

For a solid year following that, Allan never even entertained a glass of wine with dinner. Yet as time went on, and after managing a decent enough footing within the new dynamics of his home, he was able to drink again, becoming the poster boy for moderation.

And right now, ready to entertain who knows how many people in his home, he'd love nothing more than a quick nip from the bottle to give him the proper layer of chill he'd need to get through the night. Maybe during their first break, he might be able to persuade Amy Whoever (no last names in group) to sneak into the kitchen with him for a quick belt just as they'd done the last time he hosted. He hoped so.

Amy Whoever was good people. She reminded him a lot of his Samantha. The confident way she carried herself that never once crossed the line into arrogance. A natural beauty right at home in either a five-star restaurant or a company softball game and, better still, eagerly taking part in both. Allan was not ready to date. He didn't know whether he'd ever be. But if the time did ever come, at the top of his list would definitely be Amy. Their secret sip of whiskey shared at the last session he hosted had cemented that truth—a woman who drank whiskey weakened his knees faster than a punch on the jaw.

Allan hurried to his cupboard, reached for the bottle of whiskey, and the doorbell rang.

"Balls," he said, and put the whiskey back.

Maybe it's Amy, he hoped, thinking the two of them might hurry right on back to the kitchen and pick up where he'd left off.

Allan opened his front door. It was not Amy.

.　　.　　.

It was not one but two people. A man and woman. Both young, pale, and thin. Dark circles under their eyes. The man had thinning blond hair; the girl's locks were long and straight and black with what appeared to be a thinning patch on the side of her head. Putting it politely, neither looked well. And to many, that fact might have been cause for alarm. But not to Allan; he saw it as the result of grief. Lord knows, he must have appeared no better soon after losing Samantha.

Allan smiled and stepped aside to allow them entry into his home. "Hey there," he said. "I'm Allan; please come in."

The young man and woman stepped inside and immediately began scanning their surroundings.

"Nice house," the woman said.

"Thank you. Any trouble finding it?"

"No."

Allan smiled. "Well, you're certainly not required to give me your real names, but it usually makes it easier if you give some—"

"Jennifer," the woman said.

Allan extended his hand. Jennifer shook it. "Nice to meet you, Jennifer." He turned to the man. "And you are?"

The man was still seemingly entranced by the house, eyes going all over. Jennifer nudged him. The trance broke.

"Huh?" the man said.

"This is Tim," Jennifer said for him.

Allan extended his hand. Tim took it. "Nice to meet you, Tim."

Tim nodded and mumbled: "Nice to meet you."

The newly grieving, Allan guessed. The girl seemed sharper, more assertive. The guy, somewhat stoned. Again, no cause for alarm. He probably was. *Klonopin or Xanax, most likely*, Allan thought. Once again, booze was a no-no, but everything else was fair game, as long as it was prescribed by a doctor, that is. Although truth be told, Allan had smelled the skunky smell of pot on several attendees on more than one occasion in meetings past.

"This your first meeting?" Allan asked.

"Yeah," Jennifer said. Then, bluntly: "Our mom died."

Allan hid his surprise at her bluntness. Once again, though, he did not question nor judge it. It could simply be another prime example of the unpredictable behavior that loss caused in some people.

"I'm very sorry for your loss," Allan said.

Both Jennifer and Tim muttered a thank you.

Allan flashed a warm, practiced smile and gestured towards the den. "Well, why don't you come on in and have a seat? The others should be here any minute."

"How many?" Jennifer asked.

"I'm sorry?" Allan asked.

"How many others will there be?"

Allan stuck out his lower lip and gave a little shrug. "I really don't know—it varies." He chuckled and added: "It could just end up being the three of us."

Tim, still appearing a little stoned, turned to Jennifer with a confused frown. "*What?*"

Now it was Allan who frowned. First-timers usually preferred a small crowd. The way Tim was looking at his sister now, it almost seemed as though he was counting on more.

Jennifer looked at her brother sharply, as though annoyed by his ignorance. "He was just making a joke. Of course there's going to be more people coming."

Allan's gut did a funny swirl. The kind of swirl he felt when someone was eying him up in a bad part of town. The newly grieving. First-timers at group. Loaded up with benzodiazepines and antidepressants. All solid reasons for odd behavior. But these two... as much as Allan's mind justified their odd behavior with those solid reasons, his gut apparently wasn't having it. His gut felt something was off.

The doorbell rang, quieting Allan's gut before he could indulge it further.

"Ah—there you go," he said to them with a smile. "More people." He gestured into the den again. "Why don't you guys go on in and make yourselves comfortable." He then gestured toward the table of coffee and pastries. "And please help yourselves—all the coffee and sugar you can handle."

Tim and Jennifer went into the den.

Allan answered the door.

"Amy, welcome," he said.

CHAPTER 16

"Any trouble finding it?" Allan asked Amy as she entered the foyer.

"No—I've been here before, remember?" Amy said. She then mimed a quick sip from a bottle followed by a finger to shushed lips.

"Oh, right! I forgot all about that."

Seriously, man? Lame. So lame.

"Am I the first one here?" Amy asked.

"No—we have two first-timers in the den."

"Darn. Was hoping we could"—she mimed the secret drink gesture again—"before anyone arrived."

"Looks like we might just have to be ninjas in the kitchen again after first break," Allan said.

Amy raised her fist. "I'm in."

Fist bump. Sam used to do that.

Allan tapped his fist against Amy's. "See you then."

.   o   o

"Amy, this is Jennifer and Tim," Allan said when the four of them were in the den.

"Hello," Amy said pleasantly.

Tim, sipping a cup of coffee, slowly lowered the cup from his mouth and just stared.

Jennifer offered a thin smile. No hello.

Well, nice to meet you too, Amy thought. She shot Allan a quick, uncertain glance.

Allan flashed a big codependent grin for all. "Tim here was worried it was going to be a small turnout," Allan said to Amy.

"Oh yeah?" Amy said. "Most first-timers prefer a small turnout."

"How do you know we're first-timers?" Jennifer said.

Amy frowned a little. "Uh…because Allan told me in the foyer."

"What's your last name?" Tim blurted to Amy.

"Last names aren't required in group," Allan said.

"We'll tell you ours," Tim said.

Amy shot Allan another quick glance, then replied: "That's okay—I don't need to know."

"Why do you keep looking at him?" Jennifer asked Amy, gesturing to Allan. "I see it, you know. Is something wrong?"

Yeah, you're fucking weird. "No—everything's fine on my end. How about you?"

"Our mom died," Jennifer said.

"Oh yeah? My husband died," Amy replied flatly.

Allan flashed his codependent grin for all again. "Uh, Amy, can you help me with something in the kitchen for a sec? Jennifer and Tim, please help yourselves to more coffee and food."

.   .   .

"What is the deal with those two?" Amy whispered once she and Allan were alone in the kitchen.

"So it's not just me?" Allan whispered back. "They seem kinda strange?"

"Well, I would expect them to be a little strange—lost their mother; first-timers—but they're *rude*. New surroundings and loss shouldn't justify that."

"Yeah, they seemed a little off to me. Like not sad or shy off, but, I don't know…off, off."

And then like so many memories that arrived unwelcomed, and with an even more unwelcomed clarity, Amy was suddenly back in Crescent Lake with Patrick, sitting at the kitchen table, heavily shaken after her first "chance" encounter in a supermarket with what would turn out to be one half of the infamous Fannelli brothers, James Fannelli:

"He was so creepy, Patrick. I mean, I've met some strange men before, but this guy...there was something different about him. Something...wrong."

"Amy?"

Amy was still in Crescent Lake. She had not ignored her gut back then about James Fannelli; Patrick had ignored it for her. She'd told him she wanted to pack up and leave following the supermarket incident. Especially considering earlier events at a family diner when Carrie, then just six, had traded her beloved doll to a stranger for a single piece of candy. That stranger would end up being the other half of the infamous Fannelli brothers, Arthur Fannelli.

Patrick had refused to leave. Refused to let two unrelated incidents with two unrelated assholes (they'd not yet known that supermarket jerk and family diner weirdo were related and in the beginning stages of one of their sick and twisted games) ruin his family's vacation.

Bullheaded male ego on Patrick's part? Perhaps. But the truth Amy had come to back then was the same as it was now: She hadn't truly wanted to leave Crescent Lake; she'd just wanted Patrick to convince her all would be well, that he would look after his family with all the vigilance of a lion who led his pride. It was the dynamics of their relationship. Amy worried, and Patrick soothed her, even at the expense of his own misgivings. In hindsight, in *all* of hindsight's cruel truths, they were the stereotypical family who refused to leave the haunted house even after the ghosts all but appeared and warned them to get the hell out.

But they hadn't. And chaos had ensued. And her husband was dead because of it.

"Amy?" Allan tried again.

Are there ghosts here now, Amy? Are they telling you to leave?

"Amy?"

Amy snapped to. Allan immediately asked whether she was okay.

She dropped her head and nodded. "Yeah. Just bad memories, I guess."

The doorbell rang.

"I need to go get that," Allan said. He then gestured to the kitchen cabinet. "You can start your ninja training without me, if you want." He winked and smiled—not a secret naughty wink and smile as they'd shared before, but more a sympathetic one that was the equivalent of a hug.

Amy returned an equally compassionate smile that silently thanked him, not for the offer of the booze, but for the offer of understanding.

"Thanks," she said. "But something tells me it wouldn't taste as good if I started it alone."

Allan raised his fist.

Amy smiled again, and they fist-bumped.

Allan left to answer the door.

CHAPTER 17

The first thing Allan noticed as he started crossing through the den and into the foyer to answer the front door was that there was no sign of Tim and Jennifer. When he'd left them to go into the kitchen with Amy, they were standing by the coffee and pastries, huddling and keeping to themselves in their odd little way.

Allan paused in the den. "Tim? Jennifer?"

He got no reply.

"*Hello?*" he tried again.

Brother and sister finally appeared, strolling casually from the dining room and through the foyer to meet Allan in the den.

"Is something wrong?" Jennifer asked.

"I was just about to ask you the same. Where were you guys?"

"Bathroom," Jennifer said.

"I never told you where it was. I'm assuming you found it okay?"

They both nodded.

Only Allan hadn't heard a flush. Sure, the downstairs bathroom was through the dining room and in the neighboring mudroom by the garage, but the flush of their downstairs toilet was a damn powerful one that could be heard throughout the house. It had caused many a giggle during the sleepover last night, potty humor apparently still a thing amongst nine-year-old girls.

And so what do you ask next, Allan? If they actually used *the toilet? And if so, did they remember to flush? Come on.*

There was an awkward moment of pause. The three of them standing in the den, considering one another.

"Is something wrong?" Jennifer asked.

Again and again with the same stupid question. *Yes,* he wanted to say. *Yes, something is wrong. I can't put my finger on it, but something is definitely wrong with you two, and it's neither grief nor loss. You're making me uncomfortable in my home, and I'd like you to leave.*

The doorbell rang again.

"Are you going to get that?" Jennifer asked. And wasn't there the slightest hint of a smirk creasing the corner of her mouth just now? Short and fleeting, but there. He saw it.

For the second time that night, the doorbell had interrupted Allan's gut. He would not allow a third. Once he welcomed his new guests, he would politely ask Jennifer and Tim to leave.

CHAPTER 18

Allan opened the front door and was pleased to see Jon and Karen Rogers waiting. Having lost their daughter, Ella, to leukemia roughly around the same time Allan had lost Samantha, the three had formed a decent friendship, or as decent a friendship that could be formed under such circumstances. There were dinners and other social gatherings outside of support group and therapy at the clinic, but nothing heavy. The three of them enjoyed one another's company and saw chances for social outings as a sort of unspoken therapy, unspoken being the primary word considering they never discussed Samantha or Ella during their outings. It was their time to enjoy good company while leaving loss at home where it would always be waiting, undeterred by lack of invitation.

"Hey, you two," Allan said with a warm smile. No big co-dependent grin necessary this time; he was genuinely happy to see his friends. Better yet, happy to have allies—Jon and Karen would likely understand his asking Jennifer and Tim to leave. He knew Amy would.

"Everything all right?" Jon asked the moment he and his wife stepped into the foyer.

Allan was momentarily stunned. How could they know the dilemma he was facing with Tim and Jennifer already?

"Huh?" was all Allan could manage.

"It took you awhile to answer the door," Karen said.

Oh, right. Duh.

"Oh, no, no—everything's fine, it's fine. Come on in."

.   .   .

Allan led Jon and Karen into the den...where Amy stood alone.

Amy smiled and went to say hello, but got no further.

"Where are they now?" Allan asked.

Amy shook her head. "No idea. They were gone when I came in."

"Where are *who*?" Jon asked.

Allan didn't answer right away. He left the den and went into the kitchen.

"I just came from there," Amy called to him.

Allan reappeared. "Well, they couldn't have gone through the foyer; we'd have seen them." He approached the far end of the den where a sliding glass door led out onto the patio. Vertical blinds covered the sliding glass door. The blinds swayed slightly as though recently disturbed.

Allan pulled the blinds and hit the patio light. He saw nothing. Went to unlock the sliding glass door and stopped. It was already unlocked.

Amy appeared at his side. "What's wrong?"

"Door's unlocked," he muttered. "They must have gone this way."

"Gone *where*?"

Allan cupped a hand over his eyes and peered through the glass. The patio lighting offered acceptable direct line of sight, but poor periphery. For all they knew, brother and sister were cloaked in the shadows not three feet away.

"No idea," Allan said, still looking.

Amy did as Allan had done, cupping a hand over her eyes and pressing her face close to the glass for a better look. "I don't see anyone."

They both pulled away from the sliding glass door.

"You think they went home?" Allan asked.

"By slipping out the back without a word?"

"You were expecting a normal exit from those two?"

"What's going on?" Karen broke in from behind them.

Allan locked the sliding glass door, killed the patio light, and pulled the blinds closed. Turning, he said: "Honestly? I have no idea."

"We've got two new people here tonight," Amy said. "A brother and sister. Their behavior thus far has been...strange, to say the least."

"Well, that's to be expected, isn't it? First-timers?" Karen said.

Allan shook his head. "Trust us, we took all that into account. These two..." He snorted. "It's like they're playing some kind of game."

Amy spun towards Allan. "What did you say?"

Allan was momentarily rattled. He felt like he was being accused of something. "About what?"

"About playing a game."

Allan splayed a hand. "What? You were saying the same exact thing."

"I said they were odd—I never said they were playing a game with us."

"Well, haven't they been?"

"What do you mean, Allan?" Jon asked.

Allan shrugged. "I don't know exactly. It's like they're crossing the line but not crossing the line, you know?"

"No, I don't," Jon said. "Give us an example."

Amy broke in. "No. No examples. We're leaving. All of us."

Allan frowned. "*Leaving?*"

"Their game will only escalate," Amy muttered, head down, rifling through her bag.

"What the heck are you talking about?" Allan asked.

Amy ignored him, pulled her phone from her bag, and dialed. Waited. "*Please sober up*," she whispered. She hung up and dialed again. Waited. Hung up again. "*Dammit!*"

Allan put a hesitant hand on Amy's shoulder. "Amy, I felt like we were on the same page earlier. But I gotta be honest—you've lost me now."

The doorbell rang.

No one moved.

"Are you going to get that?" Karen asked.

Allan nodded absently and shuffled toward the foyer, still affected by Amy's behavior.

He opened the front door.

No one there.

"Are you kidding me?" he said to himself.

Allan stepped out onto his front step, looked in all directions, the two lanterns flanking his front door offering him a gloomy yellow lens for a short distance until ultimately diffusing into the black of night. He could see his driveway; he could see his front yard; he could see the many trees in that yard and the many silhouettes of trees beyond.

"*Hello?!*" he called. "You having fun?"

Allan stepped back inside and slammed the door.

When he returned to the den by himself, Amy asked: "Who was it?"

"No one," he said.

"*No one?*"

"Yes."

"No one—like nobody was there?"

"Amy, if someone was there, don't you think they'd be standing next to me right now? Trust me, I looked, and I saw absolutely noth—" Allan stopped abruptly, his face going queerly blank for a spell as though in the throes of déjà vu.

"Allan?" Jon said.

"I saw nothing," he whispered, still in his daze.

How the hell had he missed it the first time?

Allan snapped to, spun around, and bolted for the front door, running outside until coming to a dead stop in his empty driveway.

All of the cars were gone.

CHAPTER 19

All four hurried back inside, Allan locking the front door behind them.

"Allan, what the hell is going on?" Jon asked. "*Where are our cars?*"

"I have no idea."

"It's them," Amy said.

"Them *who*?"

"The first-timers—Jennifer and Tim."

"What? Why?"

"Because it makes the most sense."

"*None of this makes sense!*" Jon snapped. "Are you saying they're car thieves or something?"

"Let's hope that's all it is," Amy replied.

Jon gave her a crazy look. "*That's all?* You get your car stolen every day, do you, Amy?"

"Relax, Jon," Allan said. "I don't think that's what she meant."

"How did they get here?" Karen asked. "The first-timers. Did they drive?"

"Well, they certainly didn't *walk*," Jon said, his comment clearly referencing their rural surroundings.

Allan looked away in thought for a moment. "I don't remember seeing a car. I remember *your* cars, but I don't remember seeing theirs. I suppose they could have parked on the street and walked up the driveway."

"What difference does it make if they drove or not?" Jon asked. "They were here, and now our cars are gone."

"Because if they didn't drive, it means they got a ride," Amy said. "Which means there's a third involved."

Instant silence followed this prospect. Everyone but Amy began looking over their shoulders as if the potential third might be creeping up behind them.

"Well, I guess that makes sense," Karen eventually said. "The third person drops them off, leaving the two of them to take two cars—one each."

"This is *not* about stealing cars," Amy said.

Jon faced her. "Well, then do you mind telling us what it *is* about? I'm sorry, Amy, I don't mean to be an asshole here, but you've been more than just a little cryptic thus far."

Amy said nothing.

"Look, everyone just relax," Allan said. "I know we're a little freaked out, so why don't we just call the police and let them take it from here."

They all nodded.

Allan started for the stairs.

"Where are you going?" Jon asked.

"My cell's in my bedroom."

Jon pulled his cell from his pocket and handed it to Allan. "Use mine."

Allan took the phone and started fiddling with it. He handed it back to Jon. "You got a security code on it or something?"

Jon took back his phone and dialed. Frowned and pulled the phone away, eyes staying on the cell as he said: "Says I've got no signal." He looked up at Allan. "Says I've got no signal. You have trouble with reception out here?"

Now it was Allan who frowned. "Not at all."

Both Karen and Amy pulled out their phones simultaneously.

Karen looked at Amy. "I've got nothing. You?"

Amy shook her head. "Nope. Was working fine a few minutes ago."

"How is this possible?" Jon asked. "How can all of our phones suddenly have no reception?"

"Try your landline," Amy said to Allan.

Allan nodded and hurried into the kitchen. He returned with a cordless phone and a look of disgust. "Nothing," he said, holding up the phone. "Line's dead."

"Please tell me this is some kind of joke," Karen said.

Jon pulled his wife close and held her.

Allan tossed the cordless phone on the sofa. "Okay, let's everyone just think for a second. My car is still in the garage. I say we pile in and *drive* to the police, yeah?"

"*Hell* yeah," Jon said.

"What if someone else shows?" Karen asked. "For group, I mean?"

"Group started twenty minutes ago," Allan said. "I'd say we're it."

The four of them followed Allan's lead through the dining room and into the mudroom. Allan opened the door leading into the garage, hit the light switch on the wall, and froze.

All four tires on his SUV were flat. The windshield was smashed. Scraped into the driver's-side door was a question: *Is something wrong?*

CHAPTER 20

"*Jesus Christ*," Jon whispered.

The four of them stared incredulously at the battered SUV—the flat tires, the smashed windshield, and, of course, the message scraped into the driver's-side door.

"Still think it's about car theft?" Amy said.

Jon spun on her. "Okay, Amy—you seem to be the expert here. Any chance you can start enlightening us?"

Amy gave a thin smile. "Gladly. First I'm gonna need you to get out of my face."

Jon took a step back, let out a short sigh, and nodded apologetically. "I'm sorry."

"It's okay," Amy said. "Trust me, I get your frustration. And I assuredly get your fear. I've been there and gotten the T-shirt, as they say."

"What are you talking about?" Allan asked.

"Anyone here heard of Crescent Lake?" She then made air quotes, voice ripe with contempt: "*'The Crescent Lake Massacre'*? The Fannelli brothers? Monica Kemp?"

Karen's eyes lit up. "Oh yeah—I remember that."

Allan started nodding slowly as the memory trickled back. "Yeah, I remember hearing about that."

"I don't," Jon said. "What happened?"

"Let's go back in the den and I'll tell you," Amy said. She then looked at Allan. "Do you have a gun?"

"No," Allan said softly.

"*A gun?*" Jon blurted. "Why do we need a gun?"

Amy laughed—the type of laugh you couldn't help when someone asked a stupid question.

CHAPTER 21

Aunt Kat sat on her sofa, laptop on lap, surfing through Facebook. She marveled at all the ridiculous posts. *So many people posting about themselves, and about nothing at all. Look what I'm eating! Look where I am! I think this is wrong! I think this is right!* And of course there were the selfies. *Look, here's a photo of me taken by... me!* The novelty of it all was lost on Kat.

And then hypocrisy took the stand, enlightening her with testimony stating that what sustained such nonsense was people like her who bashed yet indulged all the same. No different than the reality TV bug, really—a bug that shamelessly fed on her as well. She even DVR'd them.

Kat chuckled at her shame and set the laptop aside. She looked over at Jamie and Janine, both flat on their backs in front of the TV, heads propped up by pillows.

"You guys wanna play a game or something?" she asked them.

"Nah," they said without turning around.

"Wanna snack?"

"Nah."

"Go for a walk?"

"Nah."

"Buy a puppy?"

Both girls scrambled onto their knees. "*Huh?*"

"What's with you two?" Kat asked. "Usually by now I'm tempted to slip NyQuil into your juice."

"Are you gonna buy us a puppy?" Janine asked.

"No. Tell me what's wrong."

Janine went first. "Why wouldn't Daddy let us go to the thing at our house tonight?"

"Because it's for grownups."

"But it's about Mommy," Jamie said. "And Daddy said it makes him feel better to talk about her with other people. Why doesn't he want *us* to feel better?"

Kat slid off the sofa and onto her knees like her nieces. She inched close to them. "Oh, honey, it's not like that at all. Your daddy wants nothing more in this world than for you to feel better. But sometimes there are things that work for adults that don't work for kids."

"Why can't we at least *try*?" Janine asked.

"Do you want to try with me?"

Janine frowned. "What do you mean?"

"Why don't we talk about Mommy?"

"But you knew her."

"That's not the point," Kat said. "The point is for *you* to talk about her—to talk about all the good memories you have of her."

"It makes me sad when I do that," Jamie said.

"Me too," Janine said.

Kat gave a nurturing smile. "Maybe that's why you're not ready to go to Daddy's thing just yet." She inched closer and cuddled up to them. "Listen, you're always going to miss your mommy; that will never go away. But soon a time will come when you think about her and you won't be so sad. You'll be happy."

"Happy?"

Kat dug for a good analogy. There were none. She tried all the same.

"Do you remember when we all went to Disney World? How you guys cried when we had to leave?"

They nodded.

"Do you cry when you think about Disney World now?"

They shook their heads.

"No, you don't. It's nice to talk about it now, though, right? To have all those wonderful memories?"

"But Disney World is still there," Jamie said. "We can go back."

Kat's heart plummeted. She felt momentarily ill. Forcing an analogy for such a subject...she deserved whatever sickness her guilt handed out.

"I guess I didn't explain that as well as I'd hoped," she said, offering up an apologetic smile.

"Can we call Daddy?" Jamie asked.

Kat glanced at the clock on her cable box. "Oh, honey, I'm not sure his thing is over yet."

"Can we try?"

It's the least you can do after that analogy debacle, she thought. "Okay."

Kat retrieved her cordless phone and dialed Allan's cell. It went straight to voicemail.

"Voicemail," she said to the girls. "It must still be going on."

Straight to voicemail, though? That probably meant he'd turned the phone off. No way would Allan do that when his girls weren't around, even if he knew they were with Kat. He wouldn't even dare mute the ringer. Put it on vibrate or at a lower volume tops, if not just leaving the damn thing to ring at the top of its lungs, rude interruption be damned—his girls had to be able to reach him whenever and wherever.

"Can I try?" Janine asked.

"Wait, let me try again," Kat said.

She did. Straight to voicemail again. Something with his service? A dead spot in the house?

She tried his landline. This too went straight to voicemail.

"Can you try our house?"

Absently, her head processing things, Kat said: "I just did."

"There was no answer?"

"No," Kat said, her tone still far away as she tried to make sense of it all.

Was it possible that Allan had turned his cell off for the meeting? Had taken the landline off the hook? Perhaps she'd been wrong; Allan's knowing his girls were with his sister gave him the peace of mind to temporarily turn off all devices while his support group did their thing.

The pride that such a notion gave Kat did not silence her skepticism completely. "I'll tell you what," she began, "we'll try again in a little bit, and if there's still no answer, we'll swing on by. How's that sound?"

CHAPTER 22

Back in the den, Amy told them everything. She was not vague, nor was she long-winded. She gave them the horrific details of Crescent Lake and the subsequent events thereafter in a curt and straightforward manner, never once pausing for effect or sympathy; if this turned out to be what she feared it might, then time was a factor. Time they needed to prepare.

Many questions followed. Not so much about what Amy had endured, but their predicament now. The constant *why why why*s even though the answers were obvious: The ghosts were here, they were telling them to leave, and yet no one wanted to accept it.

And so now, Amy did not find herself irritated by what appeared to be their willful ignorance, but instead sympathized with it. She'd been there, experienced firsthand the human mind's ability to ignore the obvious when it was all but slapping you in the face. To desperately cling to some alternative explanation that never failed to give hindsight a good laugh—assuming you had survived to endure hindsight's laughter, that is.

It was a universal coping mechanism—people didn't want the truth when that truth was painful or frightening. People wanted what Amy once had: a Patrick. A big lovable Patrick to tell everyone that all was okay despite the blatant clanking of chains and woeful cries in the night. To convince you the ghosts were *not* in the house.

Except they were.

Or, at the very least, hovering just outside, eager to come in. And the answers to those willfully ignorant questions needed saying, bluntly and without a fleck of sugar. Codependency had no place in this home tonight. Not if they wanted to survive. No fucking way.

"They took our cars and trashed Allan's so that we'd be stuck here," Amy said. "They cut the landline and somehow killed a signal for our cell phones to keep us from calling for help. And they left that message scraped into the side of Allan's car because they're starting to enjoy themselves. This is probably their first game—and they're having fun."

Momentary silence.

"First game?" Allan eventually said.

"Yeah," Amy said. "Tim and Jennifer seemed willing and dangerous but...*unstable*. People like that tend to follow rather than lead."

"So who's leading?" Allan asked.

(*Yes, Amy—who's leading?*)

I don't know.

(*Why not heed your own advice? Go with the most logical explanation?*)

Without conscious effort, an image of Kelly Blaine leapt into her head.

But why? She has no grudge with me. Her grudge was with Monica. I killed Monica. If anything, she should respect me.

(*People like that are incapable of respect.*)

Fine—no respect. But no grudge either—it wouldn't make sense.

Domino's voice suddenly echoed in her ear, their conversation on the phone while watching *The Joan Parsons Show* last year:

> Domino: "Ooh—she didn't like that."
> Amy: "What?"
> Domino: "That comment about Monica."
> Amy: "Why?"
> Domino: "Ego. I promise you, what Kelly just heard was 'Monica Kemp is better than you.'"
> Amy: "You think?"

Domino: *"I know."*

So *what does this mean?*

(*It means Kelly needs to prove that Monica Kemp is* not *better than her.*)

Fine. But that still has nothing to do with me. Domino *was* Monica's enemy. Domino *was the one Monica wanted to torture and kill.*

(*Which means if Kelly truly is behind this, she wants to do what Monica couldn't. She wants to finish Domino.*)

But if that's true, then why all this bullshit here? With me and these people I barely know? I don't see the connection.

(*When Monica failed to kill Domino, who did she go after?*)

Me.

(*And she failed at that too.*)

So Kelly's coming for me then? Is that it?

(*Maybe. Or maybe she's planning on raising the bar.*)

Amy's blood ran ice cold. "*Oh God*," she whispered.

"What?" Allan said. "What is it?"

The prospect grew with terrible possibility. *Kelly needs to prove that Monica Kemp is* not *better than her.*

"*Amy!*" Allan yelled.

Amy snapped from her daze. "We need to get to a phone," she said. "I need to get ahold of my kids."

"Your *kids*?"

"If this is what I think it is, then there's a chance they're in danger. I need to go now."

"Go *where*?" Allan asked.

"I don't know. I'll walk until I get a signal."

"Are you nuts?" Jon said. "For all we know, they're out there waiting for us. You can't just go wandering around in the dark hoping to get a signal."

She turned to Allan. "Your neighbors," she said. "Who are the closest?"

"Mike and Pam Rolston. About a hundred yards east, give or take. They're not right next door, that's for sure."

"Then I'll head there. If I get a signal on the way, great. If not, I use their landline."

"You'll still be out in the dark on your own, Amy," Jon said. "You're safer in here with us."

Amy's temper was nearly off its leash. "Jon, in any other situation I'd agree with you, but this is about my kids, so with all due respect, *back the fuck off.*"

Jon leaned back and raised both hands as if Amy had pulled a gun.

Amy hurried towards the front door.

"*Amy, wait!*" Allan yelled.

Allan ran to the foyer and grabbed Amy's shoulder just as she unlocked the front door. Amy instinctively spun and smashed the heel of her palm into Allan's nose.

Allan dropped to all fours and groaned, blood pouring from his nose and onto his tiled floor. He brought an exploratory hand to his face and came away with a palm full of blood.

Jon and Karen could only look on in disbelief.

"Jesus, Amy…" Allan said without looking up. "What the hell?"

Amy dropped next to him and started rubbing his back. "Allan, I'm so sorry. I didn't mean it. Just please understand, I *need* to get to a—"

Amy's cell phone rang.

Everything stopped.

They all gaped at Amy, even Allan, now wide eyed and oblivious to the blood streaming down his nose and gathering on his chin where it periodically dripped.

Amy frantically dug into her pocket and pulled out her phone.

The caller ID read "Domino."

CHAPTER 23

Mike Rolston, sixty-seven, pulled the six-pack of beer from the fridge, placed it on the kitchen counter, and then began rooting in his cupboard for a bag of chips.

His wife, Pam, entered the kitchen and spotted the beer on the counter. "What are you doing?"

Mike answered while still digging through the cupboard. "Was going to pop in on Allan, see if he wanted to have a few beers. Do we have any chips? I thought we had chips."

"Honey, Allan is hosting his support group tonight."

Mike pulled his attention out of the cupboard and fixed it on his wife. "Huh?" His expression was that of a boy who'd been promised pizza but tricked with leftovers.

"Allan's hosting his support group tonight. You knew that. I told you."

Still the dejected face of the boy with no pizza. "No you didn't."

"I did—you don't listen."

"I listen."

Pam snorted and started making herself a cup of tea.

"What time does his group thing end?" Mike asked.

"No idea."

"Nuts." Mike put the beer back in the fridge. "Are the girls there? At the support group?"

Pam nudged her husband aside and went into the fridge for some lemon. "I doubt it—I don't think they'd be ready for something like that."

Mike grunted and itched his bald spot. "So then who's watching the girls?" he asked.

Pam set the bag of precut lemon wedges on the countertop, then got the honey and a box of tea from the cupboard. "I don't know. His sister, Kathy, I would imagine."

"Have I met her?"

"Many times."

"I have? What's she look like?"

"I swear, if you weren't like this from the day I met you, I'd worry you were getting senile."

"You know what the best thing about senility is?"

Pam groaned. "What?"

"You get to hide your own Easter eggs."

She shook her head. "You never run out, do you?"

He laughed and sidled up behind her, wrapping his arms around her waist. Took a stab at a romantic one. "And every night with you would be like the first time." He kissed her cheek.

"Well, I guess that's a plus; I'm not sure the first time was worth remembering."

"Hey!"

She turned in his arms and faced him. "Oh, honey, you know I'm just teasing. It was the best thirty seconds of my life."

"Hey, I finished right on time. You were late."

Pam laughed and slapped him lightly on the chest. "You really are always on, aren't you?"

"What was it little Jamie said the last time we babysat? Oh yeah: *'On like popcorn!'*"

"Oh, *that* you remember." She pushed him away.

The doorbell rang.

Mike's eyes lit up. "What are the chances Allan's support group is finished and he wandered over *here* for a beer?"

"You wish."

Pam went to the front door and opened it. The decent glow of the porch light revealed a young man and woman. The young man had thinning blond hair; the woman, long and ink black locks with what appeared to be a sizable patch shaved into the side of her head. Both were thin and pale. Neither was smiling.

"Can I help you?" Pam asked.

"We're here for the meeting," the young woman said. Her tone was flat, her face vacant.

"I'm sorry?"

"The *meeting.*"

It clicked. "*Oh!* Oh, *the support group.* You're looking for Allan Brown's house, yes?"

"Yes."

Pam smiled a little uneasily. Not the friendliest of people, these two.

"Allan is next door," she said, gesturing to her left.

The couple turned and left without a word.

Pam shut the door behind them. "Well, you're welcome." She returned to the kitchen.

Mike had resumed his search for the missing chips. "Who was it?"

"A young couple looking for Allan's house. For the support group. They were more than a little rude, I must say."

Mike pulled his head out of the cupboard and looked at his wife with mild concern. "Yeah?"

"Yeah. They didn't even thank me after I told them where Allan lived. Just turned and left."

Mike gave a partial shrug. "Well, it *is* a support group for the grieving. I imagine they had other things on their mind."

"Good manners cost nothing," Pam said and then set the kettle on the burner.

Mike went back to checking the cupboards.

The doorbell rang again. Mike popped his head out again. He and Pam exchanged a look that said: *Now who could* that *be?*

Pam started for the door.

"Wait," Mike said, "let me answer."

Mike opened the front door. A young man and woman. Thinning blond hair for him, long and ink black with a bald patch on the side for her. Thin and pale. Neither smiling.

"Can I help you?"

"We're here for the meeting," the young woman said. Flat tone, vacant face.

Mike frowned. "Weren't you just here?"

"No."

Pam appeared behind her husband, peering over his shoulder. "You were!" she exclaimed. "You were *just* here."

"Can we come in?" the young woman asked.

"No, you may not," Mike said, and started to close the door.

The young man stepped forward and stuck his foot in the door, preventing Mike from shutting it completely. Mike went to put his shoulder behind it, but the young man beat him to it, lowering his own shoulder, the door flying open and catching Mike in the chest, knocking him back into his wife's arms.

The young man and woman stepped inside and shut the door behind them. The young woman pulled a gun. The young man held a pitchfork at his side.

Pam screamed just as the kettle began whistling on the stove.

The young woman's face was no longer vacant. She was grinning.

CHAPTER 24

Amy couldn't answer her cell phone fast enough. "*Domino?*"

"Hello?" It was an odd, sexless voice. Almost synthetic.

"*Who is this?*" Amy asked.

"Amy? You there?"

"Is this Domino?"

"Of course it is. Who else would it be?"

"It doesn't sound like you. You sound funny. Like a machine voice or something."

"You sound funny too. And the connection is bad. You keep going in and out."

"We've had no connection for nearly an hour. All our phones are dead. The landlines too. Listen to me, something very bad is happening. I think Kelly Blaine is behind it."

"*What?* What the hell are you talking about?"

"I don't have time to explain, just please trust me. I need you to get the kids and take them someplace safe." And then a forgotten truth slapped her. "Shit, are you still wasted?"

"Amy? You there?"

"*Fuck!*" Amy zigzagged throughout the house in a desperate bid for a stronger connection, asking whether Domino could hear her every few feet. Allan, Jon, and Karen looked on, wide eyed and anxious, Allan with a bloodied rag pressed to his nose courtesy of Amy.

Amy got reception halfway up the stairs.

"Amy?" the distorted voice on the phone said.

"*Yes!*" She froze on the spot, each foot on a different step, not daring to move. "Yes, I'm here. Can you hear me?"

"Barely."

"Listen to me, Domino." She spoke loudly and slowly as though trying to speak over a racket. "*You need to get Carrie and Caleb someplace safe. If you're still drunk, call a cab, call a limo, call anyone, just get them someplace—*"

"Amy? You still there?"

"*FUCK!*" Amy moved a few steps up the staircase. "Domino?"

"Yeah, I'm here. You keep breaking up. Can you get to another phone?"

Amy nodded into her cell. "I'm gonna try. I'll call you *right* back, okay?"

"I'll be here."

Amy hung up and hurried down the stairs. "Gimme your phones," she said to the group.

Without debate, Jon and Karen handed theirs over.

No signal for either of them.

She tried hers again. It too now had no signal. "*Goddammit!* It was *just* working!"

"Let me go get mine," Allan said, starting for the stairs.

"What's the point?" Jon said. "You're not going to get a signal."

Allan ignored him and bounded up the stairs.

CHAPTER 25

"This isn't happening," Allan said as he descended the stairs ten minutes later, dabbing at his nose with the rag, the bleeding now all but done.

"What?" Karen asked.

"I can't find it," Allan said. "I looked everywhere, and I can't find the damn thing."

They adjourned back to the den. Allan tossed the bloodied rag into a small wastebasket in the corner.

"Are you sure you left it in your room?" Amy asked.

"Not a hundred percent, no, but high nineties."

"Did you look anywhere else?" Karen asked.

"Yeah. Checked the girls' room, the guest room—nothing."

Amy's lips vanished in contempt. "How long were they out of our sight?" she asked.

"Who? Jennifer and Tim?" Allan said.

"Yeah."

"I don't know—they wandered a few times. Each time seemed like it was only for a couple of minutes, though. Why? Are you suggesting they went into my room and took my phone?"

Amy nodded.

"How would they know it was even up there? In my entire house, in the short intervals they were gone, how would they know to look in my bedroom for my phone?"

A pause.

"Because you said," Karen whispered.

"What's that?" Allan asked.

"You told us it was in your bedroom. You were about to go upstairs to get it, and Jon said you could use his phone instead, so you stopped."

Allan frowned. "I'm not following."

Amy said: "She's saying we weren't the only ones who heard you say your phone was upstairs."

Karen nodded.

"Wait—no, no, no," Allan said. "They were gone by then—they'd taken our cars."

Another pause. The collective chill was almost visible as the only other alternative presented itself.

Amy voiced it: "Then there was someone else in the house who heard it."

Ten minutes earlier

Last Allan remembered, he'd left his cell phone on his nightstand.

It was not there.

One hand pressing the bloodied rag to his nose, he used the other to tear his bedroom apart like a burglar ransacking the place, tossing this and that over his shoulder without a care, desperate to locate the goods.

He gave up and slumped on his bed, sighed, and murmured: *"This isn't happening."*

. . .

Tucked safely away in the bedroom closet, watching Allan's search through one of the slits in the shutters, the object of his search in her bag along with Domino Taylor's phone and a high-end cell phone jammer capable of *miles*, Kelly Blaine could scarcely contain her glee.

At one point, out of desperation, Allan had even approached the bedroom closet and opened both doors. Stood inches from her. *Inches!* And yet there she stood unnoticed, her small frame invisible behind the dense row of dresses once belonging to his wife, dresses that grief would apparently not allow Allan to discard just yet.

Such exquisite irony all but made her squeal.

Though she struggled to admit such a thing (any parallels between herself and the likes of Monica and her stupid family were *not* welcomed observations), Kelly was enjoying this "game" thing immensely.

CHAPTER 26

"*Someone else in my house?*" Allan said.

"It makes the most sense," Amy said.

"*Now?* Here *now?*"

"I don't know."

All eyes immediately scanned their surroundings.

All eyes but Amy's.

Not that she wasn't frightened. She simply knew better how to cope with fear. One might think Amy had become desensitized to fear after all she'd endured over the past few years, but this too was false. It was, she'd learned, exceptionally rare to become desensitized to fear. Even the biggest and the baddest felt it.

Domino had once made Amy watch a film on Mike Tyson's first trainer (a short, plump little gray man, Cus something, she couldn't remember his last name just now) who was explaining to a young and impressionable Tyson that there is no difference between how a hero feels and how a coward feels; they both feel the same.

What separates them is what they do.

The coward refuses to face his or her fear and wilts. The hero fights that fear and does what he or she needs to do to survive. And if Amy Lambert was anything, she was a survivor.

"I need to get to your neighbor's phone," she said.

"Wait a minute," Jon said. "You just said it was possible there was someone else in this house."

"It *is* possible."

"Well, then, shouldn't we—I don't know—*do something about it?*"

"Like what?" Amy said.

Jon looked helplessly at Allan and Karen for support.

"Where are we most vulnerable?" Allan asked everyone. "In here or outside?"

"They took our cars," Karen said. "They could be long gone."

"Or they could have parked them down the street and made it back on foot," Amy said.

"Why would they do that?"

"I told you: Taking our cars was only a means to an end—they only did it to make sure we couldn't leave. Same reason they trashed Allan's car."

"Okay, they wanted to make sure we couldn't leave," Jon said. "*Why?* What are they planning?"

Amy said nothing.

"Earlier, you said 'if this is what I think it is,' then your kids might be in danger," Allan said. "You then told your friend Domino that you thought someone named Kelly might be behind this. What did you mean by that?"

"I don't have time to explain."

"Please."

Amy sighed. "Let's just say the past I told you about might be coming back to haunt me."

"I thought they were all dead," Karen said.

"They are. Sort of. There's one…" She sighed again, frustrated.

"Kelly?" Allan asked.

"Yes."

"Who is she?"

"A psychopath. I really don't have time to explain further. I'm sorry. I hope my hunch is wrong, I really do, but right now I'm just asking you to please trust me. *Please.*"

Allan dropped his head and nodded.

Amy started for the front door.

"Wait, so if this is all about your past, then what the hell are *we* doing here?" Jon asked, gesturing to his wife and Allan.

"You're here for support group," Amy said.

"That's not what I meant. I meant why are we *involved?*"

"Bad luck," Amy said.

"*Bad luck?* I think we've all had enough bad luck for one lifetime, Amy. There's no way something so traumatic could happen to us again. Not after what we've been through."

Amy laughed. "Forgive me, Jon, but you're a fucking moron."

"*Excuse me?*"

"The quicker you get it through your head that there is no grand scheme in the universe, the better off you're gonna be."

"*Grand scheme?* What the hell are you talking about?"

"Things do not"—she made air quotes—"'happen for a reason,' Jonny-boy. They just happen. And here's another useful little tidbit for you: Life is not fair. It's just life. Sometimes it's good, and sometimes it fucking sucks. And it can *keep* on sucking—there is no cosmic rule that states one misfortune exempts you from another."

Amy took a deep breath and let it out slowly, cheeks puffing, feeling a little guilty for her outburst at these people who were not just mourning, but who were also very scared.

"Look, I'm sorry for being so blunt," she said. "I guess you could say at this stage of my life—after what I've been through—discretion is something I'm finding less and less use for. The reality is that bad shit happens to good people because bad shit happens to good people. That's it. Look no deeper."

Jon finally spoke up. "God wouldn't allow so much tragedy in one lifetime," he said.

Amy laughed again. Burst out laughing, actually; whatever guilt she might have felt for her behavior toward the Rogerses moments ago now gone in the presence of Jon's unwavering ignorance.

"Okay, Jonny-boy...okay," Amy said. "Maybe your god can talk to my god sometime. I'll give you a heads-up, though: My god has a sick sense of humor."

CHAPTER 27

Philadelphia, Pennsylvania

Kevin Lane ordered another round.

The bartender, mid-forties, close-cropped graying hair, solid build on display thanks to a tight black staff shirt, had a different suggestion. "How about a Coke instead?"

Kevin frowned. "Why?"

"Because you're drunk."

Kevin waved a hand over the bar. "Everyone in here is drunk."

"Maybe. But I got shit for serving you too much the other night. Last *couple* of nights, as a matter of fact."

"I take care of you," Kevin said.

The bartender conceded this with a little nod. "Yeah, you do—but I'm not about to lose my job over a good tip."

"Come on, man, just one more."

The bartender shook his head. "Can't do it, buddy." He then leaned over the bar and spoke in hushed tones. "Listen, man, I don't want to sound like a dick, but you've been coming in here a lot lately doing nothing but sitting by yourself and getting drunk. You might as well do that shit at home, man. Save yourself a lot of money, not to mention a DUI."

"I'm waiting for somebody," Kevin said.

"Tonight?"

"Every night."

The bartender leaned back. "Well, obviously she's not showing anytime soon, man, so why don't you—"

"*He.*"

"What?"

"*He's* not showing."

"Whatever, man—bottom line, you're cut off, all right? So, maybe it's better you just go."

Kevin Lane now had no alternative but to ask. "You know a guy named Domino? Big black guy?"

"Yeah, I know Domino. That the guy you're waiting for?"

Kevin nodded. "I was told he comes in here sometimes."

"Yeah, he does. Sounds like you're not so much waiting for him as much as you are *looking* for him," the bartender said.

"Something like that," Kevin said.

"Domino's not the kind of guy you want to be stalking, man. Trust me."

Stalking.

It sounded so ugly. But it was true, wasn't it? He'd been told this was Domino's favorite watering hole and had been frequenting it nightly ever since. He even knew where Domino lived, knowledge few had. He'd camped out at Amy Lambert's house one night and had gotten lucky when Domino showed up for a visit. All he had to do after that was follow Domino home. Tricky stuff with men of Domino's ilk, but somehow he'd managed to do it undetected.

All there was to do after that was knock on Domino's door, introduce himself (even though he was fairly certain Domino would know who he was), and then flat-out ask Domino whether he'd be willing to help him take Kelly Blaine down. After all, if anyone knew how sinister the little bitch was, it was Domino Taylor.

Problem was, Kevin Lane could never quite bring himself to knock on Domino's door. Though he'd obsessed over the girl getting her comeuppance for as long as he could remember, that obsession growing to one of disturbing proportions following her embarrassment of him on nationwide television—he seldom ate or slept; his home had become derelict with neglect, resulting in many complaints from his neighbors; he drank daily and abused prescription drugs— Kevin simply had no idea how he'd go about doing such a thing. He was a school counselor (or *had been*), not a vigilante.

Domino Taylor, however, was as close to a vigilante as you got. And he had some serious history with Kelly. It was almost perfect. It was all just a matter of presenting it the right way so Domino didn't slam the door on him or, if he did manage to catch him at the bar, toss a beer in his face and call him crazy like so many others (*so many others*) had done these past few years.

And sometimes Kevin wondered whether he *had* perhaps gone a little crazy. How could such false exploitation over the years *not* take a toll on a man? Still, the one thing he did know, the one thing he believed to be sane and just down to his very soul, was that Kelly Blaine needed to be exposed for the psychopathic killer she was. He believed Domino Taylor was his last chance.

"Yeah, I know," Kevin said. "I'm willing to take my chances, though."

The bartender shrugged. "Your health."

Kevin chuckled politely at the bartender's wit. "You mind telling me when the last time you saw Domino in here was?"

The bartender held up a hand. "Sorry, man—I'm not being a part of this."

"What if I gave you my name and number? Maybe the next time Domino comes in you can give it to him?"

"Man, what did I just say? Hey, Tommy," the bartender called over Kevin's shoulder.

A bouncer appeared next to Kevin.

"This guy's done," the bartender said.

Kevin turned on his stool and looked at the bouncer, a man who looked like something out of a fairy tale who ate children.

"Let's go, man," the bouncer said.

Kevin pursed his lips. "Fine." He looked at the bartender. "No tip for *you* tonight, pal."

The bartender snorted. "There goes my yacht."

The bouncer escorted Kevin outside and shut the door behind him. Kevin closed his eyes and stood there for a moment, listening to the ambient noises of Philadelphia nightlife all around him, people shouting, laughing, cabs honking, and he wondered whether he should take the bartender's advice and go to the nearest store, grab a cheap case of something, and sit at home to get properly shitfaced without trouble. It was still early in the evening; he could find a place still open.

And Domino Taylor would still be awake, he thought.

Hoping to catch him at his favorite watering hole had been a bust. He'd previously flirted with the idea of staking Domino out and following him on his daily routine, perhaps running into him at the supermarket: *Oh hey! Domino Taylor, right? Remember me?*

Except staking out someone like Domino was a far cry from staking out Amy Lambert. On his first night, Domino would have likely made him. And as for approaching him in the supermarket? Even if Domino did accommodate him with a friendly hello, what next? *Listen, Domino, would you be interested in helping me bring down that crazy little bitch Kelly Blaine? Oh, don't mind us folks, continue shopping, just ordinary everyday conversation here.* If Domino didn't suspect Kevin might be losing it before, he would definitely think so then. Probably stuff him in the shopping cart and kick him down one of the aisles until he took no for an answer.

So what did that leave? He knew he had to at least *try* to talk to him. Even though he had no formal plan, perhaps someone as keen as Domino would see the desperation in his face. And again, if anyone knew the real truth about Kelly Blaine, it was Domino Taylor; he might, in fact, be the only person left in this world who truly believed Kevin's side of the story.

Yes. Yes, he'd decided. Or maybe his gut full of booze had decided for him, but he'd decided all the same. He would go to Domino's. Go to Domino's and hope that the only person left in the world who might believe him was willing to help. He had to try. He was a short step above rock bottom. He had to at least try.

CHAPTER 28

Several minutes of silence passed as Amy and Jon cooled down.

Amy's words to Jon, harsh as they were, rung truer than anything else Allan had ever heard. Her choice of words about a "grand scheme in the universe" were eerily similar to his invisible "scales of justice" that seemed to cruelly insist on tilting against him ever since Sam's passing. From the cop who'd given him a ticket earlier today, to his girls' struggle to comprehend the cathartic benefits of support group when it came to their mother, to right now, knee deep in one hell of who knew what. Not to mention the slew of other bumps (and, quite often, some seriously cavernous potholes) he'd endured over the past two years as a recent widower who was desperately trying to nurture his grieving children without simultaneously losing his own shit.

And so as far as Allan was concerned, Amy's assertions were spot on. Things do not happen for a reason. Life is not fair. One misfortune does not exempt you from another. And, most of all, bad shit happens to good people because bad shit happens to good people.

And there was a sort of liberation in that for Allan, crazy as it may sound. No false hope, no complaints about the injustice of it all. It forced you to know exactly where you stood and whom you could rely on. Not so far off from the coveted here and now.

"So, are we safer inside or outside?" Karen eventually asked.

"I don't know," Amy said. "For all we know, there's someone in the house right now."

"But we're not positive about that," Jon said.

"Then how do you explain someone taking Allan's phone after Tim and Jennifer were gone?" Karen asked.

"Could be a few different explanations," Jon countered.

"Occam's razor, Jonny-boy," Amy said.

"What?"

"Basically, it means the answer to a problem is often the simplest," Allan replied for her.

Amy nodded approvingly towards Allan.

"Well, then how the hell did someone else get into your house after Tim and Jennifer had already left, Allan? Don't you have an alarm system?"

Now Amy answered for Allan: "Tim and Jennifer obviously let them in while they were still here."

Jon grunted and looked away.

"Look, whatever we decide is safest is irrelevant," Amy said. "I'm *going* next door."

"Maybe we should *all* go," Karen said.

"And what if they're out there waiting for us?" Jon said. "We'd be far too vulnerable in the dark."

"They took our cars and killed our phones, right?" Karen said. "That means they want to keep us from going for help, but most of all, keep us *here*."

"So?"

"Well, if you ask me, it means they intend on coming back."

Jon considered his wife's words, then shook his head adamantly. "No—I say we stay here. We arm ourselves and stand back to back in the den. No surprises that way. We see what's coming, and we're prepared."

"Do what you want," Amy said and started for the front door again.

Jon thrust a finger at her. "There, you see? It's like a damn horror film. Everyone always splits up and does the exact opposite of what they *should* do."

"So you propose we arm ourselves and stand back to back in the den until *when?*" Karen asked.

"Until sun up if we have to. But it'll never come to that. Allan, your kids are with a sitter, I assume?"

"My sister's. A sleepover."

"And were you planning on calling to say goodnight?"

"Yes."

Jon splayed a hand. "Okay—so when you don't call, won't your sister think something's fishy?" He spun toward Amy, who was now in the foyer. "Amy, I assume your kids are with a sitter as well?" he called to her.

Amy stopped, gave an impatient sigh, and turned back toward the den. "That's right."

"No sleepover?"

She shook her head.

"And when you don't show up to collect them, will the sitter not suspect something's wrong?"

Amy said nothing, just turned back toward the front door, unlocked it, and went to leave.

"*Wait,*" Allan said. "I'm going with you."

Jon rolled his eyes and splayed another hand in their direction. "Yes, by all means, let's split up more so—give the horror film aficionados what they want."

"I have a gun," Allan said bluntly.

Jon and Karen stood stunned.

Amy shut the door and looked hard at Allan. "You said you didn't."

"It was Sam's," he said.

"Did she hunt?" Karen asked.

"No—no way. She went to a range. It was her thing. Some people join a gym. She liked to shoot guns." He shrugged, then dropped his head, the memory painful.

"Can you go get it?" Amy asked.

Allan nodded. He returned minutes later with the gun. He handled it like a man with a critter that may bite.

Amy took it from him. Handled it like a woman who tamed critters. It was a 9mm Glock. A damn good handgun. Unfortunately, however, it was just that: a handgun.

Allan noticed her disappointment. "Something wrong? Is it no good?"

"No—no, it's great. It's just…"

"What?" Jon asked.

"Well, it's a pistol."

"So?"

"You ever fired a pistol before, Jonny-boy?"

"No."

Amy turned to Karen. "You?"

"No."

"If it was a shotgun, I'd say hurrah and place it in your laps with instructions to blow anyone away who came close. A shotgun blast spreads."

"And a pistol?" Jon said.

"They require training. *Lots* of training. Movies will have you thinking you can hit wherever you point. It's bullshit. Hitting your target with a pistol is damn hard."

Allan sighed. "She's right. I went with Sam a few times. It was exceptionally humbling."

"So then what are you saying?" Jon asked.

Amy looked at Allan. "Stay with them. Let me take the gun and go next door by myself. I'm the only one here who knows how to use it."

Allan said nothing. Amy went on.

"Do what Jon said. Arm yourselves. Knives, bats, fucking boiling water—I don't know. Just arm yourselves. The three of you together make a tougher target."

"And you?" Allan said.

"She's got the gun," Jon said.

Allan shot him a look. *Pussy*, that look said.

"Here's what I can tell you," Amy began. "I *will* make it next door. I *will* call for help. And Jon was right; people *will* start missing us eventually."

Jon raised his chin.

"Don't get a big head, Jonny-boy. You're a pussy, and it shows."

Jon frowned.

Allan bit back a smile.

"Look, I hope I'm wrong about all this, guys," Amy continued. "I hope the Kelly girl I mentioned is not involved. I hope these assholes screwing around with us are some sick groupies of Monica Kemp and the Fannelli brothers getting their rocks off by playing games on the five-year anniversary of Crescent Lake or something, I really do. And if my wish comes true, I'm gonna go next door, call the police, and they're gonna show up and find these copycat amateurs and arrest their asses."

"And if your wish doesn't come true?" Allan said.

"I spoke to my friend Domino. You all heard me. Domino's picture is in an encyclopedia somewhere under *Do Not Fuck With*. You might even say it would be far more satisfying if he found these assholes before the police—the police frown on excessive force."

Allan bit back another smile. Was he enjoying this? No. Absurd. Or maybe not so absurd. He was in the here and now, after all. Insistent thoughts of the painful past and uncertain future were forced to leave. The situation demanded it. Damn good therapy this was, albeit the cost a little extreme.

Amy went on, tucking the gun in her waist and then readjusting the strength in her ponytail as she did so. "Domino knows all about Kelly Blaine," she said. "More than you can possibly imagine. If he heard me mention her, he knows something's wrong, and he'd start calling for help. He knows I'm not one to panic."

"All the more reason you should stay here," Jon said. His tone was not one of concern—she'd just called him a pussy, after all—but that of a man insisting his plan was superior.

"The connection was shit," Amy said. "I'm not a hundred percent on what Domino heard and what he didn't. I *do* know he heard me mention Kelly's name. Either way, I *am* going next door to call my kids and make sure they get somewhere safe until we know what's what."

"So what do we do while you're gone?" Karen asked.

Amy popped the clip on the Glock, double-checked the ammunition, popped the clip back in, and then aimed the gun at the far wall. "Cover your ears."

She fired two quick rounds into Allan's wall.

Everybody flinched as though a bomb had gone off.

"*What the hell?!*" Jon yelled.

"Gotta make sure it works, Jonny-boy," Amy said. Then to Allan: "Keep safe. Grab whatever you can for defense just in case. I'll be right back. Sorry about your wall."

CHAPTER 29

Kevin Lane found it odd that a former security specialist like Domino Taylor would have a front door in such need of repair. Even with the door closed, it was apparent that the wooden frame was badly cracked. Kevin believed that with enough strength, one could still probably open the door—locked, bolted, and chained—just on the splintered, defective frame alone. Literally rip the thing open.

Still a little drunk, Kevin was not drunk enough to ignore common sense. It *was* odd that a security specialist like Domino would have his front door in such a state. What was the old saying? "Where there's smoke, there's fire"? Was the cracked frame on Domino's front door the smoke; inside, the fire? It was damn sure possible. Better still, it now gave Kevin an excuse to at least ring the doorbell. If Domino answered and treated him with less than a little kindness, he might be able to fumble out an excuse that he just wanted to chat and happened to notice his front door and got concerned. A nice little diversion into something that would make Domino appreciative for Kevin's concern, and thus perhaps receptive to what he had to say.

And if he didn't answer the doorbell?

What about the police? Call the police and tell them, *I dropped by to say hello to an old friend, noticed the state of his door, rang the bell to no avail, and now I'm concerned*?

Sure, he could do that. There were a few problems to that approach, though.

Kevin Lane's obsession with Kelly Blaine was not a secret from the Philadelphia police, or many other police forces across the state or even the country, for that matter. Living the life of a transient over the years, many was the night that, after too much booze and too little sleep, he had phoned authorities, begging for them to listen to him. His public execution on *The Joan Parsons Show* certainly didn't help paint him in a better light, either. If he were to call the police now and tell them he was standing outside Domino Taylor's front door—Domino Taylor, who happened to have a strong rapport with the Philadelphia police—would they still think him a crackpot and hang up? Maybe, maybe not.

There was something else to consider though. Another problem, if you will.

Kevin wasn't entirely sure he even *wanted* the police involved in bringing Kelly Blaine to justice. She'd eluded them so many times before, convinced them she was the victim and not the evildoer, and, of course, in doing so recently, painted him as a sex-offending liar. If this were to happen yet again, if she were to slip out of his grasp for the umpteenth time, he would assuredly and finally lose his mind. He was *terrified* to take that risk. A part of him wanted his own justice for Kelly Blaine. Even if that meant wrapping his hands around her little throat and squeezing until he heard a snap.

So what did all this mean? No police, if possible. But first why not try ringing the bell, for Christ's sake?

He did. And there was no answer. He pressed the button again, and once again got no reply. He decided to knock, first a few polite raps, and then a firm couple of thumps.

The door creaked open on the last thump.

Not only was the doorframe cracked, but the door had been unlocked. Things were no longer odd. They were unsettling.

Kevin steadied himself, took a deep breath, and went inside.

CHAPTER 30

Incredulously, Amy's biggest concern during her trek next door to the Rolstons' was not running into the likes of Tim and Jennifer. A part of her *hoped* they'd show up, try to get the jump on her. She would happily put many bullets in them and continue on her way.

No, what Amy was worried about was everyone who *wasn't* Tim or Jennifer or whoever the hell else was involved in their stupid game. As rural as the neighborhood was (and Allan was right, Amy was finding the Rolstons were anything but right next door), it was still a neighborhood. Here now, in the dark, keeping low and taking periodic cover as she moved from tree to tree, Amy would not put many bullets in anyone unless she was absolutely sure it was Tim and Jennifer. God forbid it was a man or woman simply out for a nightly stroll. This meant hesitation. Hesitation was often the difference between life and death, as Amy well knew.

Fortunately, such concerns became immaterial; she'd arrived at the Rolstons' home without incident. Amy was surprised to see that practically all the lights in the house—a sizable two-story contemporary—were on. More curious still, the lights on the front porch shone bright and welcoming.

It was as if the Rolstons were expecting company.

CHAPTER 31

After locking the front door behind Amy, Allan returned to the den.

"She gone?" Jon asked.

"She's gone."

"I was hoping she decided to stay."

"Because she's got the gun?" Allan asked.

"Because she seems to be tougher than about ninety percent of the men I know."

"If you'd gone through what she went through, I'd imagine your skin would be a bit calloused as well."

"Do you really think this is connected to all that?" Karen asked. "Or do you think maybe it's like Amy suggested: groupies or whatever playing sick games on the anniversary of the tragedy?"

"I really don't know," Allan said. "Does it matter?"

Both Karen and Jon said nothing.

Allan nodded with a thin smile that said he was disappointed to be right.

"So what do we do now?" Karen asked.

"Stick to the plan, I guess," Allan said. "Arm ourselves and stay put right here—" He pointed a finger straight down toward the floor of the den. "—and wait for Amy to return or, better yet, Amy and the police to return."

"Okay, let's think," Jon said. "You've got knives in the kitchen, right?"

Allan nodded. "Of course."

"Okay, I guess we can start there—"

"Let's go to the garage," Allan interrupted.

"Why?"

"Because I have an axe, a pitchfork, and even a machete out there. But if you'd feel safer with a kitchen knife…"

They went to the garage.

CHAPTER 32

Amy tucked the gun into her waist and approached the Rolstons' front step. She squinted from the glare of the porch lights. *Were* they expecting company? Perhaps so. Perhaps company was already there. She turned behind her and checked the driveway. No cars. None on the street either. Long rectangular windows flanked the door, and Amy bent at the waist to peek inside. She saw the interior of a nicely furnished home, and that was all. No signs of life. Perhaps they were out? Amy often left more than the usual amount of lights on in the house when she was away to give the impression that someone was home when they were not. An old-school deterrent to burglars that still held merit, according to Domino.

Was that what was going on here? Had the Rolstons gone out and left the lights on? Perhaps. No cars in the driveway didn't necessarily make it so, however; Amy could make out a sizable garage at the far west end of the house. Likely, the cars were tucked in there for the night. The only thing the empty driveway (and street, for that matter) told her was that if the Rolstons *were* home, they were likely alone. No guests.

Enough guess work. Ring the damn bell.

She did. Rang it once, and then accompanied the ring with a firm but respectful knock. Waited. Got nothing. Rang again and knocked again. Waited and got nothing. She peeked through one of the rectangular windows again, hoping to see someone approaching, or perhaps someone peeking out at *her*, justifiably wary about who was so insistent on seeing them on a Sunday night.

She saw nothing.

Amy tried a final time. Ringing the doorbell twice, knocking several times. Shifting to the adjacent slice of window to peek in right after, hoping the new perspective from this window would give her a different view of something, anything.

What Amy saw through her new perspective was just the thinnest slice of a television set down the hallway and into the adjoining den. The television was on.

Screw this, Amy thought, and pinned her finger to the doorbell, letting it ring countless times, the bottom of her fist banging against the door just after, no firm courtesy knocking anymore, but an insistent *open-up-dammit!* banging.

She pressed her mouth close to the window, screamed: "*Please open up, it's an emergency!*" In her haste and frustration, she went to wriggle the doorknob, only to fall silently stunned as the knob turned without resistance and the door opened, the sound of the television down the hall suddenly clear, as if welcoming her.

CHAPTER 33

Allan could not help but fixate on his newly mangled car when the three of them returned to the garage.

"Leave it be," Karen said. "We'll make them pay every single cent for its repair."

Allan said nothing, just guided them toward a large metal tool cabinet standing tall in the far corner of the garage.

"You really have a machete?" Jon asked.

"Yeah."

"Why?"

"Clearing brush in the backyard. My girls have a trail they like to walk. It gets overgrown sometimes."

"Hedge clippers don't do the job?"

Allan sighed and faced Jon. "I suppose they would. I think I have an old pair somewhere in here. Would you prefer wielding those over a machete, Jon?"

Jon conceded Allan's point with a little nod and a smile, a silent touché.

The beige cabinet had one giant locking door, the keyed handle long and silver. Despite this, Allan never locked it. Didn't even know where the damn key was, to be honest. He'd told himself countless times he should for the safety of his girls, not that he imagined his girls would find much interest in horsing around with axes and pitchforks and the like. Still, he supposed if they were bored enough they could access the cabinet whenever they wanted without much troub—

A sudden bolt of terror struck Allan square in the chest.

He did not bother to relay his fear, just prayed as he ripped the cabinet door open.

The cabinet was empty. Taped to the inside of the cabinet door was a single piece of paper. On it, a message.

Allan snatched the paper and read it.

You really should keep this locked ☺, it said.

CHAPTER 34

Amy stepped into the Rolstons' home. Her tread was light and deliberate, as though the floor might give beneath her. She took quick inventory of the situation. She'd rung the doorbell a zillion times, and knocked on the door twice as many. Each time she got no response. Saw no life through the windows when she peeked in after each ring and knock.

Except the television. The television was alive yet apparently entertaining no one.

Had they left it on before going out for the evening? One of Amy's neighbors had a rescue dog that used to get exceptionally worked up whenever the family would leave their house. A nice pile of poo would be waiting for them when they would return home. A veterinarian had recommended leaving the television on when they were out—a way to trick the dog into thinking there was still life in the house and it was not being abandoned yet again. Crazily enough, it had worked. No more poo waiting for them when they would return home. Could that be the case here? A dog in the house? No. Unless the dog was deaf, it would have assuredly barked its head off after her incessant ringing and knocking. And if it was deaf, why even bother leaving the TV on for it? The movement on the screen, perhaps. No, that was silly.

So what else did that leave? TV on, no one answering her banging and ringing. Perhaps the Rolstons had been watching television when they spotted Amy approaching. Took off upstairs or some-where else in the house to hide until Amy went away.

But then she'd started hollering, hadn't she? Pleading for help through the door? Surely the Rolstons wouldn't assume a solicitor would use such an approach, no matter how desperate. That would make Amy a woman in trouble. Were the Rolstons the kind of peo-ple who would turn their backs on a woman's cries for help? Who knew, in this day and age? You certainly didn't have to convince Amy that there were plenty of crazies running around. Female ones, even. Perhaps the Rolstons saw it as a ruse to get them to unlock their door.

But the door *was* unlocked. How the hell did you explain that? Sure, this part of Montgomery County was considered rural, maybe even country by some, but it wasn't Mayberry. Even the most trust-ing of souls knew better these days to lock up just in case.

Enough guesswork.

"Hello? Is anybody home?" she called. Waited, and then tried again, louder, cupping a hand next to her mouth. "*Hello?!*"

No reply.

Amy made a left, strolling cautiously into the kitchen. The gun was still in her waist. She contemplated drawing it and keeping it at her side but chose against it just now.

She noticed something odd on the kitchen counter. A teacup. Next to the teacup was a Ziploc bag of precut lemon wedges. Next to the bag of lemons was a plastic squeeze bottle of honey. Next to that, a box of tea.

Amy peeked inside the teacup. It was empty. She spotted the kettle on the stove and placed a tentative hand on it. It was still warm. So what did all this mean? Well, it was fairly obvious, as far as Amy was concerned. Someone had been interrupted while mak-ing tea. Recently.

Amy spotted a cordless phone at the opposite end of the kitchen counter. She hurried toward it and raised it to her ear. No dial tone. She mashed a few of the phone's buttons all the same and tried again. Still nothing.

A line down in the neighborhood maybe?
(*And how do you explain the cell phones?*)

Amy immediately snatched her own cell from her pocket and checked it. No signal. She powered it down and then started it back up again. All the welcoming noises chimed as the phone came to life, and for a moment Amy felt hope, only to sag at the shoulders and sigh when the screen cruelly informed her once again that she had no signal.

Except she'd *had* a signal, hadn't she? At Allan's. It was short and fleeting and choppy, and Domino sounded like a robot, but there *had* been life. So how was that possible? Though she was no expert, cutting landlines seemed plausible to Amy. But cutting signals to multiple cell phones? No, scratch that—turning them off and on? It couldn't be a coincidence. Occam's razor. Someone was controlling it. It seemed impossible, but someone was turning their signals on and off as it suited them. It made sense at Allan's. As they'd surmised, someone could have still been in the house. Tim or Jennifer

(*or, God forbid, Kelly Blaine*)

could have somehow snuck back in, hiding somewhere and using some kind of tech gadget that allowed the on-and-off jamming of their signals. That made sense.

But here? At Allan's neighbors', several hundred yards away? Either the tech gadget jammer thingy had one hell of a range or...

(*or?*)

Someone *was* home. And it wasn't the Rolstons.

Amy pulled the gun from her waist.

CHAPTER 35

Allan slammed the big metal cabinet door closed. It clanged and reverberated back open, the lock failing to catch from the impact. This time Allan slammed it shut and added his fist for good measure, his knuckles denting the metal door with a boom.

"Allan..." Karen said.

Allan turned to her, face twisted with helpless rage.

"What do we do now?" she asked softly.

Allan gave her an incredulous look. "*Seriously?* You seriously think I have an alphabet full of plans for this fucking madness?"

Jon held up a hand. "Whoa—take it easy, Allan."

"*You* fucking take it easy, Jon."

"I'm not the one punching tool cabinets."

"Yeah, you wouldn't even have the balls to punch a time clock, would you, you fucking sissy."

Jon shoved him. "Fuck you, man."

Allan stepped forward. He couldn't be sure, but he felt as though he were smiling. Grinning even.

(*Enjoying this?*)

(*Sure. The here and now—momentarily free of everything and anything.*)

Jon took a step back and raised a stop hand at Allan. "Back off, Allan…I'm warning you, I took an advanced weekend course in self-defense last summer and—"

Allan launched Jon onto the hood of his SUV with a solid right cross. Jon rolled off the hood and onto the cement floor, where he lay groaning.

Karen ran and knelt by her husband's side. She soon looked back up at Allan with disgust. "*What is wrong with you?!*" she yelled.

"He put his hands on *me*," Allan said matter-of-factly.

(*Who is this guy talking? Is this you, Allan?*)

Jon got to his feet with the help of Karen. He shook his head to clear the cobwebs, massaged his jaw, and then shot Allan a look of pure loathing. "Karen," he said, hate-filled eyes staying on Allan as he spoke, "hit the garage door opener. We're leaving."

"*What?*" Karen blurted.

"We're not spending another goddamn second here," he hissed.

"So we're going to split up?" Allan said. "Give the horror movie aficionados what they want? Your words, buddy."

"You go to hell, Allan." He spun on his wife. "*Hit the garage door!*"

Karen shook her head. "Jon, *no.*" Her head then vacillated between Allan and Jon as she spoke. "Look, we can't allow this to happen. It's exactly what they would want, isn't it? To see us turn on each other?"

"Karen, I'm only going to tell you one last time. Open the—"

"*Jon, shut up!*" she yelled. "Lose your goddamn ego for a minute and listen to me! We need to make it through this night, and the best odds we have are doing it *together*. You said it yourself, and you were *right*. Don't let pride cloud your judgment now."

"*Fine!*" Jon shoved Karen aside, changed tactics, and went for the adjoining door into the mudroom instead, slamming it behind him.

"Jon!" Karen ran after him, opening the door and leaving it ajar as she went after her husband.

Allan stood still, taking it all in. He glanced at the open door leading into the mudroom.

Raised in a barn? was his first thought, accompanied by a little smile.

Then a second thought: *That's not funny. What the hell is wrong with you?*

"Nothing's wrong with me," he said aloud.

And maybe there wasn't. But there *was* something wrong with...well...*everything*, wasn't there? If he made it through this night, he'd never have to speak to Jon Rogers again. But was now really the time for *he started it* nonsense?

"No," he said softly, feeling a little ashamed.

Living in the now, all that shit, it held merit when it came to explaining his own behavior. But did it not just as easily hold merit when it came to the notion of going after Jon and Karen? If he was living in the now, wouldn't that justify going after those who were putting themselves in danger? Those who were fleeing for all the wrong reasons?

Yes. Dammit, *yes*.

Allan went after them.

"Guys?" he called as he walked through the mudroom toward the den.

The craziest thing. He heard conversation coming from the den. Inappropriately casual talk. Like a dinner party.

Allan arrived on the scene. Jon and Karen were on their knees, Karen weeping, Jon visibly shaking, both looking up at a grinning Jennifer who was happily alternating the point of a gun between their eyes.

A young woman whom Allan had never seen before stood beside Jennifer. She smiled at Allan's arrival. The young woman was short, slender, dark-haired, attractive. Allan's machete was in her right hand.

"Allan, hi," she said. "I'm Kelly. It's nice to meet you. Why don't you join us? Therapy is about to begin."

CHAPTER 36

Make a run for it? Allan thought.

(You do that, and they're dead.)

I could make it.

(Yeah, you probably could. What about Jon and Karen? Would they make it? And what about Amy?)

Amy. Wait…did this girl say her name was—

"Kelly," Allan said aloud.

"Yes?"

"No—I mean you said your name was Kelly."

Kelly cocked her head. "So?"

"You're *Amy's* Kelly. Kelly…" *What the hell did she say her last name was? Something with a b…?* "*Blaine*," Allan blurted with no satisfaction. "Kelly Blaine. You're the one Amy feared was behind all this."

Kelly's eyebrows rose. "She told you that?"

Allan said nothing, nor did he have to.

"She *is* a clever one, that Amy," Kelly said.

There was a momentary pause where everyone in the den seemed to consider one another. Allan by the den entrance, capable of making a run for it if he chose to; Jon and Karen on their knees, bound with fear and a gun vacillating between their foreheads; Jennifer, the one holding the gun, grinning, looking twitchy, unstable;

and then Kelly Blaine, Allan's machete dangling in her hand, her manner calm, almost pleasant.

And then there was Tim. Or, the lack of Tim. His absence did not elude Allan. Nor did the fact that Jennifer was holding a gun, and that Kelly Blaine was holding his machete—and *only* his machete. His axe, his pitchfork, all missing from the tool cabinet in the garage, now failing to make an appearance here in the den with the machete. Why? Too cumbersome to wield for someone Kelly's size, unlike the machete? Perhaps. But if so, why take them then? To ensure that he, Jon, and Karen did not, most likely.

Or perhaps they aren't so cumbersome for someone Tim's size. And Tim's gone. Perhaps next door at the Rolstons. Waiting for Amy.

Allan twitched, as though common sense and bravado were warring over use of his body.

"Thinking of making a run for it?" Kelly asked.

"No," Allan lied.

"Want to get next door to Amy? Warn her, is that it?"

Allan's alarmed expression asked the question his mouth would never.

"Yes, I know she's next door, Allan," Kelly said. "I would think by now you'd realize just how far behind you all are."

Jennifer laughed again.

"Oh, and your cell phone *was* on your nightstand, by the way." Kelly produced Allan's cell from her pocket and flaunted it playfully before him. "Didn't want you to think you were getting senile or anything. See, I'm not all bad." She pocketed the phone.

"What do you want?" Allan said.

Jennifer's eyes lit up. Gun staying on the Rogers, she whirled her head toward Kelly.

Kelly smiled knowingly back at her. "Didn't I tell you?" she said. "'*What do you want?*' is almost always a sure thing. Guarantee you, further down the line we'll also get '*why are you doing this?*'"

Jennifer's laughter became the sinister giggles of a child.

"I *will* answer it, though," Kelly said to Allan. "But I'll have to answer it quickly because I've still got things to do and not much time to do them. First, Allan, I'd like you to come in here and take a spot next to Karen."

Karen gaped up disbelievingly at Kelly.

Kelly rolled her eyes and sighed. "Yes, I know your name, Karen." She sighed again and maneuvered behind Jon. "Can we please prevent any future gasps of disbelief that may derail my train of thought and simply accept the fact that, for all intents and purposes, on this particular evening, that *I*"—she tapped the flat of the machete's blade on top of Jon's head—"know"—*tap*—"fucking"—*tap*—"everything?"

Everyone nodded.

"Thank you." Kelly brought the machete down into the back of Jon's heel, severing his Achilles tendon, yet still managing to keep the foot intact.

Jon threw his head back and screamed, veins bulging on his neck and forehead like cords.

Karen cried out for her husband.

Allan stood stunned, watching in disbelief.

Jennifer giggled like the sinister child.

Only Kelly looked unaffected by it all. She held the machete up to her face and studied it with a look of disappointment. Keeping the foot intact, was not, it would seem, her intention.

"You know, in the movies they make it look so easy," she said over Jon's moaning. "One little swipe and, *whoop!*, off it goes." Kelly shook her head at the machete. "I swung this thing as hard as I could." She fingered the blade, testing its sharpness, came away with a finger full of blood and casually wiped it on Karen's cheek. Karen shrieked and immediately wiped it off. "Not very sharp," Kelly went on. She looked at Allan with the same disappointment she cast the machete. "Dammit, Allan, sharpen your machetes."

Jon had since rolled to his side, clutching his now useless ankle, grimacing, eyes shut tight against the pain. He moaned incessantly.

Karen went to cradle Jon in her arms. Jennifer looked at Kelly for approval.

Kelly nodded back. "They're not going anywhere." She turned toward Allan: "How about you, Allan? You still thinking about going anywhere?"

Allan, still rattled by the brutal scene he'd just witnessed, managed to summon what little nerve he felt was left in the tank.

"Whether I stay or run, you'll kill them," he said, gesturing to Jon and Karen.

Kelly turned to Jennifer. "Jennifer, do you think you could get the rest of Jon's foot off? No cutting or anything. Just wrench it off. Think of it as a big drumstick."

"Definitely," Jennifer said, starting for Jon.

Karen screamed and shielded her husband.

"*Wait!*" Allan said.

Kelly gestured for Jennifer to stop.

No matter what you do, they're dead. But if you run, you can make it. You can see Jamie and Janine again.

(*You'll have the deaths of Jon and Karen on your conscience.*)

My girls lost their mother. I'm NOT going to let them lose their father too. I'll run. I'll run, and I'll keep on running until I find help.

(*And they could be dead by the time help arrives.*)

Or they may not. If I escape, these psychos might panic and run themselves, fearing that help is on the way. Leave Jon and Karen alive. At least there's a chance. There is ZERO chance if I stay.

"Allan?" Kelly said. "Did I not mention I still had things to do?"

Allan nodded absently, trying his absolute damnedest to make it look as though shock was slowing his decision process, not the idea of making a run for it.

"Then please get over here and join your friends before I tell Jennifer to put several holes in their heads."

She never finished telling you what she wanted. Ask her now. Ask her and make a break for it when she's explaining.

"You never finished telling us what you wanted," Allan said.

Kelly closed her eyes and breathed in deep through her nose, showing the first crack in what had been a disturbing calm up until now.

"I no longer have the time to finish telling you. However, if you come over here and stay put, I promise you will eventually get all of the answers—"

Allan made a break for it.

He expected gunfire behind him and instinctively shrugged his shoulders and brought both hands up to protect his head as he bolted for the front door.

Except there was no gunfire. Did he care? Like fuck he did.

Allan unlocked the front door, ripped it open, and charged out into the night…

…only to stumble and fall, something taut and unforgiving like wire catching him at both ankles. Allan hit the ground of his front porch hard, his breath lost from both the impact and sudden panic of his predicament.

He rolled to one side, face now a reddish purple as he pleaded for his body to find air. He spotted the cause of his fall. It *had* been wire. Strung ankle-height across his front porch.

Allan then heard a giggle. It was not Jennifer's giggle. It was the giggle of a man. Allan rolled all the way over onto his back. He looked up and saw only the night sky, felt a queer, transitory moment of peace in its infiniteness.

Tim then came into frame, blocking out the sky as he loomed over Allan's head, smiling.

"*Whoopsie*," Tim said and giggled again. Allan now saw that the missing axe from his tool cabinet was at Tim's side.

Allan's final thought before everything went black came directly from the Amy Lambert School of Philosophy.

Life is not fair, he thought.

Tim raised the axe.

CHAPTER 37

Amy left the kitchen and crept into the den, where the television continued to provide the only noise in the house.

The television was the focal point of the den. Before it were a cushy sofa and a coffee table. The cushions on the sofa were neat and puffy, not shifted and mushed. The coffee table held nothing but a remote control and a magazine. No drinks, no snacks. Amy couldn't remember a time when she hunkered down to watch the tube without at least a drink or something to nosh on. And the sofa cushions...

She touched them, and they were cold. But would they still be warm if someone had been sitting there, say, fifteen minutes ago? She didn't know. What she did know was that they wouldn't appear as primped as they now did. After a marathon tube session at home, her couch appeared as a sad, flattened sandwich. She'd make a happier, fluffier sandwich out of it in the morning, but never during. What would be the point?

Someone had been interrupted in making tea, she thought. *Perhaps they were interrupted before they could watch TV too.*

Sure, it made sense. Turn the TV on, go into the kitchen to fix yourself a cup of tea to sip while watching, get interrupted, and thus leave behind what she was finding now.

Interrupted how, though? was the chilling thought now playing on a continuous loop in her head. Or, worse still, *interrupted by whom?*

Amy grabbed the remote control from the coffee table and turned off the television. The ambient sounds of an empty

(*is it?*)

house seemed loud at first. Automatic air whooshing from unseen vents; fridge in the kitchen humming; a clock ticking somewhere; water running upstairs—

(*wait—what?*)

Water running upstairs was *not* an ambient sound of an empty house.

Amy held her breath and closed her eyes in a bid to hear more efficiently. Water was definitely running above.

She left the den and inched toward the staircase, held her breath, and closed her eyes again. She wagered three possibilities at first: a washing machine (she'd known quite a few people who had a washer and dryer on the second floor), a broken toilet that ran unabated until you jiggled the damn handle (she knew one person very well with this particular problem, and fixing it was on her to-do list), or someone running a bath or taking a shower (the oddest and least explainable of the three).

She ruled out washing machine first. She heard no accompanying effort of a motor as it spun and churned, and certainly not the startling earthquake rumble exclusive to all washers as it neared the end of its cycle.

She ruled out the running toilet next. As someone who'd recently become an expert in the sound, she would know the bastard anywhere.

That left someone running a bath or taking a shower, the oddest and least explainable of the three. And Amy supposed she could stand there at the foot of the stairs, weighing and discarding flimsy possibilities as to why someone might be running a bath or taking a shower while the TV ran unwatched, while a cup of tea was left unmade, and while someone had not only rung their doorbell and banged on their front door half a zillion times but was now *inside their home*, desperately calling for them with just as much emergency.

She could stand there and theorize, but why even bother when the true explanation was a simple flight of stairs away? Because you could disturb someone running a bath? Taking a shower? Big fucking deal. Besides, Amy's faithful belief in Occam's razor was in full effect here, and it answered all those questions with one swooping certainty.

Question: Who would run a bath or take a shower during such things?

Answer: No one, that's who. The answer was, no one would run a bath or take a shower during such things. Simple.

And yet the water above still ran. Why?

Well, if still on the clock, and not stubbornly told by Amy that it was quitting time so that she could head upstairs in her unbreakable quest to find a working cell phone, good old William of Occam might have told Amy that the reason *why* the water above still ran was—what else?—simple.

Not good. The answer was not good.

She headed upstairs anyway.

CHAPTER 38

Allan woke before attempting to open his eyes. For a brief moment he thought he was hungover. Exceptionally hungover. There was a pounding in his head like no other. Except the pounding was more localized than a bad hangover headache that always seemed to spread right down to his toes. This one was exclusive to his forehead. Not even the back of his head had the unwanted privilege. Odd. He had no recollection of drinking the night before. His daughters had had a sleepover, hadn't they? Memories swirled just out of reach as his consciousness slowly returned. He remembered *wanting* a drink. Sharing one with Amy, the girl from support group. But then the doorbell had rung, interrupting them, and two new members had entered his home…

Everything came back at once.

He was alive. Allan had thought his (*unfair*) life was surely over the second Tim had stood over him and raised the axe. What had happened instead? Well, the localized throb around his forehead gave him a fairly good idea. Tim had obviously not brought the blade of the axe down, but the blunt end instead, knocking him cold.

Allan opened his eyes. His vision swam and made him nauseated, and he instantly shut them tight again. He went to bring a hand to his head but felt instant resistance on his right arm. He tried his left and felt the same. He opened his eyes again, determined to fight the nausea until his vision settled. When it did, he quickly discovered a few things:

He was in his den, seated in one of his kitchen chairs. The reason he could not move either arm was because his arms and torso were bound to the chair with what appeared to be miles of duct tape. Legs too.

To his left were Jon and Karen Rogers. Both were in the same exact predicament—each bound to one of his kitchen chairs with miles of duct tape.

There was no trace of the psychos.

Jon was a ghostly white and drenched in sweat. His face was a constant grimace of pain. It was then that Allan remembered how the girl had brought the machete down on the back of Jon's ankle, severing his Achilles tendon.

The girl…

Who was the girl? Kelly something. Someone Amy knew. Someone bad.

Wait. Amy. *Where the hell was Amy?*

This memory, like the others, trickled into place. She'd gone next door to ask the Rolstons for help. She'd gone alone because she had the gun. Did she make it? Did she get help? He guessed no. If she had, why the hell were they tied up in his fucking den?

Allan eventually came to a realization. Tim could have killed Allan, but did not. The girl with the machete (or maybe that other psycho girl…Jennifer, was it?) could have killed Jon and Karen while he was unconscious, but did not.

Realization: They were being kept alive for something.

But of course the realization was anything but final and only served to produce the obvious follow-up question: kept alive for what?

Amy was nowhere in sight. If she'd gotten help, there was a strong chance it would have been here by now. So that meant Amy was either dead or on the loose. If she were dead, then why the hell was he still alive? Why were the Rogerses still alive? This was about Amy, after all, wasn't it? And what had Amy said before when Jon had asked why they were involved if all of this had to do with *Amy's past?*

Bad luck was all Amy had said, and none too compassionately.

Which then made the follow-up question to Allan's discovery that much more enigmatic. If Allan and the Rogerses were only involved in this mess from Amy's past because of bad luck, why keep them alive? Surely they were nothing but an insignificant liability, yes? A potential risk?

And then just like that, Allan had an answer to the increasingly enigmatic follow-up question, yet he took no pleasure in it:

Because we are *significant*, he thought. *We're pawns.* And what was it Allan's father had told him years ago about pawns when first teaching him the game of chess?

"The thing about pawns, Allan, is that their low piece value allows you to sacrifice them relatively easily in order to gain a stronger position overall," Martin Brown had told his son.

We're pawns, Allan thought again. *Here to be sacrificed so that Kelly may gain a stronger position over Amy.*

CHAPTER 39

Amy ascended the Rolstons' stairs slowly and deliberately, gun at her side. The sound of the running water was more distinct now. It was not the sounds of someone running a bath, but the sounds of a shower.

Oh, hell—someone in the shower? No wonder they didn't hear her banging on the door and ringing the bell.

But there were *two* of them, weren't there? Pam *and* Mike Rolston, Allan had said. One of them would've had to have heard her racket while the other showered.

Unless only one was home? Maybe.

How about if they were showering *together*? Another maybe, she supposed. Personally, Amy had hated showering with Patrick. He was just too damned big and hogged all the hot water whenever he stood before the shower head. Not to mention they'd nearly broken their damn necks trying to make sex work, no matter what position they tried. Talk about Bambi's first go on ice.

Again, she could stand and theorize, or she could just finish climbing the damn stairs and find out.

Amy crept further. A step creaked below her weight, and she winced at the sound. She felt like an intruder. And she was. Except she felt like the bad kind.

The Fannelli brothers kind.

The fleeting parallel made her momentarily ill, like a hot flash or a wave of nausea. She gripped the railing with one hand and steadied herself. Breathed deeply and slowly. This was not the first time her traumatic past had her questioning a change in her psyche. She had enjoyed killing Monica. Enjoyed it immensely. What was it Monica had said as she lay dying at Amy's feet, looking up at her, smiling with a mouthful of blood from the gunshot wounds Amy had inflicted on her?

Maybe we're not so different after all, she'd said.

Amy pinched the bridge of her nose, closed her eyes, and grimaced. "*Fuck you,*" she whispered to both Monica and herself, then continued climbing.

She reached the landing without incident and now stood in the center of a long and spacious hallway. Bedrooms on opposite ends, one bathroom in between.

The bedroom doors were open. The bathroom door was closed. The running water behind it could be heard clearly.

Amy pressed her ear gently to the bathroom door. Listened for any change in the water's cadence, the verification of someone actually showering. She heard nothing but the unbroken flow of the water.

She slowly lowered herself to all fours and strained to peek beneath the door. Waited several breaths and saw nothing pass.

She stood and tried the doorknob. It was unlocked. Amy turned it slowly, as if turning it too fast might trigger an alarm. Opened the door a crack and peered inside. The humidity of the shower greeted her instantly, misting her face and blurring her vision. She inched it open another crack, allowing more steam to exit into the hallway. Her vision was better now. It allowed her full view of the bathroom's interior without committing to full entry.

The interior was modest. White tile. White walls. There was a sink and mirror; there was a toilet; there was a shower and tub. The shower's curtain was pulled tight, the color midnight blue. It did not offer any silhouetted glimpse of anything behind it.

Gun on the shower curtain, Amy slowly entered the bathroom. She dropped into a low crouch and paused by the sink, waiting. If she couldn't see them through the curtain, they couldn't see her, but that didn't mean they wouldn't have felt the bathroom's shift in temperature when she entered, the subtle breeze of an open door in a room full of mist that was now dissipating. If someone behind that curtain was waiting to yank it back and pounce, they would be expecting her to be upright, not in a crouch. They would momentarily pause, giving her the precious time to blow them away from below.

And so she waited in a crouch by the sink. And just as she heard no change in the water's cadence when she'd pressed her ear to the door, so too did she hear no such change in the water's tempo by the sink.

(*There's no one in there. There can't be.*)

Then why leave the water running?

(*A trap?*)

Possible. Lure me upstairs towards an empty shower so they can—

(*So they can what?*)

I don't know. She rose slowly from her crouch. *I don't know, and I don't care. I came here to find a phone—*

Amy's cell phone beeped. She jumped as though jolted from behind, dug the phone from her pocket and stepped into the hallway. A text message from Domino:

Where are u?

Amy instantly dialed his number. It rang unanswered before going to voicemail. She cursed under her breath and tried texting him back:

did you get hold of c and c?

An excruciating minute passed before Amy's phone beeped again:

what the hell are you talking about?

Amy cursed aloud, her thumbs working frantically on her phone, mashing buttons without care for misspellings:

somthing bad going on! kelly b behind it. go get c and c and get them soenwhere safe!!!

Another excruciating minute before:

still not following. What are u talking about?

"*Are you fucking kidding me?!*" she yelled. She went to text again but got no further; her cell started ringing in her hand. The caller ID read "Domino." He'd gotten through.

"*Domino?*" Amy answered. "*Can you hear me?*"

"Amy?" His voice still sounded odd. Sexless and synthetic.

"*Yes!* Yes, it's me. Can you hear me?"

"Barely. There's a lot of static or something. What's that noise?"

"I don't hear any—" But then she stopped. Of course she heard something. The rhythmic and unbroken fall of the shower a mere few feet behind her.

She stepped back into the bathroom and immediately pulled back the curtain to get at the faucet and found herself staring at who she assumed were Mike and Pam Rolston. Both on their knees, facing away from her, slumped onto their sides, lifeless white faces mushed against the tiles. They'd clearly been dispatched execution style—told to get on their knees and face the other way while shot from behind. And Amy might have accepted this truth—shot from behind—had a giant pitchfork not stood upright in the corner of the tub, leaning against the tiled wall. Had, upon further inspection, husband and wife not been littered about the head, neck, and back with multiple holes the precise size of the pitchfork's prongs.

"Jesus Christ…" she whispered.

They marched them upstairs with a pitchfork? No one's being forced to go anywhere with a pitchfork.

(*They must have had a gun. They marched them upstairs and into the shower with a gun.*)

Then why not use *the gun?*

The answer came too fast, tapping deep and dark without conscious effort, and Amy felt the fleeting parallel again, the hot flash of nausea…

They didn't use a gun because it would be a quick death. No fun.

Amy slowly raised the phone to her mouth, unable to take her eyes off the Rolstons as she spoke. "They're dead."

"Amy?"

"They're both dead."

"*Who's* dead? I can still barely hear you. Did you turn off the shower?"

Amy shook her head into the phone. "No," she said absently, "hold on." She bent for the faucet and froze. Slowly stood upright and brought the phone back to her ear. "I never told you anything about a shower."

"What? Yes you did."

"No—I *didn't.*"

"Well, I must have just assumed, Amy." The voice on the phone was normal now. It was the voice of a woman.

A breathless pause. Amy felt her pulse in her head. "Kelly Blaine," she said.

"That's the name my dead folks gave me."

Amy bent for the faucet again, shut off the shower, and then slowly stepped out into the hallway, looking left and right as she spoke, gun ready. "How did you get Domino's phone?"

"Watched him die, then took it. Easy peasy."

"Bullshit. You may have stolen it somehow, but no fucking way did someone like you kill someone like Domino."

"'*Someone like me?*'"

"That's right."

"Oh, Amy—you really should hush."

Amy started back downstairs, gun leading the way. "Pushing a button or two, am I?"

"Just proving your stupidity," Kelly said.

Amy's phone beeped in her ear. An incoming text while she was talking. She pulled the phone away and checked the ID of the text. Restricted number.

Please let this be Domino. Please let this be Domino warning me that Kelly had somehow gotten ahold of his primary cell. That he has Carrie and Caleb safe and sound and that help is on the way. Please.

Amy opened the text. It *was* Domino. A bloodied image of him with his throat cut. Next to his dying face was Kelly Blaine, grinning, her arm outstretched and off camera as she took the selfie.

Amy stared at the image in disbelief.

A fake. It has to be. Some kind of Photoshop bullshit.

"Did ya get it yet?" Kelly asked.

"It's a fake," Amy managed in barely a whisper.

"You mean like the two you just found in the tub?"

Amy closed her eyes and shook her head, refusing to believe. "No. No, it's *fake*. There's no way—"

"No way what? No way that *someone like me* could have managed such a thing?"

Amy felt sick. It was not like the brief waves of nausea that flashed whenever she found herself subconsciously sharing thoughts with the likes of Monica or the Fannelli brothers, but a deep, cancerous sickness, as if her body was slowly eroding, being hollowed out and robbing her of any conceivable strength.

Still, she managed to voice her denial with some measure of will in her tone. "I don't believe you. I don't care what you say or what you show me—I don't believe you."

"Suit yourself. You'll find out soon enough."

"Go fuck yourself." Amy hung up and immediately dialed 911.

"911, what's your emergency?"

Yes! Fucking YES!

"Yes, hello, I'd like to report a double murder at…"

Shit! What's their damn address?

Amy ran into the Rolston's kitchen and frantically scanned countertops for signs of mail. She found nothing.

"I don't know the address, I'm gonna find it, okay?"

No answer.

"Hello? You still there?"

No answer.

Amy pulled the cell phone away from her ear and found herself staring incredulously at the no-service message displayed.

Amy kicked the refrigerator as hard as she could, threw her head back, and screamed.

A moment passed. She stood panting in the kitchen of two dead strangers, rage and frustration pulsating throughout her body. She closed her eyes and tried to steady her breathing.

Get ahold of yourself...breathe...

She took a long, final inhale and then let it out slowly. It did not entirely defuse her rage and frustration, but it did leash it. How strong a leash would remain to be seen.

So what now?

(*Nothing's changed. We need to get to a phone that works.*)

Everything's *changed. People are dead. Domino may be dead. And Kelly Blaine is officially involved. Everything has definitely fucking changed.*

(*Doesn't mean getting to a phone still isn't the number one priority. Now that Kelly Blaine is involved, who knows how far she'll go? You thought it before: She'll try to one-up Monica to prove she's better, and that means not only you, but your* kids *are now a potential target. You need to get ahold of them now more than ever.*)

How? Fucking HOW?

(*Keep moving until you get to the next neighbor. These assholes couldn't have gotten to all of them.*)

And how far away are *these next neighbors? And in which direction? I could be wandering for hours. And what about Allan and the Rogerses? I told them I'd return.*

Amy started pacing in circles, began gnawing a fingernail on her gun hand, completely unaware that the barrel was pointed at her head as she did so.

Well, that's it then. Two birds, one stone. I head back to Allan's and tell them there's been a change of plans. I explain about the Rolstons and that Kelly Blaine is involved and then tell them all of us are venturing out on foot. Allan will know the way to go. Two birds.

(*You do realize there's a very good chance that they've already got them, don't you? Allan and the Rogerses? That by going over there you could be doing exactly what Kelly wants you to do?*)

Yes, I know that. I also know that Kelly wants me alive. I know better than anyone that it's all a fucking game. She doesn't want to kill me—not straight out anyway. Ironically, that gives me time.

(*Time for what, exactly?*)

I don't know. But I am *going to kill the little cunt somehow. I know that much.*

Amy tucked the gun back into her waist and pocketed her phone. She went to the front door, opened it, and her phone rang again. She brought all of her efforts (and thus, all of her attention) on digging her phone back out of her pocket—

(It was 911 calling back; they'd traced her cell number)

(It was Domino calling; he was *not* dead, *not* dead, *not* dead)

—that she did not see the small blue arc of light that touched her neck and crumpled her into a daze. And she certainly did not see the follow-up blow to the back of her head that knocked her out completely.

.   .   .

Amy woke, chin on her chest, groggy, head throbbing. She slowly lifted her chin and opened her eyes. Before her stood Kelly Blaine and Jennifer. Amy immediately went to lunge for them but got nowhere. A quick inspection revealed she was duct-taped to a chair.

Jennifer laughed at her feeble attempt.

Amy spit in her direction.

"Amy…" a male voice said to her left.

Amy looked left. It was Allan. Heavily taped to a chair just as she was. Next to Allan were Jon and Karen Rogers. They too were in the same bind.

Kelly clapped both hands together once. "Okay! We're finally all here. Let's let the healing begin."

CHAPTER 40

The microwave beeped, and Irene Flannigan retrieved the bag of instant popcorn. She pulled at the corners to open the bag, and steam instantly burned her fingertips. She yelped and dropped the bag on the counter, promptly swatting at it seconds after as though it were a living thing that had nipped her.

"Every bloody time," she muttered, now running her fingers under the faucet.

Caleb appeared in the kitchen after hearing her yelp from the den.

"What's wrong?" he asked.

"Just your screwy neighbor doing the same thing she does every time she makes popcorn, love—burning her fingers."

"You okay?"

Fingers still under the faucet, she smiled over at Caleb with genuine affection. Such a caring boy. She'd met few like him in her seventy years. "I think I'll live, sweetheart."

Caleb smiled and returned to the den with his sister.

The doorbell rang.

"Want me to get it?" Carrie called from the den.

Irene turned off the faucet and started wiping her fingers on a towel as she said: "No—you two stay put."

Irene opened the front door. A second door, a screen door, stood between her and every visitor to her home. She never opened the screen door for strangers, and the man standing under the porch light of her front step now was a stranger.

He was a young man. Tall and skinny and pale with thinning blond hair. He did not, according to Irene, look well.

The man smiled at Irene, and the effort appeared both disingenuous and painful, as if aggravating sore muscles in his face.

"Hi," the young man said.

"Hello yourself," Irene said. Her expression was stern. *Not buying whatever you're selling*, it said.

"I'm a friend of Amy Lambert's. Her meeting is running late, and she wanted to talk to her kids and tell them herself, you know? Tell them she was gonna be late?"

Irene frowned. "So why didn't she just call then?"

The young man started scratching the side of his neck. "Well, she's been trying to, but she hasn't been able to get through. We figured something was wrong with your phone, so I told her I'd come over, and we could use *my* phone, you know? She could talk to them with *my* phone."

The furrows in Irene's frown etched deeper. "Amy said she tried but couldn't get through?"

"Yeah. Are the kids here?"

"What did you say your name was?" Irene asked.

The young man scratched his neck again. "I'm a friend of Amy Lambert's."

Carrie appeared at Irene's side. Irene turned to her. "Carrie, go back in the den."

"What's the password?" Carrie asked the man.

"The what?"

"The password. My mother wouldn't have sent you without giving you the password," Carrie said.

The man stopped scratching his neck and now ran a firm hand through his thinning hair. "Oh, she must have forgot to tell me. She had a real sad meeting, you know? She was real sad, so she must have forgot. But it's okay, it's okay."

Carrie spun towards Irene. "*Call the police!*"

The man punched through the screen.

Carrie screamed.

The man reached through the hole he'd made with his fist and went to unlock the screen door.

"*Bastard!*" Irene yelled and sunk her teeth into his hand.

The man cried out and punched through the screen with his other hand. He grabbed ahold of Irene's hair and began slamming her head into the wooden doorframe. A final slam and Irene dropped to the ground.

The man reached through the screen door again, unlocked it, and ripped it open, the thin metal frame hitting the outside wall with a reverberating clang. He stepped inside, slammed the main door behind him, and caught sight of the two kids scurrying upstairs.

He immediately started after them, but Irene had come to at his feet. She latched onto his leg and sunk her teeth into his calf. The young man howled in pain and tried shaking her off. He resorted to stomping at her with his free leg. The third stomp knocked her out cold.

"*Fucking biting bitch!*" He kicked her unconscious body once in the stomach, pulled his knife, and took off upstairs after the kids.

CHAPTER 41

If Amy's physical strength had equaled that of her rage, she could have torn through the layers of duct tape binding her to the chair. Literally ripping Kelly and Jennifer to pieces soon after was a given. And enjoying the hell out of it all the while fell into the category of the bleedin' obvious.

"You look upset, Amy," Kelly said to her. She lit a cigarette with her black Zippo and drew on it.

Amy fought with the only weapon at her disposal. She shook her head and offered up a sympathetic little smile. "You know, for a fleeting moment, I was willing to give you the benefit of the doubt, Kelly," she said.

Kelly tilted her head, curious. "What do you mean?"

"Well, at first I worried you would try to one up Monica—I know that's what this is all about—but then I figured the better player wouldn't even bother. The better player wouldn't have to prove anything; she'd *know* she was better, and she'd be content with that. How wrong I was."

Kelly dragged hard on her cigarette. "I *do* know I'm the better player."

Amy snorted. "Clearly, you don't. I mean, look at you. Christ, you could be Monica's little sister with all your bullshit you need to prove. You even *smoke* like her."

Kelly stepped forward and stubbed her cigarette out on Amy's cheek.

Amy grimaced but refused to cry out.

Kelly stepped back with a satisfied look and flicked the dead butt at her. "Anything else you want to add?"

Steadying her breath against the searing pain, Amy calmly managed: "Monica wouldn't have lost her cool so easily."

"Stop antagonizing her!" Karen yelled.

"Shut the fuck up, Karen," Amy said. "What, you think she's going to let you go if you behave?"

Karen looked away.

Kelly slowly took her eyes off Amy and strolled toward Karen. "You know, as much as it pains me to admit it, Amy *is* correct. I simply can't let you leave here alive. I'm sorry."

Jon, pale and weak due to blood loss from his hacked ankle, croaked out: "*Why are you doing this to us?*"

Kelly spun toward Jennifer.

Jennifer grinned and clapped.

Kelly looked equally enthused. "And there it is," she said. "It's like I said: '*What do you want?*' and '*why are you doing this?*' are practically guaranteed."

Jennifer nodded, still grinning.

Kelly sidled up to Jon and ran a hand through his sweaty hair. Even gingerly swept his bangs to one side with two fingers to improve his disheveled appearance. He was too weak to resist.

"How about this, Jon?" Kelly said, still fixing his hair. "How about asking 'why *not* you?' instead? I mean really—why *not* you?" Kelly chuckled and shook her head. "You know, sometimes I think the cruelest trick God ever pulled was giving people the free will to think they mattered."

Now Amy chuckled.

Kelly looked over at her. "Something funny, Amy?"

"Kinda, yeah. Now I'm the one who's pained to agree with *you.*"

Kelly gave an amused little bump of the eyebrows. "How so?"

"Earlier I was lecturing them about how foolish it was to think that life was fair. That there was no cosmic balance in the universe that made you exempt from further tragedy just because you'd already endured it."

Kelly left Jon and stood before Amy. "Really? Maybe we're not so different, you and I."

Monica's dying words to Amy surfaced instantly, stinging like a slap: *Maybe we're not so different after all...*

Amy tasted bile. "Fuck you, you little cunt. Just get on with whatever bullshit you have planned."

"Amy..." Allan said.

Amy turned her head toward him. "What? *What*, Allan? Are you gonna tell me you're starting to think like Jon and Karen over there? That life *is* fair?"

"No, I'm not. *I'm not at all.* I just...I guess I just don't see the need to expedite things, for Christ's sake."

"Oh, I see," Amy said. "You prefer to drag it out, do you? You're enjoying this that much?"

Jennifer laughed. "I kinda like her," she said to Kelly, gesturing to Amy.

"Fuck yourself, junkie whore," Amy said.

Jennifer appeared momentarily rattled.

"What, you're shocked I figured it out?" Amy said. "Christ, you're a poster child."

Now it was Kelly who laughed. Jennifer frowned her way, and Kelly waved an apologetic hand.

"It's funny you mention dragging things out, Amy," Kelly said. "I've arranged a little something especially for you, but I'm going to need your full cooperation in order to make it work."

"And if I refuse?"

"Well, then I'm going to have to call Tim—you'll notice he's not here—and tell him to kill Irene, Carrie, and Caleb, and then bring their bodies back here for you to identify."

CHAPTER 42

Carrie and Caleb rushed into the first bedroom with an open door. Carrie shut and locked the door behind them and ran to the bedroom window.

"*What are you doing?*" Caleb asked in a loud whisper.

"We'll go out the window," Carrie whispered back.

Caleb joined his sister at her side. Looked out the window. "It's like a million feet!"

"*Where the hell are you, you little shits?*" a voice echoed from the hallway. "*If you come out now, I promise I won't hurt you…*"

"We need a phone," Carrie whispered.

Brother and sister searched the room. It was a guest room with little else but a bed and accompanying furniture. No phone.

"Wait, look here," Carrie said. She was squatting by the base of the bed, pointing to a lonely phone jack.

They immediately checked the closet in hopes of finding a phone they could plug into the jack. Oddly enough, the only thing the closet contained was a generous supply of Boston Red Sox memorabilia. Irene Flannigan had kept no secret about her love for the team, having first settled down in Boston for a number of years after leaving Ireland before relocating to Pennsylvania. There were Red Sox pennants, shirts, hats, balls, a couple of bats, and then—*saints be praised!* as Irene might say—an official Boston Red Sox telephone, cheap and plastic and seemingly decades old, but a phone all the same.

Caleb snatched the phone and handed it over to his sister. They ran it back to the wall jack.

"*We've got your mom, you know!*" the voice boomed from the hallway.

Carrie and Caleb instantly locked eyes.

"*If you come out now, I'll tell them not to hurt her…*"

Carrie started to cry. She put a hand over her mouth to stem the noise. Tears ran down her cheeks.

"He's lying," Caleb whispered. "He's just trying to find us. Hurry up and plug in the phone."

"What if he's not lying?"

"*Plug in the phone, Carrie!*"

Carrie unwrapped the cord that encircled the plastic phone and plugged it into the wall. Brought the receiver to her ear.

Caleb didn't need to ask. The deflated look on his sister's face told him. Her tears had started up again too, rolling down her cheeks and onto her shirt.

Caleb snatched the phone from his sister anyway, brought it to his ear and began tapping the small plastic switch hook over and over again like they did in the old movies he watched. It was indeed dead. Maybe had never worked.

"*That Irish bitch downstairs is still alive, you little shits… If you don't come out, I'll kill her right here and now, I swear to God!*"

Carrie and Caleb fixed on each other again. The panic in their eyes vibrated.

Carrie wiped away her tears. "What are we gonna do?"

Caleb looked at the closet again. Then the bed. Then the bedroom door. He started to take off his shoes.

"What are you doing?"

"Take off your shoes," he said.

CHAPTER 43

Blown the plan. He'd blown the fucking plan.

It was supposed to be simple. Tell the old Irish lady that Amy was running late and she wanted to call and say goodnight. And here, use good old Tim's phone, because we *tried* calling your phone, old Irish lady, and we couldn't get through. The old Irish lady would then no doubt check her phone, Tim would hit the cell jammer in his pocket, and *voila!* No signal. Then, let's check good old Tim's phone, turn off the cell jammer in his pocket, and would you look at that! *His* phone works. Why don't we just use that one, yeah? We'll sort yours out in the morning, old Irish lady. Besides, Mommy wants to say goodnight before it gets too late.

Simple.

And if there was any funny business during any of this? Well, Tim was to take care of it. It was the only reason Kelly sent him in the first place. Otherwise, they could have easily called from Allan's house and avoided all this legwork.

Problem was, if they did that, then they risked Amy suddenly blurting out during her goodnights that they should call the police or run and get help or who knows what. Such a thing would ruin the final stages of Kelly's plan (though she hadn't completely explained to him what those final stages were just yet), and there would be no one there to contain the mess.

Yup, that's why she'd sent him. To make sure it ran smoothly and that there was no funny business—but, if there was, to contain the mess.

Simple.

Except there *was* funny business. Lots of it. Now he needed to contain the mess.

How, though? Call Kelly, tell her what happened, and ask what *she* thought was the best way to contain it? Probably. Except he feared his failure to carry out the plan would result in her holding out on him. And he was sick. Incessant cold sweats like some malevolent flu. He needed a fix so badly, perhaps as bad as he ever had. It would be so easy if Kelly had just ordered the old Irish lady and the kids dead in the first place. The old Irish lady was out cold downstairs, so she would be a piece of cake. And he was going to find the kids eventually. The cell jammer was on so even if the kids had a cell, it was useless. And as for the landline, he'd taken the phone off the hook in what he assumed was the old Irish lady's bedroom. So no way were the little shits calling for help in any way whatsoever. He just needed to find them.

And then what?

Contain the mess.

How? He couldn't think. His craving for dope consumed his every thought, made it impossible to improvise.

He needed to call her. Call her and hope she had a plan B and that she wouldn't be too angry and that she would still give him all the dope she promised him because he was pretty sure he'd never felt this sick before and he needed it bad and he was so sorry and it would be so fucking easy if she would just let him kill the fucking kids and the old Irish lady so he could get back to Kelly quickly and get what was his and do up and feel better and—

A slight bang from the room down the hall froze his rambling mind and spun him on the spot. Knife leading the way, he hurried toward the room down the hall.

He tried the knob. It was locked. He brought his mouth to the door. "I know you're in there, you little shits. This is your last chance to come out while I'm still in a good mood."

No response.

"Have it your way, then…I'm gonna kill your fucking mother and make you *watch*."

Tim took a step back and kicked the door with everything he had, the wood edging by the knob cracking and giving, the door flying open with a bang.

He grinned with success. Grinned wider when he saw two pairs of shoes sticking out from beneath the bed.

"Gee…" he sang. "I wonder where they could be hid—"

Eyes on the shoes under the bed, Tim did not see the Boston Red Sox bat fly out from behind the wall and blast him smack between the eyes. The surprise of the blow magnified the impact tenfold—the equivalent of one hell of a sucker punch. Tim dropped instantly, asleep.

"Carrie, come on out," Caleb said, panting, Red Sox bat in both hands. "It's okay, come on out."

Carrie emerged from the closet and instantly looked down at the unconscious Tim in the doorway. "Is he dead?"

"I don't know." Caleb put the bat on the bed, bent and retrieved his shoes and put them back on. Carrie immediately followed suit and did the same.

Finished, Caleb picked the bat up off the bed and held it over his shoulder.

"We have to get past him," he said, gesturing to the unconscious man blocking the doorway.

"What if he wakes up?" Carrie asked.

"Then I'll hit him again."

Caleb quickly stepped over the unconscious man and into the hallway. He turned back to his sister and waved her on. "*Come on,*" he whispered.

Carrie hesitated. She looked down at the man as if he were a decaying bridge she had to cross, fearing it would give out on her.

Caleb waved her on again. "*Come on!*" he whispered louder. "Don't look at him, just come on."

Carrie took a step forward, her left foot coming down beside the man's knee, her right beside his waist. The bridge was sturdy thus far, yet she broke the cardinal rule and looked down all the same.

The man's eyes were open.

She screamed.

The man reached up and snatched hold of her wrist, yanking her down with one convulsive jerk. Carrie fell on top of him, screeching wildly as she struggled to pull away.

She did not have to wait long.

Caleb brought the baseball bat down onto the man's head once again. The man instantly released his grip on Carrie and brought a feeble hand up to defend himself from the blind assault behind him.

On all fours, Carrie scurried back into the bedroom and pressed herself up against the furthest wall. Panting and wild-eyed, she watched her little brother bring the bat down again and again, each blow gaining further momentum and impact, the man long since unconscious once more, his legs now doing what Carrie thought to be such an odd thing for an unconscious man to do as they juddered and convulsed rapidly, reminding her of some robot short-circuiting, trying to run even though it lay flat on its back.

It was Irene who stopped Caleb's assault. She came up behind the boy, waited for one of Caleb's swings to clear so she would not catch an inadvertent wallop, and wrapped both arms around him, pinning them at his sides.

Caleb went berserk. He screamed and yelled and fought Irene's hold on him, but it was not long before her soothing words in that familiar Irish brogue penetrated his fury and assured him he could stop.

Caleb dropped the bat, turned in to her, and started to cry.

Carrie slowly emerged from the bedroom. She ran to Irene and Caleb, and Irene opened her arms, allowing Carrie to join their huddle. Carrie began to cry too.

The three of them stood there in the hallway for a moment, locked in an embrace, brother and sister sobbing, Irene (now sporting a sizable egg on the right side of her brow) constantly repeating words of comfort as she rubbed their backs and ran alternating hands through their hair.

When the cell phone in the dead man's pocket rang, all crying, all nurturing, all everything but the ring of the cell phone stopped.

CHAPTER 44

"You want me to do *what?*" Amy said to Kelly even though she'd heard perfectly well.

"I want you to call your kids and say goodnight," Kelly said. "Here's the rub, though: You're gonna have to play it supercool. No tears, no weird behavior or warnings, just tell 'em you love them and all that crap and that you'll see them in the morning—which of course you won't."

"Why?"

"Because you'll be dead, dummy."

Amy gritted her teeth. "No—why the stupid charade with making me call my kids?"

"Honestly? It sounds fun. How's that? Nothing profound. I think it would be fun to watch you call your children and pretend to say goodnight when really you're saying goodbye." She smiled. "Fun, fun, fun."

"Why don't you just kill me?" Amy asked. "You've got me; you won. Monica never came this close."

"I *am* going to kill you."

"No, me. *Me.* Just me." She then flicked her chin towards Allan and the Rogerses. "Why all the bullshit with them? With the Rolstons?"

"Well, it's gotta look like a killing spree, doesn't it? The Rolstons just seal the deal. That and they were the nearest help. That's called planning ahead, sister." She tapped her index finger against her temple and winked.

"Killing spree?" Amy said.

"I couldn't just kill you straight out, Amy. Well, I *could*, but with my ties to Monica? I'd be brought in for questioning. That stuff takes forever. So annoying."

"So then what? You stage a killing spree for two houses, and Amy Lambert just happened to be in one of them? Those are crazy odds, Kelly. You'd still be questioned."

"Very true. Unless I'm looking at the spree killer right now."

"What?"

Kelly smiled. "What, you think today's date escaped me? I'm thinking that on the five-year anniversary of the Crescent Lake Massacre, Amy Lambert finally snapped. What do you think?"

"I think you're fucking crazier than I thought. Good luck proving such a thing."

Kelly gave a little shrug. "Everyone tied up and dead? The only one who is *not* happens to be sprawled out on the floor with a single gunshot wound to the head, the weapon in her hand in what looks to be an obvious suicide?" Kelly lit another cigarette. "That'll be you, by the way."

Jennifer laughed.

"What about your buddy Tim? You said he's at Irene's house right now with my kids. That's one hell of a loose end."

"Not if he does as he was told. He's simply going to pretend to be a friend of yours from group who graciously offered the use of his phone because you couldn't get through to Irene. He'll explain that you were going to be staying late and you wanted to say goodnight to your kids. It's not brain surgery."

"Irene will never buy it. She's too cagey. Tim's a twitchy junkie who couldn't sell water to a guy on fire."

"You better hope she buys it. Lord knows what a 'twitchy junkie' like Tim would do if Irene puts up a fight."

Amy chuckled dryly. "This is going to be your downfall, Kelly. You're reaching too far. This 'fun' game of yours with me calling my kids has too many moving parts. If you were smart, you'd kill me quick and be gone." She chuckled again. "It's going to blow up right in your fucking face."

"You think so, huh?" Kelly stuck her cigarette in her mouth and pulled out her cell phone. She spoke as she dialed, cigarette bouncing between her lips with each word. "Why don't we just call and see?"

Finished dialing, Kelly put the phone on speaker and held it to Amy's mouth. She then took a final deep drag of her cigarette and let the smoke filter out with her words as she said: "I'd make it convincing if I was you." She exhaled the last of her smoke in Amy's face and grinned. "Showtime, baby."

CHAPTER 45

The phone continued to ring in the dead man's pocket.

"Get back," Irene Flannigan said to Carrie and Caleb.

She approached the man as cautiously as she would have if he were still alive. And she supposed it was possible he could be. His head was a bloodied, dented mess, and he'd been convulsing dramatically when she'd come up behind Caleb and stopped his assault, but she'd heard stories of men and women walking away from car wrecks, only to die hours later from extensive injuries.

But those had been internal injuries, hadn't they? This man's *head…*

Still, she could not be too careful. Thoughts of his gruesome face springing to life as she rifled through his pockets were constant. She eventually averted her eyes from his face, keeping her focus on the chirping phone buried somewhere in one of his many pockets.

"*Gotcha*," she soon whispered and pulled the cell free.

It was a flip phone, nothing of the increasingly popular smart phone variety. The message flashing on the small square of the phone's front read that it was a restricted number.

Irene flipped the phone open and held it to her ear for a moment before saying anything. She could hear very little on the other end.

And then a voice she recognized instantly.

"Hello?" Amy said.

"*Amy?*"

"Irene?"

"Yes, it's me, love. Are you all right? I don't even know where to begin—"

"Listen, Irene, I can't talk long. The meeting is about to start again, and I'm going to be running late. Uh, I guess if we're talking, that means my friend got there okay and you're using his phone, yeah?"

Irene glanced over at the dead man. What Amy was saying was impossible. *Friend?* A man who attempted to kill her children? No chance in hell. Something was very wrong. Instinct told her to play along.

"Yes, that's right, love. He's in the kitchen now with Carrie. She's making the poor lad draw her a unicorn."

A pause.

Then: "Is she? How did the unicorn turn out?" Amy asked.

"Well, *I* think it turned out rather well. I'm not sure your friend would be inclined to agree."

Another pause. Then sounds of a slight disturbance on the other end followed by two identical phrases from another woman's voice spoken back to back, one echoing in the background, the second blaring directly into the phone.

In the background: "What the fuck is going on?" Into the phone: "*What the fuck is going on?!*"

CHAPTER 46

Kelly held the phone up to Amy's mouth. It rang several times before it was answered. The recipient did not say hello. For a moment, Amy thought they'd been disconnected.

"Hello?" Amy said.

"*Amy?*" It was Irene.

"Irene?"

"Yes, it's me, love. Are you all right? I—"

Just get it done. Play her stupid game and wow the audience with your performance.

Just saying goodnight, kids. Mommy won't be home until late. I love you both very much.

Pretend to fight back tears. Pretend it's killing you. Play her stupid fucking game. It's not over yet. You're gonna kill this little bitch slow. Somehow, some way, you're gonna kill her slow.

"Listen, Irene, I can't talk long. The meeting is about to start again, and I'm going to be running late. Uh, I guess if we're talking, that means my friend got there okay and you're using his phone, yeah?"

Is that what it meant? Amy wondered. *Did* Twitchy Tim actually talk his way into Irene's home without bother? Amy would have wagered everything against such a result. There was more going on here than she knew. There had to be.

"Yes, that's right, love," Irene replied. "He's in the kitchen now with Carrie. She's making the poor lad draw her a unicorn."

Unicorn.

It registered almost instantly.

"Is she?" Amy said. "How did the unicorn turn out?"

"Well, *I* think it turned out rather well," Irene replied. "I'm not sure your friend would be inclined to agree."

Amy was not aware of any changes in her face, but clearly something new was there. The subtlest of smirks, most likely. She sure as hell *felt* like smirking.

Whatever it was, Kelly saw it. She straightened up and kicked Amy's chair. "What the fuck is going on?"

Amy said nothing.

Kelly brought the phone to her mouth. "*What the fuck is going on?!*"

"*Excuse me?*" Irene's voice was stern through the speaker phone.

"Where the hell is Tim?"

"Was that his name?" Irene said. "He never gave it."

Amy succumbed to the smirk.

"Listen to me, you old Irish cunt—"

"*No*—you listen to *me*. Let Amy go, whoever you are, or—"

"Or *what?* What possible leverage do you have over me, lady?" Kelly pulled her gun and jammed the barrel into Amy's forehead. "Do you know I'm holding a gun to Amy's head right now?"

"*Amy?*" Irene called from the phone's speaker. "*Amy, can you hear me?*"

"I hear you, Irene," Amy responded, wincing as the barrel dug into her brow.

"Yes, she hears you," Kelly said, digging the barrel in harder. "Big fucking deal. I hope you're smart enough to know that if you call for help, she's dead, lady. I don't care if the police kick down the fucking door, it's more than enough time for me to put a bullet in her head. Are we clear?"

Silence.

"*Are we clear?*"

"Yes," Irene finally replied.

"*Good*. When I have things arranged on my end, I will let Amy go unharmed, and you will get a call from me as to where you can collect her. But until then, *you do not call anyone*, and *you fucking stay put*. Take a good look at Carrie and Caleb there…" A deliberate pause. "Do you really want to explain to them how you got their mother killed because you couldn't follow simple directions?"

"No…no, of course not." Kelly's last comment sapped the assertiveness from Irene's voice. She sounded meek now.

Kelly lowered the gun. "I hope so."

"What do you—?"

Kelly hung up.

"Told you," Amy said. "You reached too far, Kelly. Bit off more than you can chew. Eyes were bigger than your stomach." She looked up. "Wait, I think I've got one more…" She then nodded once emphatically and added: "Flew too close to the sun."

"*Amy,*" Allan said.

"No, it's okay, Allan," Kelly said. "She's being funny. It's *funny*."

Kelly walked over and stood in front of Allan. "You have kids, right, Allan? Of course you do. I was all over your upstairs. I saw their bedrooms. Where are they tonight?"

Allan didn't reply.

"At a friend's house?" She then shook her head. "No, it's a school night. For that we would need someone like a relative, yes?"

Allan's eyes twitched.

Kelly's sparkled. "That's it, isn't it? A relative. But who?"

Kelly wandered into the kitchen and stopped at the refrigerator. Everyone in the den looked on, the kitchen a mere few feet from their captive spots.

Kelly began slowly circling her index finger over the ornaments stuck to the fridge. "It really is amazing what a refrigerator can tell you about a family," she said dreamily, eyes never leaving her search on the fridge.

Her wandering finger stopped on something. "'*Dad and His Deejays,*'" she said, touching the magnet. "Very cute." Her finger continued exploring. Stopped on something else. "'*Aunt Kat and*

Her Kittens,'" she said, plucking the magnet from the fridge with one hand and removing the traffic violation beneath with the other. She read the violation and turned to Allan. "'Disregard for Stop Sign'? I do hope the 'Deejays' weren't with you at the time, Allan. Maybe they were with Aunt Kat? Being 'kittens' that day?"

Kelly wandered back into the den and whispered something to Jennifer. Jennifer disappeared, returned with a roll of duct tape. Began taping everyone's mouth shut.

Kelly produced Allan's phone, showed it to everyone first—*nothing up my sleeve!*—and then began flipping through its contents, all the while muttering: "K, K, K, K, K—*ah!* 'Kat.'" She turned her head towards Allan and smirked. "*Aunt* Kat, I presume."

She hit the number and brought the phone to her ear, waiting with a pleasant calm, casually checking a fingernail and frowning at it before nibbling away the imperfection and spitting it at Allan.

Someone answered.

"No, it's not Allan, Kat," Kelly said. "I'm a *friend* of Allan's. I help run the support group with him... Right... He's tied up with a few guests at the moment, and he asked me to call and see if Aunt Kat wouldn't mind bringing her Kittens back to Dad. Turns out he had a pretty rough session tonight and he's missing his Deejays." She winked at Allan.

Allan went insane. He fought his binds until his chair fell over. Kelly squatted next to him in his upturned chair and stroked his brow as she continued her conversation.

"Uh huh...what's that? You did? Well, that's weird. Oh well, you've got us now." She chuckled affectionately at something Kat said and then replied: "You sure you don't mind? Great. See you soon." She hung up, tapped Allan on the head, and pointed at Amy. "Blame her," she said.

Kelly then got into Amy's face. "Got any more jokes, Amy? How about the one with the girl who got a widower's sister and kids killed for no good reason other than being a smartass?"

CHAPTER 47

Kat hung up. "Guess who that was?"

Both girls said "Who?" simultaneously.

"That was your daddy. Actually, a friend of your daddy's. He says he misses you guys and wants you to come home. Is that okay?"

Both girls nodded and smiled.

Kat smiled back. "Well, then get your stuff and let's get going, Kittens."

CHAPTER 48

Kelly handed Allan's machete to Jennifer, turned back, and faced the group.

"We're going to be having some new members joining our group soon," Kelly said. "So we'll need to make room."

She began walking down the line of chairs, stopping before each captive to address them personally. "Amy? Since it was your wit that prompted me to invite our new guests, you can stay."

Amy tried yelling something through the duct tape over her mouth. Kelly smiled, patted her head, and casually moved down the line to Allan, whom Jennifer had since sat back upright in his chair.

"Allan? Since our new guests know you so well and will likely feel more comfortable in your company, you can stay too."

Allan too attempted to yell something through his tape.

Kelly shook her head, pursed her lips, and gave a silly little frown. She glanced back at Jennifer. "You think they'd be grateful."

A laughing, grinning machine not thirty minutes ago, Jennifer now accommodated Kelly's wit with a pained smile. She was sweating. Her complexion was growing paler by the minute.

Kelly acknowledged her need with an understanding little nod. She held up a finger. *Soon*, the finger said.

Kelly moved down the line. Stopped between Jon and Karen.

"That leaves you two, I guess. Logic would say I get rid of Karen because Jon here is all but useless. Except his constant moaning is annoying the hell out of me. Putting him down would be a mercy killing for him *and* my ears." She glanced over at Allan. "Maybe I let Allan choose. After all, they're his guests. What do you say, Allan?"

She walked over and tore off his duct tape. He did not wince from the sting, just began pleading instantly.

"Please, just please listen to me…please call my sister back and tell them to turn around. I will do absolutely *anything* you want, just *please* call them back. *PLEASE.*"

"You'll do anything I want?"

"*Yes*—yes, absolutely."

"Choose then."

He let out an exasperated little cry. "*Okay!* Okay fine, I'll choose! But you have to call first. Call first and *then* I'll choose."

"Here's the problem with that though, Allan," Kelly said. "If I call them back and tell them not to come, then we won't need the extra room, and then choosing won't be necessary."

"*Fine!*" Allan blurted. "*That's fine!*"

"I don't think that's fine. I don't think that's fine at all. If we do that, then Amy here wouldn't have learned her lesson. This is all her fault, after all. The reason your sister and kids are coming over is because of Amy. So, you might want to start directing your anger a little more her way and a little less my way, don'tcha think?" She now got nose to nose with Allan and enunciated the next part slowly and clearly: "*You're…going to watch…your little girls die… because of Amy Lambert's…big fucking mouth.*"

Tears started down Allan's cheeks. "*Please…*"

"Choose."

Allan said nothing.

Kelly stood upright. "How the hell are you even conflicted? You have a chance to save your *children* by sacrificing one of *those two*—" She flicked a dismissive hand towards the Rogerses.

Sacrificing.

(*"The thing about pawns, Allan, is that their low piece value allows you to sacrifice them relatively easily in order to gain a stronger position overall."*)

Nothing easy about this.

(*She's right, though. It's Kat and the girls. How are you even conflicted?*)

Because I don't trust her.

(*What choice do you have?*)

We're pawns. We're here to be sacrificed so that Kelly may gain a stronger position over Amy, remember?

(*Except now she's allowing you to play. So play and be ruthless. Living in the here and now—you don't get to just turn it off and on as you please, pal. Choose one. Sacrifice one of the pawns. It may just give you a stronger position over her.*)

"Time, she's a-wasting, Allan. Better choose soon, or Kat and the Kittens will be here any minute—"

"I choose Jon," Allan said.

"*No!*" Karen cried.

Kelly took a step back. "Really? Why Jon?"

"Who gives a shit why? I chose. Call my sister."

"Well, we have to carry it out first," Kelly said.

"*Bullshit!* I chose like you wanted. *Now call my fucking sister and tell them to go back!*"

"Please don't," Karen sobbed.

Allan looked down the line of chairs toward Karen. He was amazed he was able to make eye contact with her. "Karen, I'm so, so sorry. He would want the same thing. Jon? *Jon?*"

Jon slowly lifted his head. He was no longer moaning or grimacing. The continuous pain and blood loss now made him look drugged. Face sluggish and pale and coated in a slick sheen of sweat, he struggled to keep his head from lolling to one side.

"Jon, right?" Allan said. "You'd sacrifice your life for Karen's? You'd do that, right? *Jon?*"

Jon nodded once before his head dropped. To Allan, it looked as if he'd fallen asleep.

"*No...*" Karen continued to sob.

"Well, I guess chivalry isn't dead," Kelly said. "Very noble of you, Jon."

Kelly whispered something into Jennifer's ear. Jennifer nodded and lunged forward with the machete, burying it in Karen's forehead. She then let go of the handle and took a step back, the machete staying put, standing to attention like an odd horn. Only this wasn't the oddest thing. The oddest thing was that Karen was still alive. Odder still, she began to giggle. Blood running down both sides of her face, eyes fluttering rapidly like some type of nervous tic, she actually started giggling.

"I think...I think something's wrong," Karen said and giggled again, eyes still fluttering. "I think something's wrong," she repeated. "Jon? I think something's wrong."

Jon said nothing. He couldn't—as Allan had guessed, he had passed out moments prior.

Kelly whispered something to Jennifer again, and again Jennifer nodded back and approached Karen.

Karen actually greeted Jennifer with a smile. "Hi," she said to her. "I think something's wrong—"

Jennifer yanked the machete free from Karen's head. Karen's bizarre chatter stopped instantly. Her fluttering eyes rolled back until only the whites showed. Her head dropped forward a second later. Blood immediately began soaking her front. A few of her fingers twitched.

When Jennifer returned to Kelly's side, Kelly looked at her and said: "Good for you—" She then gestured to Jon. "I couldn't even get that one's ankle off. Gotta join a gym or something."

"What the fuck was that?" Allan asked. It came out as barely a whisper.

"What was what?" Kelly asked.

"I chose Jon. You *know* I chose Jon." His voice started to rise.

Kelly's reply was dreamy, as though replying to Allan while thinking about something else. "Yeah..."

"*So then why did you kill Karen?!*"

Kelly brought her full attention back to Allan and gave a bored little shrug. "I don't know."

"You wasted all that time having me choose!"

Kelly nodded. "I guess I did, yeah."

"*Call them!*" Allan screamed. "*I did what you wanted, and I chose, NOW CALL MY FUCKING SISTER!*"

Kelly shook her head. "I don't know...you may be right—we wasted too much time choosing."

"*What?!*"

"They're probably going to be here any minute. I mean, what would I even say? 'Allan changed his mind and doesn't want to see his kids after all'? Kinda makes you look like a jerk."

"*No no no no no no no no...*"

"Yeah, you'd look like a total jerk. Your sister would have to turn around and head all the way back home. Your kids would be sad, asking things like, 'Why doesn't Daddy want to see us?' Total jerk. I'd actually be doing you a favor if I didn't call."

"*NO! You call them! You call them now!!!*"

Kelly maneuvered behind Allan and tore off a piece of duct tape.

His head whipped over his shoulder toward her. "*I'M GONNA FUCKING KILL YOU, YOU FUCKING LITTLE CUNT! I SWEAR TO GOD, I'M GONNA FUCKING KILL—*"

She taped his mouth shut. Walked back and faced him again. Allan continued to scream through the tape, his face purple, eyes bulging, snot flying.

Kelly brandished Allan's cell and then promptly stuffed it back into her pocket again. "Now you're not a jerk," she said. "You're welcome."

CHAPTER 49

Amy tried speaking through her tape, her efforts so incessant that Kelly could no longer ignore them. She huffed and tore off Amy's tape.

"Yes, Amy?" Kelly spoke with the tone and manner of a parent finally addressing a nagging child.

"You're reaching too far again, Kelly. What's your plan now? You can't use me as the killer anymore—after what happened with Tim and Irene and my kids, you'd never be able to sell it."

"And your point is?" Kelly said.

"My point is actually for Jennifer."

Jennifer, sweating and slightly shaking now from withdrawal, said: "Huh?"

Amy locked eyes with her. "Think about it for a minute, Jennifer. Kelly here needs a plan B she can sell. Tim's already gone. Where do you think that leaves you?"

"What do you mean?"

"You know what a patsy is, Jennifer?"

"No."

"Don't listen to her," Kelly said.

"A patsy is someone who is easily manipulated and taken advantage of. Someone to *blame* for something. Two addicts like you and Tim? Do the math."

Jennifer glanced over at Kelly.

Kelly closed her eyes and calmly shook her head. "Don't listen to her," she said again.

"Hell, I'd be shocked if Kelly had intended for you and Tim to survive the night even if the plot worked out the way she'd planned," Amy said.

"That's not true," Jennifer said. "We made a deal."

"That's right, you did," Kelly said. "I intend to honor it."

Amy laughed. "What was the deal, Jennifer? Do as she says and you'll get all the heroin in the world? Let me ask you something: If you and Tim were to go missing, would anyone notice?"

Kelly raised the gun on Amy. "Shut up."

Amy continued, undeterred. "*Someone who is easily manipulated*," she said again. "Your addiction checks off that box, Jennifer. All we have to do now is wait and see if plan B includes blaming you for anything."

Kelly pressed the gun barrel against Amy's forehead. "I said *shut up*."

Amy's eyes stayed on Jennifer as she said: "If it weren't true, she wouldn't be getting so agitated now, would she, Jennifer?"

Gun still pressed to Amy's head, Kelly glanced back at Jennifer. "Don't listen to her. She's just trying to mind-fuck you."

Jennifer rubbed a hand vigorously up and down the arm holding the machete as if trying to warm herself even though such an assumption contradicted her incessant sweating. She was also shaking considerably now. "What *is* plan B?" she asked Kelly.

"You're going to get what I promised you," was all Kelly said.

"I need a hit," Jennifer said.

"She'll hold out on you until you do as she says," Amy said. "Makes it easier to manipulate you, Patsy—I mean Jennifer."

Kelly dug the barrel into Amy's head and glared at her. "I would really, *really* consider shutting the fuck up." She then pulled the gun away with one demonstrative gesture, twirled on the spot and addressed everyone: "Okay! Plan B? Everyone wants to know what plan B is, yes?" There was an exasperated condescension in her tone and theatrics. She maneuvered behind Amy and taped her mouth shut once again. Then, looking at Jennifer: "Wait here."

"*I need a hit*," Jennifer said again.

Kelly's flared nostrils betrayed her patient smile. "If you just wait here and keep an eye on them, I will set you up for *life*, Jennifer. You will never have to go on the street for it again."

Amy mumbled something into her tape. Jennifer looked at her as if she not only understood what Amy had just mumbled, but was also considering it.

"Jennifer?" Kelly said. "Who are you going to believe? A woman who will say *anything* to save her life, or someone who has already shown you kindness and supplied you with the purest dope you've ever had? The purest dope that will be *all yours* when the night is done? Tim's gone now, remember? *All yours*."

Jennifer started to nod, slow and tentative at first, and then soon faster and with more assertiveness, the sickness, her debilitating need overriding all else. "Okay," she said. "Okay."

"Thank you." Kelly left the den.

The mudroom door leading into the garage could be heard opening and slamming shut in the distance. Echoes of clanging and banging inside the garage. Sounds of the mudroom door opening and slamming shut in the distance again.

Kelly appeared holding a can of gasoline. She raised it for all to see.

"Plan B," she said.

CHAPTER 50

Kelly began sprinkling gasoline all throughout the den, talking as she did so.

"It has been my experience that fire is one of the true constants you can rely on in this world. I'm actually a little ashamed it took me this long to consider it for plan B."

She stopped speaking just then and intentionally sprinkled a generous amount of gasoline at the feet of Allan and Amy, winked at them, and then carried right on speaking while attending to the rest of the den.

"People consider forest fires a tragedy. They try to stop them. But forest fires are, in fact, nature's way of cleansing the earth. Even the Native Americans knew that. They did not try to fight the fires that occurred for centuries in dry habitats, but instead let them run their course. They knew how beneficial they could be in cleansing the environment."

When the can was empty, she set it on the floor and removed her black Zippo. "I guess you can say that's what I'm doing here," she said. "Cleansing the environment. Creating my own little forest fire, if you will. All traces of you and your home will be gone, but in time, a new house, a new family will appear. It's kinda cool when you think about it."

Kelly lit a cigarette with the Zippo, snapped it shut, and took a deep drag on it to ensure the tip glowed strong. She exhaled with a grin, looked at Jennifer, said, "Watch this," and then flicked the lit butt into an area of the den she'd sprinkled heavily.

Everyone's eyes, including Jennifer's, bulged in horror as they tracked the path of the cigarette to the floor where it landed and sat smoldering and harmless.

No fire.

There was a unanimous sigh of relief from the three, Allan and Amy from their nostrils, Jennifer from her mouth.

Kelly laughed and lit another cigarette. "Big myth," she said. "You see it a lot in movies, but the truth is, cigarettes don't burn hot enough to ignite gas vapors."

All eyes went back on the cigarette as though needing more confirmation despite the experiment they'd just witnessed. The cigarette still smoldered harmlessly on the floor.

"A *match*, on the other hand..." Kelly handed Jennifer the Zippo, stuck the cigarette between her lips, and pulled out a pack of matches. She lit one and flicked it into Amy's lap.

Amy screamed into her gag, the single paper match flickering on her lap.

Kelly laughed and retrieved the match. Blew it out, went to toss it, and then hesitated.

"Wait," she said. "The embers on a match still burn pretty good after you blow them out. I wonder if a recently burnt match would fail to burn hot enough to ignite our party like its friend the cigarette. I want to wait until Allan's sister and his Deejays arrive, but it's too damn tempting not to try right now." She glanced over at Jennifer. "If it gets too bad, we can always put it out, right?"

Jennifer nodded back without smiling. Her agreeability at this stage was simply to advance things as quickly as possible. To placate the god who would soon take her away and make it all better.

Kelly took a final drag of her cigarette, tossed it (once again, all eyes followed its path with dreadful anticipation, prior display be damned), and then lit a second match. She brought the burning match right before the tip of Amy's nose.

Amy turned her head and shut her eyes.

"Make a wish," Kelly said, blew the match out, and dropped it into the puddle of gasoline at Amy's feet.

Nothing happened.

"Poop," Kelly said.

Amy's head whipped back and dropped down, frantic eyes on the now lifeless match at her feet. Her exhale of relief was so strong her torso appeared to shrink.

"Shall we try again?" Kelly asked. "What about you, Allan? You wanna try one?"

Allan screamed muffled hate into his gag.

"*Fine...*" she said with mock hurt. "I guess we'll have to wait until our guests arrive."

The doorbell rang.

Allan's eyes stretched impossibly wide, rage dilating his pupils demon-like, his muffled tirade into his gag a muzzled dog's.

"Now that's what I call right on cue," Kelly said with great delight.

She left to answer the door.

.   .   .

Kelly put on an unassuming face before opening the front door. Her goal was to greet with courtesy and respect, but little enthusiasm; she was playing a member of a grief session, not a host to a party.

She opened the door and found herself staring into the barrel of a pistol; behind the barrel were the half-crazed eyes of Kevin Lane.

"Evening, Kelly," Kevin said and rammed his fist deep into her stomach, crumpling her instantly.

CHAPTER 51

Earlier

Parked on a rural side road some fifty yards away from Allan Brown's residence sat Kevin Lane's battered Oldsmobile. Kevin Lane was not inside. What was inside—in the glove compartment, to be exact—was a piece of paper spotted with dried blood. On the paper was a message that initially looked to Kevin as if it had been written by two different people.

The meat of the message was perfectly legible. And that made sense; the man who'd written it had been very much intact.

The slices of text holding that meat together were a different story. The script was nearly illegible. And sadly, this too made sense to Kevin; the man who'd written those had been moments away from death.

The note read:

save amy

ALLAN BROWN
125 HENKEL ROAD
WESTMORE

kelly blaine did it

The conflicting emotions Kevin Lane had faced while standing in a dead man's home (with two other dead men to boot) were not gentle as they flew at him. They'd *crashed* into him, each with its own justification.

Domino is dead. Call 911.

He's dead. He can't be saved. If you call 911, the police will get involved.

If the police get involved, you lose any chance at getting your hands on Kelly. She could slip away again.

But I have proof! Domino managed to scribble this note just before he died. How could the police ignore that?

Do you want to take that chance? See her somehow walk yet again? See her glance your way before she's out the proverbial door with that faint, almost imperceptible smirk of hers? Implying that she once again, for the umpteenth time, fucked you right in the ass?

No. No, I surely don't.

This note, this address, it's everything you've been waiting for. You happening upon it was no coincidence. You've been given a final chance. Use it.

It came at the expense of a great man's life.

So then do him proud. Use it. Save Amy and bring the devil's child down.

Yes. Yes, I'll bring her down. I'll bring her down and prove to the world that she IS the fucking devil's child. Yes. YES.

And so Kevin Lane had become a vigilante. Taking a gun with him. Speeding toward Allan Brown's home. Parking fifty yards away so he could make the rest of the way on foot undetected. Carefully navigating the perimeter of Allan's home until he found a window with a curtain that wasn't drawn. A window adjacent to the patio around back that just happened to give a decent view into the den and the horrific goings on therein, giving him once again the conflicting emotions of both anxiety for the captives (two of them looked dead) and exultation for the opportunity to right the wrong that had consumed his every waking moment for the past several years.

And the wrong was there. Holding court. Not the blameless victim with the faintest of smirks he was used to, even as far back as Stratton Grove when Kelly Blaine was still a kid, but large and in charge, despite her diminutive stature. Parading about with a cool, confident smile, sometimes even a grin (he never thought he'd see the day, wondered whether she even had *teeth*) as she tormented the people before her, one of them Amy Lambert. *The* Amy Lambert.

And who was the girl standing next to Kelly? The one holding a...*a machete?* What role did she play? She was assuredly an addict; years of working with troubled youths had allowed Kevin to spot an addict as easily as the average person spotted a redhead.

It quickly made sense. Kelly had employed the help of a junkie to assist her, plying the girl with drugs to do Kelly's bidding. Her bidding for what, though, was what Kevin wanted to know. What was Kelly's end game?

Or *did* he want to know?

Did the specifics of whatever sick plan she'd concocted really matter? It would all become irrelevant anyway once he got his hands on her. And he *would* get his hands on her. Finally.

But how?

He'd brought a gun with him. Start shooting through the window?

No. Absurd. Though he was donning the hat of the vigilante tonight, he was still a counselor by trade; he'd probably end up shooting the hostages as often as he shot Kelly and her helper, if he managed to hit Kelly and her helper at all.

He would need to get close. Did, in fact, *want* to get close. How often had he fantasized about wrapping his hands around Kelly's little neck and squeezing for all he was worth? To watch the very life drain from her black eyes with each passing second, with each tightening squeeze. Call him a would-be cold-blooded murderer all you wanted, but in Kevin Lane's eyes, he was ridding the world of evil. No different than an angel striking down a demon.

Whichever method he chose to enter the home and take Kelly and her assistant down, it had to be soon; a second, careful reconnaissance along the perimeter of Allan Brown's home gave him a second window with a decent view into the den, this one at the front of the house, facing the captives.

And it was at this view that he noted the exceptional amount of blood on one of the captives he'd presumed dead. That one, a woman, was definitely gone. He was sure of it. The other, a man, looked equally gone, though he spotted no blood on him. Unconscious maybe? Who cared? Either way, his next move had to be soon, or Amy Lambert and the man next to her whom he assumed was Allan Brown would quickly join the other two captives in their tragic condition.

Kevin Lane backed away from the window, popped the clip on his pistol to check the ammo, and then rammed it back in with an exceptionally satisfying click: the sound of justice ready to be had.

Until headlights approaching in the distance forced justice to wait.

. * .

For the second time that day, Jamie and Janine Brown heard the F-word from a family member.

First from Dad when a car blew a stop sign at an intersection and nearly T-boned them this morning. And now from Aunt Kat when, just as she went to turn in to her brother's driveway, a man leapt smack in front of her car, both hands on the hood, demanding she stop.

"*What the fuck?*"

No giggling from the girls in the back seat as they'd done with their father this morning; they were too shaken by what appeared to be a lunatic now hollering through Kat's driver's-side window, telling them they needed to leave.

Kat reached into her glove compartment, pulled out a can of Mace, cracked her window an inch, and aimed the can directly at the man. "You back off right now, or you're getting a face full of pain, buddy!"

The man raised both hands in surrender. "Please, listen to me," he said.

"You've got three seconds," Kat said. "Then I'm spraying you *and* calling the police."

"*Good!*" the man cried. "I *want* you to call the police! But not just yet."

"One..." Kat said.

"Please, listen to me—"

"*Two…*"

"My name is Kevin Lane. Inside that house is a serial killer named Kelly Blaine. She's holding the people inside hostage. She's already killed one of them."

Kat lowered her can of Mace. A fan of *The Joan Parsons Show*, she remembered the episode featuring Kelly Blaine and Kevin Lane well. And now, despite the dark, despite her panic, she recognized the man by her driver's-side window as indeed *the* Kevin Lane.

This did not stop her from being ready to spray him full blast in the face at any moment, however. She remembered Kevin Lane looking unstable on *The Joan Parsons Show*. He looked more so now. And if the allegations Kelly Blaine had proclaimed about Kevin Lane on that show were true—a sex offender—then she was taking zero chance with her Kittens in back.

"You better talk fast and convincingly, pal," Kat said to him.

. . .

Driving away from her brother's house, Kat pulled out her cell phone. The man had begged her to wait thirty minutes before calling the police. Claimed that she would be putting her brother's and everyone else's life inside in mortal danger if she called any sooner. Told her—no, *begged* her yet again—to let him take care of things first, that he was the only one capable of doing so.

And it was the begging that made Kat disobey. It reeked of desperation.

It had been a year, but Kat remembered the show well enough. Remembered the rage in Kevin Lane's eyes when he spoke to Kelly Blaine via remote camera. Despite his claims, Kat's gut told her this man was harboring an ulterior motive that had long since jettisoned rational action. In its place, at the expense of everything else, was good old-fashioned revenge. Revenge that could cost her brother his life.

No way was she taking that chance. She called the police right away.

CHAPTER 52

Kevin Lane bent over a writhing Kelly Blaine and checked her for weapons. He found her gun and tucked it into the waistband behind his back.

"Got anything else I should know about, Miss Blaine?" he asked and promptly kicked her in the gut, what little air she'd recovered from his initial blow whooshing out of her again.

He found nothing more after a second pat-down, snatched a good handful of her long dark hair, and began dragging her into the den by the scalp.

·   ·   ·

"Kelly?" Jennifer called from the den.

Direct line of sight from the den into the foyer was impossible no matter where you stood. The distance was too great, the angles too sharp. But Amy believed this was not the reason Jennifer called out. She did not even believe Jennifer called for Kelly because she was taking a while to reappear. No, Amy believed Jennifer called out because the distinctive bass of a male's voice from the foyer was clearly audible to all, and last everyone checked, one woman and two little girls were the only ones slated to arrive.

"Kelly?" Jennifer called again.

A man appeared in the den. Gaunt and unshaven, eyes red from lack of sleep and possibly sanity, he was still recognizable as Kevin

Lane. In his left hand was a gun pointed directly at Jennifer. In his right hand was Kelly Blaine, dangling by a fistful of hair, her face contorting from both the pressure on her scalp and what Amy was sure were injuries Kevin had inflicted on her in the foyer.

"Drop the machete," Kevin said.

"Who are you?" Jennifer asked.

Kevin thrust the gun forward. "Drop the machete or I will kill you here and now."

Jennifer dropped it.

Kevin's nose wrinkled as he began sniffing loudly, head going all over the den. "What the hell is—is that *gas*?"

Both Amy and Allan nodded quickly.

"Jesus Christ," Kevin said. He jerked Kelly's head upwards. "You and fire..." He shook his head and chuckled. "Crazy fucking pyro."

He's loving this, Amy thought. *Please don't milk it. Please don't make the* same-exact-fucking-mistake *Kelly made—thankfully—and start playing with your dinner. Kill it quick and eat it. Please just kill it quick before it bites back.*

Amy tried yelling through her gag to bring Kevin's attention back to priorities.

(*And those priorities are?*)

Nevertheless, it did the trick. "Untie them," he said to Jennifer, gesturing toward Amy and Allan with the gun.

Jennifer balked.

Kevin thrust the gun forward again. "I'm doing you a favor by keeping you alive, whoever the hell you are. You can either do as you're told, or I can kill you right now, and I can untie them myself."

Jennifer walked toward Amy and removed the tape over her mouth.

"You okay?" Kevin asked.

"I'm okay," Amy said.

"You're Amy Lambert, right?"

"Yeah."

Allan screamed through his gag. It was not a scream demanding his gag be removed next, but a warning scream, his eyes wide and wild and fixed on Jennifer who had subtly moved away a step while Kevin's attention was on Amy. In Jennifer's hand was Kelly's black Zippo lighter, little black lid open with its windproof flame burning tall for all to see.

Again, Kevin thrust the gun forward. "You put that away, girl, you hear me?"

"Put the gun down or I'll drop it," Jennifer said. The hand with the Zippo was shaking badly. Withdrawal coupled with adrenaline.

"Put it away *now*."

"You shoot me, and I'll drop it. It'll stay lit, and the whole room will go up." Her shaking increased.

Oh God, she's going to drop it by accident.

Kevin sneered. "I'm only going to tell you one more—"

"*Jennifer*," Amy cut in. "Jennifer, listen to me. Kelly would have killed you no matter what happened here tonight. Do you really think she wanted any loose ends? You mean *nothing* to her. Please, put the lighter away—"

"I don't care about her!" Jennifer yelled. "I just want to leave!"

"Okay," Amy said. "Okay, then leave."

"*What?*" Kevin said. "She's an accomplice to—"

"*Shut up!*" Amy yelled. She turned her attention back to Jennifer, her tone calm and soothing again. "You can go, Jennifer. No one's going to follow you. I promise. Just please put the lighter away first."

Her whole body was shaking now. Her sweating profuse, skin a sickly white. "You won't follow me?" she asked.

"No, no we won't. You have my word. All you have to do is put the lighter away and leave. That's it. Okay? Jennifer? That's it. Just put the lighter away and leave."

"You promise?"

"I promise on the lives of my children," Amy said.

Jennifer started nodding. "Okay...okay."

She went to close the Zippo, and Amy's greatest fear became real.

Jennifer's sweaty and shaky hands fumbled with the lighter, lost hold of it, clumsily batted it from one hand to the other in a desperate attempt to snatch it back, and then ultimately failed as the open Zippo hit the gasoline-soaked rug.

Fire consumed the den almost instantly.

CHAPTER 53

Jennifer turned and ran. Kevin Lane fired shots after her and missed.

"*Untie us!*" Amy screamed.

Kevin, still gripping Kelly Blaine by the scalp, dragged her with him towards the row of chairs, his gun arm draped across his brow, shielding himself from the growing flames all around them.

He tore furiously at Amy's tape.

"*Do Allan!*" Amy cried. "*Do Allan first! He's stronger! He can help!*"

Kevin instantly obeyed and began ripping Allan free. The flames at Allan's feet from where Kelly had intentionally sprinkled gasoline burned Kevin as he worked on freeing Allan's ankles, causing him to curse and cry out and release his hold on Kelly so he could maneuver behind Allan, tilt his chair, and drag him back to a better spot to finish the job.

And Kelly made a run for it.

Kevin spun toward her fleeing shape through the smoke and flames. "*NO!*" He fired two shots after her, missed, and then immediately gave chase.

"*What the fuck are you doing?!*" Allan yelled. "*Get back here!*"

CHAPTER 54

Officers Dixon and Lawler pulled their cruiser into Allan Brown's driveway, quite honestly—as they would later say to all who asked—not knowing what to expect. They'd received a call from a woman claiming to be Mr. Brown's sister. She'd claimed she was on her way to her brother's house to drop off his daughters when a man by the name of Kevin Lane literally stopped her and told her to turn around. Mr. Lane had claimed Kelly Blaine was inside the house with several hostages, one of them dead.

Both officers were quite familiar with Kevin Lane and his erratic antics over the years when it came to Kelly Blaine. And it was for this reason that they pulled up to Allan Brown's house not only clueless about what to expect, but also with their caution tanks fairly low. Lane was nothing but a nutty blowhard as far as they were concerned. They'd even volleyed lighthearted guesses back and forth to one another en route to the Brown home as to what was waiting for them:

> "Kelly Blaine is probably a friend of Allan Brown's. Probably in there having a dinner party."
> Laughter.
> "Probably right. Lane parked down the street and has probably been peeping in on them the whole night, waiting to see if she butchers the guests."
> More laughter.

"Dude's got a serious hard-on for that girl."

"Well, that was the whole thing, wasn't it? Dude was suppos-edly fondling her back when she was a kid at the youth ranch where he worked."

"Plus a few other girls."

"Sick fuck. Think we can find a reason to lock him up tonight?"

"Sounds good to me."

What Officers Dixon and Lawler found that night instead—or so they thought—was a reason to shoot Kevin Lane stone dead.

When they rolled up Allan Brown's driveway and saw the rag-ing blaze in the den clear as could be in contrast with the dark of night, saw Kelly Blaine burst out the front door, running toward their cruiser, screaming for help, saw Kevin Lane appearing in the doorway seconds later wielding a gun and firing after her, Officers Dixon and Lawler drew their own weapons and blew Kevin Lane away.

. . .

Kelly Blaine collapsed into Officer Dixon's arms.

"Help them!" she sobbed. *"They're still inside! Please help them!"*

Officer Dixon held her at arm's length, looked her up and down. "Are you all right?"

"YES!" Kelly cried. *"Just please, help them!"*

Dixon and Lawler dashed for the house.

When they disappeared inside, Kelly dashed too.

CHAPTER 55

Officers Dixon and Lawler finished helping Allan with Amy's binds. There was no time to work on Karen's or Jon's; the fire's strength was growing stronger by the second. Dixon and Allan lifted Jon's chair with him in it and, braving the flames, staggered toward the sliding glass door at the back of the den. Lawler and Amy did the same with Karen, chair and all, toward the sliding glass door.

Dixon set his end of Jon down and went for the sliding glass door's lock. He struggled with it.

"*Just break the fucking thing!*" Allan yelled.

Dixon drew his gun, took a step back and fired multiple shots into the door. The glass did not shatter; it produced a giant spider web pattern, endless cracks from top to bottom. Dixon kicked at the glass, and it broke free in chunks. Allan immediately helped him, the two clearing a hole sizable enough for them to snake everyone through.

Again hoisting chairs and bodies as one, they carried Karen and Jon Rogers through the hole in the sliding glass door and onto Allan's back porch.

Lawler urged Amy to set Karen down. Amy obliged. Lawler immediately inspected Karen's head wound, aided by the light of the blazing fire inside.

"Jesus Christ," he said. He checked her pulse, dropped his head, and muttered: "She's gone."

Dixon told Allan to set Jon down. He did.

Lawler left Karen and checked Jon's pulse, looked up at Dixon, and said: "We got a pulse on this one."

Dixon nodded, pulled out his radio, and called for assistance.

Lawler turned to Allan. "Kevin Lane do this?"

Allan, hands on his knees, panting, looked up at Lawler with wide, dumbfounded eyes. "*What?*"

"Did Kevin Lane do this?" Lawler asked again.

Amy, equally bent over with hands on knees, stood up and yelled: "*KELLY FUCKING BLAINE DID THIS!*"

Lawler and Dixon exchanged a look. *Ohhh shit*, that look said.

CHAPTER 56

Irene Flannigan's doorbell rang.

The three of them close together in the den, waiting with ex-cruciating patience for Amy Lambert's captor to phone back with further instructions (cherry on top a dead man decomposing up-stairs), Irene, Carrie, and Caleb twitched and sat up like dogs' ears when the door's bell chimed.

"You think that's the police?" Caleb asked.

"They told us we weren't allowed to call the police, didn't they?" Carrie said to Irene.

Irene didn't answer, just said: "You two stay put, got it? *Stay right here.*"

Both kids nodded.

Irene snatched a butcher knife from the kitchen and went to the front door. Unlocked the bolt, left the chain on, and opened the door a few inches, as far as the chain would allow, the screen door behind it as mangled as ever.

In the glow of the porch light, a small young lady with long dark hair and dark eyes greeted Irene with a concerned smile. "Irene Flannigan?"

After what they'd just endured, courtesy was something Irene was fresh out of. "And just who the hell might you be then?"

The young lady spoke quickly and with what appeared to be great anxiety. "I was with Amy Lambert this evening. We planned an escape together. She told me that if I managed to get away and she didn't, would I please come to this address and take you and her kids to someone named Domino Taylor and tell him everything. She said he would know what to do."

"She mentioned Domino, did she?" Irene asked. Mentioning Domino was something, but Irene's tone was not without skepticism.

"That's right," the young lady said.

"I see," Irene said. "And the password Amy gave you would be?"

The young lady did not respond straight away, only stared at Irene for a moment as if she misunderstood the question.

Irene tightened her grip on the knife at her side. Readied herself to slam the door shut and bolt it in an instant. "You've got three seconds to—"

"Unicorn," the young lady said.

Irene exhaled, slid the chain, and opened the door.

The young woman smiled and stepped inside.

CHAPTER 57

Irene Flannigan's landline rang. Kelly Blaine answered it.

"Flannigan residence," Kelly said.

"It's me," Amy Lambert replied.

Kelly left the den and went to the kitchen. She pulled back the curtain on the kitchen window an inch and peeked outside. Flashing red and blue everywhere. "Figured you'd be calling," she said.

"I'm surprised you actually went to Irene's," Amy said. "You had to know I'd realize that's where you were heading."

"I did, yes."

"Are my kids okay?"

"They are, yes."

"Irene?"

"Yup."

"So what's your plan then?" Amy asked. "The game's over."

"Oh no, it's not. Not yet."

"You can't be a ghost on this one, Kelly. Everyone sees you now."

"I know that."

"So what is it then? You gonna treat this like a bad movie? Hold Irene and my kids hostage and demand the police call you a chopper?"

Kelly laughed. "No. I wanna make a trade."

"What kind of a trade?"

"Irene and your kids for you."

A pause.

"Should I repeat myself?" Kelly said.

"No—I heard you."

"Strange. I wouldn't think you'd hesitate over such a request."

"I need to know they're alive first."

Kelly went back into the den. Irene and the kids sat huddled together on the floor. Kelly raised her gun on them. Carrie whimpered and tucked her head into Irene's side. Irene squeezed her tight. And though Caleb did not make a sound when the gun was raised—did not even flinch—Irene pulled him in close and squeezed him just as she'd done his sister.

"Say hello," Kelly said, holding the phone out to them.

No one said anything.

Kelly cocked the hammer on her pistol. "Say hello."

"*Hello!*" Irene yelled.

Kelly moved the phone closer to Carrie. "Now you," she said. "How about an '*I love you, Mommy*'?"

Carrie hesitated.

Kelly aimed the gun right at Carrie's head. "Or how about a '*Goodbye, Mommy*'?"

Carrie screamed.

Kelly laughed. "Ooh, that'll work." She brought the phone back to her ear. "Some lungs on your daughter."

Amy went to say something, but Kelly took the phone away again. Held it before Caleb.

"Your turn, little fella," she said.

"I'm here, Mom," Caleb said.

Kelly nodded and lowered the phone. "Good boy."

"Fuck you," Caleb said.

Kelly laughed. Irene pulled Caleb in tight and hushed him.

"I like your son," Kelly said once she was back on the phone. "Good potential. I'd love to keep him for a while."

Amy ignored Kelly's comment. "Now what?" was all she said.

"Well, do you believe they're all alive?"

"Yes."

"Well, then let's make a swap, lollipop."

CHAPTER 58

Irene and Caleb were ushered out first. Caleb spotted his mother among the sea of uniforms and flashing lights and sprinted into her arms. Amy showered him with love then held him back at arm's length and checked him up and down. "Are you all right?" she asked.

Caleb nodded and dove into her again. Amy started to cry.

Irene came over, and Amy pulled her in with them. They all cried together.

"Mrs. Lambert?" an officer said behind them. Still in the embrace, Amy turned her head. The officer was holding out a cell phone. "It's her," the officer said.

Amy pulled away from Caleb and Irene and took the phone. "We're not done yet," Kelly said.

"Send out Carrie," Amy said. "Then I'll come in. I promise."

"Gee, lady, you mean it? Honest and for true?"

"Look, Kelly, I—"

"Oh, shut the fuck up. You want your daughter, then you better get your ass in here first. You've got one minute."

.   .   .

Amy went through the front door. Kelly was in the hallway, Carrie on her knees before her, Kelly's gun pressed to the back of her head execution style.

"Shut the door and lock it," Kelly said.

"Carrie, honey, are you okay?"

Carrie started crying. She could only nod.

"*Shut the door and lock it*," Kelly said again.

"Why?" Amy asked. "You're only going to have to unlock it again when you let Carrie go."

"I'm not letting Carrie go," Kelly said.

"*What?*"

"I'm just not comfortable letting her go. You're too crafty, Amy. Too tough. You and me alone? I feel like you'd try to pull something. I'm not the biggest girl, in case you didn't notice. Even with a gun, I still wouldn't feel a hundred percent safe alone with you."

"This is fucking bullshit."

"You always talk like that in front of your daughter?"

"We had a deal," Amy said. "Honor it and let my daughter go."

Kelly pretended to consider. Then: "Nope."

"If you let my daughter go, I will not try anything. I will do *exactly* as you say. I swear."

"See? There you go promising again. Why on earth would you think that holds any value for me?"

Amy said nothing.

"How about this?" Kelly began. "I can't promise you're going to walk out of here alive, Amy, but I *can* promise you that your daughter will."

"And why should your promises hold any value for *me*?" Amy said.

Kelly dug the gun barrel into the back of Carrie's head. Carrie winced and cried harder. "I'd say under the circumstances, they would be fucking priceless."

Amy turned and shut the front door. Locked it and turned back toward Kelly and Carrie.

"Good," Kelly said. She took the gun off Carrie and waved Amy closer with it. "Come closer."

Amy shuffled forward a few steps.

"Closer."

Two more steps. She was close enough now to reach out and touch her crying daughter kneeling before her. And she did, taking Carrie's face in her hand and gently raising it to hers.

She did not say anything to her daughter, only smiled down at her with endless love.

"One more step," Kelly said.

Amy did.

Kelly took the gun off Carrie and raised it on Amy, the tip of the barrel no more than a few inches from her forehead. It was then that Amy noticed it was not the 9mm pistol Kelly had been carrying at Allan's house, but a six-shooter.

"Put your hands in your pockets," Kelly said.

Amy did.

"Good." Kelly opened the revolver's cylinder chamber and dumped all six bullets into the palm of her hand. She tossed all but one aside, the bullets clattering then rolling once they hit the wooden floor.

She held the single bullet up for Amy to see, slid it into one of the six empty holes in the cylinder chamber, gave the chamber a solid spin, and then slammed the chamber shut with the heel of her palm, midspin.

"I know I'm going to prison, Amy," she began. "And I'm sure you know someone like me could never tolerate being caged. So, I don't plan on leaving here alive. However, I'd like to test something."

"And that is?"

"Back at the house you said you agreed with me that life was not fair. You said something like there was no balance in the universe, and that one tragedy did not make you exempt from another. Was that the gist of it?"

"Something like that."

"Well, I'd like to test it again. Lord knows you've endured tragedy countless times, so one would say further testing was unnecessary, but still, I'd like to try one more time. Let's see if life will be fair to you just this once."

"By playing Russian roulette?"

Kelly smiled.

"I thought you said you had no intention of leaving here alive."

"I don't. Even if I win, I'll still pluck one of those bullets up off the floor and put it in my head."

"If you're going to kill yourself no matter what, why not just let us go?"

Kelly laughed. "Amy...you know I can't do that."

Amy dropped her gaze to Carrie, caressed her face again, and then looked back up at Kelly. "Win or lose, my daughter leaves?"

"Yes."

Amy nodded. "Let's play."

CHAPTER 59

Kelly held up a coin and looked down at Carrie. "Heads or tails, Carrie?"

Carrie wept silently.

"Hey!" Kelly flicked her on the top of the head. "Heads or tails?"

Carrie tucked her head and whimpered.

Amy saw red. "*Don't hit my fucking kid.*"

Kelly smirked and held up an apologetic hand. "Sorry. How about you choose then?"

"Tails."

Kelly flipped the coin, caught it, then slapped it on the back of the fist holding the gun. "Tails it is," she said. "Choose."

"You go first," Amy said.

Kelly smiled. "Hoping to get lucky right from the start, are we?"

"You and I don't believe in luck."

"Touché."

Kelly cocked the hammer, stuck the gun in her mouth, and pulled the trigger.

The gun clicked empty.

She pulled the gun from her mouth and aimed it between Amy's eyes. "One in five chance now. You ready?"

Amy just stared at her.

Kelly pulled the trigger.

The gun clicked empty.

Kelly smiled again. "Starting to get interesting." She cocked the hammer, stuck the gun in her mouth, and pulled the trigger.

The gun clicked empty.

"Uh-*ohhh*..." Kelly aimed between Amy's eyes again. "One in three." She nudged Carrie with her foot. "They teach you about odds in school, Carrie? How risky is a one-in-three shot?"

Carrie looked up at Amy. "Mommy?"

"It's okay, baby." Amy's heartache was crippling. "Mommy wants you to put your head down and cover your ears, okay? Don't look up, no matter what."

Carrie stared up at her mother.

"Just do it, honey," Amy said softly.

Carrie did as she was told.

Kelly steadied the gun, cocked the hammer—and paused. Held the gun between Amy's eyes for several seconds, milking it. Loving it.

Amy contemplated going for the gun. But if she missed...

"*Just fucking do it,*" Amy said through gritted teeth.

Kelly pulled the trigger.

The gun clicked empty.

Amy exhaled, shoulders dropping. Her legs felt weak. Her vision swam. But now it was Kelly's turn—and a one in two, no less. Fifty-fifty.

Except Kelly wasn't raising the gun on herself as swiftly as she had on previous turns. Instead, her gun arm dangled at her side as she considered Amy.

Oh, Christ, she's not going to take the chance.

She's going to shoot me.

All she has to do is pull the trigger twice and fast and I'm dead.

I have to go for the gun.

(*And suppose you fuck up and she decides to shoot Carrie instead?*)

I...oh God...

"Fifty-fifty odds," Kelly said as she started to raise the gun.

A sickening bit of irony hit Amy just before Kelly pulled the trigger and ended it: Amy had expected Kelly to play fair.

CHAPTER 60

Kelly Blaine cocked the hammer, stuck the gun in her mouth, and blew her head off.

CHAPTER 61

One month later

Amy replaced the old flowers in front of Patrick's grave with some new ones. She then sat, as she always did, over a spot on the cemetery grass she liked to think was his lap.

"Me again," she said. "They finally caught that girl I was telling you about before. Jennifer? The junkie who was helping Kelly Blaine? They finally got her, so I guess that's something. Still won't bring Jon Rogers' wife back, but at least they got her."

She paused there for a moment. Dropped her head.

"Sometimes I wish it was like that for us. That it was me who died and not you. I'm strong for the kids, but sometimes my head feels like it's going to explode. You were always so much better when it came to dealing with drama."

She knuckled away a tear and looked up at a cloud. She wondered if somewhere, somehow, Patrick could see the same cloud.

"Speaking of drama, Carrie's still sleeping with me, and I have the gall to give her shit about it sometimes. Here I am, thinking *I'm* about to lose it, and I have the absolute gall to give our eleven-year-old daughter shit for being scared and wanting to feel safe by sleeping with her mother at night."

She shook her head at herself and fingered the cigarette burn on her cheek that was nearly healed but would leave a scar.

"Caleb? He's still a rock, you know? He's still like he was right after we first encountered Arty and Jim at Crescent Lake. Insisting on sleeping by himself. Puttering around without talking. No tacks in my slipper this time, thank God, but it's got me worried. I'm beginning to think Domino's death affected him more than we initially thought. He was like a statue at the funeral. No tears, no nothing. And never mind the fact that he killed a man. *He* never minds the fact that he killed a man. When the therapist asks him about it—when *I* ask him about it—he just shrugs as if it was a job he had to do, no big deal. It scares me, honey."

She looked up at the sky again. "His school called me in again. His third fight this month. Remember that little boy who used to cry when Carrie would squash a bug in front of him?" She dropped her head back down to Patrick's tombstone. "I worry about our baby boy, honey. Carrie is so easy; she displays her emotions on a billboard. But Caleb…" She looked away. Fixated on another grave and its engravings for a spell in a bid to tamp down her anxiety.

"You know I tell Caleb that you and Domino are together now?" she eventually said. "That the two of you are watching over us? He smiles, but I think he's just placating me. You believe that? A nine-year-old boy placating his mother?" She chuckled without humor. "Still, *I* like to believe it. I like to think you and Domino are living it up somewhere, drinking scotch and shooting the shit and watching over us like guardian angels. It helps me sleep better at night."

Amy stood and brushed her butt and legs off.

"I went through hell again, baby. And I survived again. I'd like to think this was the last of it, but I think you and I know better by now. Christ, I'll probably go home to find aliens on my doorstep. I guess the Lamberts are just lucky that way." She chuckled dryly again, looked up at the sky, and closed her eyes.

She brought forth an image of Patrick and her in bed on a Sunday morning, sleeping late and cuddling, the kids barging in and piling into bed with them, bouncing and laughing, and Amy felt a transitory moment of peace. She savored it awhile.

Finished, Amy touched two fingers to her lips and pressed them to Patrick's gravestone. "You know," she began, "I don't believe the world is fair, and I don't believe the universe has balance…" She flashed a shrewd little smile toward Patrick's grave. "But I like to think that somehow you and Domino made sure that little bitch ate that bullet."

She chuckled, anything but dryly this time, and pressed two kissed fingers to Patrick's grave again. "See you soon, baby."

CHAPTER 62

Three months later

Living in the now, Allan thought as he stood outside Amy Lambert's door. He closed his eyes, took a deep breath, and repeated the mantra his therapist had provided him, the mantra that had become his best friend these past three months:

Life owes me nothing. I can't change the past. The future is unwritten. But I'm here. Now. And then his own little addendum that he believed made the mantra that much stronger: *Alive. I'm here. Now. Alive.*

He opened his eyes and exhaled long and slow.

He rang the doorbell.

Amy answered in a T-shirt and sweats, her long brown hair in a ponytail. "Allan, hi!"

Allan pulled a bottle of whiskey out from behind his back. "Thought you might want to finally sneak that drink in the kitchen."

Amy laughed. She then raised her fist.

They fist-bumped, and Allan's smile became his whole face.

Amy stepped aside and invited him in.

ABOUT THE AUTHOR

A native of the Philadelphia area, Jeff has published multiple works in both fiction and non-fiction. In 2011 he was the recipient of the Red Adept Reviews Indie Award for Horror.

Jeff's debut novel *Bad Games* was a #1 Kindle bestseller that spawned two acclaimed sequels, and now all three books in the terrifying trilogy have been optioned as feature films and are currently being translated for foreign audiences.

His other novels, along with his award-winning short works, have also received international acclaim and are eagerly waiting to give you plenty of sleepless nights.

Free time for Jeff is spent watching horror movies, The Three Stooges, and mixed martial arts. He loves steak and more steak, thinks the original 1974 *Texas Chainsaw Massacre* is the greatest movie ever, wants to pet a lion someday, and hates spiders.

He currently lives in Pennsylvania with his wife Kelly and their cats Sammy and Bear.

Jeff loves to hear from his readers. Please feel free to contact him at http://www.jeffmenapace.com/contact.html to discuss anything and everything, and be sure to visit his website at www.jeffmenapace.com to sign up for his FREE newsletter (no spam, not ever) where you will receive updates and sneak peeks on all future works along with the occasional free goodie!

Connect with Jeff on social media:

http://www.facebook.com/JeffMenapace.writer

http://twitter.com/JeffMenapace

https://www.linkedin.com/in/JeffMenapace

https://www.goodreads.com/JeffMenapace

https://www.instagram.com/JeffMenapace

OTHER WORKS BY JEFF MENAPACE

Please visit Jeff's Amazon Author Page or his website for a complete list of all available works!

http://www.amazon.com/Jeff-Menapace/e/Boo4Ro9MoS

www.jeffmenapace.com

AUTHOR'S NOTE

Thank you so much for taking the time to read *Bad Games: Malevolent*. Who would have thought there would ever be a book four??? Wanna hear something crazier? Book five is already in the works! I don't want to spill too many beans just yet, but what I can tell you is that it will take place ten years in the future, and Carrie and Caleb will play far more significant roles now that they're adults.

Once again, I want to thank you for reading. If you enjoyed *Bad Games: Malevolent*, I would be extremely grateful if you left a review for it on Amazon. Good reviews are very helpful in the success of a book. It doesn't have to be anything super-long (though feel free to make it as long as you want), just a line or two would be awesome. It would truly mean a lot.

Thanks again, my friends.

Until Amy battles zombies...

Jeff

Printed in Great Britain
by Amazon

35129344R00139